Edward Healy Thompson

The Life of Marie Eustelle Harpain

Edward Healy Thompson

The Life of Marie Eustelle Harpain

ISBN/EAN: 9783337412609

Printed in Europe, USA, Canada, Australia, Japan

Cover: Foto ©Raphael Reischuk / pixelio.de

More available books at **www.hansebooks.com**

THE LIFE

OF

MARIE-EUSTELLE HARPAIN,

The Sempstress of Saint-Pallais,

CALLED

"THE ANGEL OF THE EUCHARIST."

"Ego sum qui humilem in puncto elevo mentem; ut plures æternæ veritatis capiat rationes quam si quis decem annis studuisset in scholis."—*Imitatio Christi*, iii. 43, 3.

LONDON:

BURNS, OATES, & CO.

17 & 18, PORTMAN STREET, PORTMAN SQUARE;

AND 63, PATERNOSTER ROW.

DUBLIN: KELLY, 8, GRAFTON STREET.

1868.

ADVERTISEMENT.

———◦○◦———

THE materials for the Life of Marie-Eustelle Har pain are twofold. Ten months after her death there was published, with the sanction of Mgr. Ville-court, the Bishop of La Rochelle, afterwards raised to the Cardinalate, a work entitled " *Recueil des Écrits de Marie-Eustelle ; née à Saint-Pallais de Saintes, le 19 Juin,* 1814 ; *morte le 29 Juin,* 1842." To this pub-lication the bishop prefixed a letter addressed to all the faithful who should read the work. In it he gave an account of the circumstances which led to his acquaintance with the eminent virtues which had adorned Marie-Eustelle, and of the high esteem he had conceived of her sanctity from their very first interview. The peculiar motives for caution which existed during her life no longer operated to impose silence, and her bishop was therefore free to lead the way in proclaiming her merits to the world. The work in question may be considered in a certain sense to be his own, so far, at least, as the fullest responsibility was concerned ; for he himself examined all Marie-Eustelle's manuscripts, and compared the copies taken of them with the originals, in order to ensure the most perfect accuracy. The few changes and omissions made were such as he himself authorized or suggested. They amounted only to the correction of some grammatical errors into which the writer had accidentally fallen in her letters — letters, it may be observed, which it never crossed her mind would ever be given to the public,—and the suppression of a few repetitions. In addition to the letters, the work contains an unfinished account of her interior life, written by herself under obedience ; three fictitious dialogues embodying various observations and opinions of this holy girl, obtained from an authentic source ; and some hymns and canticles of her own composition.

It was through this publication that Marie-Eustelle first became known in France. The pious author of the "Life of Auguste Marceau," with whose name we are not acquainted, as he does not append it to his writings, but which is probably no secret in his own country, shared the general enthusiasm which the work excited. Nor was this feeling of a merely temporary character. He was continually seeking in its pages wherewithal to feed and sustain the love of Jesus in his own soul ; and several years after the book had first come under his notice he resolved to visit the places which Eustelle's presence had rendered sacred in his eyes. This purpose he put in execution, and sought, moreover, the acquaintance of all who had known or had been connected with her ; in particular, he spent long hours with her mother and sisters, closely questioning them, and treasuring up every minute incident or characteristic trait patiently gathered from their lips. But not satisfied with availing himself of all these opportunities and advantages for the gratification of a legitimate and pious curiosity, he strove to make his visit profitable, and to carry back something of Eustelle's spirit with him on returning to the world. He went often to pray where she had prayed, and spent a whole novena before that tabernacle of Saint-Pallais where her life had consumed itself in one long act of love. Here he seems to have largely partaken of the communications he had desired, his expressions of love to the Blessed Sacrament reminding us, by the intensity of their fervour, of those of Eustelle. He thus became specially fitted for the office of her biographer. It was in one of those moments of ardent devotion, while adoring in the church of Saint-Pallais, that, "penetrated with grief," he says, "for having as yet done nothing for the Lord," he formed the resolution of writing, if it were but a few lines, to draw his brethren to the love of the Divine Sacrament, borrowing, to that end, the words of her whom he has aptly called "the Angel of the Eucharist."

But he did not enter hastily on his work, about which he felt a certain timidity; nor was it his purpose to compose a complete biography of the holy sempstress of Saint-Pallais, which he modestly esteemed to be a task appertaining to some more competent pen. Five years later he sent his first pages

to Cardinal Villecourt, being desirous of taking his
Eminence's advice before proceeding any further with
his undertaking. What was his surprise and dismay
when he received in return a bundle of papers, many
of which were in the cardinal's own handwriting, and
found that that venerable prelate had himself contemplated writing the biography of Marie-Eustelle,
and now transferred the task to himself! His Eminence had gladly availed himself of the opportunity
to commit to able hands a work which he was extremely desirous to see completed, but with the
execution of which his own imperative duties were
necessarily always interfering. The diffident and
humble writer did not share these feelings of satisfaction. It had never been his own intention to
compose a life, and now he learned with grief that
—to use his own expression—"a voice which would
have echoed through the whole world, the voice of a
Prince of the Church, was going to betake itself to
silence in order to leave him place to speak." The
very desire he had entertained of ministering to
the glory of Jesus in the Adorable Sacrament of the
Altar had thus become, in his estimation, the actual
cause of diminishing the glory which would otherwise
have accrued to Him. This misfortune he bewailed
before the Lord, and represented touchingly to the
cardinal; but his Eminence viewed the matter otherwise, and was inexorable.

Nothing remained but to set to work with a good
will, the grace of God assisting. Imploring, therefore,

the special aid of the Sacred Hearts of Jesus and Mary, he took up his pen on the 19th anniversary of Eustelle's passage from earth, with the pure intention, as he solemnly avers, of making Jesus loved in the Blessed Sacrament. His thoughts, he declares, dwelt not for a moment upon Eustelle for her own sake ; he desired nothing for her personal exaltation or renown, regarding all the rich graces with which she had been adorned as bestowed with one sole object—*the glorification of the Divine Eucharist.* It was for this end that her heart was, so to say, transformed into that of her Lord, and that she was converted into a mirror to reflect the flames of His love. Her mission, he says, is not closed, and to this mission it is that he associates himself.

We subjoin the cardinal's letter on the completion of the work, which was submitted to him before going to press.*

" MY VERY DEAR * * *,

" I had read with much satisfaction the very interesting book you wrote on the Commandant Marceau ; but I may say that I have been much more delighted with the perusal of your manuscript on the Life and Spirit of Marie-Eustelle. There is but one

---

* It was published in two volumes, under the title of " L'Ange de l'Euchariste ; ou Vie et Esprit de Marie-Eustelle, d'après les Documents les plus authentiques. Par l'auteur de la Vie du Commandant Marceau. Ouvrage recommandé par le Cardinal Villecourt."

reproach I should be inclined to make you : it is the having named me so frequently. For the rest, you have painted her to the life, and I have reason to believe that she will have placed you amongst those to whom she will grant her special protection; for I entertain no doubt but that she has received in Heaven the recompense of her rare virtues. I shall await with a religious impatience the publication of a book calculated to produce the greatest good alike for the conversion of sinners and the perfection of the just. Your style, always modest, has nevertheless the refinement and elevation becoming the subject of which you treat. The very intimate knowledge I had of the virgin of Saint-Pallais, whose bishop I was, and the communications which Providence willed I should have with her, had suggested to me the idea of devoting some of my few leisure moments to writing a biography of her; but I rejoice sincerely before God that you should have taken this labour on yourself, and, above all, that you should have availed yourself so well of the notes with which I supplied you, when I became acquainted with your purpose. . . I have announced the approaching publication of your book to some pious souls wholly devoted to the Adorable Eucharist, and emulous of walking in Eustelle's steps, whom they have taken as their model. You may rely on their eagerness to procure your conscientious work, for which I confidently anticipate great success. Accept, my very dear * * *, the assurance of my warmest affection. I join thereto, since you desire it, my paternal benediction in Jesus and Mary Immaculate,

"CLEMENT, CARD. VILLECOURT.

"Rome, December 8th,

"Feast of the Immaculate Conception

"of the Blessed Virgin."

It will be seen from the above that the materials for a biography of Marie-Eustelle are both abundant and reliable, for every care and diligence has been used from the first in collecting and certifying them, and they have been submitted to the scrutiny and have obtained the sanction of high ecclesiastical authority in the person of one who was at the same time the most competent and important of witnesses. The present work is of course grounded throughout upon that of the French biographer, with such reference as was desirable to Eustelle's fragmentary account of herself. But we have endeavoured rather to reproduce the life as it has impressed ourselves, than to follow in the track of another, however superior to our own we must confess his qualifications to be. We have avoided so far as was possible, not only translation, but paraphrase, being convinced that such a process robs a work of all freshness and impress of originality. Nevertheless, when the observations of the respected author were such as we should naturally have desired ourselves to make, or the particular expressions he had used appeared to be more appropriate than any we could have chosen, we have not scrupled to adopt and interweave them with our own. No entire passage, however, has been appropriated without being expressly acknowledged.

In illustration of Eustelle's feelings and character we have availed ourselves of her letters to a considerable extent; quoting them as occasion seemed to require, but referring immediately to the original collection, instead of selecting from the large extracts to which the biographer has given a separate place in his work. The selection is necessarily somewhat of an arbitrary kind, as much has been omitted which would have equally, possibly better, served the purpose; for, as Eustelle's letters occupy the larger part of two volumes, it is difficult to feel assured that the best choice has always been made. The necessity of placing a limit to such extracts has often compelled us with reluctance to make omissions and curtailments; yet, without quoting at some length from her own writings, it would have been quite impossible to do justice to our subject; for Eustelle's soul is in those letters.

It only remains for us to add that, having communicated with the present estimable Curé of Saint-Pallais, we have learned with pleasure that veneration for this holy girl still prevails in her native place, but is still more abundantly manifested by persons living at a distance; and that very lately he had received requests for Masses of thanksgiving for graces believed to have been received through her intercession. "Our bishop," he continues, "interests himself much about our dear Eustelle, causing every particular relating to her to be registered, and seems disposed to call the attention of the Holy See to her and to introduce her cause at Rome." In so doing (we may remark) he would be but carrying out the intention of Cardinal Villecourt, who at the time of his death was engaged in collecting materials for the same purpose. For ourselves, as in duty bound, we declare, in obedience to the decrees of Urban VIII. and other Sovereign Pontiffs, that in all that we have written regarding the life and virtues of Marie-Eustelle Harpain, we submit ourselves without reserve to the judgment of that same Apostolic See, which alone has authority to pronounce to whom rightly belong the character and title of saint.

CONTENTS.

PART I.
𝕿rial and Conflict.

CHAPTER I.
CHILDHOOD AND FIRST COMMUNION.

Influence of the French nation for good and for evil. Many
special devotions due to France; especially to its women.
Marie-Eustelle an instance of this. : Her humble origin and
destined renown. Character of her parents. The intelligence and sensitive nature of the child. Her sweetness
of disposition. Talent for ornamental work. Tendency
to self-conceit; for which she afterwards reproached herself. Preparation for first communion. Serious reflection.
An act of self-denial. General change of demeanour.
She makes her communion on the feast of Corpus Christi.

CHAPTER II.
DECLENSION AND CONVERSION.

First fervours. Desire for the religious life. Beginning
of apprenticeship. Frivolous companions. Self-love and
self-flattery. Love of pleasure; especially of dancing.
Abatement of piety. Mental struggles. A momentary
fault repaired. Increasing disquiet and conflict. Pleadings
of grace. Temptation to despondency. A victory over
human respect. Promise made in confession. She breaks
it. Distress of conscience. Disrelish for worldly amusements. A good confession and devout communion.
Thankful remembrance of this in after years.

CHAPTER III.

EFFECTS OF ONE GOOD COMMUNION.

CHAPTER IV.

FREQUENT COMMUNION.

CHAPTER V.

PERSECUTION AND PERSEVERANCE.

CHAPTER VI.

THE LOVE OF JESUS AND THE LIFE OF LOVE.

CHAPTER VII.

MORTIFICATION AND INTERIOR TRIALS.

CHAPTER VIII.

FRUITS OF SUFFERING AND SPECIAL VOCATION.

CHAPTER IX.

VOW OF CHASTITY AND ITS FRUITS.

CHAPTER X.

WORKS OF MERCY.

CHAPTER XI.

VOW OF POVERTY AND SELF-DETACHMENT.

PART II.

The Ways of Peace.

CHAPTER I.

EUSTELLE AND ANASTASIA.

CHAPTER II.

THE SACRISTY AND THE ALTAR.

CHAPTER III.

THE THREE DIRECTORS.

CHAPTER IV.

THE TWO ATTRACTIONS.

CHAPTER V.

SECRETS OF THE INNER LIFE.

CHAPTER VI.

EXCESSES AND MARTYRDOM OF LOVE.

CHAPTER VII.

EUSTELLE AND HER BISHOP.

CHAPTER VIII.

EUSTELLE'S SPIRIT AND CHARACTER.

CHAPTER IX.

THE LAST DAYS OF EUSTELLE.

CHAPTER X.

CONCLUSION.

ERRATUM.

Page 222, line 26, for " key of the sanctuary " read " key of the church."

PART I.

TRIAL AND CONFLICT.

CHAPTER I.

No country has exhibited so great a power in modifying the ideas, tastes, manners, and morals of the other members of the European family as France. A peculiar national character or comparative isolation has, it is true, tended to neutralize or counteract its operations in some instances, but, in the end, its influence has never been altogether resisted. The power thus exercised has undoubtedly been beneficial in contributing to general polish and refinement; but it must at the same time be confessed, that it has not unfrequently helped to destroy the simplicity and efface the originality of traditional manners and customs, with which so much that is good is often intimately bound up, and to introduce the elements of that corruption which is attendant on luxury and the cultivation of the more frivolous arts. The effects of the dominion which France has exercised over social habits have, indeed, been strikingly various, but still more remarkable is the phenomenon presented when we pass to a higher order of things. Here we see her with curses in one hand and blessings in the other. If in her we behold the source of that devastating flood of irreligion which

B 2

was let loose on Europe in her Great Revolution, and the main instrument in tearing down and demolishing the venerable edifice which mediæval Christianity had reared, we also see her foremost in the work of reparation and reconstruction. If her blood has been spilt in unjust wars of aggression, no nation has been so prodigal of that same blood in propagating the Gospel of Christ. If the holy institutions and memorials of past ages have been swept away by her levelling hand, with no less zeal has she set herself to work to build again the desolate places. If her press is the fount from which the poisonous waters of corruption are perennially issuing, none can be said to supply the antidote more abundantly. There is scarcely a work of charity in which she has not taken a generous initiative; scarcely a devotion which does not seem to well forth with renewed warmth from her Catholic heart.

The gift of piety, indeed, has been pre-eminently attributed to this great people by no less an authority than that of Pius VII.,* when, on the occasion of his being dragged a captive through France, he became the object of an enthusiastic and affectionate homage such as has never attended the triumphant march of the greatest temporal monarch. We see this spiritual excellence continually exemplified in the share

* This opinion had been previously expressed (as Father Lallemant remarks) by the Venerable Cardinal Bellarmine. "Of all the gifts of the Holy Spirit, that of piety seems to be the portion of the French. They possess it more strikingly than any other nation. Cardinal Bellarmine, when he came into France, was charmed with the devotion which he everywhere observed; and he said afterwards that Italians scarcely seemed to him like Catholics when he compared them in piety with the French."—*Spiritual Doctrine*, p. 180.

which the devout French people have so largely taken
in the propagation or renovation of those sweet
devotions which cluster round the Sacred Humanity
of Jesus and His Blessed Mother, or which are
directed to that tenderest work of mercy, the relief
of the suffering souls in Purgatory; and every day
we are being called to witness the formation of fresh
associations and confraternities instituted with these
objects.   True it is that no devotion is really novel
in the Church, but the Good Householder who brings
out of His store things both new and old has His own
times and seasons and His own appointed instruments
for carrying on this dispensation.   Thus, while we
cannot fail to perceive the prominent part which it
has pleased Him, for His own inscrutable reasons (as
well as for others which may be more obvious to us),
that France should assume, in the progressive development and evolution of the special devotions to which
we allude, not less remarkable is the share which
women have had in this work.   The great expansion
given to the worship of the Sacred Heart, took its
origin, as all know, in France, and was due to a humble
religious lately raised to the altars of the Church.
Closely united with this worship is that of the
Adorable Sacrament, where again we find France in
the foremost ranks; and again it is a woman—only
one still more humble and obscure than the religious
of Saint-Paray—who is the instrument employed to
kindle afresh the flame of love to the Blessed
Eucharist through the length and breadth of her
native land, and, what adds to the marvel, the utterly
unconscious instrument: for all that Marie-Eustelle
was conscious of was the consuming love which
glowed in her own bosom; and when the almost

illiterate sempstress of Saint-Pallais penned those lines which, since her death, have been given to the world, she little knew that they would be seen by other eyes than those of the persons to whom they were addressed, still less that her burning words— to her dull and cold as compared with what they strove to express—should so inflame the hearts of thousands—priests, religious, seculars—that (as her biographer says) it may not be rash to regard "the great cry of love uttered by Marie-Eustelle as the first signal of that immense Eucharistic movement which has since manifested itself in Christendom, and which, it is hoped, will convert the treasures of God's wrath into riches of mercy." Upon the saintliness of this remarkable girl, and upon the work in which she has been the providentially ordained agent, the Church has pronounced no judgment; when mentioning her therefore in connection with the Blessed Mary Margaret, it need scarcely be observed that we simply indicate a certain analogy, and that no direct parallel or comparison is, or could be, contemplated; for which, in the absence of such authoritative judgment, the essential elements are wanting. Marie-Eustelle, moreover, received no Divine intimation that she was to be the means of reviving and spreading devotion to the Blessed Sacrament; but it would seem as if He who said that He had come to "cast fire on the earth," and who willed only that it should be kindled, had lighted up a furnace of love to the greatest miracle of His love in the breast of this poor girl, that its heat, radiating as from a burning centre, might renew the flame of devotion to the Adorable Eucharist in the hearts of a cold and selfish generation.

On the road which leads from Angoulême to Saintes, the traveller, when approaching the term of his journey, will observe some modest dwellings dotted along the highway, bordered, as it so frequently is in France, by a formal row of tall trees. At the western extremity of this unpretending little village he will descry the meandering stream of the Charente; green meadows form the background, and a hill upon which antiquated houses peep from the midst of verdure, closes the horizon of the landscape before him. This little village is the *bourg* of Saint-Pallais, and the decayed old town is Saintes. The earthly glory of this ancient place has long passed away; but time was, some two thousand years ago, when that hill was the site of one of the most opulent of the Romanized cities of Gaul. Flanked with high walls, it could boast its spacious amphitheatre, its triumphal arch, its capitol crowned with majestic towers; but of all this splendour nothing now remains but a few crumbling ruins, which the inhabitants still point out with a certain local pride. Saintes, however, has inherited a purer and less perishable glory than any which the relics of Roman magnificence can confer; for this venerable city dates its Christianity from almost Apostolic times, its earliest pastor, St. Eutropius, having received his immediate mission from Pope St. Clement, the disciple of St. Peter and St. Paul. Saintes' first bishop was a martyr, and so also was her last, the pious and intrepid De la Rochefoucauld, who was numbered amongst the victims of September, 1792.

The little satellite at its feet, while sharing the honours of the mother-city, has its own special boast in the venerable pontiff from whom it derives its

name, St. Pallais, Bishop of Saintes, and the friend
of St. Gregory the Great, who raised upon its terri-
tory his own Episcopal church and a superb abbey.
Both these religious edifices have been desecrated by
the Revolution, the abbey being converted into a
barrack, the cathedral into a stable; and the King
of Kings, driven from His palace, has taken refuge in
a mean-looking building which serves as the parish
church.   But poor as are its externals, the glory of
this latter house was to excel that of its magnificent
predecessor.   Thanks to the humble maiden who
worshipped within its walls during her brief earthly
sojourn, and whose piety towards the Adorable
Eucharist was to console the angels of the sanctuary
for the insults that had been offered to the Lord of
heaven and earth, the little church of this hitherto
unknown village has attained throughout the Catholic
world a celebrity which it can never lose.   The child
destined by God to confer such lustre on her obscure
native village was born on the 19th of April, 1814.
Those were days of stirring interest and of great trans-
actions on the world's stage; the fall of Napoleon,*
the return of the Bourbons, the occupation of French
soil by foreign armies—all these things filled the
minds of men, and busily employed their tongues.
Who gave a thought to the little infant carried for
baptism to the parish church of this insignificant
village on a morning of that eventful month of an
eventful year; and, if a thought had been given,
who would have suspected that the influence of that
poor child would ever extend beyond the narrow
domestic sphere in which her lot was cast?   That

* Napoleon signed his abdication at Fontainebleau on the
6th of April in that year.

child has stirred the hearts of thousands, not with the temporary excitement which attends the steps of those great ones who figure on the public theatre of life, but with those deep and lasting emotions which bear fruit for eternity. True it is that few bestow a thought upon her even now, beyond the limits of that class whose minds dwell on invisible things, to whom the spiritual is the substance, and the material the shadow; for when we spoke of the fame of Saint-Palla:s and of Eustelle who has immortalized it, it was not to secular notoriety that we alluded. There are two histories proceeding simultaneously on this globe of ours, and embracing in their framework the same external facts. Like dissolving views, they occupy the same field, but the vision of the one excludes in a sense that of the other. The one history presents what we may call a kaleidoscope of secular vicissitudes, a history of which none but Christians have the key; a history which is by turns a scandal to the moral sense, a disappointment to the insatiable longings of man's heart, and a perplexing enigma to his intellect. The other is the history of God's Church, the spiritual drama in which the affairs of eternity are being enacted; in which the great conflict between light and darkness is being continually carried on; for the sake of which the visible shell with its material accidents, and the chain of earthly events alone exist. The supernaturally enlightened eye views this external shell but as a vesture which shall be changed, a scroll which shall be folded up, and regards the sequence of worldly incidents only as the phantasmagoria of some empty show. With those who live in the things of time and sense it is quite otherwise. To them the visible and palpable alone have any substantial being. What wonder, then, if saints and holy persons and events of the most momentous importance in the spiritual order should pass unnoticed, except when they chance to come forward on the world's platform, and that they should then be noticed only to be misjudged! To Marie-Eustelle, unconnected as she was through life with any matter of public interest, has necessarily fallen the milder lot of being unobserved or ignored.

René Harpain and Marie Picotin, the parents of the subject of our biography, had three years previously to her birth lost their first child, also a daughter, six weeks after it saw the light of day.* Eustelle was therefore the eldest living member of her family. The first recorded incident of her life, and one at the recollection of which the pious girl always shuddered, is the delay of her baptism for five days. Few reasons can be considered adequate to excuse procrastination in an affair of such vital importance; in this case, the absence of the godfather appears to have been the motive. The child received the name of her grandmother, who held her at the baptismal font, and had thus for her patroness the Queen of Virgins and a virgin martyr, the first of her sex who at Saintes had the glory of shedding her blood for Jesus. The babe's parents, as we have said, belonged to a humble class of life; nobility of birth was not hers, but she had the higher honour of

* René Harpain and Marie Picotin had five children:—Marie-Anne, born the 8th of September, 1811, who survived only six weeks; Marie-Eustelle, born the 19th of April, 1814; Marie, called Angèle, born the 27th of March, 1817; Charles, born the 17th of June, 1820; and Madeleine-Anastasie, born the 12th of February, 1824.

reckoning among her forefathers a sturdy confessor of the faith. Her paternal grandfather, Michel Harpain, had firmly maintained his fidelity to God during the worst days of the Revolution and of the national apostacy; when so many abandoned or abjured, and so many more from fear concealed their faith, nothing could induce this good man to acquiesce in the slightest act of compromise, and in spite of scorn, ridicule, abuse, and even blows, he continued punctually to discharge all his religious duties. We know, too, that whoever remained true to his God during those terrible times, was so at the imminent peril of his life. His son, René, did not inherit his father's fervour. It is true that he ordinarily acquitted himself of those obligations which are absolutely essential to the preservation of the character and privileges of a Catholic, but he did no more; in short, he seems to have been one of those unsatisfactory members of the Church, unfortunately too numerous at all times, who concentrate all their energies on the honest discharge of the laborious duties of their state in life, and thus contrive to satisfy their consciences, leaving piety to the women and the aged.

The state of France during the years when René must have received his youthful impressions and formed his habits was necessarily highly detrimental, in a religious point of view, even to those who were blessed with truly Christian parents; and a rank crop of indifferentism has been the baleful result of that disastrous period amongst classes whom the poison of scepticism and infidelity did not so directly taint. How full of peril Eustelle esteemed her father's spiritual condition to have been, her own words testify. "Oh, how many prayers," she says, "have I addressed to Heaven that the bad examples of this perverse age and evil counsels might not cause him altogether to abandon the precepts of the Lord! To a Christian family there is nothing more bitter than to see any of its members forgetting the holy laws of the Gospel. O my God, Thou knowest all the thoughts of my heart in this matter, and Thou knowest with what unreserved self-devotion I have conjured Thee to accept the sacrifice of my life, that my father should not become the miserable victim of eternal reprobation!" After her death, the father was made acquainted with his child's magnanimous act of love; and, roused from his lukewarm state, he hastened to cleanse his soul by confession, and to unite himself to his long-neglected Lord by a worthy communion. The memory of his pious daughter, and, doubtless, her protection never forsook him in his last agony; and there was good reason to hope that her prayers helped to open for him the gates of heaven.

Of her mother, Marie-Eustelle speaks in very different terms, noticing in particular amongst the virtues which adorned her character, and which were nourished at the source of holiness by a faithful use of the means of grace, her sweetness, gentleness, and unalterable patience. A dangerous illness which attacked the infant when she had scarce left her cradle, alarmed the mother, who (as we have seen) had already felt the bitterness of loss in the early death of her first child; but God, who had taken the first in her innocence, had other designs in regard to the second : she was to live to glorify Him, and win for herself a brighter crown. Gratitude for the restored health of her treasure quickened the zeal of

Marie Harpain in the fulfilment of that most sacred of maternal duties, the watching for the first dawn of reason in the soul of her infant, in order to turn its first voluntary aspirations towards God. Eustelle could only stammer a few words when already she repeated in her mother's arms the Our Father and the Hail, Mary. The love which little children have for verbal repetition, and the singular pleasure they take in this exercise, even before they can realize the sense of what their tongue utters, are among those helps to Christian instruction which we must refer to the special appointment of God's creative wisdom. The words are learned first with a vague apprehension, which tends to arrive at comprehension as their meaning seems insensibly to filter into the mind and to inform the outward symbol—a process, indeed, which never ceases so long as there is a continuance of intellectual or spiritual growth. As respects abstract conceptions, words, in children, precede the corresponding ideas: to wait to teach the words which embody faith and the acts of religion until the infant mind can grasp their import, is to give the devil no slight start in a race where he already possesses so many terrible advantages. It was the more needful in Eustelle's case thus early to occupy the ground, on account of the great precocity both of her intelligence and her affections. Very few days sufficed for this quick and lively child to acquire the first elements of reading. To love, she needed no prompter or instructor, for her heart opened to the smile of kindness as the rosebud to the sun: "I loved very easily and very warmly," was her own account of her early dispositions. The New Testament and the Imitation of Christ were her first books. She was ready, however, to pick up whatever came in her way, and, through some unfortunate chance, she thus more than once lighted upon some of those licentious songs by which Satan's agents minister to low tastes and corrupt the morals of the poor. The child, ignorant of the sense of what she had contrived to decipher, ran to her mother to have it explained. The prudent matron had the tact to conceal her feelings of horror, and smilingly cautioned her little one against repeating the words. " You are very lucky, my dear," she said, "to have told only *me*. Be sure and always do the same : come to me when you want to know anything, and then you will avoid being laughed at." And as Marie-Eustelle, like most other little girls, had a great dread of being laughed at, she heartily congratulated herself on her happy escape.

To this remarkable precocity were conjoined qualities which are its frequent accompaniment : the finest sensibility, a lively imagination, and an intense relish for pleasure. This last disposition, it may be observed, is not seldom the mark of a sensitive temperament ; exquisite appreciation of enjoyment usually, though not invariably, corresponding with acute susceptibility of painful impressions. At present Marie-Eustelle's mother was all in all to her : her little joys and sorrows all centred in this dear mother. It was to her fond caressing arms that the child daily hurried back from school, to which, notwithstanding their scanty means, her parents sent her at six years of age. Looking up into her face, if, with the divining penetration of childhood, her eye detected the slightest shade of sadness, she would strive to comfort her after her fashion. "Mother dear," she would say, "you are sorry about something ; come listen to what

I have been learning in my class;" and then followed some Gospel story or, perhaps, one of La Fontaine's fables. We need scarcely doubt the efficacy of the consolation thus administered, or, rather, the irresistible charm of the consoler: Marie-Eustelle's mother doted on her, and was not a little proud of her besides, for she was as artlessly graceful and pretty as she was intelligent and loving. Years after, when the tomb had closed over the saintly girl, the good woman still reverted to the early beauty of her darling when describing her in her own simple way to Eustelle's future biographer.*

The Harpains had not intended to be at the expense of schooling for Eustelle longer than might suffice to perfect her in the art of reading; they were poor, and had their living to gain; but the wonderful progress of the little girl, now in her eighth year, and her eagerness to learn, induced her mother to make fresh sacrifices, in order to give her the advantage of being able to write. While thus, as she thought, simply consulting her daughter's interests, and forwarding her advancement in life, she was unconsciously seconding the designs of God in order to far higher ends. Eustelle must know how to write: this was needful for the accomplishment of her peculiar mission; but the benefit which for the present the child derived from the acquisition of this additional knowledge seemed very questionable. The school-mistress could not resist the temptation which solicits so powerfully the self-love of the instructors of children, to show off such of their young charges as do them the most credit and are most endeared to them by

---

* "Elle était jolie *comme un cœur*," was the familiar but untranslateable expression which she employed.

their docility and proficiency. When the Curé visited the school to examine the classes, Marie-Eustelle was sure to be pointed out for special notice, and opportunity afforded her for display. Nor was she by any means indifferent to these little distinctions, nor slow to profit by the cruel kindness shown her; the effect on her character, indeed, soon betrayed itself at home, and her good mother, indulgent as she was—perhaps only too indulgent—took the alarm, and besought the school-mistress not to allow of anything which might flatter her little pupil's vanity. Whether this appeal was successful we know not, but it may not have been easy for the amiable teacher to conceal a preference which the child's warm affection for herself only rendered the stronger; for, instead of eagerly running off as soon as recreation hour arrived, Eustelle would hang lovingly about her mistress or remain to cheer her with her singing, which she had noticed was particularly pleasing to her. And then the little creature had so many engaging ways: who could help loving her? who could help petting her? The sweet disposition of this charming child made her also much beloved by her companions. She was always prompt to render any little service, and ready to comply with the passing wishes of others; and there is, perhaps, no quality so winning, so generally attractive as this peculiar facility of temper. It was at this time that Eustelle's remarkable skill with her needle began to manifest itself. It was enough for her to see any kind of ornamental work to be able at once to copy it; and adepts in the art well know that such a talent is extremely rare. Eustelle's family still preserve one of her early achievements—a piece of carpetwork, which, as executed by so young a child, excites the admiration of connoisseurs. This talent was hereafter to prove of special service, by becoming the means of securing to her that independence which was necessary to the fulfilment of the designs of Providence.

At ten years of age the child was taken from school. She could read fluently and write legibly ; if not always in strict accordance with the rules of grammar and orthography, this was of no great consequence in one destined for no higher position than that of dressmaker or lady's maid. But slender as was the little budget of knowledge which Eustelle carried back from school, it was by no means inconsiderable in her own estimation. It had been sufficient to distinguish her amongst her young companions, and it was amply available for shining in the family circle gathered under René Harpain's humble roof. Like the "dying fly" which "spoils the sweetness of the ointment," there was in her heart a root of bitterness which had begun to poison the gifts of nature which adorned her, and to wither the work of grace in her young soul. The compliments inconsiderately lavished on her, the excessive fondness of her father and mother, who could absolutely refuse her nothing, all combined to foster the predominant passion. "My pride," she says, speaking of herself at this period, "made me unbearable." She adds that she soon became "disobedient and unsubmissive to her parents, hasty in temper, and impatient," and felt all the passions beginning to bud within her. "How long," she exclaims, "did I continue innocent and pure? Thou only knowest, O my God. Alas! I did not long preserve the whiteness of that mysterious robe with which Thou clothedst me on the day of my baptism. I hastened

/　　c

to enrol myself in the number of those who have pierced Thy Adorable Heart, and to sacrifice the title which the waters of regeneration had given me to the heavenly country. O Divine Liberator, is this what Thou shouldst have looked for after so many benefits? Where were the love and gratitude I owed Thee? O Jesus, wherefore did I so soon close my eyes to Thy light?" That these self-accusations were not altogether groundless, at least as respected her childish domineering temper, we have the testimony of a surviving relative, who says that she repeatedly saw Marie-Eustelle "slap" her little sisters when not quick enough in doing what she bid them. Nevertheless, it is impossible not to feel that, as seen by her subsequently in the light of her intense love for her Lord, past faults were magnified into serious offences. Such are the exaggerations common with saints and saintly persons; exaggerations, however, rather as respects what they convey to our minds than what they represent to the minds of those who utter them. For it is impossible to suppose that the Spirit of Truth, when He enlightens a soul as to the nature of its past faults, can create other than a more accurate estimate of their magnitude; still less that He can be the source of distorted or disproportioned images. The soul thus favoured begins, in fact, to have a more just appreciation of the hateful character of the slightest offence against God, and to regard even venial transgressions with a horror which souls less illuminated scarcely feel for mortal sins, and consequently applies to what are commonly esteemed light failings terms which ordinary Christians reserve for sins of the deepest dye.

The serious business of life begins early with the children of the poor. Our little Eustelle was now ten years old, and her parents judged it time for her to acquire the practical knowledge which was to enable her to earn her bread. But before entering on her apprenticeship, which must withdraw her from the paternal roof and the maternal eye, Eustelle's mother was anxious that she should make her first communion. She would not allow her child to be launched into the world and encounter its perils alone, without having been fortified by this great act. Jesus must have first possession of her young heart. Eustelle was accordingly kept at home for the present, her mother employing her in little domestic matters. The Curé of Saint-Pallais, M. Maupontet, was not only willing, but desirous that the usual age at which the children made their first communion should be forestalled in Eustelle's case, on account of the early development of her understanding. From some unexplained cause, however, there was a further delay of above a year.

As yet nothing peculiar, it will be observed, had distinguished the subject of our biography in the supernatural order; nothing to mark her as the special object of our Lord's regard, and destined, although her brief career was to be passed in the world, to be one of His chosen spouses. The first arrow of His love which was to wound her heart was to proceed from the Tabernacle, where her whole life was one day to centre and all the affections of her soul were to be treasured up. The announcement of her approaching communion aroused her spiritual senses: she seemed, so to say, to awake; and her first waking act was serious reflection: How much happier she

would be if she were better, more obedient, and if she
fulfilled her religious duties more perfectly!—such was
the tenour of the child's thoughts. She was in this
preparatory state of mind when, one day, her eyes,
wandering during Mass, were arrested by the sight of
a young person engaged in devout prayer. Eustelle
had from her very infancy felt an attraction towards
pious people, and as she continued looking at this
girl, the modesty of whose expression and whole
attitude specially charmed her, a ray of light seemed
to enter her soul, piercing it at the same time with a
sense of remorse, and inspiring the desire to imitate
what appeared so lovely. Nor did she allow this
aspiration, the fruit of Divine grace, to die away without effect; for she formed an immediate resolution
which involved no little sacrifice in the pleasure-
loving girl : she would avoid for the future joining
the parties of children, boys and girls, who, bent on
fun and amusement, used to go the round of the village. Innocent as they were in intention, these
childish frolics frequently led to mischievous results.
Marie-Eustelle probably was too young to appreciate
the full extent of the evil of which they were often
the occasion, but she could feel the essential incom-
patibility of such exciting diversions with delicacy of
conscience and a tender love of God. An acute and
accurate perception of this truth would seem to be
among the first revelations of grace to very young
souls, and they often yield an unhesitating assent
which we fail to see in maturer years, when the soul,
grown cunning against herself, or from habit less alive
to the deceptions of her artful enemy, will find a thousand ingenious and plausible reasons for endeavouring
to combine, to a certain extent, the service of two

masters. This little act of self-denial, as might be anticipated, appears to have been rewarded by more pressing solicitations of grace, with which she further corresponded by a determination to avoid whatever might prove an obstacle to her due reception of the precious favour for which she was preparing.

A great change was now observed in Marie-Eustelle by all her friends. Not only was she assiduous and attentive at her prayers, but her behaviour was marked by a more modest reserve, greater patience, and increased gentleness. The devotion which pleased her most was the Way of the Cross, and she went through this pious exercise four times a week with the view of obtaining the grace of making a good first communion. This grace was not denied her. The great day came at last: it was the feast of Corpus Christi, that day set apart for the special honour and adoration of the Holy Eucharist, when Marie-Eustelle was to receive Him who is Life and Love Eternal, and first to experience a foretaste of those passionate movements of her own soul towards this sweetest and most wonderful of mysteries which were hereafter to make her untaught tongue so eloquent on the inexhaustible theme. "Jesus," she says, "then entered into my soul, which as yet understood Him not. Yet how happy I was! and what generous resolutions I seemed to myself to make! Alas! very soon I was shamefully to forget them." It appears that it was then that for the first time she had been admitted to the sacrament of penance, an unaccountable delay, since she was now twelve years old. While alluding to the circumstance she makes no comment, but, after mentioning that on the day of her first communion she received the additional grace of another sacrament, she adds, "I confess, father, that I received confirmation with a very imperfect comprehension of its value, and accordingly I failed to draw all the profit from it that I might otherwise have done." She was soon to need all its fortifying power against the attractions of the world, which were about to solicit and lay siege to her young and impressionable heart.

CHAPTER II.

DECLENSION AND CONVERSION.

ALL for God or all for the world! Chosen souls know and feel intimately that with them at least so it must be. And the devil, too, knows it full well, and takes as much pains to seduce such a soul to live an ordinary life as he does to beguile the common run of Christians into committing mortal sin. To whom much is given, of them much is required; and when Jesus addresses any soul with a peculiar message of love—when, in those voiceless words which are unmistakably audible to the inner ear, He whispers, " My child, give Me thy heart "—then, what is pardonable, what is excusable, what is, perchance, scarcely blamable in others becomes an infidelity in this soul to its Heavenly Lover. He is a jealous Lover, our God, and His love is a consuming fire.

Marie-Eustelle persevered for some little time in her good resolutions. The sweetness of her first communion was still fresh in her memory, and acted as a preservative against external allurements. She had

"tasted that the Lord is sweet." The perfume of
life and salvation, the odour of the Beloved's oint-
ments after which the virgins run, make the soul
which is embalmed therewith despise the delights of
earth, and render her keen to detect the taint of death
which exhales from them ; so that even after Eustelle
was tempted to turn aside to these false pleasures,
the recollection of the true blessedness she had enjoyed prevented her from yielding herself up unreservedly to them, or partaking of them without
remorse. But at present she was still at home,
shielded as yet from trial ; and under the influence
of the salutary impressions she had received her pious
dispositions grew and flourished. They led her to
seek the society of persons consecrated to God. The
"Filles de la Sagesse," a Congregation founded by
the V. Grignon de Montfort, at the beginning of the
18th century, for the combined object of visiting the
sick in hospitals and educating girls belonging to the
poorer classes, had a house at Saintes. Thither, at
the further extremity of the town, the little girl
would eagerly run on Sundays after attending the
religious offices of the day at her own parish church.
From these good sisters their young visitor had
always a kindly welcome ; and she would return, after
these expeditions, musing within herself whether the
Lord might not call her to serve Him in this holy
Congregation. Her mother was the affectionate and
trusty confidante of all these little spiritual "castles,"
as the aspirations of young hearts so often prove,
and smiled complacently as she listened. But if the
fervent desires of the innocent child to give herself to
God in holy religion were not to find their accomplishment, we shall see that it was not because piety

waxed cold with advancing years, but because another
and a singular vocation was to be hers.

The critical time was now come for leaving the
maternal wing. True, Eustelle was not to be far
removed from her home, to which it appears she
returned at night ; but to spend the whole day under
another roof is to lose in a great measure the benefit
and safeguard of parental influence. A perilous
spirit of liberty and a sense of independence are apt
to spring up in the bosom when the eye of affectionate
control no longer rests on the young brow ; and then
Marie-Eustelle as yet so little knew her own heart.
To this self-ignorance, and consequent self-confidence
and self-conceit, she referred her infidelity to grace.
" At the period of my first communion," she writes,
" I was a little changed ; I had sentiments of piety,
but self-love still reigned within me. When I was
present at Catechism and the instructions given to the
other children of my age, I always inwardly flattered
myself with the notion that I knew more, and was
better and more devout, than the rest. Fool that I
was ! expecting to raise the edifice of my sanctification
on the ruinous foundations of pride and self-love.
Alas ! at the first tempest all crumbled down : the
just chastisement of my foolish pretension. One of
the children who made her first communion at the
same time told me that my devotion would not last
long ; that soon I should be like the others. This
prediction was only too faithfully accomplished."

She was fourteen years old when she was bound
apprentice to a needle-woman, and she soon became
an especial favourite with her companions. Her
beauty, her sweetness, and engaging manners made it,
indeed, impossible to see and converse with her

without loving her. These girls were what the world reckons modest and well-conducted young persons, but they possessed only the outside coating of virtue, —in short, just so much personal propriety of demeanour as was needed to satisfy the requirements of the class to which they belonged. They were frivolous-minded and devoted to all those amusements which supply at once an outbreak for the animal spirits of the young, and a field for the pasture and gratification of their vanity. Eustelle must of course share their pleasures. Natural friendships, and early friendships peculiarly, live on companionship; it is essential to their maintenance, and they crave it as the condition of their very existence. Eustelle was accordingly besieged with solicitations, and unfortunately there was a pleader within to second the tempter without. She yielded, and soon became passionately fond of dress and of dancing. The first of these tastes she had little means to gratify, but, as she observes, the disposition was not the less reprehensible on that account. For the satisfaction of the other, there appears to have been ample opportunity. "I can truly say, father," she writes, "that I loved dancing as much as it is possible to love it; I counted the moments till the hour came for indulging in this amusement, so full of peril to youth. I cannot calculate the number of thoughts, desires, looks, and words which on these unhappy occasions may have rendered me guilty in the sight of God. And I was but fourteen years old! Already, however, my whole thought was to please and make myself loved. When I tell you this, it is all one with saying that my soul could no longer be innocent." If innocence, in the strict, or, rather, in the larger sense of the word, was compatible with an attachment to these giddy diversions, it is clear that piety and the love of heavenly things could not subsist in such company. We have but óne heart; and when we strive to divide it between opposite objects, the one half, irresistibly, draws the other to it. But if Eustelle was bitterly to reproach herself with these hours of forgetfulness of God and the holy strictness of His requirements, still more did she deplore that she should have carried the vain thoughts which had begun to make such havoc in her soul into God's Presence in His sanctuary; for she confesses that often at this time she went to church merely to see and to be seen. "O my Saviour, O Jesus," she exclaims, "Thy love kept Thee enchained for me in the holy tabernacle or on the altar; and the time which I spent near Thee seemed so very long to me. The celestial intelligences surrounded Thee, prostrate in wonder and reverence; and I, a miserable nothing, dared to maintain in Thy Presence an attitude of so little respect; and one so little worthy of Thy greatness. Thy Adorable Heart was consuming with love for me; and mine, in return, was burning with a strange and profane fire. The excess of Thy charity prompted Thee to renew upon the altar the sacrifice of Calvary; and I assisted thereat only to renew Thy sufferings, and to rob Thee of hearts created to love Thee, and for whom Thou wert offering anew Thy Blood and Thy infinite merits!"

But although Marie-Eustelle had thus lamentably fallen from the fervour of her first communion; although all her good resolutions of giving herself wholly to Him who had then so lovingly given Himself to her, had been scattered to the winds; although she had begun to turn her face from the Living God to follow vain baubles, yet she never altogether forsook His service or neglected the imperative religious duties of a Christian. She assisted at the offices of the Church on Sundays and festivals, offered her morning and night prayers, punctually observed the prescribed days of abstinence, and still approached the sacraments, but this very rarely ; for she, whose hunger for the Blessed Eucharist was hereafter to feel insufficiently appeased by a daily reception, was at this period satisfied to partake of the Bread of Life only twice a year. All these religious acts were performed, she tells us, with coldness and indifference ; yet, poor in merit as they might be, her adherence to them testifies to her desire not to alienate herself from God, and they doubtless exercised a powerful restraining influence over her. We have the testimony moreover of her bishop, afterwards Cardinal Villecourt, who became intimately acquainted with the secrets of her conscience, to her freedom, even in her giddiest days, from the guilt of mortal sin. He likens her in this respect to St. Catherine of Genoa, whose first fervour suffered a temporary abatement from her having permitted self-love to insinuate itself into her heart, in consequence of having hearkened to the solicitations of friends, who prevailed upon her to indulge in some diversions, and to discontinue a life of such entire seclusion, so calculated, they said, to foster a melancholy disposition.

We have already observed that Marie-Eustelle could not abandon herself with the unreserve of her thoughtless companions to a life of dissipation. Grace in her heart did not suffer it to rest. " In the midst of the storm which the world and my passions excited in my soul," she says, " a heavenly voice from time to

time made itself heard. It was the voice of God my
Redeemer, calling me to Him. Ah! then it was I
felt the weight of my chains; but I loved them still:
I should have wished to give myself to God and the
world at the same time." In those moments of conflict and hesitation, when on the one side she was
stung by remorse and urged by a desire of sanctification, and on the other drawn to the world and its
pleasures, which she could not resolve to abandon, the
idea of the utter impossibility of her ever being able
to resist her temptations and correct herself would
take possession of her mind; and this artful suggestion
of the enemy furnished her with a pretext to remain
in the state she was in. Three times, in particular,
she was so powerfully moved, and experienced such a
gush of re-awakened fervour, that she imagined that
an entire change was about to take place in her; all
that, in fact, was needed was a generous resolution
on her part, but from this, and from the sacrifices
it involved, she shrank back. "The infernal lion,"
she says, "held me bound under his cruel dominion,
and laughed at my feeble resolves: what did he not
do to hinder his prey from escaping him!" But if
the devil had matter for triumph in the success of his
worldly baits, he met with a discomfiture on his first
attempt to seduce his intended victim from the strict
path of honesty. She was one day alone in a house,
where she was engaged on some needle-work, when
she felt tempted to appropriate to herself a trifle
which lay before her. In recording her youthful
faults, which she is assuredly far from desiring to ex-
tenuate, she says that the coveted object was too
insignificant to make it worth the mention. It was
probably so valueless an article that the mention of it,

from its very triviality, would have sounded absurd.
Nevertheless, whatever it may have been, it was not
hers : this she felt, and an instant's reflection led her
to replace it. Satan was vanquished this time, and she
was happy at having repaired her momentary fault :
"but I was wrong," she adds, "in not considering that
it had been the consequence of my want of self-watch-
fulness."

Some months elapsed after this little incident,
when her disquiet and perplexity, so far from abating,
began to increase beyond measure. God would not
suffer her to find any rest or sweetness in the pleasures
which yet so strongly attracted her, for they were
ever rendered bitter to her by self-reproach. Thus, at
once unable to give them up and unable to enjoy
them, pressed by the solicitations of grace, to which
she could not bring herself to yield, and held captive
by the worldly chains which she felt powerless to shake
off, her inner life was one of almost ceaseless conflict
and disturbance. Eustelle in after years could not
find words of sufficiently tender plaintiveness to deplore the long resistance by which she had grieved
the Heart of her Beloved. No wonder, indeed, that
saints and saintly persons, whom God has specially
sought to win to His love, should speak in terms
which seem to us overstrained of their past insensibility, when they remember how patiently and perse-
veringly their Eternal Lover had stood knocking at the
door of their closed heart, and how He would take no
denial, as one who had rather a boon to crave than a
priceless treasure to bestow. But Jesus did not content Himself with continually pressing her inwardly
by His grace. He had other ways of addressing her.
He would set before her a living picture of the joy

and peace which are found in His love. When
Eustelle was at church her eyes would often wander,
as eyes are wont to do when thoughts are gadding
here and there, but at last they would become fixed
on one object. What was it that had thus the power
to arrest her roving imagination ? It was the sight
of a pious girl at the foot of the altar. We have
already seen how readily Eustelle was moved by witnessing more than ordinary devotion; and now,
Sunday after Sunday, festival after festival, as she
gazed at this girl, she seemed to behold an angel
in visible form adoring the Hidden God in the Tabernacle: "She loves Jesus," she would inwardly murmur, "and is happy in her love." Then, as she
returned home, she would ask herself why she could
not be like her: why could she not do what so many
others have done ? Had she not the same grace, the
same Divine assistance ? At such moments she appeared to be all but ready to give herself unreservedly
to God, but the enemy of souls did not fail speedily
to place before her mind's eye a picture of all the
difficulties she would have to face in renouncing her
inclinations and breaking with the world. He reminded her of the gay circles she must forsake, the
company she must forego, the pleasures and diversions
she must sacrifice. What, he suggested, would be
said of her by those friends who so petted and caressed
her ? She would become the laughing-stock of those
by whom she was now lauded and admired. And, after
all, was she not very young to begin to lead so dull
and melancholy a life ? Had she not a right to partake without reproof of some enjoyment and recreation
at fifteen ?

Reasonable as such a plea might be judged by many

who are far from ranking with the world's votaries, it failed, as did all else, to silence the voice of conscience, or, rather, that of Jesus, who wanted all her heart, and would have nothing short of all. We cannot bargain with God, or make our terms with Him. Vain to say, He is contented with this or that in another, if it fails to satisfy Him in us; or, He permits this or that in others who, we have no reason to doubt, are His sincere and faithful children, if in us He will not tolerate it. Perhaps He has more to give to us than to them, but the condition of His giving is the complete surrender of self. If we obstinately withhold what a God deigns to ask for, we shall forfeit what He would have bestowed; and, perchance, even what we have shall be taken from us. A voice which transcends reason, addressing the soul in its very citadel, where the pure intelligence apprehends what the reasoning faculty may fail to grasp, is able to silence in honest souls all captious and plausible ratiocinations. This voice within us is an illumination of supernatural grace; and it is the test of our sincerity with God whether we will give heed to it, or whether we will consent to talk it down and overrule it by the help of our discursive reasoning powers. Such a sin against grace would seem to be more heinous, or, at least, more dangerous, than a conscious yielding to temptation, for it is a darkening of the light within us. Eustelle never fell into this snare: all the art of the enemy could not succeed in deceiving her, or in making her wilfully deceive herself. "Notwithstanding all the efforts of hell," she says, "I felt that it was necessary to break my chains." It was strength and courage which alone were wanting. Unable to seduce her reason, Satan now endeavoured to tempt her to despondency. "What!" would she say to herself, "shall I never arrive at a perfect conversion? I am unable to conquer myself; my passions are too strong for me. Shall I never, then, love my God? Shall my conscience never be at rest? Shall my soul never taste of peace, never arrive at knowing its God, and seeking Him alone? Will this God of goodness never satisfy my desires? Yet it seems to me as if I desired to save my soul." The spirit of evil would now maliciously suggest to her to lay the blame, as it were, on God Himself. "It is all over with me," she would passionately exclaim; "God does not will to save me; His mercy is not for me; it is not for me He suffered on Calvary; I shall never have a share in the benefits of redemption." And then a doubt would be whispered to her mind, and she would hesitatingly say, "God is not just: He wishes you to be His, but refuses you His help." If these sentiments had been the deliberate utterances of her heart, they would have been nothing less than fearful blasphemies against the Divine mercy, goodness, and justice; but, as the Bishop of La Rochelle truly observes, such thoughts cannot be imputed as crimes to persons in the state of agitation and perplexity in which Eustelle describes herself to have been; they cannot be said to consent to what passes in them; and he suggests as one proof that the soul does not adhere to the extravagant ideas with which the devil fills the imagination, its continuing to feel itself urged to seek God even while it appears, in its anguish and perturbation, to be bringing accusations against Him. The apparent inability to correspond with the powerful pleadings of grace which stirred up in Eustelle's mind this painful conflict, and

by which other servants of God have often been
severely tried, is, we need scarcely say, only a secret
form of unwillingness; as the holy girl afterwards
well knew, deploring her long resistance to the tender
invitations of her Lord. She willed the end, but as
yet did not will the means.

She was soon to receive a more abundant supply of
fortifying grace, a favour which may be regarded as
the reward of her fidelity to Christian duty and her
courage in braving human respect. She had been
taking part with her companions in an animated ball
on the evening of Shrove Tuesday. Such diversions,
we know, are common in Catholic countries, however
much disliked or discouraged by the clergy, as by all
who take a serious view of the design of the Lenten
fast.* The Church, indeed, sufficiently marks her
sense of the need of preparation for that penitential
season by the change of tone and aspect which she
assumes in her public offices for nearly three preceding
weeks. But the Carnival dissipations are dear to
thoughtless and tepid Catholics, and zealous priests
have contended, with comparatively small fruit, against
their wild excesses. Those who wish to save their
souls, but yet to get as much out of the world as they
can—and such a class is very numerous—naturally
like to narrow the season of penance as much as possible, and to take their fill of enjoyment to its very

* St. Francis de Sales used to call the season of the Carnival
his "bad days," because of the grave transgressions of God's
law to which it so often gives occasion. These sentiments
have been common amongst all holy persons. It has not been
unusual for communities during the week preceding Lent to
fast on bread and water, keep continual silence, and redouble
their austerities and prayers, in order to make amends to
Jesus for the offences offered to Him, and to obtain mercy and
grace for sinners.

D

verge. Supper had followed the ball in question, and the dancers were all at table, when twelve o'clock struck. No one noticed the circumstance, not even Eustelle at first, but soon the thought crossed her mind: Ash Wednesday had begun. "It is midnight," she said to the person next her, "and we are eating meat; I won't go on." But her companions did not look at things so closely: to them the morrow will not have commenced until they have had their night's rest and opened their eyes to another sun; they were in no hurry for the morrow. And so Marie-Eustelle, only a moment before the queen of the party, became at once a butt for the silly pleasantries of her careless friends; but she summoned all her courage, although it required no little in one so sensitive, and—" among the faithless faithful only" she—came off victorious in the trial. Who can say what may have been the value in God's sight of her fidelity? Certainly her conversion followed soon after.

In the year 1829 there was a Jubilee of fifteen days. These are always seasons of rich outpouring of grace, and this particular Jubilee was one of special benediction at Saint-Pallais. "Never," says its good curé, the Abbé Jossier, "shall I forget the edifying spectacle of which I was the happy witness;" and he proceeds to describe how the inhabitants of town and country vied with each other in their zeal; how the poor labourers might be seen crowding in before dawn to hear the early morning instructions; and how one infirm woman, who could only crawl along by supporting herself on her hands, actually used to leave her humble dwelling at two in the morning, that she might arrive in time for the exercises. Marie-Eustelle, feeling herself more and more powerfully drawn to

God, resolved to partake of the precious favours and blessings which the Church then proffered to her children, and for this purpose went to confession to the holy ecclesiastic just named, who had recently been appointed to the charge of that parish. He was struck with the clearness and simplicity with which his young penitent expressed herself, and, discerning the workings of grace amidst the faults of which she accused herself, as well as great capabilities for high sanctity, moved also, no doubt, by the Spirit of God, he said to her, "My child, God has special designs in your regard : be faithful." He then required from her a promise to renounce dangerous pleasures. His words made a deep impression upon her, and she never forgot them. "And has the Lord," she inwardly said to herself, "particular designs with respect to me ? And shall I not love this good God? Is it possible that I can continue to offend Him ?" She asked permission to make some addition to the penance prescribed, and imposed upon herself the obligation of eating only dry bread at breakfast during the six days of the following week. Her confessor agreed, and added, " See what confidence I place in you ; I will give you only a week's trial, and will then admit you to communion." She had, indeed, firmly resolved not to go back, but henceforward to avoid sin and its occasions. To this end she placed herself under the protection of the Blessed Virgin, and said the rosary every day, begging that Good Mother to obtain for her the grace of a perfect conversion.

As yet her conversion—to use her own expression —was but a mere *outline* (n'était qu'*ébauchée*) : its solidity had to be tested by trial, and there was great reason to fear, for she was still very feeble of purpose.

D 2

For a few weeks she adhered to her resolutions : but
it was Lent, and therefore not so difficult for her to
refuse to take a part in worldly amusements without
provoking remark.   The real trial was to come when
this pretext for seclusion was removed.   Accordingly
no sooner had the Church laid aside her weeds than
Eustelle's promises to God and to her confessor were
put to the proof.   Her parents were invited to a supper, and she consented to accompany them.   Perhaps
she felt it impossible to refuse ; such refusals, indeed,
may be said to be almost impossible to very young
persons ; they 'lack those plausible excuses under
which in after-years timid piety can shelter itself, and
so avoid passing that implied censure which the world
so deeply resents, and which a sensitive nature shrinks
from appearing to inflict.   She might hope, too, that
the party would be a mere social meeting, though probably she had no very distinct notion of what her
behaviour should be in case it proved of a more lively
description.   Unfortunately a musician was present, and
a dance was proposed.   Eustelle of course was expected
to join, and she seems to have yielded without a struggle ; less, however, from human respect than from the attraction of pleasure which suddenly revived within her.
The first notes of the music, the sight of the dance
forming in which she had so often mingled with wild
delight, recalled the old associations and silenced
the voice which reminded her of her solemn engagement.   One of her friends, to whom, it would
seem, Eustelle had mentioned her promise, whispered,
" What will your confessor say, who thinks you so
devout ?"   " Oh ! it will only be just this once," she
hurriedly replied.   Nevertheless, it was not the only
occasion on which she gave way : seldom, indeed, is

it that "just once" has no followers. What could
not have been so securely anticipated was that, by
God's mercy, she no longer took the same pleasure in
these amusements. She could not, it is true, help
yielding to temptation when placed within its influence, but her exposure to it was hardly of her own
free election. Her disposition to draw off from them
was perceived by her companions, to their great displeasure; but, hoping that it might be a temporary
scruple, they assailed her through her parents, representing to them the perfect innocency of their recrea-
tions, and the ridicule their daughter would incur
by secluding herself from society. Even Eustelle's
good mother was won over by their eager remonstrances; but when, on her child's return one evening,
she witnessed her misery and remorse, she promised
to leave her free for the future to follow her own
inclinations, and Eustelle, on her part, declared
that she would henceforth resist all the entreaties of
her friends.

Her distress on this occasion and her growing disinclination for these gaieties had probably been height-
ened by an incident to which she alludes in her unfinished manuscript—a quarrel between the relative
who escorted her and an individual in the company.
Anyhow, she availed herself of the circumstance as a
temporary excuse for declining invitations; but she
afterwards reproached herself with a want of generous
boldness for not avowing her real motive. The truth
was that, by God's grace, she now felt a total disrelish
for worldly dissipation. The hand of God was indeed
there: for it must have been in the course of one
short week that this striking revolution was accomplished, and that an amusement which had possessed

such irresistible charms in her eyes came even to excite repugnance and disgust. "Our Lord," she writes "had detached me from it. From the instant of which I speak I never again experienced the faintest desire or felt the least attraction for the pleasures of the world." A sudden transforming change had passed over her inner being during that Easter week. What she had hitherto so loved she loved no longer. Her will had acquired a fixity of resolve which God's special grace can alone impart. Henceforth the world shall be nothing to her : she mentally tells it so; she has turned her back upon it, and another horizon has opened on her view. Upon its borders was beginning to arise that luminary which was to be the light of her eyes and the joy of her heart during the remainder of her earthly sojourn. The Sun of the Eucharist had begun to dawn. Marie-Eustelle was to owe all to the Eucharist : it was the source of her sanctification, and became, as it were, the very main-spring of her existence ; and to this it is we owe the burning eloquence of this illiterate girl when she speaks—and seldom it is that she has any other theme—of Jesus in the Sacrament of His Love. At this time she felt a mixture of wonder and envy at the sight of frequent communicants, and the desire to unite herself to her Lord in this Divine Banquet began to spring up in her soul.

When she approached the tribunal of penance preparatory to her Paschal communion, her confessor expressed his surprise and disappointment at her infidelity to grace after the dispositions she had evinced, and the promises she had made ; he also pressed her most earnestly no longer to delay a sincere conversion. She told him all that had passed, assuring him that henceforth, with the help of God's grace, the world should be nothing to her; and after thus purifying her soul by a good confession she had the happiness of communicating. The recollection of this communion, which sealed her irrevocable return to God, draws from her a jubilant song of triumph in after years:—"Holy Angels, rejoice: I belong to Jesus for ever. Inhabitants of the holy Sion, celebrate the victory of the God who crowns you; break forth in rejoicing: I belong wholly to Jesus. His love has triumphed; His Eucharistic Presence has restored me to life; and, even as the Redeemer of men conquered the devil and hell by rising victorious from the tomb, so, enthroning Himself as a king upon my heart, He triumphed over all the enemies who oppressed my soul, and who had so long hindered Him from reigning therein."

Through her whole short life, indeed, we always find her recurring to this time, and mingling the notes of thanksgiving for her conversion with those of tender sorrow for her resistance to grace. "Oh blessed a thousand times be the excess of Thy ineffable mercy!" she exclaims: "would that I had a million voices to proclaim the prodigies Thou hast wrought for me! Divine Redeemer, when I travel back in thought to those unhappy days in which I so blindly took pleasure in that which offended Thee, my heart is pierced with grief, and feels ready to break: would that I could sorrow with an infinite sorrow! Thy paternal voice, which had so often sounded in the depths of my heart, had always found it closed against Thy loving solicitations; that heart was forming guilty projects, whilst Thou wast preparing for it the kiss of peace and reconciliation. I was Thy enemy, the slave of Satan; and Thou, Infinite Love, wast dwelling with complacency on the days when, by Thy grace, I should become habitually Thy tabernacle, those days when Thou wast to take in me Thy dear delight. Thou hast Thyself deigned to say it to me, O Eternal Truth—Thou hast said to me that Thou wouldest no longer keep any of Thy secrets from me. O Goodness, O Love, O Mercy! now may I borrow the language of the prophet-king, and with him exclaim, Thou hast broken my bonds; I will offer to Thee the sacrifice of praise, and call upon Thy Adorable Name. With St. Augustine I will say, Too late have I loved Thee, O Beauty ever ancient and ever new. But now, at least, receive this remainder of my life, this remnant of my youth, which I ought to have consecrated wholly to Thee. Alas! that I should have waited to the fifteenth year of my life to make Thee the entire offering of my heart. Can I so much as endure the thought that a single instant of my existence has not been given to Thee? Nevertheless, blessed be Thou, O Divine Spouse of my soul, who hast arrested me in the midst of my fatal career, and hast not permitted me to sacrifice all my days to the world and to the devil. A thousand acts of thanksgiving to Thee for this, O good Saviour. I am Thine: complete the work of Thy grace."

CHAPTER III.

EFFECTS OF ONE GOOD COMMUNION.

EUSTELLE'S confidence in the firmness of her late resolution proceeded from no vain presumption. She knew herself to be all weakness, but she knew also that God would be her strength, as of all who, by His grace, have hearts generous enough to believe that He can and will do great things in them. We receive according to our faith. As with Mary, whose vocation, immeasurably exalted as ·it was above all others, is the pattern of the vocation of her children, so with us ; we also may have a share in the blessing with which the mother of the Precursor was inspired to greet the Mother of God : "Blessed art thou that hast believed, because those things shall be accomplished that were spoken to thee by the Lord." Each of us has his vocation of God, and although an angelic messenger does not come in visible form to acquaint us with it, yet as certainly—although, perhaps, but dimly discerned at first and gradually unfolded—it will be made known and proposed to us, if we have ears to hear ; and this either by the secret intimations of grace, in concert with which it may be that our angel guardian has some special enlightening office, or by the outward course of God's providence, or by the voice of those who have the care of our souls. And when we know, or in so far as we know, the will of God in our regard, the believing heart-utterance of " Be it unto me according to Thy word " becomes the signal for the influx of all those strengthening graces which we need for the accomplishment of the Divine purpose. Accordingly, one of the most remarkable fruits which Eustelle gathered from this communion in which she made a complete surrender of herself to her Lord, was a wonderful increase of the gift of fortitude. From this moment she was emancipated for ever from " the degrading tyranny of human respect ;" and, in spite of her natural sensitiveness, she not only despised all the sarcasm and ridicule of which she became the object in the little circle which constituted her world, but even courted it to a certain extent ; neglecting no opportunity of publicly declaring how much she repented having loved the world and its maxims, and how resolved she was to condemn them henceforward in her conduct. · Sometimes she even put herself voluntarily in the way of those from whom she had reason to expect the most mortifying remarks ; she would patiently listen to the end, and then withdraw, happy at having gained a victory over human respect, and suffered something for her Lord.

Regularity, as we all know, is one condition for the satisfactory performance of any business ; and if this be the case in all secular affairs and undertakings, no less is it requisite in those of our souls ; indeed, there are obvious special reasons which render the adoption of some kind of rule of life, varying of course with our state and condition, one of the first and most necessary steps in the spiritual course. Marie-Eustelle accordingly resolved to hear Mass daily, and every evening pay a visit to the Blessed Sacrament ; to say the rosary, and never to omit some spiritual reading. She would also confess and, with the permission of her pastor, communicate frequently. But our Lord gave her early to understand that external exercises, however holy, do not constitute true piety. From the instant of her conversion her chief study was "to shun company, avoid dangerous employments, watch over her senses, renounce her inclinations, her natural vivacity, sensibility, self-love—in fact, to free herself from all those different ties and attachments which bind and fetter the heart." Henceforth she had absolutely no friends : not only were the former gay meetings abandoned, but she even gave up her accustomed walks with her companions. Amongst them, it is true, there were some with whom she might without detriment have kept up intimate relations, but no exceptions were made : "None at this time suited me," she said, adding these remarkable words : "Besides, I perceived (j'entrevoyais) that hereafter Jesus was to be in the place of all to me ;" and meanwhile she was doing her part : she was making room for Him who was to possess her whole soul.

Some may be disposed to think that, in this unsparing renunciation of all the endearing ties of friendship, this holy girl suffered her zeal to carry her beyond the bounds of discretion, particularly as in after-years we find her admitting of some relaxation in the matter. There is, however, no real ground for a supposition which she herself never appears to have entertained. Of course it cannot be denied that faults of what may be called pious indiscretion may occur in the early days of conversion, although we can hardly be too slow in hazarding a censure in any particular case. We are, perhaps, not a little disposed to over-estimate the claims of the world upon us, while we are absolutely in the dark as to the special demands of God on any individual soul. That might be dangerous to one person, and at one time, which would be profitable to another, or to the same individual under other conditions. Jesus was hereafter to be all in all to Eustelle; and when He had completely filled her heart and appropriated it to Himself, so that she had come to love all in and for Him alone, affectionate intercourse with a few who were like-minded, or with such as she desired to bring to a like mind, would no longer be liable to the same perils. At present she had too recently broken through earthly attachments for there not to be considerable danger lest much of mere natural love might insinuate itself into the purest friendship. Moreover, the higher the grade of sanctity to which God would call a soul, the deeper must the foundations be laid. In proportion as that soul is to share in the power of the risen life of Jesus, the more entire must be its conformity to the death of Jesus. All Christians, indeed, in order to partake in the benefits of redemption, must die with Christ. They must die to sin. Christ suffered death for us all, not only as our sacrifice and expiation, but as the pattern and model of the death which He would accomplish in each of us. He comes, then, again to die in every regenerate soul; but this death—which in all Christians alike must glorify God by condemning sin in the flesh—in the perfect works a complete mortification and crucifixion of the whole natural man, with all his affections, wills, and desires. After this mystic death comes the resurrection, when the soul clothes itself with wings, like the butterfly, and comes forth from its chrysalis, as St. Teresa has so beautifully described. Absorbed in divine charity, and purified from its human dross, it is then made fit to do great things for God.

The change which was wrought in Eustelle was as

signal as it was sudden.   Recording (under obedience)
the graces she received, she declares, to the glory of
God, who so mightily assisted her, that three or
four months after her conversion she experienced in
herself neither passions, habits of sin, nor the slightest
inclination to sin.   Those passions, it must be remembered, were in her very strong, for she more than
once alludes to their ardour.   A certain vivacity of
nature, with the impatience which is its usual accompaniment, was also one of her characteristics; again,
a sensitive temperament like hers, allied to an acute
intelligence, is apt at once keenly to feel and vividly
to perceive the faults and foibles of others; and without the restraining influences of grace, we know that
the lively tongue of thoughtless youth, and of girls
especially—and Eustelle was but fifteen—is prone anyhow to give itself a good deal of licence in the way of
playful censure, the temptation to which is commonly
increased by friends, who are amused with sallies
from which malice seems altogether absent.   Of this
character no doubt was that habit of "backbiting" to
which Eustelle says she had been previously addicted,
but which, like other habitual defects, no longer
formed matter for self-accusation in confession.   Purity
reigned in her heart, and "the law of clemency" and
charity ruled her tongue.   No more acts of petty
disobedience to her parents, no more impertinent airs,
no more indocility, no more caprice; it had become
her joy to manifest towards them all love, submission,
and respect, recognizing in their authority over her
that of God Himself; no more wandering looks or
distractions in the holy place, where she had eyes for
Jesus only,—and this entire transformation had been
effected without effort or struggle: all the virtues

seemed to have entered peaceably, as if infused simultaneously into her soul, and to have there taken up their abode without opposition. One would have thought that they had all been natural to her, and so it even seemed to herself. Yet she never for a moment forgot that this facility in well-doing was the supernatural gift of God, and that the fruits of a victory which her own strength could never have won might be easily lost by her frailty. It was, then, with the most faithful and watchful care that she kept guard over her treasure. For instance, one day she was asked by an acquaintance to accompany her to a neighbouring promenade of public resort. If balls were objectionable, the most timorous conscience, it was urged, could not condemn so harmless a recreation. "True," replied Eustelle, "but I am so weak that I do not like to expose myself to the temptation of being led on further. Do not, then, be displeased with me if I decline to go." But her friend *was* displeased : not all Eustelle's gracious sweetness could make a refusal acceptable which was based on such grounds.

Of the persecutions to which this innocent child was subjected through her fidelity to the impulses of grace we shall have to speak presently ; but we must pause a moment to consider what was the power which in so short a time had achieved this complete triumph over a nature so passionate and energetic as was Marie-Eustelle's, and that at an age when the world, of whose bitter deceptions the young heart has had no experience, was opening out all its attractions before her, and had even already succeeded in drawing her within its charmed circle. Such a triumph raises in us, perhaps, more wonder than that which

we feel when witnessing the perseverance of those
chosen souls who have never hearkened to its solicitations, and thus have never come under the influence
of its blandishments, or the return of such as have
discovered its emptiness and experienced its treachery.
It was the triumph of the love of Jesus, but of Jesus
specially in the Sacrament of His Love.   It was the
triumph of the Holy Eucharist.   Eustelle expressly
asserted that it was to the Divine Eucharist she was
indebted for her speedy emancipation from the bonds
of sin.   It taught her the difference between earth
and heaven, God and the world.   As in that Celestial
Banquet she received a wonderful increase of the gift
of fortitude, so also does she seem to have derived an
abundant measure of that of wisdom.   The Eucharist
taught her, not merely by the spiritual light which It
imparted, but, so to say, by Its very taste, in virtue
of that transcendent *sapience** which is the crowning
gift of the Holy Ghost.   She had tasted " the Bread
containing in itself all sweetness," and henceforward

---

* " Wisdom is defined to be a knowledge acquired by first
principles; for ' the name *sapientia*, wisdom, comes from *sapor*,
savour; and as it is the property of the taste to distinguish the
flavour of viands, so,' says St. Isidore, ' wisdom, that is, the
knowledge that we have of creatures by the first principle, and
of second causes by the first cause, is a sure rule for judging
rightly of everything.'   .   .   .   The taste of wisdom is sometimes so perfect that a person who is possessed of it, on hearing
two propositions, the one formed by reasoning, the other inspired by God, will at once distinguish between the two, recognizing that which comes from God by a certain natural
relation, as it were, between itself and its object, ' *per quan-
dam objecti connaturalitatem*,' as St. Thomas says; pretty
much in the same way as one who has eaten sugar, afterwards
easily distinguishes the taste of sugar from that of other sweet
things, or as a sick man knows the symptoms of his disorder by
his experience and sensations as well as the physician does by
his knowledge."—" The Spiritual Doctrine of Father Louis
Lallemant," pp. 150, 151.

she relished and cared for nothing else. That one passion, a passion for the Eucharist, expelled every other passion from her bosom, and wellnigh every other thought from her mind. As the bee round the honey-cup, so was she to hover perpetually round " the chalice that inebriates,"* making mystic music within her—aspirations of love and adoration and longing desire—gazing into the fathomless depths of this miracle of miracles, feeding on its memory, feasting on its anticipation.

Her confessor allowed her to communicate once a fortnight, and this permission seemed at first to fulfil all her desires ; but, each communion increasing her hunger for this divine food, the interval began to appear very long. To wait fifteen days before again receiving her Lord ! If only she might communicate every Sunday : but she did not venture to ask for this privilege. Meanwhile she continued to prepare herself for so great a favour, and no sacrifice seemed too great which would make her a less unworthy tabernacle for the King of Heaven. We have her own testimony, indeed, that ever since her conversion not one act of self-renouncement but was made from the love of Jesus, and, in particular, in order to prepare herself for more frequent sacramental union with her Lord. It was not long before this boon was accorded to her, and she was allowed to communicate every Sunday. Imitating, probably unconsciously, St. Aloysius Gonzaga, she now divided the week between thanksgiving for the last and preparation for the next communion, but her desires always kept running in advance of what she enjoyed, and each communion only increased her longing for the next. Never-

* Ps. xxii. 5.

theless, she left the matter with perfect simplicity in the hands of her director, receiving with joy any permission he might grant for an additional communion, but never murmuring if he judged proper to withhold it; for she considered that such was the will of her Lord, whom he represented. That good Lord, she tells us, had made known to her that nothing would please Him more than the renunciation of her own will, and that He wished her to direct all her endeavours to that end.

In proportion as she strove to divest herself of everything which could displease Him, Jesus poured fresh torrents of joy into her heart. Replenished with these heavenly consolations, borne on the wings of grace, led as it were by the hand along the course upon which the love of Jesus had launched her, "what wonder," she exclaims, "that I made progress in piety! Oh, how happy I was! how full of confidence in the God who had so loved me!" As God gave Himself liberally to her, so she in return gave herself unreservedly to Him; and not only did she refuse Him nothing, but she cast about her for something more to give. "How sweet it is," she said, "to deprive ourselves of creatures, that we may enjoy the delight of conversing with God! How He compensates to us and rewards us, even in this life, for the privation, if, after all, it is one!" And then she would turn with childlike simplicity to her Saviour, and ask what more she could do than she had done, and whether He wished for anything else, for that she was consumed with the desire to fulfil His whole will. One day the thought of her beautiful hair crossed her mind. Vanity, once a ruling passion with her, she now held in abomination: she will

E

deprive herself of woman's fairest ornament, that
which the Apostle calls her " glory," and which all,
from the highest to the lowest, instinctively prize.
But she must obtain her mother's leave. Poor
mothers ! they take as much pride in a daughter's
beauty, often even more, than does the vain girl herself. But Marie-Eustelle will wind her arm caress-
ingly round the good woman, and look up in her eyes
with that winning grace which has often extracted far
different permissions. Not many words are needed.
" Dear mother," she said, " allow me to get rid of
all this long hair, which makes me lose so much time
in a morning, and is really a great trouble to me."
Her indulgent parent could never say her nay, and
no sooner had the reluctant assent been extorted, than
she ran up to her room, where the scissors quickly
performed their relentless work. She replaced the
hair which had shaded her brow by a bandeau, and
rejoiced in being able to make this public profession
of desiring to please no one except her Divine Lord.
Her mother herself related this fact to her biographer,
adding, with a smile, " But the poor child could not
succeed in disfiguring herself : she preserved her
bright and fresh complexion up to the illness of her
last years, and her modesty itself served her as adornment."

Prayer was now her delight. She was up at four
in the morning, and as the whole parish was beginning
to be in arms against her, she used to walk to Saintes,
that she might there adore in peace and (as she hoped)
unobserved the God of the Tabernacle, to whom she
had given herself. Not, however, unobserved : one
day a lady stopped a woman of the peasant class,
whom she met in the streets of the town, and said to

her, "My good dame, I think you are from Saint-Pallais. There is a young girl belonging to that village, whom I find every morning in the church here; go as early as I may, still she is always there before me. There she remains on her knees, without movement, for an extraordinary length of time. If care is not taken to prevent it, she will injure her chest irreparably. Pray tell her mother." The person addressed was that mother herself. She was deeply affected; but what could she do to moderate a flame which God Himself had kindled, and which every day burned more intensely?

God draws the souls whom He specially loves into solitude: "I will lead her into the wilderness," said the Holy Ghost of old to typical Israel, "and there will I speak to her heart." So it was with Eustelle; and never was she less solitary than when alone. Often she would run and hide herself in the garden, behind a thick hedge, to kneel and pray. Afraid of being sought out, she would say to her mother, "Mother dear, if any one comes to see me, do please say I cannot come." The truth was, her heart had been wounded with Divine love, and as the wound deepened and widened, conversation with creatures became every day more and more irksome. Marie-Eustelle, in fine, was become not only a true and sincere convert, but an entire conquest of the Saviour's grace,—the captive of Him who has Himself become a prisoner in the Tabernacle, that He may draw all hearts to the captivity of His love.

CHAPTER IV.

FREQUENT COMMUNION.

MGR. DE SÉGUR has inscribed on the frontispiece of his beautiful work entitled *La Très-Sainte Communion*, "We need saints more than ever, and it is communion alone which makes saints ;" and (to add a still higher testimony) our Holy Father, Pius IX., writing to this same prelate, thus expresses himself :—
" Very dear son, we warmly congratulate you on the zeal with which you labour to excite the faithful to a more frequent approach to the Holy Table." We have seen how it was communion which laid the foundation of Eustelle's saintliness, and it was communion also which reared the edifice. True as this is in all cases,—for it was of all, without distinction, that Jesus spoke when He said, " He that eateth My Flesh and drinketh My Blood, abideth in Me and I in him "—it would seem as if in her case this golden, this vital truth had been laid palpably bare before our eyes, that we in these latter days might the more vividly realize and appreciate it. Days these are in which it would appear that God, in His wonderful dispensations regarding His Church, designed to place in a fuller and more touching light every mystery which displays the unutterable love and tenderness of the Sacred Humanity of His Incarnate Son. As the Evangelist who closed the Gospel history, and whose Apocalyptic vision seals the Inspired Record itself, is especially the Apostle of Love, so may we not say that the Church in these latter times is in every act and word perpetually proclaiming, with increasing earnestness and emphasis, while in her own deep

bosom—the hearts of her united faithful children—
she is ever and ever more intensely musing on the
thought, that God is Love; and where is this His
character exhibited in a more transcendant manner
than in the Holy Eucharist?

Casting forward an anticipatory glance, we shall
find Marie-Eustelle all her life long regarding frequent
communion as the chief source of the Christian's
strength in his conflict with sin and the powers of
evil, the great means of sanctification for all, without
exception. It would be a mistake to suppose that
she was drawn to it only by those transports of joy
which she experienced in connection with the Holy
Eucharist ; these were but the exceptional and
gratuitous favours of God. During those years of
interior trial which followed her sunny spring-time of
grace, when all hell seemed to be conspiring to fill her
soul with obscurity and anguish, she never omitted
one of her accustomed communions. When approaching the altar she would say, "Lord, my soul is in
thick darkness ; I know not whether I am guilty, but
by Thy grace I believe I have fought and resisted.
Lord, I have not willed to sin. I come, then, to
receive Thee with confidence, that I may resist with
still greater courage." She would then draw nigh
without fear, relying on the assurances of her confessors, who had encouraged, nay enjoined her to
disregard all such disquieting apprehensions. Immediately a heavenly light filled her soul, and she discerned, as in the clear brightness of day, that she
was free from the offence she dreaded. And what
she practised in her own case, she urged upon others
with what may be called even a holy vehemence. A
good religious, after hearing a sermon on unworthy

communion, was so impressed with fear that she felt she had no longer the courage to receive her Lord. Eustelle, in visiting her, discerned the traces of inward discomposure on her countenance. "What is the matter, sister?" she said; "confide your grief to me, and if I can console you, I will do so with all my heart." No sooner had the nun told her the cause of her sadness, than Eustelle began to speak with so much love and unction of the confidence which ought to animate us at the thought of the excessive goodness of the Saviour, that peace descended at once on this troubled soul. "Oh! if I could but make you understand," she said, "how good, how loving, how merciful He is. You will promise me, will you not," she added, entreatingly, "never to deprive yourself of one single communion without some well-grounded reason? Oh, my dear friend! believe me, our Lord loves you; and how you will grieve Him if you abstain from receiving Him through an unreasonable fear. You are too mistrustful: our Lord loves the souls which go confidingly to Him. How He loves to communicate Himself to such! He fills them to overflowing with His graces. He speaks to them as one friend speaks to another, as a father to his child, as a husband to his spouse, as brother to brother. Oh, my good dear friend, if I could but put into your heart what Jesus has put into mine! I will beseech Him to give you light." And much more she said, not like one who is merely repeating what she knows and believes to be true, but with that vivid conviction which comes of experimental knowledge. The religious from whom these particulars were derived regretted that she could not recall to mind all her words on that occasion. "Eustelle's prayers were

heard," she said; " my confidence is now as great as
was my former distrust ; but it is chiefly since her death
that I have possessed it in such abundance.   It would
seem as if in departing she had poured into my heart
the fulness of her own.   After God, I owe this blessing
to my faithful friend Eustelle."

" When I omitted my communions out of scruple,"
writes another of Eustelle's friends, " she was ex-
ceedingly pained, and used to reproach me with
much warmth.   '*One communion less,*' she would
say to me, '*is one degree less of glory.*'"   To another
we find her writing, "I am ignorant whether you
have not permission to communicate, or whether you
refrain through some disquietude of conscience.   As
for your disquietudes, I take them upon myself; I
will place them this evening in the sweet Heart of
the good Jesus, whom you must love more than
yourself.   Oh, how good is this God, so full of love !"
And again, probably after a reply, "I know that you
have been permitted to continue your communions ;
however, if need be, you could speak to M. ——.
This being the case, either go to communion as usual,
notwithstanding your disquietudes, or go and speak to
the Curé.   I believe the devil has got some advantage
over you this week."   In her zeal to urge pusilla-
nimous souls to share in the heavenly banquet, she
would proffer her word as security, and add, " I
answer for it, I will answer for it ; only go on."   In
one of her letters to a person consecrated by vow to
God, we find her writing, " What I blame you for is
your not giving to your soul more frequently the
sacred nourishment of the Divine Eucharist, that
pledge of the tenderness and charity of a God ; that
aliment deprived of which our soul remains without

strength, warmth, or life. Oh, if this light of angels
did but shine in our hearts, what would not our
works be! Alas! why should there be so much ice
in the midst of such flames?" To another timid soul
she uses these encouraging words :—" Dear friend,
draw near to-morrow without fear to the Altar of the
Lamb ; go to satisfy your hunger and quench your
thirst. It is the love of a God-Man which invites
you ; it is Jesus, that dear Brother, that only Benefactor ; He opens His Heart to you, hasten to enter
It ; you will find therein the plenitude of all goods.
Be not discouraged at the sight of your infirmities,
but, animated with a sweet and loving confidence, let
your soul detach, purify, and raise itself above all that
might stain it, to unite itself, even in this life, by
anticipation, to its principle and its beatitude—to
Jesus, the Love Unknown." Marie-Eustelle had
apparently taken up her pen that day only from a
view to securing the morrow's communion.

It need scarcely be observed that all those upon
whom she thus urges a frequent participation of the
Bread of Life, notwithstanding presumed unworthiness,
were persons who were known to her as desirous of advancing in the love and service of God, but who were
either timid, scrupulous souls, fearful of making a sacrilegious communion, or labouring under some erroneous
view of the severity of God or a mistaken notion of
humility. Eustelle well knew that the sin of sacrilege
cannot be committed unwittingly and unwillingly.
Whoever communicates in good faith, and with the
sanction of his confessor, may make a more or less profitable communion, according to his dispositions, but
cannot commit an offence of the character he dreads ;
while the false views of God's rigour and of the true

nature of humility, which withhold some from frequent approach to the Table of the Lord, are an injury to the sublimest and dearest of His attributes, or, rather, to that which includes and sums up all, His Infinite Love, and proceed from a subtle form of pride suggested by the father of lies. Eustelle is evidently addressing herself to combat an argument which had been advanced, savouring of Jansenism, when, in one of her letters, she warns her friend against falling into the snare of the devil, who had suggested to her to give up frequent communion and follow the example of so many others, of whose salvation, after all, she could not be assured. "You are too weak," she says, "for a monthly communion to keep up in your soul the life of the Divine Model which you are bound to copy within you: an imitation without which we cannot be numbered among the predestinated. The words which our Lord in the Gospel addresses to His Heavenly Father, He says also to us, when He prays that we may be one with Him, as He and His Father are one. See in these words the Saviour's desire: how they tend to the most perfect union! Think not to attain to this union by forsaking the means which establishes it, maintains it, and preserves it; that which causes it to grow in time, that it may be consummated in eternity. To bargain with God, as you would be doing by adopting this course, would be to constrain Him to withdraw His graces from you. He has a right to expect from you the most perfect life and the most generous love. Under the pretext of avoiding pride, you would neglect the means of its destruction. Humility, humility, confidence! Destroy the self-love which is in you, and, for this end, communicate with humility. I am very desirous that you should give up your own notions; they pain me. Adieu. Give yourself to Jesus through Jesus." "Do not," she said to some one on another occasion, "deprive yourself without reason of communion; it is the life of our souls. Will you let your soul perish away for trifles to which great and generous souls pay no attention, because they abandon themselves in a sentiment of confidence and love to Him who knows the frailty of human nature? He has been pleased to clothe Himself therewith for the love of us, and in order to supply for our weakness, by expiating the faults which through it we may commit." All her advice tends to the same end. "Oh, do not so easily abstain," she again repeats to this same timid soul, "from so great a good, from the *only good.*" And in a little note to one who placed confidence in her, we find her encouraging her to ask permission for an additional communion. In this instance again it would seem that the backening cause was that fear which perfect love casts out. "God," writes Marie-Eustelle, "does not like little souls which stick at trifles, and sometimes neglect what is essential." But not only was she solicitous to deter persons from drawing back through timidity, and to urge them to more frequent communion, she was also watchful for opportunities to recommend it as the sovereign means of acquiring sanctity to any of her friends who had begun to take to heart their soul's salvation. Thus she hears that a former intimate friend of hers, now in service at Bordeaux, is determined to labour in good earnest to advance in holiness; forthwith she writes, "It is above all in the holy use of the Sacraments that you will find the graces and lights which you need in order to make continual progress in the paths of virtue. The Sacrament of the Eucharist is the master-piece of the power, the wisdom, and the goodness of a God. What sentiments ought to animate your soul in the presence of this Jesus, who, God as His Father, Eternal as His Father, before whom the universe is but a speck, who, by a single act of His will, could reduce this universe to nothingness, abases Himself, through the excess of His love, to become our Food under the species of bread ! Dear Marie, it is at that source of all good that you must often go and draw. Ob, if the people of the world did but know what exquisite pleasures are tasted at that sacred banquet, I do not doubt but that they would renounce all their false joys to come and take long inebriating draughts at the fountain-head of everlasting truth. As for you, who have already tasted of this ineffable joy, be diligent to increase it by as frequent communion as may be. Place all your delight in this divine aliment. Let Jesus in the Eucharist be all in all to you." And again, in another letter, " I would fain persuade you to make this Bread of Angels your delight as often as possible. In your sorrows, in your trials, go and take refuge in this asylum of peace; seek the shade of the Tabernacle. · There reposes our tender Father, our compassionate Brother, our heavenly Friend, the God of angels, adored by them in heaven, and on earth by those souls which a bright ray of faith has enlightened." We find her writing in the same strain to a youth[*] of her own parish, for whom she had a tender charity, who was studying at the little seminary of Pons. She would bespeak this innocent

* Armand Guérin, afterwards a priest; he will be noticed again later.

soul for Jesus: "Ah, brother of Jesus, child of Mary," she writes, "consume yourself at the Eucharistic flame; have no soul, no heart, spirit, intention, love, life, breath, taste, but only for the Eucharist: in a word, let your entire being be ever flowing in one perpetual sacred stream towards this Jesus so unknown, so lovingly hidden in the prison of the Tabernacle. Let Him be ever our joy, our peace, our aim. In as far as it depends on yourself, frequently approach the Holy Table, to taste the sweetness of this delicious honey."

Marie-Eustelle's active charity in inviting guests to the banquet of the Lord became so well known, that a learned and experienced priest appears to have given her the special charge, particularly during his absence, of several persons, who, to use an expression which alone accurately describes their state, were "afraid of the good God," commissioning her to urge them on. Traces of this may be noticed in her letters, as where she says, "I have lost my rights; your spiritual father has returned." Need we add, that Eustelle, thus devoured as it were with zeal to bring all over whom she had any influence to the Table of the Lord, was ready herself to endure any fatigue and any privations rather than sacrifice one single communion? For instance, she once consented, at the earnest solicitation of some pious ladies, to go and pass a few days with them. They lived a few leagues from Saintes, and nothing but the exceeding charity of this holy girl, which made it impossible for her to refuse where it was question of serving others and helping to bring them nearer to God, could have overcome the reluctance with which she always left her beloved Saint-Pallais. Besides, she had to set off too early in the morning to receive her Lord, a privilege which at this period she enjoyed daily. Nevertheless, she hoped that by hastening her steps she might reach her destination in time to secure this blessing. The distance, however, was considerable, and the exertion must have been very trying to one suffering as she then was from extreme weakness and a most distressing cough ; but to her this was a small matter, so as she could but compass an object so dear, the one great object, indeed, of her life. On she pressed, but when she reached the church she found Mass very far advanced, though not quite completed. There was still the priest at the altar, a Sacred Host in the ciborium ; a priest to give It,—this was all Eustelle desired or needed. She communicated after Mass, and her joy was full. She then devoted herself to those for whose satisfaction she had come, and all were so charmed and edified by her easy cheerfulness, almost gaiety, her amiability, and the unaffected piety and fervour which breathed in her conversation, that she had soon won every heart. Her presence alone, all embalmed, so to say, with the fragrance of her recent communion, seemed to do good even to those who had no opportunity of speaking with her. Long was the short stay of the "angel" of Saint-Pallais remembered in that household.

From the very hour, then, of Marie-Eustelle's conversion, and the complete change effected in her by her participation of the Eucharistic banquet, to her last days, this servant of the Lord was a fervent apostle of frequent communion. Imbued with the same spirit which animated the saints who were intimately conversant with the feelings and desires of the Sacred Heart, she knew that the "delights" of Jesus "are to be with the children of men."[*] Did He not say to St. Gertrude, who enjoyed such familiar communications with her Lord, " Whosoever hinders souls from receiving Me is an enemy to My happiness ?" And the same truth was expressed by Father Avila when he said, " Those who blame frequent communion act the part of the devil, who bears an implacable hatred to the Divine Sacrament." But it needs not to quote the revelations or the words of saints when Christ Himself has plainly spoken by the infallible voice of His Church, and has expressed by her mouth His divine aspiration :—"Our desire would be that all the faithful should communicate each time they assist at Mass." Such was the formally expressed wish of the assembled bishops, in union with their head, Christ's Vicar on earth, at the Holy Council of Trent.

CHAPTER V.

PERSECUTION AND PERSEVERANCE.

WE have been led in the last chapter to anticipate a few incidents in Marie-Eustelle's life, for the purpose of illustrating the distinctive character of her piety. As each individual has his peculiar outward features and bodily constitution, as each child of Adam has his inherent natural qualities, so each member of Christ's mystical body, each child of grace, has his spiritual stamp and impress, which he has either received or is in process of receiving through the

* Prov. viii. 31.

co-operation of his own will, or which at any rate subsists in the Divine intention regarding him. When the God-Man condescended to be baptized of John in the Jordan, and the Holy Ghost visibly descended on His Sacred Humanity, anointing Him for His mission, while the voice of the Eternal Father declared Him to be His Beloved Son, immediately (we are told) Jesus, coming forth from the waters, was "led"— another Evangelist says "driven"—into the desert. It was the first step in a course of which our Lord Himself testified that it was all marked out to Him by His Father, and that of Himself He did nothing. The baptism of the Head is the model of that of the members in their several measures. Upon each soul regenerate in baptism the Holy Ghost descends, while the Father receives it as His dear child in His Only-Begotten, the Firstborn among many brethren ; and this same Spirit takes possession of it for a determined and special end, to seal it with its appointed image, and to impel it, albeit with the free acquiescence of its will, along its predestined road. These roads differ, although they have all the same goal. Marie-Eustelle was led by the road of love. This was the distinguishing feature in God's dealings with her soul. From first to last she was constrained to do all through love ; for, as we shall have to notice hereafter, she had even a kind of inability to do otherwise, or to act in any other spirit, or from any other motive, however good in itself. And this love all centred in that mystery of love, that concentration of all love, so to speak—the Holy Eucharist. Here, then, as before observed, we have the key to all which this holy girl said, and to all she did ; and in order rightly to understand and profit by her example, it is well that we should thoroughly realize, from the first, the special and peculiar characteristics of her vocation,—a point, indeed, of much importance in studying the lives of God's saints or of His most favoured servants.

To return to our narrative. So great a change could not take place in Marie-Eustelle without attracting notice in a little neighbourhood where every one, of course, knew every one else. One would have imagined, however, that it might have escaped animadversion. In an unpretending village, whose inhabitants were almost exclusively the humble sons and daughters of toil, one would have thought that the spirit of the world and the pride of life could scarcely be so rife, but that a poor child of fifteen might renounce dancing and the desire to attract admiration, might dress plainly and give herself to prayer and retirement, without exciting a clamour of indignation and calling down on her a very storm of contempt and invective. But the world is everywhere, and not in great cities alone, although it may there have fuller scope for its display and the opportunity of exhibiting more tempting and perilous baits. The world, at any rate, was not banished from Saint-Pallais, which seems to have been a miniature Paris for frivolity, dissipation, and heartless secularity. " The world," says Eustelle, "had loved and caressed me when I seemed to be all for it. What, then, had I done by embracing the cause of piety to make me so culpable in its eyes? It could not have treated me with more rigour if I had been guilty of the greatest excesses." We might add, that it would probably have been more indulgent. Its condemnation at least would have had none of the acrimony and

fierceness which characterized its censure of so utter
a rejection of all its principles and maxims, a censure
the more bitter in the present case as this rejection
implied a contempt of all it had to offer, and was not
the result of the disappointments of life or of the dis-
enchantments of age. For it was one in the first
bloom of her youth and loveliness, to whom as yet it
had proffered nothing but smiles and soft words, who
had dared to throw its favours in its face and turn
her back upon it in scorn. This was the offence.
Eustelle might have been forgiven her faithful fulfilment of the imperative duties of her religion; some
virtues and a certain degree of modesty would have
been esteemed even by the world as an adornment in
one of its votaries. Much may be tolerated, nay
admired, so as we break not with it, and do not
openly declare ourselves against it. Whoever is not
against it, the world will still reckon to be on its side.
But Eustelle's whole conduct proclaimed her its sworn
enemy: she had chosen the Beatitudes of the mountain, and must abide by the consequences of her
choice,—the obloquy and hatred of the multitude at
its feet.

It seemed as if there were now no other topic of
general interest at Saint-Pallais than the conduct of
this poor girl. The needlewoman's humble apprentice
engrossed everybody's attention; no one talked of anything but Eustelle; she became the object of the most
cruel sarcasm and ridicule; and the rancour and viru-
lence, not to say fury, with which she was assailed
would be hardly credible were it not so well attested.
She was pointed at in the streets, and addressed in
terms of grossest abuse; she was made the subject of
vulgar talk in the public-houses. Did her neighbours

F

see her enter any dwelling, they would crowd in after her, and begin laughing and railing at her, accusing her of follies and absurdities which were the merest inventions of spite and illnature. Great as is the world's hatred of the true Christian character, when it sees it faithfully portrayed in the life of perfection, the cause of provocation in the present instance would scarcely seem adequate to the indignation evoked. Did we not remember that the devil and his instigations are always to be taken largely into account, we should be disposed to wonder at the display of so much active malice against a gentle and unoffending girl; marvelling, however, not so much that men and women could be so malicious, as that they should bestir and excite themselves for so small a matter. But even good and respectable people—the *soberly* religious, as they would have called themselves—joined in the clamour against her, and perhaps of all Eustelle's tormentors these were the most pertinacious and teasing. They would come with an air of compassion and inform her of all that was said of her, assuring her that she had brought these annoyances on herself by her eccentric modes of proceeding. It was well to serve God, but extremes should be avoided: her devotion was simply ridiculous. Why should she debar herself every pleasure? Was there no amusement that was innocent? Nay, even some who desired to pass, not for good Christians only, but for persons of no ordinary piety, were amongst the bitterest of her censurers. Marie-Eustelle held her own with firmness; although as yet the light she had received was imperfect, compared with that which she afterwards enjoyed, yet she clearly perceived that the reasons they urged were contradicted and refuted by the inspirations of grace within; she judged it best, therefore, to hold no further intercourse with them than such as courtesy and propriety demanded. Nevertheless, whenever she was brought into contact with them she showed them all cordiality and sweetness, and a ready disposition to serve them; but this amiable behaviour had no success in allaying their irritation. When they perceived that Eustelle's piety was not after the pattern of their own, that she did not care to listen to gossip, even when it concerned herself, their spitefulness knew no bounds. They taxed her with hypocrisy, and declared that the motive of all her devout practices was the desire to impress her confessor with a good opinion of herself. All her confessions and communions, they said, were so many affectations on her part; her whole life was a mere piece of acting, devised to attract notice and make herself remarked: she was idle and useless at home, and spent nearly all day in church, outdoing religious themselves in the length of her prayers. Among her traducers was even one who had herself a title to that honourable appellation. True, she was but a poor old woman, possessing a slender amount of knowledge—self-knowledge unfortunately included,— ignorant of her own ignorance, which is the worst and most incurable kind of ignorance. She had been a lay-sister in a community of Benedictines at Saintes before the Revolution, and, valuing herself on her religious profession, she could neither comprehend nor endure that any one living in the world should approach the altar so frequently: that was a privilege reserved to the cloister; she counted up the communions of the *lingère* of Saint-Pallais, and every one in the number exceeding her own was felt to be an

affront to herself as a nun. Her antipathy was so
enduring and obstinate that even when Eustelle's
saintliness had triumphed over the prejudices of her
neighbourhood, this old woman still let no occasion
pass of exhibiting her dislike, which died only with
its holy object, for Eustelle preceded her to the tomb.
A few other religious there were who, from a motive
of jealousy, as Cardinal Villecourt avers, could not
bear to hear her praised. But these were lamentable
exceptions, and, as that venerable prelate observes,
the same thing occurred in the case of St. Catherine of
Siena, whose reputation for saintliness excited an ill
feeling in the breasts even of some who were consecrated to God. Want of humility—need it be said?
—has always been the root of such deplorable exhi-
bitions. These unworthy religious, confounding the
sanctity of a *state* with that which is personal, have
been ready to believe that, because their condition is
the highest and most perfect, it has therefore a kind
of monopoly of perfection. But, as St. Francis de
Sales observes, perfection belongs to all states, and
St. Jerome had long before pronounced that a humble
married woman is better than a proud virgin.

It was Eustelle's frequent communions especially
which roused so much ill-feeling. Nor is this surprising, seeing that, it is especially against the Sacrament of the Altar that Satan directs all the fury of
his malice. Eustelle, while deploring whatever was
offensive to God, cheerfully and even joyfully accepted
all the persecutions of which she was the object. They
served her, too, not a little, helping as they did to
unveil still more clearly the perversity of the world,
and the utter futility of its judgments. She was
more severely tried by the attacks made upon her

through her parents. These good people were besieged by representations and remonstrances on the
part of so-called kind friends. "Such and such persons are very pious," it would be said, "but they do
not push things so far. Why should not your daughter
be satisfied with doing as they do?" These and such-
like remarks, by their constant repetition, so worked
upon the minds of Eustelle's parents that they also
took part against her. Neither of them had received
any high amount of religious instruction, and even
her excellent mother, finding nothing to reply to the
arguments that were used, believed that there was
some justice in what was so confidently and so
generally asserted. Distressed and annoyed, she
joined with her husband in finding fault with her
daughter, and insisting upon her changing her mode
of life. They neither questioned their own right to
require this sacrifice from her, nor doubted her submission to their positive commands; Eustelle, so
docile and obedient, could not, they thought, resist the
will and authority of her parents. But that obedience
and docility had its root in the entire submission of
her whole soul to God; she obeyed them for God, she
could not obey them against God; it was His sovereign
will which traced out for her the course she followed;
and with what power that Divine will acted upon and
ruled her will they knew not. Hence they encountered an unexpected firmness on her part, which to
them bore only the appearance of obstinacy. Her father
grew angry; he was, as we have seen, no very strict
observer of his own religious duties, but with a confidence which was in the inverse ratio to his qualifications for forming a just judgment in spiritual
matters, and with a not very uncommon misappre-

hension of the proper limits of parental authority,
he determined to interpose with a decided prohibition. Accordingly one day he signified to his daughter
that it was his will and pleasure that she should discontinue communicating every Sunday, adding that
if she disregarded this injunction she would have
cause to repent it.   But Eustelle calmly replied that
it was painful to her to hear him talk like one who
lacked faith ; that such language did not comport with
the spirit of true religion ; besides, it was fruitless to
return to the subject, for that no one would ever
succeed in making her change her resolution.   What
answer her father made in return, or whether he
made any answer at all, we are not told, but, as we
hear no more of the matter, we may conclude that, if
not convinced, he was at least wise enough to see that
authoritative interference was useless.

Eustelle's persecutors, however, had not given up
their point.   They now carried their complaints to
her confessor.   He had by no means escaped their
censures, as his penitent's change had been imputed in
no small degree to his influence ; nevertheless, they
hoped, by representing to him the mistaken character
of Eustelle's piety, and the injurious effects it was
calculated to produce, to gain him over to their side.
The list of charges brought before this court of final
appeal is somewhat amusing.   Her modesty was
excessive ; she never turned her head or noticed anybody in church ; she did not raise her eyes ; she was
always praying.   If every one else were as much
absorbed, and always engaged in contemplation, there
would be no use in books, and no need of booksellers ;
in short, not a look or act or movement on her part but
had been watched and noted down to be represented

in as exaggerated a light as possible. According to these fault-finders, her conduct had caused quite a scandal in the parish, it had prejudiced the interests of religion itself, and a stop ought to be put to such vagaries; not that they could pretend that any of these items of accusation constituted an offence in itself, but they were instances of the eccentricities in which she indulged, and they then proceeded to descant on the evil effects of singularity in devotion, begging her director to use his authority to induce her to leave off such mischievous practices. No doubt the modesty and recollection of Eustelle were singular—that is to say, she possessed these virtues in a singular degree; but no one could with justice reproach her with the slightest affectation of singularity, or with making a display of superior piety. Gladly indeed, would she have subtracted herself from the eyes of others, to be alone with God and unseen by man.

When Eustelle herself was addressed with taunts and reproaches, it was her custom to keep silence, but her silence only irritated her enemies the more, and was imputed by them to pride. All her attempts to disarm them by kindness and by suppressing the faintest show of displeasure were worse than useless. Had her sole or main object been to pacify her tormentors they might at last have succeeded in wearing out her patience, but that patience had its root in charity, and so its work was perfect. She repaid the ill-services of her neighbours by fervent prayers on their behalf, and inwardly rejoiced in having something to offer to Jesus, her only friend, her happiness, her all. In a letter written at this time, we find her regarding these venomous assaults as so many arrows of love from the Sacred Heart of Jesus. "How good," she says, "is Jesus to treat me thus! Bless Him for it, and pray Him to enlighten these persons and to forgive them. My soul ardently aspires with all its powers after persecution and the contempt of creatures. It desires to be known by God only, and to remain hidden from men ; it strives to withdraw itself from the eyes of all : on Jesus alone it fixes its gaze ; Jesus alone fills its every thought ; Jesus alone is its aim and occupation." And yet these arrows from whose points she extracted such sweetness were often sharp beyond measure to flesh and blood. For not only was she treated as a hypocrite and a deceiver, but attempts were made to injure her character. A good priest who was a native of her parish, has recorded that nothing was esteemed too horrible to lay to the charge of the maid of Saint-Pallais (il n'est sorte d'horreurs qu'on n'ait dites de la vierge de Saint-Pallais). On one occasion such infamous language was used with regard to her that a sister who was present burst into a flood of tears. She could not help retailing all to Eustelle, who answered with much simplicity, "Tell them, should they ever talk about me again, that I love them with all my heart and pray for them."

The injurious suspicions set afloat by malignant tongues led to a system of most impertinent espionage into her conduct. When she was given some employment in the sacristy, people would stealthily scale the windows outside to peep in and see what she was about. Once, when she was receiving a visit from a stranger, some individuals, actuated by a malicious curiosity, suddenly burst into the room ; when, finding themselves in presence of a personage whose character and quality they had little anticipated, they stood confounded with shame. Eustelle understood all at a glance, but she had the generosity to appear ignorant of their motive, and to relieve their embarrassment by giving them a kindly welcome. Upon another occasion a young person who was under obligations to Eustelle opened a letter addressed to her, out of a like spirit of inquisitiveness and a desire to discover some evil to justify the manner in which she was treated. When Eustelle was made acquainted with this act of meanness and treachery she only said, "Poor child!"

We may insert as belonging to this subject, although it occurred at a later period, when Eustelle had become a daily communicant, a little dialogue which took place between her and a lady who, with an utter want of good feeling and propriety, intruded her remarks and advice upon the saintly girl. There were several other persons present, to one of whom we owe the preservation of the anecdote. Eustelle was already, it must be observed, suffering extremely in health. "You are going to die soon, Mdlle. Eustelle," said the individual in question, with an air of assumed flattery, "may I beg you to remember me when in Paradise?" "If I reach it before you, I promise not to forget you," was the reply. But this was not exactly the answer desired, as it did not furnish a ready handle for the next proposed remark: however, no matter—the remark must be made, whether naturally suggested or not. "Then, mademoiselle, you look to going straight to Heaven? But you will begin by passing through Purgatory." Eustelle having rejoined that such was her expectation, and that in Purgatory one could glorify God, this strange woman continued, "To go to Heaven one must be a saint, and as for you, mademoiselle, your piety is very ill-judged; you are full of obstinate notions; you communicate every day:" this was the chief grievance, no doubt. "You would be doing much better if you took care of your health. Such and such persons," she continued, naming them, "are better than you are, and only communicate once or twice in the week." "Madam," answered Eustelle very calmly, "I know that I cannot compare myself with the persons you mention; but it is not because I esteem myself better than they that I receive our Lord so often; it is in order to become better than I am." "If you were in a convent," sharply retorted the lady, "you would have to obey." "I should obey those to whom I owed obedience," replied Marie-Eustelle; and then she went on to explain that she did not act without the counsel and direction of those to whom God had committed the care of her soul, but that she did not consider herself under obligation to submit herself in this matter to all the world. The lady, however, would not be satisfied, and continued in the same strain, endeavouring to humiliate her by mortifying remarks. She even went so far as to say, "I once heard a preacher observe that it was not those who went to communion most frequently who were the greatest saints; and he added, 'those who pass for devils are often angels, and those who look like angels are often devils.'" Marie-Eustelle thanked her for her charitable advice, and when the person from whom these particulars were derived afterwards told her friend how much she had suffered during this conversation—"Oh, it is nothing," replied Eustelle gaily; "as for me it does not trouble me in the least; only it is impossible for me to deprive myself of the favours our Lord is willing to grant me, to please this dear lady." It might have been thought that in one who had the slightest claim to be reckoned a gentlewoman—and this individual was evidently of a class superior to that of Eustelle—such undisguised impertinence was barely possible. Unusual we may hope it to be; and yet it is astonishing to what lengths a passion for setting others to rights, when fortified with no small stock of religious self-sufficiency, will carry some persons. The Pharisaical spirit seems to blind those possessed by it, not merely to their own faults and secret springs of action, but to all sense of propriety and even of common civility.

To resume the regular order of events. Eustelle was now to be tried in a manner calculated to test the solidity of her virtue, and her true love of obedience. Her confessor, to whom false reports were continually brought, and to whom special complaints were made of the great length of time that Eustelle remained in the church, bade her stay no longer in the morning than the half-hour occupied by Mass, making no exception as to the days when she had received communion. This latter injunction must have been designed to prove her spirit of submission, otherwise it would appear a somewhat startling concession to worldly opinion. Be this as it may, Eustelle neither reasoned nor remonstrated, but complied with all docility. No sooner was Mass ended than this admirable girl, even when she had approached the altar, punctually departed, bearing away her Treasure with her. No one could deprive her of that. In this assurance, and in the fulfilment of her Lord's will, signified to her by His minister, she found her consolation, as we learn from her answer to a friend who, in after days, said to her, "You must have felt very sad having to leave the church so soon?" "Why so," was Eustelle's prompt reply, "since our Lord wished it to be so? I used to retire to my room at once, and there no one could prevent my being happy. The idea of complaining never crossed my mind." Her confessor, however, recognizing the spirit in which she acted, and touched by her resignation, soon had compassion on her and set her once more at liberty.

The divine consolations with which the soul of Eustelle was continually replenished rendered all tribulations light and easy to her, while they detached her more and more from the love of any enjoyments which earth can bestow. She had no one at this time to whom she could open her heart, or at whose lips she could seek counsel, except her director, and he maintained a profound silence on the subject of the persecutions of which she was the object, a silence which she respected as dictated by her Lord, and on her part never alluded to them : it sufficed her that Jesus knew them all. He had won her, and was winning her yet more and more entirely to Himself. The arms of His love were around her, and she knew it—Oh, joy unutterable !—but He was drawing her into a still closer embrace. Her perfect passiveness and docility enabled Him to do as He would ; for we have the awful power, not only of resisting His will, but of interrupting or interfering with His work : God alone knows how much we all deprive ourselves of by this restlessness of ours. Had Eustelle turned aside for some human consolation ; had she at this

time poured out her griefs, as without sin undoubtedly
she might have done, into the bosom of some pious
friend; had she, under the specious plea of seeking
advice or direction, but really with the object of self-
relief, broken upon the marked reserve of her director,
how much might she not have foregone of the tenderness of her Heavenly Spouse, and of the rich and precious favours He had in store for her. True it is that
many of us need these supports, and He allows us to
profit by them; His love has even provided them for
our weakness; but there are elect souls, souls who
have received their ten talents, His dear and chosen
spouses, to whom He wills to be all in all; and it is
not too high a price to pay for so inestimable a favour,
to forego all solace from human affection, all consolation and sympathy, however holy. Shall we call such
love exacting? Yes, it is exacting, and so is love
always. It exacts by its very nature; it exacts love
in return proportioned to what it gives, and it is
grieved and repulsed when it finds not all it seeks.
If such be the case in that affection to which we pre-
eminently give the name of "love," shall it be less so
in the love of Him who has espoused our souls to
Himself—a love, which the human affection so dimly
images? Shall He, our Divine Lover, who has an
infinite love to bestow, expect less than the whole of
our finite heart? Eustelle from the hour that she
gave herself to Jesus never wounded the exquisite
sensitiveness of His Sacred Heart by looking to any
friendly supporting arm except His own, or seeking
solace by confiding her pains to any other ear. Her
pains and her joys were alike locked within her own
bosom. We shall, it is true, find her less reserved in
her communications with a chosen few hereafter,

but times will be changed then; and what Eustelle
shall speak in those days shall be from the exuberance
of divine love, irrepressibly seeking a relief for pains
how different from any which human agency can
cause! But we must not anticipate.

At the period on which we are engaged all her
efforts were directed to the acquirement of the greatest purity of heart, with the view and hope of
becoming a more frequent partaker of the Bread
of Life. The obtaining of these dispositions was the
subject of continual prayer, and she was answered by
a growing facility in well-doing,—our Lord in all her
difficulties seeming to lead her by the hand,—and by
an ever-increasing attraction to that heavenly magnet,
the Holy Eucharist. "Oh, how I already loved Him
then," she exclaims, "in that Adorable Sacrament!"
And this was but the beginning, the prelude, the dawn
of the meridian fervours which were to succeed. It
was the sweet spring-tide also of the mystic life, when
God gives the tender young souls He is attaching to Him
milk and honey from His choicest stores, and makes
them to bask in the cloudless sunshine of His smile.
The dryness and the desolation and the tempest and
the darkness will follow—that heavy weight of inward
trials, compared with which the world's persecutions
are as light straws and feathers. All this has to be
passed through before emerging into the serene splendour of settled summer, when the soul, purified by
suffering and arrived at perfect union with its God, is
sometimes permitted even here below to enjoy a bliss
which the Beatitude of Heaven can alone surpass.*

---

* It is, of course, not intended to assert that any strict rule
can be laid down as governing God's dealings with souls which
He calls to high perfection. His way with one soul differs from

CHAPTER VI.

The Love of Jesus and the Life of Love.

Six days without uniting herself to Jesus seemed very long to Eustelle, but she did not presume to ask for more. No doubt a larger allowance would have drawn down fresh persecutions, not only from her worldly neighbours, but from those who were actuated by a mistaken piety, and who were more irritated by her frequent communions, as they esteemed them,[*]

His way with another, and He can effect His work of purification in a manner altogether hidden from us. The early season of abundant sweetness may in some cases not be recognisable, and states of trial and consolation may occur alternately through life. Again, we find certain trials spared to certain saints; and, as might naturally be expected, the experience of the converted will vary from that of such as have not only kept their baptismal innocence but have striven after holiness from the first dawn of reason. Still, this succession of states is so frequently met with in the lives of holy persons, defined with more or less of clearness, that it is common for spiritual writers to speak of them as constituting the different stages of the spiritual life.

[*] Religious practice must have been at a low ebb in this district at that time, or weekly communion would have excited no surprise or animadversion on the score of frequency. The Church of our day clearly does not regard it in that light. "Frequent communion," writes F. Dalgairns, "is a relative term, the meaning of which depends upon the custom of the age. In the middle ages once a month, in the time of St. Francis of Sales, once a week would be considered frequent. In our time, according to the general estimation, a Christian who communicated once a week would not be considered a frequent communicant. . . . . I assume as certain that all ordinarily good Christians may communicate every week."— *The Holy Communion, its Philosophy, Theology, and Practice,* 2nd Edition, p. 290.

To this passage F. Dalgairns has appended the following note:—"'Never have I regarded weekly communion as frequent,' says St. Alphonsus; 'that person alone who communicates several times a week is considered to be a frequent

than by anything else. No fear of rousing additional
irritation against herself could, however, deter Eustelle
from seeking the favour for which she so ardently
longed. To obtain it she adopted a pious device.
The good priest of Saint-Pallais was at this time removed by his bishop to a larger and more important
parish. Marie-Eustelle would naturally have been
grieved at the loss of his counsel and direction, but
she permitted herself no murmur at a privation which
the Providence of God imposed on her; nay, she
believed that He who orders all things for the good of
those who love Him would enable her in some way
to derive profit from what bore the semblance of a
loss; and so indeed it proved. It occurred to her
that she might seize the opportunity afforded by this
change to make her confession in the middle of the
week instead of on Saturday, as heretofore. By this
means she obtained another communion on the
Thursday without prejudice to the Sunday communion, which she was permitted to receive as usual.
Some time afterwards, the new priest asked his penitent why she came to confession on Wednesdays
instead of on Saturdays. She said it was because the
Wednesdays seemed to suit her better, but that she
would readily conform to his wishes; accordingly by-
and-by he changed the day, but allowed her to continue her two communions. This was an immense
gain; and Eustelle testified her gratitude to her Lord
by the most energetic efforts to adorn her soul with
every virtue, that it might be less unworthy of the

communicant.' It is very important to remember this maxim
of the saint. It is evident that many more good Christians
might communicate weekly if they were not withheld by tra-
ditionary rigorism."

Guest it now so often entertained. Jesus in the
Eucharist was more than ever her one abiding thought,
her one only aim.

About this time Eustelle underwent a fresh trial.
Her apprenticeship was over, and she must begin to
earn her own livelihood.   The skill she had acquired
with her needle afforded fair prospect of success, and
it seemed reasonable to expect that she would find
sufficient employment ; but at first very few orders
came in, to the extreme vexation of her parents.
Whether the prejudices created against her by the ill-
natured stories that were current had any share in
causing this disappointment, it is impossible to say ;
at any rate Eustelle's father and mother were fully
persuaded that it had everything in the world to say
to it.   When there is a stock grievance against a
person it is sure to be made responsible for all accidents and all failures.   How was it likely, they said,
that people would wish to employ a young woman who
lived so solitary and morose a life ? Of course this
could not go on, their daughter must turn her thoughts
to domestic service.   Eustelle herself felt that if such
a state of things were prolonged she would have no
alternative but to comply.   Poor people naturally
do not expect their grown-up children to continue to
be an expense to them when they are capable of
shifting for themselves, and that, too, after having
provided them at no little sacrifice with the instruction
necessary for earning their own bread.   Eustelle,
indeed, could not for a moment contemplate the idea
of being a burden to her family ; nor did she feel any
repugnance to service in itself, to which, as being a
state of subordination, her humility and love of
obedience would naturally have disposed her.   But

she dreaded the obstacles which such a condition would throw in the way of the one great object of her life, and the restrictions it would necessarily put on her devotion ; and an interior voice seemed to sanction and assent to this her disinclination.

While matters stood thus, one of the best families in the town of Saintes, which had previously testified a desire to take Marie-Eustelle into their service, made a definite proposition on the subject to her parents. They had by some means become acquainted with her great merit ; and they knew that they could reckon upon finding in her the most scrupulous probity, and that she would conscientiously devote to their interests every moment not given to God. Eustelle would, indeed, have proved a blessing to any household she had entered, and must have won a position which she would have been far from seeking; for, notwith-standing the simplicity which attended all her words and acts, and from which she had made it her rule never to depart, there was in the manners of this peasant girl a certain indefinable air of distinction which at once inspired a sentiment of admiration, tempered, young as she was, by what might almost be called a feeling of reverence. For this native grace, this look of inborn nobility had a peculiar type and character of its own. Her demeanour was not so much that of one above her station—though she might have adorned any station, however high—as of a being of a superior order. There was more in it of the angelic than of the noble. Cardinal Villecourt, her bishop, has left on record a description of Marie-Eustelle's personal appearance. It is with regret, he says, that he speaks of these exterior qualities, which would have lost their fairest ornament without that supernatural grace and inexpressible dignity which was the fruit of her habitual converse with God. Ever dwelling in the presence of the Supreme Lord of all, what wonder if the manners and ways of the celestial court unconsciously hung about her, and that some rays of light from the Eternal Throne should illuminate her meek countenance. " Since we must describe her," says the bishop, who had undertaken to write the biography of this saintly girl, and who concludes, therefore, that his readers will expect a portrait—"since we must describe her, let us do so. In stature, she was considerably above the middle height, her complexion was delicately fair, tinged with a rosy bloom, her eyes full of sweetness, her voice very pleasing, her countenance perfectly un- affected and graced with heavenly modesty. When she spoke, you might have thought you were listening to a young queen formed by all that surrounded her to express herself in the terms of the greatest purity that our language can afford, while at the same time she preserved the utmost simplicity in tone and manner. It will be easily judged how great a trea- sure a family would have possessed in her, and what sacrifices they would have made to secure her."

Eustelle's mother pressed her to accept a situation which offered many advantages, and which insured her a future maintenance. There seemed no motive for refusing. In the retirement of her own room she laid the matter with tears before the Lord, to obtain light and guidance where they are never denied ; for in her perplexity she dreaded either to resist a secret divine inspiration, or to sin by dis- obedience to her parents' will. One day, while the matter was yet in suspense, her mother surprised her weeping, and asked the cause. "O my good mother," replied Eustelle, "to go into service, and no longer be able to hear Mass daily!" Moved to her inmost soul by this touching exclamation, this excellent woman immediately assured her daughter that she did not wish to constrain her to adopt a line of life which would thwart her pious inclinations, and she might consider the affair at an end. A few days afterwards, Marie-Eustelle was asked to undertake the care of the linen in a boarding-school for boys. This offer she accepted, for although the work required would occupy a considerable portion of her time, it would nevertheless leave her free in certain respects; and on her return home in the evening she could devote herself to her exercises of piety. But at the end of a year she gave up this employment on account of the unavoidable contact into which it brought her with the pupils. Such bashfulness may appear to some excessive; but Christian modesty is a virtue ever shy and timid. It must be remembered, too, that Eustelle was at this time little more than six-teen. She was soon rewarded by a most surprising influx of work. A sort of emulation seemed suddenly to arise for the favour of employing her. The diffi-culty was no longer to procure orders, but to satisfy demands. She was now free to choose, indeed she was fain to choose, between the numerous applicants for her services, as more work was offered than she could possibly undertake. In her selection she was guided by spiritual motives, not by views of profit or human prudence; she determined to confine herself to those families from whom she was likely to derive edification, as, from the nature of her occupation, she was necessarily obliged to remain for many hours beneath their roof.   According to the usual practice, she used to repair to the house of her employers at eight o'clock, and remained there till the evening. But much had taken place before eight o'clock.   Curtailing a repose which her delicate frame greatly needed, she rose very early, and like "the hart panting after the fountains of waters," she fled to the holy place.   There she assisted at the Adorable Sacrifice, and then remained, like the lamp which burns and consumes before the Tabernacle, until the hour for labour summoned her away.   If there happened to be no Mass at Saint-Pallais, she crossed the Charente, and went to the old cathedral of St. Pierre at Saintes.

As in her eagerness she had often forestalled the dawn, so also was she often beforehand with the guardians of the church, and would find the door still closed.   There she calmly waited, without moving, her face towards the door, adoring her Beloved upon whose threshold she stood.   There was another pious girl, afterwards well known to Eustelle, who used like her to seek the courts of the Lord before the break of day.   A little tacit emulation arose between them as to which should arrive the earliest ; but Eustelle had always the happiness of being first to offer to Jesus this morning tribute of adoration.   On these occasions, as her friendly rival afterwards related, Eustelle would smile with a sort of childlike pleasure at the serious air with which the other confessed herself to be the laziest.   When the welcome moment came and the doors were opened, Marie-Eustelle proceeded straight to the High Altar and prostrated herself before it, after which she went to kneel in the Lady Chapel, where the Blessed

Sacrament was also reserved,* and there she remained for about an hour and a half absorbed in prayer. On quitting the church her whole soul was like a chamber full of light, so vivid was the apprehension which at the foot of the altar she had acquired of the things which appertain to Eternity and the soul's salvation.

As we are now entering upon the period of Eustelle's life at which her devotion began to assume its more striking characteristics, it may be well perhaps to pause and ask a question or two which some may possibly be asking themselves. Eustelle was not a religious, she never had a call to the religious state, she lived in the world, and had her bread to make. Was she right thus to peril and waste the health absolutely needed for the duties of her condition in life? And if she was right, which few can be disposed to deny, when they consider the extraordinary graces which rewarded her self-sacrificing love, what of us, men and women of the world, who yet desire to please God and grow in holiness? How is Marie-Eustelle an example to us? Are we acting over-cautiously, and to the prejudice of our souls' interests, when we have regard to the measure of our strength, and refrain from what we believe would too severely tax it? Are we losers thereby? Would it be better to exert ourselves to the utmost, and leave consequences to God, as Marie-Eustelle did? And if not, how is she an example to us? Souls truly solicitous to advance in divine love,—and it is of them alone we speak,—will be sometimes haunted by problems of

---

* The practice of reserving the Blessed Sacrament in two tabernacles in the same church ceased when the diocese of La Rochelle returned to the Roman rite.

this character, when they read of what saintly persons of feeble and delicate frames have accomplished in despite and in defiance of their infirmities. Yet the solution, after all, would not appear so very difficult. One thing is clear, that whatever sacrifice of health or strength duty to God may require, it must be made, and this obligation binds the imperfect no less than the perfect ; nay, there are cases where the exercise of heroic virtue is imperatively demanded of the ordinary Christian ; such as dying for the faith, if need be.   But in the cases contemplated, it is evident that no such obligation exists, and therefore no rule of general application can possibly be ascertained for the guidance of individual souls.   As God has His special graces for each, so has He His special demands on each.   To discover what these demands are must be the object of every one of us ; we must lay ourselves open to the influences of His Spirit, and cheerfully and faithfully follow them wherever they may lead, seeking direction, in case of doubt, where God has provided it.   But to imitate noble ventures in the mere spirit of imitation, or, as men have recourse to a recipe, without any corresponding inward movement prompting us thereto, might be presumptuously to go beyond our grace, a course which has not unfrequently led to lamentable failures, and which, at any rate, can but serve to foster self-love, and prepare the way for future despondency.   It is, then, in her docility to grace that Eustelle, as we conceive, offers to us so beautiful a model.   She was literally as clay in the potter's hands, and, just as nothingness opposed no obstacle to the original *Fiat* of the Creator, so did her self-annihilation leave perfect freedom for the building-up of the new creation within her.   As the feather rests on the still air, or flies on the wings of the wind, so was this holy girl borne and wafted by the breath of Divine grace. Such is the road to sanctity, and not to the highest sanctity alone, but to all measures and degrees of it, as God may have allotted them in the kingdom of His Son. In this respect Marie-Eustelle can doubtless be unreservedly proposed for imitation to us all.

We have it on Eustelle's own testimony, that her Divine Lord, who early inspired her with a strong attraction for retirement and prayer, was also her sole instructor. She felt no pleasure save in His presence and at the foot of His Tabernacle. During the hours she spent there she was taking her lessons in meditation from her Heavenly Teacher. At first she allotted a quarter of an hour to this exercise, then half an hour. Difficulties now beset her, and, like other holy souls before her, who have been similarly tried in the beginning of their spiritual course, she was tempted to give up mental prayer, and in fact, as she confesses, had the weakness to abandon it altogether for a short time, limiting herself to her ordinary devotions. But she soon perceived her error by the detriment and loss of which her soul was conscious, and she now took the firm resolution never to omit the practice of meditation for a single day, but on the contrary to devote as much time to it as possible ; nor could she afterwards recall to memory a single deviation from this rule. As Marie-Eustelle began her day with Jesus in the Sacrament of the Altar, so the same invincible attraction brought her back every evening to His Presence, as the declining sun announced the close of man's day of labour. The hour of rest was come, and Eustelle's rest was before the Tabernacle.

With her it was not so much a holy practice thus to visit her Lord, as that her natural place and position seemed to be there, when no forcible reason detained her elsewhere. As water forcibly dammed up flows down impetuously the instant the barrier which checked its course is taken away, and rushes to seek its level, never resting till it has reached it; so Eustelle, when the obstacle that restrained her was removed, followed her soul's bias. Every moment she could spare from the duties of her condition was passed before the Altar. As for Sundays and festivals, they were to her a banquet that endured well-nigh the live-long day. Her time was then all her own, or, rather, it was God's,—with her the same thing: she could give it all to Him. When her sisters on these days asked her to join them and their companions in their walks, Eustelle would not go. Believing that some scruple deterred her from taking this recreation, and anxious to enjoy her company, these young girls would remind her that many pious persons made no difficulty in permitting themselves such relaxations. To which Eustelle would sweetly reply, "I do not blame them, but take it not ill if I abstain from doing so." It does not appear that these good girls *did* take it ill; they probably grieved a little, and wondered not a little.

But it was not only her own powerful attraction which, as it were, riveted Eustelle to the sanctuary: Jesus would not let her go. For it was His will that she should die, not merely, as all must, to sin and every sinful inclination, but to all inclinations and all sentiments without exception which were not for Him. Often and often did she hear in the depths of her heart these tender and loving words: "I am to be all-sufficient to you." And with what sweetness and winning tenderness were they uttered! Some—we might rather say many—never go into this secret cabinet of their souls; numbers, perhaps, hardly know that they possess such a privileged chamber within them. Privileged indeed—for it is there the Beloved makes His voice to be heard in those special addresses which are meant for ourselves alone. Each one of us is His special care, and He might have much to say to each, if only we had ears to hear. Every spiritual sense of Eustelle was awake to catch these tones; she was in the perpetual attitude of the young Samuel when the word of the Lord, rare and "precious" in those sad days, passing by the elders of Israel and the high-priest himself, who bore on his breast the Urim and Thummim, spoke to the child sleeping under the light of the lamp in the Temple. And to him that hears more is given. Eustelle heard and obeyed; Jesus would not let her leave Him; and so it was that, if the thought for a moment crossed her mind of refreshing herself with a walk after the conclusion of the morning offices of the Church, immediately her Heavenly Friend would whisper, "Cannot I be in place of everything to you? Cannot I refresh and recreate your spirit?" and then He told her how that if she would deprive herself of all creatures, the joys which should be given her should surpass every earthly satisfaction and even all that she could conceive: "I am infinite, and all that I have is the possession of those who love Me." But He told her at the same time that He did not wish to force her will, and that He left her entirely free to acquiesce or to resist His solicitations, only the degree of her generosity towards Him would be the measure of His love for her ; " And, O my daughter," said this dear Saviour to her, " My Heart burns with the desire to communicate Itself to thee."   Eustelle, then, might have resisted without positive sin—she had her Lord's word for it ; but had she disregarded this tender appeal of the Eternal King for the poor love of His creature, would not the voice have soon been silent ? And had Jesus been silenced, she would have been left, like others whom He has never so addressed, to walk in the ordinary path—if indeed she had persevered in that lower level : for in truth she would not have been like others to whom such great favour has never been shown, and who, faithful perhaps to their inferior graces, fulfil their less exalted calling acceptably.   Surely it cannot be a light thing to wound the Heart of an Incarnate God.   We think too little of this. We will not give our God credit for the feelings of that Human Heart of His ; we will not listen to Its pleadings ; we treat them as though they were but figures of speech, and Himself almost as an abstraction.   Alas for the silence of rejected love, and a heart estranged for ever !   Did not David dread this terrible silence more, far more, than the chastising hand ? or, rather, did he not love the one and dread the other ?   " Thy rod and Thy staff have comforted me," he says ; but at the thought of the other he cries, " Be not Thou silent to me, O Lord, lest I become like them that go down into the pit."*   But Eustelle responded with all the fervour of her loving nature to her Saviour's invitations.   " Was it possible," she exclaims, "for me to withdraw myself from the ravishing attractions of this Love of Angels ? Jesus so good !   Could I refuse to quench the thirst

* Psalm xxii. 4 ; xxvii. 1.

which my soul made Him endure on Calvary, and
which I knew He still felt in those moments when He
solicited me to be all His own."

Instructed by her Lord Himself, and thus docile
to His voice, Marie-Eustelle rapidly scaled the sublime
heights of prayer. Often she was so absorbed in God
that she seemed to be rather there whither her heart
always tended, in the Tabernacle or in Heaven, than
where she was in the body. One fair-day, being
obliged to go to Saintes, a friend upon her return
pitied her for having had to encounter the disagreeable
crowd of buyers and sellers, and the idle and curious
throng present on such occasions. But Marie-Eustelle
had been perfectly unconscious that any thing unusual
had been going on; she had passed through this concourse of people and had heard and seen nothing.
Another time she traversed a street where a house
was on fire, and never so much as noticed it. Amongst
her papers was found after her death this note, probably written with a view to insertion in the narrative
of her life, which she had been enjoined to commit to
writing: "The presence of Jesus is so intimate to me,
that it appears impossible for me to lose the sense of
it, and this presence fills my soul with a joy indescribable." A memorandum was also found containing
the following resolutions, which point to practices
which were as so many golden steps helping her to
mount towards God:—

> "To speak little.
> To pray much.—Presence of God.
> To cling to nothing.
> To let all that passes, pass.
> To attach myself to Jesus alone, who alone is
> Eternal and Everlasting."

These words were added in conclusion :—

"God alone in my spirit, to enlighten it.

God alone in my heart, to possess it.

God alone in my acts, to sanctify them."

Again, we find her writing, "Let us look at ourselves in God. Let us sleep, let us sweetly repose, in this beloved Presence ; this is the beatitude of the saints in Heaven ; it should be ours on earth."

A pious person once asked Marie-Eustelle to teach her how to acquire the gift of prayer. In her reply she begins by congratulating her correspondent on the desire she had expressed. "Your heart," she writes, "understands those sweet and tender words which Jesus, in His love, causes the faithful soul to hear when, speaking to it in the silence of prayer, He deigns to make her understand that, as He wills to be Himself all to her in all things, so must she use all her endeavours to attain to that divine life by which the soul sees Jesus in all and all in Jesus. Faith alone, practical faith, enables us to live this life, which gives us to taste, even here below, the earnest of heavenly blessedness. An excellent means to obtain this fruit of faith is prayer. The Holy Spirit tells us that the earth is full of desolation because there is no one who considers in his heart. O what good reason you have to devote yourself to this holy exercise!" Eustelle, however, felt abashed at a request which had alarmed her humility, and she here interrupts the expression of her joy, which at first had swallowed up every other sentiment, to allege her own unfitness to give advice on such a subject. "Is it to me," she says, "that you should have recourse to learn the way which leads to the gift of prayer? Do I indeed know whether I myself know how to pray? I reckon myself in this matter to be only a poor neophyte, like those young bees who, but just hatched, want to leave the hive and fly, like their parents, but who, for want of well-developed wings, fall to the ground." Nevertheless, her charity and zeal got the better of her reluctance, and she consents to answer the question which the humility of her friend had prompted, begging our Lord to inspire her to frame her reply according to His will. Eustelle here evinces her discretion and acquaintance with the spiritual life by being in no hurry to adduce, as many might have done, her own experimental knowledge, as if all must be led by the road she herself had followed. She knows that the Spirit of God conducts souls by various paths, and requests, what she thinks will not be denied her, to have, at their first interview, a more unreserved communication as to her correspondent's special attraction before giving any detailed advice. Of one thing, however, she is always certain : the Tabernacle is the first and last stage on the way of life. To the love of Jesus in His Adorable Sacrament she may direct all alike, and, indeed, it would be difficult to find one single letter of hers in which allusion to it is not made. "Be of good courage," she says, " go to the Tabernacle ; Moses had recourse to it in all his needs, and he was heard : how much more shall your prayers be answered by recourse to that of which the Tabernacle of old was but the figure."

We have a letter addressed by Marie-Eustelle to a friend upon the same subject, which we give at length :—

"It is essential, as a disposition to holy prayer, to labour to acquire interior mortification, which con-

sists in demolishing our little natural inclinations, for
the more pains we have taken to empty our soul of
ourselves, the more will the Heavenly Spouse fill it.
Before putting some precious liquor into a vessel, we
take care to cleanse it; in like manner, our soul needs
to be pure in order to contain the perfume of prayer.
Go to Jesus stripped of yourself; remain at His feet,
like His lover Magdalen.   Prayer is an elevation of
our heart to God; the knowledge of what He is, and
of what we are, is sufficient to keep us in an attitude
of the deepest humility in His presence.   God is more
intimately within us than we are in ourselves.   Hence
Jesus Christ said, 'The kingdom of God is within
you.'   Accustom yourself to see our good Saviour
present in your soul and reposing on your heart,
especially during prayer.   Be in His presence like a
sick plant which we expose to the benignant influences
of the sun; like a poor man at the door of the rich;
like a drop of water which loses itself in the ocean;
as a nothing which loses itself in its all.   Say, like
the blind man in the Gospel, 'Lord, make me to
see.'

"The Divine Eucharist above all should be the
subject of your prayer.   When your heart unites
itself to this Saviour-God, the contemplation of this
favour ought to occupy your soul and set it on fire
with heavenly love; remain at these times calm and
peaceful before Jesus, like a statue which its owner
has placed in a niche.   Listen to Jesus, and answer
Him interiorly; He will understand your language
well.   Love Him sweetly, without fear, without disquiet; allow yourself to be penetrated by His love;
desires sometimes suffice in prayer, and the most
perfect confidence ought to be the fruit of it.   In fine,

do not be disheartened by the difficulties which you may encounter; the devil knows the good which results from this exercise, and so he endeavours to turn away souls from it. But be of good courage: love much. For this, time is required; the gardener who sows does not gather the fruit immediately; he waits till the seed he has committed to the ground sprouts and grows; so, too, he grafts, or his tree remains only a wild stock; if it be required, he supports it with a stake; and he dresses and prunes it when the time comes. It is only after all this care has been bestowed that the tree bears flowers which turn afterwards into fruit. Thus it is with our soul. The gardener who cultivates it is Jesus, but we must co-operate with Him in the care He bestows: this co-operation is easy, for grace is there to aid us. Reckon, then, confidently on His help; love prayer: for *it is prayer alone which disposes us in a perfect manner for Holy Communion;* make it your delight."

It was, we have reason to believe, at the pressing instances of her friend that Marie-Eustelle traced this simple but beautiful little treatise—for such we may call it—on prayer. It concludes with a few modest words, in which we recognize her abiding lowliness of spirit and her delicate tact; for she ends by abdicating the office of instructor to become a petitioner for the help she is herself bestowing. "Pray our good Master that He may give me a little humility, for I need it much to cure my pride. Adieu. Your friend, Eustelle, the poor and un-worthy servant of Jesus." We see how she always brought everything to bear on one object; how she regarded everything as gravitating round that one centre—Jesus in the Eucharist.

It may easily be imagined how much this tender lover and adorer of Jesus in His Sacrament took to heart the desolate condition of churches, and especially how deeply she was grieved to see the August Prisoner of Love so poorly and meanly lodged. She was moved to tears at the sight, and the zeal of God's House devoured her soul. But what could she do, a poor young girl, alike without fortune and without influence, except pray, and lament, and weep, and offer her longing desires? Suddenly it strikes her that, if she has not money, she has what she can convert into money—a talent: she can embroider. And so she resolves to work a beautiful altar-cloth for the solemnity of the Quarant' Ore. But when and how? The labour of her hands is all bespoken for others during the whole day : her time is not her own, for she needs it in order to live. But there is the night. She could do this little work for Jesus during the hours which she will steal from repose ; and Eustelle feels all the happier at the thought that her offering will be made by means of some little sacrifice. And so, every night, when all was quiet, and she saw her mother well asleep, she rose softly from her bed, where she had lain watching her opportunity, lighted her lamp, and was soon busy with her needle. Every stitch was a prayer, for every stitch was an act of love ; and are not our acts of love prayers, as our prayers are acts of love? God alone knows how many nights were thus spent ; Eustelle did not count them, but they were counted in Heaven. Who knows (as her biographer says), if during these laborious nights, which followed, be it remembered, laborious days, this generous-hearted girl was not all unconsciously helping to found those many pious

H

institutions which have since sprung into existence, directed to the maintenance and adornment of God's House and to His due honour in the Tabernacle where He dwells with us? Sacrifice lies at the foundation of all great and good works, and they who reap are rarely they who have sown. The "Quarant' Ore," however, was drawing near, and Eustelle, notwithstanding all her exertions, had not yet completed her work; nor could she fail to perceive that it would be impossible for her to finish it within the time remaining. Accordingly she begged the assistance of some other young women in her pious undertaking, and even remunerated several of them out of her slender earnings for their share in the work. But she was a thousand times repaid when the looked-for day arrived, and she beheld the altar on which Jesus was enthroned, adorned with the vesture which her love and devotion had provided.

We cannot conclude this chapter better than by quoting the words of the venerable prelate whose preparatory notes for the work which he had contemplated, but which another executed, terminate with this touching incident in the life of the sempstress of Saint-Pallais. "I find it," he writes, "difficult to abstain from a reflection which many have made before me, that it is often those who gain a bare subsistence by the labour of their hands who show the greatest generosity in the adornment of the holy place, and in the relief of those who suffer want, and with whose privations they are acquainted by their own painful experience. The day will come when, before the tribunal of the Sovereign Judge, a comparison shall be instituted between these poor who have denied themselves a portion of the bread needed for their sustenance that they may give it to the hungry, and those rich men who, while themselves suffering in health from the very excess of good-living, have not permitted these poor Lazaruses even to gather up the crumbs which fell from their table. Here, on the one hand, will be seen a young needle-woman who, after having toiled all the day to gain a frugal livelihood, has spent her night also in working for the decoration of the altar of the Eucharistic God; and there, on the other, will appear an opulent family, whose splendid mansion, it may be, stood within the very sight of a church bare of all adornment, and have never so much as thought of bestowing the smallest donation upon it. O generous Eustelle, just it is that all the treasures of heaven should have been thrown open to thee. But O ye rich, without pity, without love, for the beauty of God's House, you shall be found deserving of no pity at the hands of that same God, who will render to every one according to his works."

CHAPTER VII.

MORTIFICATION AND INTERIOR TRIALS.

IF no one has ever attained any high perfection without a correspondingly diligent use of the great means of prayer, so neither has it been acquired without the exercise of mortification. Self-denial in some form and degree is, indeed, a condition required of all followers of Christ, who has declared that who-ever does not renounce himself cannot be His disciple. It is the very condition of membership with a Crucified Lord. It is implied in our Baptism, in which we mystically die to sin that we may rise with Jesus. The thorough destruction of the old man within us is the life-long work of the Christian. If few comparatively address themselves as vigorously as they might to this task, fewer still perfectly accomplish this victory over nature during their mortal probation; else would Purgatory be less fully peopled than it is. It is in the Saints, and in such as come before us with the mark of saintliness on them, that we witness this conflict heroically carried on. It is as distinctive a trait as is their continual practice of prayer. The two go hand in hand and mutually assist each other.

Eustelle was well convinced that exterior mortification is, as regards the interior life—to use her own expression—but "the bark of the tree." Nevertheless she desired to add to the acts of inward self-denial, in the unceasing practice of which she lived, such outward penitential exercises as might be permitted her. Very holy souls, whatever may have been their special attraction, have never been without this desire. She had not yet reached the age when the Church's precept of fasting becomes binding, nevertheless she began to impose certain privations on herself at meals. On Fridays she limited herself to a piece of dry bread in the morning, and deprived herself of her evening collation altogether. Later, she says, her Lord inspired her with the resolution to eat only black bread,* and usually to drink nothing but water.

---

* This is a kind of bread which in England we know only ... Bread is, unfortunately, much adulterated in this ... but our poor would be far too fastidious to content

She modestly adds that this privation was the less in
her case because the black bread did not constitute
her whole food.   Her mother, alarmed at the dete-
rioration in her health which began to manifest itself
after she had continued this diet for some years,
spoke to her confessor on the subject, and Eustelle
was forbidden to persevere in it.   Yet it would appear
from her own account that she was more than doubtful
whether her maladies did not proceed from a different
source, and were not, mainly at least, to be referred
to her severe interior trials, of which we shall presently have to speak.   Be this as it may, it is certain
that in the manuscript she left, Eustelle passes very
lightly over her corporal austerities, finding herself
checked in the practice of them.   She says that, being
desirous to wear a hair shirt, she procured one, and
was then forbidden to use it.   Her confessor, however, at last acceded to her earnest request, so far as
to permit her to wear it for eight hours four times
a week.   She does not herself describe this instrument
of penance, but one' has been preserved by her
family, and was seen by her biographer, who says
it was a wide belt of iron tissue armed with sharp
points.   It was not surprising, considering Eustelle's
fragile and suffering health, that the Bishop of La
Rochelle, to whom, after giving his provisional consent for its limited use, her director referred her,
should have absolutely forbidden her to employ any
instruments of penance.   The enlightened eye of the
pastor of the flock doubtless perceived that Jesus in
her case contented Himself with the desire of afflicting
her body ; to carry it into effect was not what He

themselves with the extremely coarse description common
amongst the French peasantry.

required. He destined her for another kind of martyrdom—the martyrdom of love.

But in mentioning these circumstances we have been led to forestall events; we shall hereafter give an account of Eustelle's first interview with the Bishop. For the present, we need only add that, as he did not speak so positively with respect to the use of the discipline, she caused one to be made, hoping that he would soon give the half-promised sanction, but to the last he continued to withhold his consent. This is all she has left on record concerning the matter, and if we had no other source of information we should have been led to conclude that she had never used the discipline at all; yet it is clear, from the testimony of survivors, that such was not the case. It is probable, therefore, that when the question was brought under the Bishop's notice, she was already no stranger to its use. Her family preserve, as a relic, this instrument of penance. It is of iron, armed with points. When her work kept her at home, if any interruption occurred which gave her a few moments of leisure, Eustelle would retire to a little outhouse attached to their small abode, to pray or give herself the discipline. One of her young sisters, curious to know why she always disappeared in this way, took a ladder one day and peeped down through an aperture into the cell-like chamber. Eustelle, who had just concluded her prayer, was at the very moment looking up to heaven: their eyes met; she blushed deeply, and, coming out from her place of retirement, gave her inquisitive sister as sharp a reprimand as her gentleness ever allowed her to administer. The relator of this anecdote also mentioned that Eustelle during one whole winter purposely wore shoes which let in the

wet ; that she put on cotton stockings in the winter,
and woollen ones in the summer, seeking by all these
ingenious devices to have something to suffer for
Jesus.   We much suspect that if the Bishop had
been aware of these practices, he would have forbidden them as absolutely as he did the discipline
and hair-shirt ; for with Eustelle's feeble constitution
they could scarcely be less injurious, if, indeed, they
were not more so.   But no doubt she considered
them as trifles not worth the mentioning ; and we
may feel certain that they are only specimens of
the many ways in which she contrived to afflict
nature, and thwart its inclinations, but to which she
never alluded, or in which she was never detected.

Although it cannot be classed among corporal
austerities, the vigorous self-denial which Eustelle
exercised in the control of all her senses must be
reckoned as belonging to that branch of mortification
which regards the exterior as well as the interior.
She had made a pact with her eyes, her ears, her
mouth, to see, hear, and speak only what might be
conformable to the will of Jesus ; and this, not merely
in such things as might be in any way displeasing to
Him, but also in things allowable and innocent.   The
liberality of His love evoked in her a corresponding
generosity of spirit ; besides, it would seem that her
Lord left her in no doubt as to the stringency of His
demands.   To content Him she would refuse nothing,
and He wanted everything.   But then He gave
Himself in return.   Never did she unnecessarily raise
her eyes, whether in the church or in the streets.   If
she entered a house or any place where there happened
to be objects calculated to excite her interest or to
satisfy a harmless curiosity, immediately she heard

the inward voice of Jesus pressing her to deprive herself of this gratification for the love of Him. If she were walking in a garden gay with flowers, she would gently close her eyes to the glories of God's natural kingdom, to contemplate inwardly the ravishing beauty of Jesus. If any one plucked and handed her a fragrant flower, she would deny herself the little passing satisfaction of enjoying its perfume, always, however, avoiding observation as much as possible. But here it may be objected, Was not this an excess of rigour? Why has God lavished beauty on His material creation, and made it so sweet and lovely, but that it might speak to us of Him and tell us, as by a parable, of His unfathomable wisdom and ineffable love? Was the rose given its scent only that we should turn away from it as from a temptation? Was nature decked in such glorious apparel that we should shut our eyes to its splendour, as if, like the world's pomp, it was set as a snare to our souls? Rather, were not all these visible things invested with such varied charms that in them we might admire and adore their unseen Maker? Now as to the excess of rigour, the reply is easy. Those holy persons who have turned away their eyes from the beautiful works of God, and have refused the pleasure which their senses might receive through them, have not rejected this satisfaction on the score of its sinfulness, but have sacrificed it as an offering of love to Him whose whole life on earth was a sacrifice of love, or have abstained through fear of resting in creatures and in the pleasure they afford—a danger which must more or less exist in the case of such as have not yet arrived at the state of perfect union with God. The scent of a flower, it is true, conveys no temptation to the soul—it is simply a delight ; but who does not know that it is possible to relish such delight as a mere luxury ? Nay, even the beauties of a fair landscape, the glowing tints of a magnificent sunset, although they speak to a higher sense, may be regarded with a mere poetic eye, and be made to minister to the soft day-dreams of the imagination.   And yet, doubtless, creatures were designed to lead us up to God ; and it is well to rise heavenward by the contemplation of them, and to make the works of the Creator a ladder whereby we may mount up to the Creator Himself.   But saints, instead of ascending the ladder step by step, and so making their way to God, seem to take a bolder flight and to spring up direct to their Sovereign Good, passing by and overlooking all that is finite—albeit afterwards descending, so to say, to creatures by viewing them in Him whose work they are.   They do not so much see God in creatures as creatures in God : this is the higher way of the two, though not the way for all. It is the eagles of the spiritual life who go straight to the Primal Light, not only soaring above and beyond the finite to fix their gaze upon the Infinite, but at times so absorbed in the heavenly vision as to be insensible to the material beauty spread out before their eyes.   Thus a St. Bernard could travel all the day long on the borders of a beautiful lake and never so much as observe it, so rapt was he in the thought of God and in the contemplation of His perfections. Nor do such saints stand in any real contrast with those who at first sight appear to have followed a different course, at least on certain occasions, and under certain circumstances.   When we read of a St. Mary Magdalen of Pazzi seizing a flower and running round the garden with it in an ecstasy of

Divine love, who would think of her as one who was
elevating her mind to heavenly things by the help of
creatures, and using them as a stepping-stone to attain
to the Creator? Nay, rather, with her soul all immersed in the contemplation of the Eternal Beauty,
and burning with the love of Him who is the Increate
Source of all created loveliness, she was kindled into
fresh rapture at the sight of the work of His hands,
bearing the stamp and impress, however faintly, of
His Adorable Attributes.* It forms, then, part of the
process of detachment from all earthly things, in the
case of those who aim at high perfection, often to put
aside, and close their eyes and other senses to, objects
which are even serviceable to the advancement of
ordinary Christians, and which may be profitable in
their own case also, when God so wills it. "The
Spirit breatheth where He will." At one time He
will direct the soul which He is guiding to reject what
at another time, perhaps, He may incline it to accept.
Or, again, He will lead certain souls by an altogether
different course, and prompt them to seek aid habitually
in those very things which He teaches others to
sacrifice. God in all things and by all things: "He
that eateth," as the Apostle says,† "eateth to the Lord,
for he giveth thanks to God. And he that eateth not,
to the Lord he eateth not, and giveth thanks to God."

Eustelle, if not led by the road of severe penitential

---

* That Eustelle was keenly sensible of the beauties of God's
creation, and felt the parabolic import of material things, is
abundantly evidenced by many constantly recurring allusions
in her letters, where she unconsciously displays the poetic
feeling which she so largely possessed. An incident still more
illustrative of the observations made above will be noticed
hereafter.

† Rom. xiv. 6.

austerities, was certainly drawn to follow that of an entire and perfect detachment from all things, a detachment of which love was to be the impelling motive. Whatever was connected with religion would naturally possess great attractions in her eyes; yet even here the spirit of sacrifice was active in her; and when it was possible to satisfy her piety without any additional accidental gratification resulting from the act, she elected to forego it. For instance, if a funeral procession passed in the streets, she offered a prayer mentally for the soul of him who was being borne to his grave, but would not turn her eyes to look at it. Another mode in which her spirit of detachment manifested itself was in hindering, as far as kindness allowed, all expressions and demonstrations of esteem and affection towards herself. She discouraged all those caressing ways of which young women are often so prodigal to each other, and of which so attractive and amiable a girl as Eustelle was sure to be the object. "One day," writes a friend of hers, "she invited me to take a walk with her into the country." Eustelle, no doubt, had her own object in so doing, but her friend was charmed at so unusual a proposal. "I accepted with pleasure," she continues, "and in the overflowing of my heart, knowing as I did the tender interest she took in me, gave free utterance to all my sentiments of affection for her. But I thought I perceived that these demonstrations were not agreeable to her. Then I said, 'Eustelle, may I not be allowed to love you, then?' She replied with much kindness, 'Ah, Mademoiselle, undoubtedly; but let us love God before and above all; let all the sentiments of our hearts be for Him alone!' I cannot describe the tone in which she uttered these words, but they seemed to lay bare her whole soul to me. She was so filled with God, that she could not without pain see any one not loving her Jesus as she loved Him."

Another field for self-denial she found in the repression of all eagerness, exercised even upon the most lawful and laudable object. Thus on one occasion, when she received a letter which she knew would interest her greatly—and we know what her subjects of interest were—she felt herself interiorly pressed not to read it immediately, and so she laid it down and did not open it for a month. This divine attraction for mortification pursued her everywhere, and she never disregarded it, never evaded or escaped from it. Such continual surrender of every passing wish, every harmless inclination, is, perhaps, more wonderful than the self-infliction of the severest penitential austerities ; and if not more meritorious, is, at least, more *certainly* meritorious. For with these self may mingle,—nay, it has sometimes altogether dictated acts which have thus become simply acts of self-torture, suggested by a subtle pride ; but this renunciation of the will in all things, this readiness to part with anything and everything at a moment's call, with all that .helps to constitute the ease, freedom, and satisfaction of daily life, admits of no possible delusion, and furnishes no allurement to pride or vain glory. In this silent, ceaseless immolation of herself, Eustelle lived. "It was Jesus," she said, "who subjected me to this mysterious death, that He might give me a large share of the true life." In her last years, having deeply realized the spiritual benefit which flows from such a course of hidden self-sacrifice, she thus speaks of it to her director : "O my father, how profitable to the soul is this interior death ! What se-

curity it gives to the mind, and what peace to the heart!
How free one then is! How the soul mounts aloft when
it is independent of created things! Oh if people did
but know the value of this interior despoilment!"
Then, recollecting herself, she added, "And I who
talk about it, can I dare to flatter myself that I
practise it, as far as I comprehend it?" She used
to say that she who has for her spouse a God, poor,
suffering, dying in abasement and humiliation, ought
to refuse Him nothing. To one of her friends who
seemed to hesitate in making certain sacrifices, she
wrote, "Love for Jesus what He has loved for you.
Shut up your whole soul in His Heart. There live by
His life, and learn to die, that you may live." One
of her maxims, indeed, was that (speaking generally)
extraordinary graces are the fruit only of a total death
to all that is not Jesus. "Let us go and repose," she
said, "on the Heart of Jesus, not only for the sweetness and lights which He communicates, but, above
all, to learn the ways of crucified love. It is only by
this last knowledge, followed by practice, that it will
be given to us to enter into familiarity with Jesus."
Writing to a friend whom she was tenderly exhorting
to embrace the Divine will in all her pains and distresses, she expresses a wish dictated by a charity
truly supernatural, when she says that she would
beseech our Lord to make amends to her for her
sufferings, but not to remove them; so much value
did she set upon them. Then, yielding to one of
those transports which often forced from her bosom,
all glowing with divine ardour, sentiments of heroic
and magnanimous love, she exclaims, "For great souls
Thabor is on Calvary."

Nor was Eustelle, when insisting on the priceless

value of sufferings, merely testifying to a profound
conviction, but speaking from her own most intimate
and experimental knowledge. For two years she
was allowed to taste all the delights which attend the
faithful practice of virtue and the perfect accomplishment of God's will; if we desire to know what these
are in their fulness, we have but to listen to the
varied strains in which the Psalmist of Israel declares
them: "I have been delighted in the way of Thy
testimonies, as in all riches. How sweet are Thy
words to my palate! more than honey to my mouth.
I have purchased Thy testimonies for an inheritance
for ever, because they are the joy of my heart." So
David sings in the 118th Psalm, that marvellous
treasury of deep spiritual experience. To the intrinsic
joys which are contained in the fulfilment of the
holy law of God, were added in overflowing measure
the sensible realization of the presence of the Spouse
of her soul, the ineffable caresses of His love, and the
intimate communications with which He favoured her.
Saints have spoken of these things, yet could not find
words to express them, and then their silence or their
reserve has told more eloquently of what no human
tongue can adequately describe. Holy Job had experience of that cloudless and serene time which
preceded the season of darkness and trial, and which he
emphatically designates as "the days in which God
kept him"—days when God was "secretly in his tabernacle," and "the Almighty was with him;" when he
"washed his feet in butter, and the rock poured out
for him rivers of oil."* Satan was to be allowed to
try him, for the manifestation of God's glory in His
servant, and for his own greater purification and

* Job xxix. 2—6.

reward. Eustelle also was to pass through the re-
fining furnace ; and she received previous intimation
of the coming trials.· Jesus gave her interiorly to
understand that the peace and security she had
hitherto enjoyed were soon to be troubled, at least in
the inferior region of her soul, and she accepted at
once with submission and adoring love all the
afflictions and probations through which it might
please her Lord that she should pass.

It was not long before the storm burst upon her.
Her soul was assailed with a multitude of interior
pains and temptations, the very remembrance of
which made her afterwards shudder. So far from
being able to exaggerate their amount, she declared
that she was quite unable to find words to signify
their number or their force ; nay, that there were
some she suffered which she was not able to comprehend, far less to describe. She was first beset by
a host of distractions during her prayers. It was as if
she had stirred up a swarm of teasing insects, which
never ceased buzzing around her, and of which it
was utterly impossible to rid herself. Yet Eustelle
had given no occasion for this disturbance of the
imagination by over-interest in worldly affairs or
attention to trifles ; on the contrary, her soul was
continually in the attitude of prayer, separated alike
from earthly cares, earthly hopes, and earthly enjoyments. Whence, then, did this inroad on her peace
and recollection come? and how were these intrud-
ing thoughts to be resisted? Their origin cannot be
doubtful. Unlike those ordinary disturbances for
which we have ourselves to blame, or which are the
result of a constitutional difficulty in fixing the
attention, and to consider which as a trial sent to us,

as persons advanced in the spiritual life, would be a simple and hurtful delusion, these were plainly the work of Satan altogether. Such distractions are an infliction, to be endured rather than directly resisted. Like the flies, they may be flapped away, but they return with the retreating hand. It is sufficient that the suffering soul protests against them, and peaceably removes them so far as she is able.

But Eustelle had other and worse trials to come. All Hell now seemed to conspire against her, and from the infernal abyss shapes and forms of horror arose and embodied themselves in revolting images before the mind of this pure virgin. Eustelle's faults before her conversion had not passed beyond such as girlish levity and vanity will produce in those who would shudder at the thought of grievous sin. Her impassioned nature, it is true, had made her ardently love and eagerly pursue what she loved, but her life had been innocent, and for these last two years no thought of earth had come near to dim the lustre of the inner sanctuary of her soul. If there was a virtue she supremely loved, as most dear to the Heart of the Spouse of virgins and to that of Mary Immaculate, it was the angelic virtue of purity. The torment she experienced may, then, be imagined when, night and day, she became a victim to these abominable sug- gestions, these impressions of evil, these images of sin. "I was at first," she said, "a little frightened." We seem almost to expect her to say more; but the humble Eustelle never uses amplified expressions to portray her own feelings and sufferings, whether bodily or mental; all her fervour of language and eloquence of tongue are reserved for the one enduring passion of her heart. Of herself she always speaks in

the plainest, the most moderate, and the most simple
terms. She was only, as she says, "a *little* frightened·
at first :" that was all which the proud prince of
darkness could effect in the soul of a timid young
maiden. Faith is an invincible shield, and the Lord
can be a lamp to the soul of His servants even in
darkness. In the midst of the obscurity in which
Eustelle was plunged, one ray of light pierced the
gloom, illuminating her mind to discern, with a
clearness never before realized, this great and animating truth—that the crown of the elect is never
more beautiful and resplendent than when it has
been obtained by victories won against repeated assaults. She resigned herself therefore to the combat,
persuaded that He who permitted her to be assailed
by her enemies would never withhold His aid. She
had already received so many proofs of His goodness that she felt that the least mistrust would have
been an injurious affront to His infinite mercy.
Well, indeed, is it for those who will rest satisfied
with this single ray of light in darkness, and act upon
it. It is the trial of faith. Such a trial had the
widow of Sarephta, when the prophet bade her go and
prepare for him of her scanty store—all that remained
to her to save herself and her son a few hours longer
from the death of famine. "Fear not: the pot of
meal shall not waste, nor the cruse of oil be diminished." Why? Because "thus saith the Lord
God." The light came with these words, and this
blessed woman gave it entrance. God sends power
with His words—this is why we are responsible for
not giving credence to them—power to convince
in that deep intellectual region of the soul where
conviction takes place — not logical proof, not

I

mathematical demonstration, not ocular evidence, but
something infinitely above these, and immeasurably
surer, inasmuch as what is divine is higher than what
is natural ; only the will can resist the one, while from
the constitution of things the human intellect is forced
to accept the other.   This is why the fool, while
unable to deny the testimony of his senses or the first
principles of reason, can say in his heart, There is no
God.   How often did our Lord utter these words,
" Only believe," so incomprehensible to the men of this
world—all immersed in their fleshly nature and filled
with the pride of human wisdom—according to whom
belief is a necessary act, an irresponsible acquiescence
of the reason.   When the servants of God have for a
moment faltered and leant to this human reason after
God has spoken, severe has been their punishment.
Witness the dumbness of Zachary ; while " Blessed art
thou that hast believed," was the first inspired laudation
bestowed on the Mother of God after Gabriel's Ave.

Eustelle believed the testimony of God within herself, but, although she could repose with perfect confidence on His protection, this reliance did not relieve
her from the pain which her pure soul endured in the
continual vision of these horrible images which a
legion of malicious spirits seemed engaged in presenting before her.   Others were busy at the work
of striving to create perplexity in her mind by filling
her memory and understanding with darkness ; and
then labouring to persuade her that she had consented
to their suggestions.   In all these trials, although she
firmly believed that God was with her, protecting and
supporting her, nevertheless this protection and support did not make itself sensibly felt.   At these terrible moments Jesus seemed to abandon her to herself.

She could not discern in what manner He sustained her; that He did sustain her, she was assured, for her heart was never separated from Him, but during the whole course of this violent tempest clave firmly to Him. She knew well that it was through no strength of her own that she resisted, and that her good God was ever, though secretly, present with her. Her temptation she describes as threefold: first of all there were the infernal suggestions themselves; next, Satan's endeavour to bewilder her and persuade her that she had given some momentary consent; the third appeared to wait until the second had been brought to bear with some effect upon her; it was a mingled feeling of vexation and discouragement—vexation that God should leave her so long to do battle with these ignoble demons; and a discouragement tending to make her lay down her arms in despair, as too feeble to pursue the conflict. For she seemed to hear the devil saying to her, All your efforts to vanquish me are useless; it is I who shall conquer, you cannot escape from my hands.

These temptations were succeeded by an indescribable state of inward dereliction. It was no longer her God concealing Himself, but her God abandoning her. The heaven was become as brass above her head, and the earth as iron beneath her feet. If she cried on the Lord in her agony, there was none to hear or to answer. He was silent to her. Silence of God to the soul!—we can scarcely estimate the profound misery of this trial; it needs to be far on the road of sanctity to appreciate its severity. All good Christians, or, at least, the most part, we may suppose, know what it is to suffer at times from sadness and oppression of spirit, and a subtraction of sensible devotion; but, afflicting as this may be, it is at least a tolerable state to those who have never been introduced into that close familiarity with their Lord which highly-favoured souls have been privileged to enjoy. For them the veil has been, so to say, raised which curtains the face of our God from us. True, we know Him to be very near to us, but to them it has been given to feel His presence with an ineffable actuality, to feel it more intimately than we feel the presence of the friend who converses with us; nay, almost more intimately than the consciousness of their own being. What, then, must it be to lose this presence? It is as if the sun went out at mid-day. Eustelle describes her condition in few but most touching words. She would have none of creatures, and God would have none of her, or, rather, He made as though He would not. Rejected by Him whom alone she loved, she took refuge, all unworthy as she was, in the Adorable Wound of His side, casting herself upon His pitying mercy; but the Heart of Jesus appeared to repulse her more coldly and contemptuously than when on earth He turned away from the Canaanitish woman. She seemed to hear Him pronounce these heart-breaking words: "Go, I reject you; henceforth you are as nothing to Me." "O my father," she exclaims, "what a terrible sentence for me who had given up all that I thought could be displeasing to Jesus; who desired nothing but Him; who had felt consumed with the desire to love Him alone, or to love nothing except for Him! Ah, this dear and tender Master wished, if I may be permitted so to express myself, to assure to Himself the effect of these words; He wished me to love Him only for Himself, and not for my own satisfaction. Oh, how

I bless Him for thus dealing with my soul. I blessed Him even in the very midst of these dreadful trials."

Other temptations came to add their gall to this special cup of bitterness : temptations to vanity, to blasphemy, to despair. No one can imagine, she says, what these last made her suffer. To crown all, she fell into a state of most miserable scrupulousness. Still ardently desiring as ever to unite herself to Jesus in the Eucharist, she was seized with the apprehension of committing a sacrilege. At this stage, however, her confessor promptly intervened ; he bade her confess only once a fortnight, and, above all, not to omit any of her usual weekly communions. She obeyed, and (as before noticed) never missed one ; indeed, she adds, "to forego this aliment of life would, I confess, have been more painful to me than all my trials." This prompt remedy dissipated the illusion. Scrupulosity, that most intractable of tempers, alike the plague of directors and the torment of souls which are subject to it, was no foible of Eustelle's. She acted always with that docility, simplicity, and straightforward common sense in spiritual as in other matters which is so foreign to the disposition of the scrupulous. She did not parley, she did not return to re-open settled points, she obeyed. With her, as with so many of the saints, scruples were simply trials and temptations. By-and-by we shall find the enemy returning in a fresh form, to be summarily dealt with in a similar manner.

Delivered from this particular affliction, she was soon to suffer in a new way. She was now so overcome by dryness and languor in prayer that she seemed utterly unable to acquit herself of this exer-

cise. She had already experienced the silence of her
Lord, and the absence of all response to her supplications—God did not speak to her, and now she was
almost unable to speak to God. The devil was re-
doubling his efforts to dishearten her altogether, and
induce her to abandon what she seemed powerless to
perform. To yield ever so little to such a suggestion
is indeed most perilous; to give up prayer is not
merely to be vanquished, it is wilfully to disarm ourselves and part with our sole weapon. Armed with
that weapon Satan knows that the soul is invincible;
and never is it more so than when, wielding it in
darkness and desolation, it seems to beat the air in
vain, and yet manfully, albeit blindly, continues the
combat undismayed. Eustelle was thus faithful. The
Sovereign Guide of her soul was there to uphold her,
and He had too well taught her the efficaciousness of
mental prayer for her ever to give way to the solicitations of the tempter. Satan now changed his tactics
a little. He suggested to her that she did not acquit
herself properly of her vocal prayers; that they were
totally devoid of merit; and that she only irritated
the Lord by praying in such fashion. Nay, he even
succeeded in so bewildering her memory that she
could not even recollect whether she had said them at
all. Night and morning the same thing would occur,
and poor Eustelle, fearful that she had not fulfilled
this daily duty, would begin again and again what
she had already faithfully discharged. Her forgetfulness was all the more extraordinary that the extreme
difficulty and lassitude with which she had accomplished what to her was now a most laborious task,
ought at least to have ensured the remembrance of
the act. It was a curious and singular sort of temp-

tation, as she herself observes ; but the evil one has countless devices and strives to weary his adversary when he cannot terrify or seduce him. Her confessor bade her on such occasions not repeat her prayers, but replace them by meditation. Still tormented by this disquieting scruple, she had recourse to what, she says, may seem a somewhat ludicrous remedy. On finishing her prayers she wrote down the day of the month and the week, as well as the hour of the day in which they were said. She had succeeded : the devil was defeated.

One might have hoped that the tempter would now confess himself vanquished, for he had been foiled in all his varied assaults, and the fortress, so far from being captured, had remained intact at every point. Yet all had been but the prelude to a still fiercer onslaught. As in a storm the gale will seem to have expended its fury, and to retire sighing and moaning into the distance, and then, after a temporary lull, will return with a terrific reinforcement of power, as if animated by a determined will to uproot, throw down, and sweep away all that opposes its progress, so did the enemy of souls rush again upon Eustelle. Or, like some great tidal wave, the flood of evil came towering onward to burst in one accumulated torrent over her soul. That "water insupportable" of which David speaks,* had indeed swallowed her up alive, if the Lord had not been with her. Not only were these hideous temptations increased tenfold in intensity, but they were unintermittent, while at night the power

---

* "Nisi quia Dominus erat in nobis. . . . . Torrentem pertransivit anima nostra : forsitan pertransisset anima nostra aquam intolerabilem."—Ps. cxxiii. 1-4. The whole of the psalm may be applied to this species of infernal attack.

of the prince of darkness seemed to wax greater, and his legion of satellites to become bolder and more insolent. Poor Eustelle dreaded the close of the day; it brought to her no rest or suspension of suffering. The whole infernal troop seemed then to be gathered about her, holding her, as it were, bound down and forced to be the witness of the horrible spectacle that was enacted before her eyes. Often she was so exhausted in mind and body with the conflict, that she felt (she said) like one in the very agonies of death. An interior voice, however, still whispered to her that in all this she was innocent; but she had not a moment's breathing time, not so much as might allow her to thank her Lord for the assistance she knew He was rendering her. One shock succeeded another, and it is only a marvel that the commotion raised within her did not cause some serious bodily injury. She records a precious favour which at this period she frequently received. In the height of the storm, when, the devil attacking her on all sides, she knew not which way to turn to repel his assaults, dreading defeat, yet not defeated, she would raise her hands and heart to Jesus; and then, even as He appeared to His disciples walking on the stormy billows of the Sea of Galilee, so did He manifest himself to Eustelle's soul, with majesty and sweetness incomparable, saying, " I am with you, fear nothing." At His presence the tempest was stilled, the spirits of darkness vanished, and all was peace. Then, blessing her Deliverer, she composed herself to sleep, a refreshment which she sorely needed. Unused as yet to intellectual visions, and considering herself unworthy of such favours, she was at first a little troubled by them. Humility always fears delusion; but it is a characteristic of heavenly communications that if in the beginning they cause alarm, this alarm is speedily followed by confidence and security, whereas in the case of Satan's apparitions simulating the divine, whatever cheating consolation they may seem at first to yield, they afterwards leave the mind a prey to apprehension and disturbance.   So the Heavenly Spouse told St. Catharine of Siena, but He gave her a still surer token to preserve her from the illusions of the devil. As He is the Truth itself, so, in manifesting Himself, He fills the soul with a more certain knowledge of the truth.   He teaches the creature what He Himself is and what it is itself; whereas the father of lies, who is all pride, can only impart to others of his own and puff up the soul with presumption and vain self-esteem.   Both these tests were verified in Eustelle. These visions were followed by peace of mind and deepened sentiments of self-abasement : "The goodness of the Lord," she says, "reassured me, and made me acquiesce humbly and simply in the favours He showed me.   I begged of Him grace to correspond by a profound humility and an ardent love."

We may here remark, that theologians are of opinion that intellectual visions are less subject to illusion than any others.   The visions presented to the bodily eye are obviously the most open to deception.   Angels of darkness have not lost their marvellous natural powers, and, if God do not forbid their exerting them, they can easily assume before the eyes of men any appearance they please.   Thus Satan can at will transform himself into an "angel of light." Interior visions, of which the seat is the imagination, and which present a visible form to the inward eye, are likewise open to the same kind of deceptions.

Satan, unless God withhold him, has access to the imagination, but the pure intellect is beyond his reach : God, who made us, has alone an entrance there. In these visions the soul sees without the help of images, yet with more vividness and with a fuller realization than by means of the external or internal senses, and, moreover, with an inexplicable certainty. What we call the intellect has not the same dependence on the body; it needs not the bodily organs for its activity, and is therefore not so subject to those peculiar deceits to which the soul is liable through its connection with an animal nature. Eustelle calls the visions with which she was favoured at this time *intellectual*, and we may presume with certainty that they were of that order, since she referred all her experiences, at a subsequent period, to the judgment of competent authority.

She was subjected to another severe trial, which she endeavoured, but felt herself incompetent, to describe. She attempts to convey some notion of it by the help of a comparison, however inadequate, with the sensations of persons sailing for the first time on a rough and stormy ocean. When the vessel goes down into the trough of the sea, the mountain billows toppling over and threatening to burst upon the frail craft, their soul sinks, and they seem ready to die; then, as the vessel mounts again and rights itself, they will experience a momentary sense of relief, to be followed by a renewed accession of terror at the next downward plunge. While occupied in prayer, or listening to the explanation of God's word, or even while engaged in conversation, analogous alternations, without any assignable cause, would take place within her. On these

occasions she had neither image nor representation
present to her mind, but suddenly she would feel
her soul overwhelmed, oppressed, as if with a sense
of suffocation; then again all would be changed:
tranquillity was restored, a bright light seemed to
fill her whole being, pure, transparent as crystal; she
was happy, and felt like a criminal whose chains
have been struck off. But this joy was only momentary, as she was instantaneously immersed in the
horrors of her previous state. These alternations
would continue for about a quarter of an hour;
they resembled nothing else which she experienced
in the way of interior pains; and it is difficult to
assign them any special object, as they seem to have
been accompanied with no temptation, except to that
weariness and despondency of mind which their
harassing nature was calculated to produce; and
this we may conceive to have been the aim of the
evil one. But, indeed, he loves to torment when he
can do no more, of which we have numerous instances
in the lives of the saints. It gives a terrible insight
into the power of this lost one to tear, rack, and
agonize souls delivered into his infernal clutches;
but, blessed be God, no one is so delivered who desires
to escape, and who calls upon the name of the Lord.
With that defence there is no weak woman, no tender
child, who is not invested with a panoply which
renders them invulnerable, and who does not possess
a power infinitely surpassing that of Satan and all
his angels. What matters, indeed, the amount of
our own native strength? for, however great it might
be, it would prove as nothing when opposed to that
of the lowest of angelic natures. We can borrow
the strength of the Omnipotent God, or, rather, it is

within us, it is ours to use, if we be members of His Incarnate Son. "His truth shall compass thee with a shield ; thou shalt not be afraid of the terror of the night. Thou shalt walk upon the asp and the basilisk : and thou shalt trample under foot the lion and the dragon. Because he hoped in Me, I will deliver him. I will protect him because He hath known My Name."*

CHAPTER VIII.

Fruits of Suffering and Special Vocation.

The interior pains to which Marie-Eustelle was subjected extended over the greater portion of her remaining life, before the close of which, however, she was to enjoy a season of unclouded peace. It is interesting to learn from her own recorded testimony what was her state of mind during the continuance of her trials, and what was their practical effect upon her. One point is particularly remarkable from its connection with her peculiar attraction. She says that, seeing how much she owed to God's justice on account of all the indifference and failures of her early years, it was natural that she should think of discharging this debt by offering her trials and inward pains in expiation of her faults ; nevertheless she was drawn in quite a different direction. Our Lord seemed to require her to suffer all for the love of Him. Love, not penitence, was to be the prevailing sentiment. Ever since her conversion, she believed that He

* Psalm xc. 5, 13, 14.

moved her thus to act. " All through love "—these
words were continually sounding in her ears. Eustelle, as we have seen, was all attention to catch the
accents of the Divine voice, and all docility to obey
them ; she had, so to say, no notions of her own ; at
any rate she never followed, nor so much as adverted
to them. They must have died as fast as they were
born ; if, indeed, her heart was not too full of a
prepared conformity to the suggestions of grace as
they arose, to leave room for any self-originated ideas.
In accordance, then, with these inward promptings to
which she was so sensitively alive, she resolved henceforward to make her whole life, as it were, one prolonged thanksgiving ; not that she had become
indifferent to feelings of holy sorrow or put away the
desire to atone for her past faults, but all was
summed up and comprehended in the act of love
which she was perpetually forming ; and seeing that
this habitual occupation of her soul was what Jesus
seemed to require of her, she felt assured that divine
charity, thus reigning within her, would super-
abundantly discharge her debts. Believing such to
be His adorable will, she accepted, not with resignation only, but in a spirit of love and gratitude, all
those apparent rigours which she knew to be in truth
so many rich gifts of His bounty and goodness. She
is never weary of speaking of the benefit of these
trials. " Not for the whole world," she said, " would
I have been exempt from them—nay, not for all
heaven itself, would I have refused the smallest drop
of the chalice which His love presented to me. I
continually blessed Him for them, and even prayed
Him to add to my trials, exclaiming sometimes, ' More,
Lord, yet more ! '"—an heroic act, upon which few but

saints could venture. She who was so discreet in
speaking of the graces which had been showered upon
her, could not refrain from confiding her joy in grief
to a few chosen friends. "Bless the Lord with me,"
she writes, "help me to thank Him for the dear
crosses He sends me;" and again, "Blessed be God
for all the crosses He deigns to send me. I am
unworthy of them; I hope, however, not to be
deprived of them. Do not speak of them to any one."
Here are no requests for prayers to be delivered from
her fearful trials, or at least, for some mitigation of
their severity. She rejoices unaffectedly at them, and
cannot conceal her joy. Yet some prayers she did
request, although not prayers for alleviation or
comfort; for, in the very letter in which she calls her
crosses dear (*aimables*), she adds, "I acknowledge that
nature complains; beg of God that grace may be
fully victorious. My soul is sorrowful." Her correspondence with her directors, to whom she was more
explicit, testifies at once to the untold anguish she
endured, and to the estimation in which she held
those pains which come direct from the Saviour's
bountiful hand. An extract from a letter written to
a friend in affliction will serve to exemplify her value
for such gifts. "Try not to lose," she says, "the
fruit of the trials to which our Lord subjects you at
this time; they are the flowers of His Passion, of
which you must form a nosegay to place upon your
heart with joy, tenderness, and love. Oh! understand better the interest which Jesus, so good, takes
in your soul by thus dealing with it. It is upon
Calvary that the lovers of the Saviour are born, and
it is there that He presents them with His diadem
of ignominy and suffering. Let us love, good friend,

to second the desires of the Heart of Jesus; let us unite to His Cross all that He sends us, and all that we are; the day will come when it shall be given us to gather with joy the sweet fruits of the mysterious tree upon which we have been redeemed."

In her sufferings Eustelle not only rejoiced, but sang; for love is the nurse of poetry, and especially suffering love. Divine love has formed no exception, only its strains are more jubilant than sad, because its sorrows are the seeds of joy—rather, they are themselves joys disguised. It was in a loathsome dungeon, deprived at once of light and air, that the Blessed Jacopone of Todi broke forth in that beautiful canticle on the delights of suffering :—

> " O giubilo del cuore,
> Che fai cantar d'amore !"*

The poor sempstress of Saint-Pallais was no mean poet in her way, and has left stanzas full of tender grace, characterized by a facility and flow suggesting the idea of improvisations, and such almost they probably were.

Never once did the thought occur to her, of entreating for the cessation of her trials. Even when they were at their height, she was always, as she herself averred, greedy for more ; and Heaven, she adds, was not niggard of them, for they were her daily bread. Alike in solitude and in company she was a prey to these torments, and she was sometimes compelled to leave those with whom she was conversing, because, notwithstanding her astonishing self-control, she felt unable to conceal her inward perturbation.

* " O joy of the heart,
Which makest us sing of love !"

Yet had any one at such moments asked her if she would be freed from her sufferings, she would have protested that she desired nothing but the good pleasure of her Lord. If ever she desired anything, it was an increase of their severity, and within her heart she was continually exclaiming with all the energy of her will, " Yes, Lord, I will be faithful to Thee ; nothing on earth or in hell shall be able to separate me from Thee. To conquer or to die; or, rather, to die in order to conquer, if need be !" And as she never desired the removal or abatement of her afflictions, so never did her confidence in Jesus flag or waver; on the contrary, it always rose with the struggle. Jesus was always " her sweet and unvarying hope," and she used to tell Him that even were an assurance given her of her eternal reprobation she would still hope in Him. Nevertheless, the violence she had to put upon herself began seriously to affect her naturally delicate health. Some sign of suffering would thus unavoidably betray itself at times in her countenance, and then people, always keenly on the watch to lay everything to the charge of what they called over-piety, would come and tell her that if she did not take care she would go mad. She paid small heed either to these remarks or to the state of her health, for which, indeed, she says she was in no degree responsible. Her only occupation was with the life and health of her soul ; her only thought, her only desire, to avoid for the love of Jesus all that might have in it the shadow of sin. Ever since her conversion, she had neither feared nor hated anything but sin ; and " the very thought of saddening the Heart of Jesus, that tenderest of fathers, that best of friends, of Jesus, Love Eternal," was sufficient to make her almost die in imagination through the very apprehension of such a calamity.

On the festival day of St. John the Evangelist one year, she felt herself suddenly delivered from her state of anguish and temptation. This reprieve lasted eight days, and it was during the interval that Jesus made her know by means of a secret illumination of a peculiar kind which lasted the whole time, the priceless value of trials and sufferings and the benefit which accrued from them to her soul. She was already convinced that so indeed it was, but now she gained a far deeper insight into this truth, which became, so to say, sensibly evident to her mind. So intense was the love of suffering which this ray of light was the means of kindling within her, that she confesses it was nothing but conformity to the will of her God which made her contentedly acquiesce in being without them for this brief season. She felt a certain uneasiness and wonder; she seemed to want for something: it was the Cross she wanted, and truly, as she observes, she had it because she had it not. Accordingly, when, after this short breathing-time, her trials recommenced, she experienced the pleasure of one who has found again a lost treasure.

The combination of inexplicable joy and sorrow which we meet with in souls whom God designs to raise to a high degree of perfection, has something in it that is very wonderful and inscrutable. It is a state altogether supernatural, and which quite baffles description; in attempting to paint it we appear to be stating contradictions. It is, in fact, a faint reflex of what was exemplified after a transcendent manner in the Human Soul of Christ alone, who was the Man of Sorrows and yet enjoyed uninter-

K

ruptedly the beatific vision. What wonder, then, that
bearing a resemblance, however distant, to so high a
mystery, words should be incapable of conveying an
adequate idea of its nature. It was not only that
Marie-Eustelle rejoiced when she lay plunged in
the abyss of sorrow, because, as she herself says, she
regarded her varied crosses as a pledge of the love
of her Heavenly Master—as the prelude of the
special graces with which He willed to enrich her,
and as a means of pleasing Him and conforming
herself to His likeness : this is intelligible, and when
she speaks of her heart overflowing with joy at suffering something in gratitude for what Jesus had
suffered for her, we understand her meaning, however imperfectly we may be able to imitate her.
What she experienced at times was more than this—
a state the description of which, at least, is familiar
to us in the lives of God's most favoured servants,
and may be best exemplified in her own words. In a
letter to one of her directors, she says : "At this
moment, my soul at once enjoys and suffers. I have
joy because our Lord makes me feel His Divine
Presence, and fills my soul with consolation; but
this is only in its superior part. Interior pains and
temptations ceaselessly agitate my soul in its inferior
part. Some days ago, being alone with our Lord,
as I knelt on the *priedieu* in our Lady's chapel, I
experienced an abundance of consolation, of which,
without doubt, I was very unworthy. Oh! how good
He is, the God of Christians, to those who love Him."
Another time, writing to this same priest, she tells
him, that for three weeks the Lord has inundated her
soul with consolations; that the lights and graces
with which He favours her so "suffocate" her that

she would desire to cry out to the whole world, "Love God;" then, after many such-like aspirations, bespeaking a soul rapt in God and all absorbed in joy akin to that of the blessed, she thus concludes: "In speaking to you of the graces which God vouchsafes to me, I must also tell you of the temptations I experience at the same time. The more the Lord manifests Himself to my soul in its highest region, the more I suffer in its inferior region, and sometimes scarcely know what this means; only I recognize that God would thus make me feel my weakness, and give me to comprehend that, notwithstanding all His favours, the glory of which belongs to Him alone, the least breath of wind would be able to strike me down and lay me low if I were deprived of His help."

Her passion for the Cross was greatly increased by a vision with which it pleased our Lord to favour her. It was not a vision of the night, neither did it take place while she was engaged at her devotions. She was sweeping her room preparatory to hastening to church, as soon as her little household business should be despatched. There, at the foot of the Tabernacle, she was doubtless already in heart, but nothing was neglected on that account. Eustelle's haste consisted in early rising and economizing of time: to bustle or hurry she was a stranger. And so she was industriously sweeping her room when suddenly, on turning, she beheld Jesus Christ before her, arrayed in the garb of His Passion, as He appeared when Pilate showed Him to the people with the words: "*Ecce Homo*—Behold the Man!" The Head of the Redeemer was crowned with thorns; His Hands were bound; and His Body all covered with His Blood.

She beheld Him, not for a moment only—and that would have been a sight never to be forgotten—but for eight or ten minutes. What passed in the tender and loving heart of Eustelle it would be impossible to describe. She begged pardon of Jesus for herself, and for all who had caused her any sorrow, and Jesus asked her to make amends to Him for the insensibility of men by her love and gratitude. This vision is not mentioned in her manuscript; nor, indeed, with the exception of the intellectual visions already alluded to, with which she was comforted during her inward conflicts, are any there recorded; she was, however, favoured subsequently with many, chiefly in connection with the Mystery of Love which her life was spent in honouring. Were it not for her letters to those ecclesiastics who, at different times, had the charge of her soul, we should know little or nothing of them, for in all her numerous letters to seculars she never makes the least allusion to the supernatural favours she had received.

One of the precious acquisitions which she said she owed to her long martyrdom of interior suffering was an abiding sense of God's presence. It seemed quite impossible for her to lose it; indeed, her very pains and trials made its recollection imperative : hence her eyes were ever towards the hills whence help cometh. Often, too, did she invoke the sweet and powerful name of Mary; and the deepening tenderness of the devotion which, like all holy souls, she had ever felt for the Mother of God was another of the sweet fruits which her crosses bore. "Oh, what help," she exclaims, "did this good and loving mother obtain for me ! How sensibly I experienced her protection during those years of conflict ! How often did she save me from shipwreck!" Mary she called "her hope in life, in death, and for eternity."

It has been observed that her inward trouble, when at its height, had occasionally betrayed itself by external marks of suffering on her countenance, but this was almost entirely due to her enfeebled state of health. Save for this circumstance all would have been well-nigh veiled from sight. She had acquired such complete self-command that not only did no complaining word ever escape her lips, but no complaining look—that mute testimony of suffering which it costs our sensitive self-love so much more to suppress, and which in her case needed the exercise of heroic fortitude—ever appeared to tell tales which the tongue did not reveal. So even and cheerful was her habitual manner, that people used to say, "Oh, *she* has no troubles : one can see that in her face." Eustelle had a double motive in putting this constraint upon herself. She did not desire to have any confidant of her sufferings but Jesus : they were all for Him, and she was satisfied that He alone should know them. Her other motive regarded her neighbour, the love of whom, for Jesus's sake, is part of the love of Jesus, and is never divided from it. She knew how little a sad countenance is calculated to recommend piety and virtue, or attract souls to their practice. Sister Anastasia, the religious who knew her so well, better, indeed, than any one, since with her alone did Eustelle depart from the reserve she maintained towards all others, bears testimony to the constant equanimity she displayed, even in the midst of the greatest sufferings, never losing her calmness of spirit, regarding everything in God, and receiving all with thanksgiving from His hands. Another nun,

Sister St. Vincent of Paul, has given the same witness to Eustelle's constant cheerfulness, speaking of her as always gay in the midst of her many occupations. One day, however (it was at the period of her most cruel trials), one of her friends noticed a certain air of sadness about her. A shade excites attention on the face of the habitually uncomplaining which would scarcely be remarked on that of ordinary persons; but in the serene heaven of Eustelle's brow a cloud was actually a marvel, and so her friend asked what ailed her. Eustelle made no reply, a significant silence which was remembered. Another time, when saying the rosary in church, she had such a seizure at her heart that her voice failed her, and she could not continue to bear her part. "Pray for me," she whispered to a friend next her; "beg the good God to give me courage." The most poignant suffering could not elicit more. Truly (as her biographer observes) did she exemplify in herself the saying of the holy Curé of Ars in those very days, "The saints do not complain."

Eustelle enjoyed the sweet privilege of those who do not pity themselves, and therefore are not beggars for the pity of others, the privilege and the talent of consoling. Complainers, if not absolutely selfish, generally abound in self-love. Self shuts out charity and, where its sway is powerful, stunts and will even stifle that beautiful human compassion which is the most touching and most divine-like of purely natural gifts. We all instinctively feel this to be so, and never look for much consolation from those who besiege us with lamentable applications for the same relief. We go to such as have few but kind words, and those not of themselves—who never say nay when

help is needed, whose ears are open to hear the tale of
woe, and who have a calm loving smile inviting confidence. And this is because we want sympathy, not
mere pity; pity, after all, can be had pretty cheap;
selfish as men are, it abounds, thank God, and often
even in those who not only lack Christian graces, but
are poorly provided with moral virtue. It abounds,
so that we make not too large or prolonged calls upon
it; but pity only does not console : it is sympathy we
crave. And if human sympathy in its mere natural
character be so winning and so engaging, what must it
be where a drop of charity from the Sacred Heart
has mingled with it and exalted it to a sublimer order
and a purer excellence! What must it be in those
specially favoured souls who have had near com-
muning with Him who came to heal every sickness
and comfort every sorrow; who have reposed in the
mystical sleep of contemplation on the bosom of Incarnate Love, and drunk, like the beloved disciple, long
draughts of compassion at its fathomless source; who
have themselves had the consecration of suffering and
sorrow,—suffering and sorrow borne for Jesus and in
union with His Cross and Passion, and, as such, divinely
fitting them for the quasi-sacerdotal office of pouring
a healing balm into the broken heart! The power
which Eustelle possessed of calming troubled spirits
and comforting afflicted souls was most remarkable.
" When my soul was sad, my refuge, after Jesus and
Mary, was the soul of this angel of peace:" such
was the testimony borne to her after death by an
inhabitant of Saintes who had the blessing of knowing her. One day, in particular, she recalls when,
oppressed with mental pains, she sought Marie-
Eustelle, and had several hours' conversation with

her, during which her friend said such beautiful, such
touching, such sublime things about the joys of suffering, that she left her filled with an ardent desire
to imitate her in the love of our Crucified Lord and
in courage under trials. On another occasion we find
a deeply afflicted lady hastening to Vespers at Saint-
Pallais during the Quarant' Ore, where she knew she
would find Eustelle, to seek some assuagement of her
bitter sorrow. Poor Eustelle was quite exhausted
with the fatigues she had gone through; no matter,
she never gave a care to herself, and at once devoting
her every thought to this suffering sister, was not
content till she had succeeded in sending her back
calmed and consoled.

Innumerable instances of the same character were
perpetually occurring; for, as those who lived within
the circle her saintly presence blessed, came to know
one from another where they could find what gold
cannot purchase, all ran to tell their griefs to Eustelle.
As we read of these things, our minds revert to that
beautiful tradition of the Child Jesus while living
His hidden life at Nazareth : such was the ravishing
sweetness and benignity of His countenance that the
sad and the sorrowful used to say, "Let us go and see
the Son of Mary." Son of Mary!—that dear name
sums up in it all tenderness and compassion, and
Jesus was known as Son of Mary before He was
known as Son of Man. The Son of Man—need we
say?—is compassionate, too, ineffably compassionate,
but He has the majesty of His divine mission about
Him and can also speak words of reproof for sin ; but
the Son of Mary, as He leaves His Mother's arms,
seems to exercise as yet only that sweet Mother's
office, the sceptre of which was to be placed in

her stainless hands on her glorious coronation-day. In her pitying charity and supernatural sympathy Eustelle's resemblance to her Beloved, the Son of Mary, and to the Mother of Mercy, His Mother and ours through Him, will be frequently recurring to our minds at every stage of her life. For as she was drawn by love and to love, so did she draw others to and by the same blessed cords : it was her mission, a mission which it pleased her Lord should be exercised in the world ; and on this topic it naturally falls to us now to speak, as it was at this period that the subject of her vocation was first broached by her pastor.

Eustelle was about twenty years old when a fresh priest was appointed to the parish of Saint-Pallais. M. Jouslain was young, full of zeal, and endowed with high qualifications for his office. Mgr. Villecourt has given a striking testimony to his merits, of which he could speak with the less reserve as death prematurely deprived the diocese of La Rochelle of this valuable pastor. M. Jouslain was not slow to distinguish the extraordinary merits of Eustelle. Enriched as she was with so many special graces, living in the world a life altogether unworldly, it is not surprising that he should have been led to believe that she must have a vocation for the religious life, which attracts to it so large, so preponderating a majority of such as follow the path of perfection, and are free to make their own choice. Whether he acted hastily in this matter we have not the means of judging, but that he was mistaken the sequel proved, and that the idea originated with himself seems equally clear. Always submissive to him who spoke in God's name, and was invested with His authority, Eustelle,

when assured by her pastor that she was called to
the religious state, prepared at once to obey. Her
attraction for the contemplative life, her wish to be
hidden and forgotten by the world, made her give the
preference to cloistered communities. There were
only two of this character at that time in the depart-
ment of La Charente Inférieure, the Sisters of
Providence and the Sisters of Our Lady of Charity,
called "White Ladies" at La Rochelle, from the
colour of their habit. M. Jouslain had been connected with this last community while he was pro-
fessor at the diocesan seminary, and his spiritual
ministrations at their convent had left on his mind
feelings of respectful attachment which doubtless influenced him in directing Marie-Eustelle's choice.

The Order of Notre Dame de la Charité,* founded
by P. Eudes, of Caen, was commenced in 1641,
and finally established in 1651. It was confirmed by
Alexander VII., and has received the approval of
several succeeding Popes. Its object is to offer a
refuge and the means of reformation to those unhappy
women who have strayed from the path of virtue.
God has abundantly blessed the labours of the devoted
sisters, who now possess houses in no less than
seventeen French towns. Besides the three ordinary
religious vows, the nuns bind themselves by the
additional vow of labouring for the salvation of souls.

---

* This order has now an off-shoot in England. A colony
from the parent-house at Caen came to Bartestree, near Here-
ford, on the 17th of August, 1863. The house was founded by
the late Mr. Biddulph Phillips, of Longworth. There is another
community of this order at Drumcondra, near Dublin. The
object of the Order of Our Lady of Charity is the same as that
of the Good Shepherd, and the habit is very similar. The
orders themselves are distinct, but both owe their foundation
to P. Jean Eudes.

None can be admitted into the community but such as have previously led irreproachable lives. However complete a conversion may subsequently have taken place, and whatever the quality of the individual, no relaxation of this rule is ever allowed. This regulation has been judged imperative on account of the peculiar mission of these religious, the very colour of their habit being significant of the purity considered needful for those who are to be brought into contact with souls that have been deeply stained by sin. It was natural that M. Jouslain should feel a strong persuasion that Marie-Eustelle had her appointed place amongst these white-robed virgins—perhaps only too natural, for the designs of God baffle all our notions founded on appearances and probabilities.

When Marie-Eustelle announced her purpose to her father, he was thunder-struck, and declared she should never have his consent. Eustelle had foreseen the opposition she would have to encounter, and the painful scene through which she must pass. She dearly loved her parents, and suffered greatly at having to inflict so rude a blow upon them, but, silencing her own heart, she gently but firmly represented to her father that if an advantageous match had presented itself, he surely would not have been opposed to it on the mere ground that it would separate her from him. She added, "I have chosen Jesus Christ for my spouse; let me go, then, where the noblest and the most beautiful of spouses wishes to lead me." The argument was unanswerable, but the wounded heart will not be satisfied by arguments: her father remained sullenly silent. Entreaties and caresses, which are often more powerful than reasons,

wrung a reluctant consent from her mother, but the
sterner parent was not accessible to prayers any more
than to just representations.   Accordingly, Eustelle
set out for La Rochelle the next day, hoping to move
her father more easily by means of a letter.   From
the convent she wrote to him in the most respectful
and tender terms; her truly pious mother joined her
supplications to those of her daughter, begging her
husband not to oppose their child's happiness; but
all she could obtain from him was a consent that was
worse than a refusal from the harsh expressions which
accompanied his forced acquiescence.   He was an ill-
instructed man, very indifferent to the affairs of his
own soul, and therefore little able to appreciate the
motives which actuated his daughter, or to comprehend the superiority of religious vocation to the
claims of parental authority.   She was his daughter,
she made his home comfortable, he thought he had
a right to the comfort this insured to him.   So think,
or so feel, at least, many fathers who cannot plead
as much in their excuse as could poor René Harpain.

Eustelle was now at the convent; the first step, and
that which apparently offered the only difficulty of
any moment, had been surmounted; nevertheless, two
unanticipated obstacles interfered with the accomplishment of her purpose.   One was purely material, and
came from the religious themselves.   It is a wonder
that it had not been foreseen, or that inquiries had
not been previously made upon the subject.   This
obstacle was the want of sufficient pecuniary means
in the postulant.   The other obstacle was of a personal character.   Her attraction to pure contemplation made her experience an invincible repugnance
to the repetition of long vocal prayers.   Had God

designed her for the cloister, this apparent difficulty
would, no doubt, have vanished, for how many souls
have its holy precincts enclosed in all ages—not to
speak of the ecclesiatical state itself—who have found
the obligation of saying office no hindrance to the
practice of the sublimest contemplation. It does not
follow, however, that it would be wise for secular
persons who possess this attraction to hamper themselves with such exercises; nor would a prudent
director enjoin what would seem like a counteracting
of the operations of the Holy Ghost, the true Director
of souls, who is manifestly leading them by an opposite
path. But this same Divine Director, when He calls
persons into religion, is well able to provide that its
obligations shall offer no obstacle to the highest modes
of prayer; and, as a matter of fact, we know that saints
have understood how to associate contemplation with
vocal exercises, while to many a holy priest the
daily recitation of office has been one prolonged act
of sublime meditation. But this is precisely the
point. Eustelle was not designed to enter the religious state; she had not herself felt any inward call
thereto, much as she appreciated its happiness and
privileges; she had become a postulant from a spirit
of obedience, ready to esteem it a high honour and
grace should her Lord be pleased to receive her
amongst His consecrated spouses. But owing to the
cause just mentioned, the religious rule did not hold
out to her the attractions it would otherwise have
possessed in her eyes; and dear to her as were the
solitude and seclusion of cloistered life, the convent
did not seem her appointed home. Nor was it. She
returned to Saint-Pallais after a fortnight's stay, to
the great delight of her disconsolate parents.

When Mgr. Villecourt revealed to the world the seraphic love and exalted holiness which the simple externals of the young postulant had veiled from sight, the nuns were full of regret at having failed to secure for themselves so rare a treasure. As for Eustelle, she ever cherished the memory of the short stay she had made amongst these daughters of Mary, and speaking one day of this failure to a friend, she said, with her characteristic humility, " I was too weak ; " as if so high a vocation had been beyond her poor strength. At another time, casting her eyes on some little object which recalled this brief episode in her life, she exclaimed, " O my God, Thy holy will ! " they were words expressive of perfect acquiescence and deep submission, not of fond regret or secret disappointment : Eustelle was never disappointed, for she always found what alone she sought and longed for, the accomplishment of that same holy, mysterious, and ever-adorable Will of God.

CHAPTER IX.

VOW OF CHASTITY AND ITS FRUITS.

EUSTELLE had returned to Saint-Pallais, but the experiment had not satisfied M. Jouslain, who remained unshaken in his persuasion that her vocation was to the religious life ; he even inspired her with fears lest she should be rebelling against grace. Poor Eustelle suffered much from this new trial. We have seen how docile and submissive she showed herself to the will of God as signified to her through His ministers, and how attentive and faithful she was to the inward movements of His Spirit. Now the two were in apparent contradiction. Her director told her she was resisting grace, but the interior voice seemed to forbid any fresh step akin to that which she had been permitted recently to take. The question had been practically asked, Was the religious life her calling? She had herself no secret misgiving as to the negative character of the reply which she had received, but he whose opinion she was bound to respect thought otherwise. What was she to do? M. Jouslain certainly displayed a pertinacity in adhering to his own views not a little surprising in the face of circumstances which, one would think, might at least have suggested a reconsideration of the subject. Anyhow, his conduct was peculiarly trying to Eustelle, not only from the nature of the dilemma in which it placed her, but because the crosses which good men are often permitted to manufacture for the good, are especially hard to bear. God's providence, however, soon relieved her from this distressing embarrassment by the removal of M. Jouslain to another parish.

Although Marie-Eustelle was not to enjoy the honour of ranking among the consecrated spouses of Jesus in religion, yet was she not to lose the privileges and advantages specially attached to religious vows. It was during the severe inward trials which we have described, that the Lord first suggested to her the idea of dedicating herself to him by an irrevocable vow of chastity. " Ever since my conversion," she said, " this Good Master had inspired me with a special love for this beautiful virtue." The desire she had to consecrate her virginity to God, came, she doubted not, from Him alone. She wished to belong wholly to Him, to give Him the absolute empire over her affections and her thoughts,—in short, to keep back nothing of the holocaust which she longed with an intense desire to offer to Him. Such aspirations, indeed, can have no other source than the Divine Object to which they tend. Poor human nature is incapable of making such a sacrifice even to God, save by divine grace, while to offer it to creatures is simply impossible. Not even when, in a generous act of self-devotion, it gives its life for another, or consumes it in a service of love, does it make that other the lord of its whole being. There is, and must be, a reserve. True sacrifice is for God only : it is the Creator's inalienable property, and, if we would, we cannot offer it but to Him. Self opposes ; the very nature of things opposes : we can give to others what is His due, or we can keep it for ourselves—we can be wickedly idolatrous in our earthly affections, or in our selfish attachments—but never can we give to created nature, or grasp for ourselves, what we *can* give to Him ;—our whole being. To Him we can give it, because it is His, and He can enable us to make the gift. No man, as the Apostle says, liveth to himself, and no man dieth to himself, so that, living and dying, we are the Lord's. Since, then, He alone could have inspired Eustelle with the desire to make this unreserved sacrifice, He also must have willed every portion of that sacrifice.

Great is the happiness of those for whose whole being God, who can claim it as His property, thus condescends to become, so to say, the suitor ; one while entreating for it with pressing gentle urgency, at another demanding it with the passionate vehemence and imperiousness of ardent love. Alas !

we often rejoice and hug ourselves at the thought of the many earthly blessings, comforts, solaces, and sources of enjoyment which our good God *spares* us— the very expression manifesting our intimate knowledge that He·does but allow us to retain what He has the right to claim, and might require us to renounce ; we rejoice and are grateful—it is well when we are so ; and this is all at which the greater number of us can arrive. But we ought never to forget that the measure of God's requests is the measure of what He has to give, infinitely disproportioned as our offerings must always be to His gifts ; and while we gladly concede what He asks of us, we ought to admire their glorious vocation of whom He has asked more—nay, asked all. "My dear Saviour," says Eustelle, "had often made me hear this language : ' I am a jealous God ; I desire to possess your heart entirely, because I desire to give you without measure My grace and My love.'" Enlightened by this same grace, she desired to embrace that "better part" which He who "feeds among the lilies" held out to her acceptance. Among all the radiant virtues that sparkle in the crown of Christian perfection, that of virginity seemed to shine before Eustelle's eyes with a brilliancy all its own. Long had her gaze been fixed upon it, and at last she communicated her wish to her confessor, and begged his permission to take a vow of perpetual chastity. As yet she was ignorant, she says, how strict were those rules of prudence and precaution which the Church has prescribed for the observance of directors in reference to persons living in the world and desiring thus to bind themselves ; and that they must necessarily undergo a probation sufficiently long to test their constancy, and to guard

L

against the danger of a passing ebullition of fervour being mistaken for a well-grounded purpose dictated by the Spirit of God. Such vocations, of course, exist, but they demand even greater circumspection and examination than a call to religion; not only because they are more unfrequent, and, as such, more doubtful, but because, although in both cases the vow is irrevocable, it has safeguards and securities in the conventual life which are wanting amidst the perils and temptations of the world without. For this reason, directors will often authorize secular persons to make only a temporary and renewable engagement, until they can be safely permitted to bind themselves by a lifelong tie. This seems to have been the course adopted by Eustelle's confessor.* She was two-and-twenty when she applied to him on the sub-

---

* This priest must have been M. Jouslain's successor. His name is not given; but on the 25th of August, 1837, he was superseded by the Abbé de Laage de Saint-Germain, who remained in charge of that parish during the rest of Marie-Eustelle's life. The removal of his predecessor to another cure gave occasion to many valuable letters addressed to him by his former penitent. It is difficult, however, to reconcile the dates. Marie-Eustelle was, according to her own statement, twenty-two when she first spoke to her director, who kept her waiting two years. Now, as she was born in 1814, she must have made her vow in 1838, when (as we have seen) M. de Laage was already installed as Curé at Saint-Pallais. It may be, however, that she still remained under the direction of her late confessor, so far, at least, as regarded this vow, although she is not likely to have taken it without the consent of her actual pastor. It is well to add that, although Eustelle has made no comment upon her director's conduct beyond what has been noticed above, we have good authority for believing that the ecclesiastic in question was deficient in the knowledge and experience necessary for dealing with high and difficult questions, and not equal to the office of directing a soul called to such eminent perfection. We shall recur to this subject when we come to speak of Eustelle's directors.

ject, and notwithstanding all her solicitations, prayers, and even tears, he made her wait two years before he would give his consent to the irrevocable vow. " At last," she writes, " the happy day arrived when I had the privilege of being admitted into the ranks of the spouses of the Saviour. Never shall I be able to find words capable of expressing my feelings on this occasion. I was almost beside myself; it was a real intoxication of joy and happiness."

It was on the 2nd of February, the Feast of the Purification of Mary, when she presented her Son to His Eternal Father in the Temple, that Marie-Eustelle made her vow of perpetual virginity, and gave herself at the same time by a solemn engagement to His Immaculate Mother. That she might preserve a continual memorial of this great event in her life, she drew up and subscribed two forms of consecration, one to Jesus, and the other to the Blessed Virgin, which she always bore enclosed in a cross upon her bosom. She begged that they might be laid in the grave with her, but for some unexplained reason her request was not complied with. Probably the very veneration of which she had by that time become the object was the cause of this disregard of her last wishes. On the borders of the tomb, the remembrance of this consecration is still to her a source of exceeding joy. " O wonderful favour !" she exclaims, " of which I was most unworthy. Yes, my tender Master, Jesus, my God and my all, I was unworthy of so great a benefit after having wandered away from Thee by my iniquities. I deserved nothing but to be banished for ever from Thy paternal Heart, from that Heart which I had so deeply grieved, and of which I so often re-opened the wounds by attachment to earth, to vanity, to nothingness. I, so poor, so weak, so destitute of all virtue, to see myself raised to the dignity of Thy spouse! Ah, my Saviour! to testify my gratitude for so great a boon, I will follow Thee, I say not to Thabor, but to Calvary. It is on Thy Cross that Thy true spouses are formed; it is there that henceforth I will be fastened with Thee, to live and die with Thee. Creatures shall be nothing to me; I will be nothing to myself: Jesus alone, He is my sole possession; Jesus in all, He is my sole desire; Jesus everywhere, He is my whole ambition; Jesus Crucified—behold all I love, all I desire to know!" Here, as everywhere, love is always the theme, love the prevailing motive. Her very penitential regrets become plaints of love. She laments, not that she had angered God against her, not that she had imperilled her soul : she speaks only of grieving His Heart and reopening His Wounds; she seems unable to think of aught else but of having been the cause of sorrow to Him; and this, not because she has forgotten or become insensible to all the rest, but that heart, affections, and her whole soul itself seem to have been altogether transferred to her Beloved, so that she can think and feel only for and with and through Him. Her vow was the signal for a fresh outpouring of graces. "Oh, how abundant in my soul was the grace of the Saviour," she writes, "after I had made this irrevocable engagement! With what liberality did Jesus recompense the trifling sacrifice I had made of myself to Him, and which had been inspired and carried into effect by His grace! One would have supposed that this act was to add something to His glory. O Divine Jesus! it is because Thou lovest us; it is our interests Thou seekest, when Thou seemest

to be ambitious of winning our love. O Infinite
Goodness ! O Love ! O Jesus ! "

Before proceeding to describe Eustelle's manner of
life at this time, certain outward circumstances of
which were changed when she was twenty-three years
of age, we will notice some of the interior fruits with
which her Heavenly Spouse requited the offering she
had made. Her biographer, who diligently collected
every available document, as well as questioned every
relative and friend of the holy girl, says that her last
four years were years of peace.* This would imply
that her interior trials, if not removed entirely, were
at least superseded in the main by an abiding state
of consolation. If so, this change in her interior
state, this dispersing of the heavy clouds with which
her soul had so long been overshadowed, was the immediate consequence of her espousals. There can,
indeed, be little doubt but that her most afflicting
temptations were banished for ever. Hell was no
longer suffered to vex the soul of the spouse of Christ
with its accursed visions ; yet all her inward trials were
certainly not immediately removed, for so late even
as April, 1839, we find her, in a letter to the ecclesiastic just mentioned, alluding in very strong terms
to the multiplied conflicts, perplexities, and disquietudes to which she was subjected, but it is the
last occasion. We meet with similar passages during
the previous year, 1838, and one especially in which
she speaks of suffering particularly during prayer,
while at other times the reverse had been the case.

---

* As the writer in another place speaks of the last *three*
years of Eustelle's life being years of uninterrupted peace of
soul, it may be inferred that in his former statement he must
have included the time when her temptations began to abate.

"God be blessed," she writes, "I abandon myself to His good pleasure : if He were to slay me, I would still hope in Him, as said the holy man Job, whose sentiments I am not worthy to adopt." In another letter, dated December 28th of that same year, she says that some of her pains have diminished, and that the holy presence of God, which had been entirely eclipsed, had begun to rekindle in her heart the charity which had seemed to be extinguished, and that she now prayed with more facility. "But our Lord," she adds, "will not discharge me of my cross ; He loves me too much for that." Yet her letters at this period are remarkable for recording the abundance of joy and consolation that co-existed with her sufferings. We have already noticed this peculiar condition, and it seems to have marked this transitional period of Eustelle's spiritual life. Soon we hear of no martyrdom but that of pure love.

One result, then, of her vow was an increased manifestation of the love of Jesus to her and in her, for she returned love for love with all the energy of one of the most loving of hearts. At the same time she experienced a great additional attraction for recollection, solitude, and silence. Converse with creatures became more than ever irksome to her, and as much as possible she fled their society. No better evidence can be adduced of the tenderness of her charity than the sweetness and cheerfulness with which she responded to every appeal, notwithstanding the sacrifice it must have involved of her own personal inclinations. How numerous were the applications for advice, consolation, and help of all kinds, which summoned her from her beloved retirement, we shall presently see. Her love for mental prayer, in like

manner, received a signal increase. We have observed
how, even four years previously, her attraction to it was
so great as to make her feel a difficulty in following
any long exercise of vocal prayer. Now it became
wellnigh an impossibility, and she reduced her
devotional exercises almost entirely to that of contemplation—for, as usual, she gave herself up
unreservedly to the impulse of grace. It was with
her as with one in a boat on the open sea, who spreads
every sail and scuds before the wind. The Holy
Spirit of God, our Director in the spiritual course,
blows straight for the heavenly port. It is He
teaches us to pray, and Himself prays within us; but
prayer is a divine art, and it pleases Him to impart it
in different modes and degrees to different persons.
To know and to follow this leadership is also a great
art. It is the art of learning how to learn. It might
seem as if those who were called by God to high perfection and sublime ways of prayer would have little
difficulty in acquiring what the Holy Ghost takes so
special a delight in communicating to them—bestowing,
so to say, singular pains and attention on their instruction. Yet the lives of many such chosen souls
tell us of trials and difficulties encountered in this
lofty study, and concur to prove that it is a very
delicate point to recognize the leadings of this Spirit
of prayer, and an arduous task to be faithful to them.
Any preconceived notions or the slightest precipitation
are often sufficient to render his voice indistinguishable,
and then labour is spent in vain. We may gather
manna at the wrong hour, or we may gather more
than He wills, or we may gather it when He desires
there should be Sabbath in the soul. Few, in fact,
are thoroughly docile, and all internal obstacles may

be summed up in this one defect, want of docility—a great impediment in the acquisition of all learning, but much more so where God is the instructor, who, unlike other teachers, can give, not knowledge only, but the capacity to receive it, so that we put no hindrance in His way.

In the case of persons led, like Eustelle, to the heights of mystic prayer, even the director may not seldom add to the trials and perplexities which beset their path. Unless he himself have a deep experimental knowledge of these ways, nothing but a profound and scientific acquaintance with mystical theology can compensate for this deficiency; and in the absence of such qualifications, which are of too high an order to be generally reckoned upon, he may fail to possess the necessary discernment. The reader will remember what St. Teresa had to suffer from her directors. Nevertheless, souls tried in this manner will still have the merit of obedience and the exercise of humility. No one is competent to direct himself: God will therefore either send such souls sufficient guidance in His own good time, or Himself graciously take upon Him their immediate and special direction. And so it was with Eustelle. She had no director in the art of prayer, and seems, indeed, to have been unconsciously withheld from seeking one. "Our good and amiable Saviour," she writes, "was my sole director in the holy exercise;" and she adds with some *naïveté*, "I should have thought I was committing an indiscretion by asking my ordinary confessor to lay down rules for me; his multiplied occupations made me feel the necessity of respecting those moments which he employed with so much zeal in the conversion of sinners." What follows, however, shows that she was far from undervaluing the assistance of directors in this exercise. She continues, "But at the same time I understood how important it was that directors of consciences should bestow the utmost care in leading to the practice of prayer the souls which Heaven has committed to their charge. By devoting themselves to this work, they will, indeed, singularly in another respect abridge their toil; for a soul given to prayer easily avoids a multitude of falls which without it all the advice of confessors is unable to prevent." But not only did Eustelle not undervalue the assistance of a good director in the exercises of the spiritual life, but it would appear that she subsequently believed she had incurred some risk by her want of a sufficiently enlightened guide when she first entered the higher regions of prayer, a subject to which we shall have to recur. Nevertheless, as this was through no fault of her own, and as the silence which she for some time kept with respect to those extraordinary things which were passing within her proceeded from no defect of humility, we may the rather believe that the circumstances in which she was then placed formed part of her Lord's peculiar design concerning her, and that He willed at that period to be her sole instructor.

Taught, then, at the fountain-head of knowledge, Eustelle's purity of conscience, rectitude of intention, simplicity, humility, and fidelity to the slightest movements of grace, made her learn with a rapidity which is one of the striking characteristics of her whole spiritual progress. "As for me," she says, "instructed in the school of Jesus Christ Himself, notwithstanding my profound unworthiness, I en-

deavoured to be attentive to all His lessons, and to
imprint them deep in my heart. In my ignorance, I
conjured Him to impart His light to me; often did I
say to Him, 'Lord, show me Thy ways, teach me to
do Thy will, for Thou art my God; lead me in the
way of Thy holy commandments and in the paths of
virtue.'" At this period she made regularly three
set hours of mental prayer, a large portion of time for
one who had to gain her bread by daily toil. It was
by mental prayer that she prepared herself for confession, for mass, for communion. As, however, she
strove to preserve herself invariably in the presence
of God, her prayer might be said to be wellnigh
unceasing.

The same inward light which manifested to her her
call to contemplation displayed also to her the rigorous
and minute self-renunciation which Jesus demanded
of her; indeed He appeared at that time to be extremely severe with her on this point, so great was
the abnegation and perfection which He claimed of
her. But Eustelle understood it all: this severity
was but the expression of His love. She could refuse
Him nothing, nor did she experience the least difficulty
in detaching herself from everything, great or small.
"Jesus was all I desired," she says, "all that I loved.
Every created object seemed to disappear at the sole
thought of Jesus." Accordingly, nothing which she
sacrificed for His sake was in her estimation a sacrifice
at all. In all her actions, pains, labours, conflicts,
privations, she continually repeated to herself these
words: "It is for Thee, my Saviour, it is for Thee.
All to please Thee; all for Thy love." How far she
carried this spirit of despoilment we shall soon see.

As, since her conversion, she had never felt affection

for any sin whatsoever, so in like manner did she seem to have a natural inclination to every virtue. But now she was as if enamoured of them afresh, and, as she calls them up in succession before her, she cannot say which is loveliest or dearest in her eyes, so powerfully was she attracted towards them all. Confidence and love were, as ever, the two virtues by means of which she looked to compassing all the rest; nevertheless those which are the most necessary for progress in the interior life were the chief object of her assiduous cultivation.

But of all the rich fruits which she derived from her consecration vow, the most striking was an increase in that already intense and absorbing love with which Jesus had inspired her for the mystery of the Adorable Eucharist. She is at a loss to find words to express the love she felt—the very thought of that Divine Sacrament seeming to transport her out of herself. At the time she made her vow she was permitted to communicate three times in the week, but she was burning with the desire for a daily sacramental union with her Lord, though she submissively awaited the manifestation of His will through her director, hoping that, if it were His good pleasure, she might ere long enjoy this blessing—a happiness which, in fact, was soon afterwards accorded to her. Some time later, our Lord made known to her His desire that she should devote herself entirely to this one object of honouring Him in the Blessed Sacrament. She thus relates what took place within her, in a letter to her former director :—"Accustomed to detail to you with all simplicity what passes in my soul, and convinced that you will not abuse my confidence, I must tell you that while engaged in making my thanksgiving after communion, a few days ago, I felt a sudden and very lively movement of joy in my soul, such as I had not experienced for a long time. It seems to me that our Lord then gave me to understand in a very special manner that He desired that I should wholly employ myself in honouring Him in the Sacrament of His Love, and that I was to make it my one sole occupation; that although many souls served Him faithfully, yet few rendered Him this interior homage, which alone was efficacious in forming true adorers in spirit and in truth. Whereupon I represented to our Lord the depth of my misery, and how unworthy I, a miserable sinner, was of such predilection. Then He made me understand the infinite riches of His mercies, suggesting to me that He loved to lavish His gifts upon the weakest of His creatures when He found them submissively disposed to further His designs." After pouring forth her whole soul in mingled expressions of gratitude, humility, admiration, and love, she says, "I am now much more tranquil; I mean as to my soul and the interior pains which I generally experience. Temptations have been less strong and less frequent for some time past. I have more facility in prayer; the presence of my Lord is more sensible; I am now in the state in which I was about three months ago."

The assaults of the evil one were evidently growing weaker, and, what is more, they were becoming intermittent. It was like the weather clearing after a stormy day: the clouds were breaking, and gleams of sunshine were bursting forth in the rents of that curtain of darkness which had so long swathed her about, revealing those bright fields of azure which were soon to fill the whole firmament of her spiritual being. For years she had lain submissively under a sunless sky, beaten with the rain and the tempest, and had never ceased thanking God for these afflictions —as men thank Him for peaceful and prosperous days, or, rather, with an effusion and a constancy with which they rarely requite His good gifts; and now she was to reap the blessed harvest of the seedtime of sorrow. Truly she had followed the advice of the son of Sirach: "When thou comest to the service of God, prepare thy soul for temptation. Humble thy heart and endure; incline thine ear and receive the words of understanding; and *make not haste in the time of clouds*. Wait on God with patience; join thyself to God and endure, that thy life may be increased in the latter end." "My soul is happy," she writes to her director. "After many and painful trials, of which God alone has been the witness, I am at peace, as much as I believe it is possible to be in this life. Ah, it is too much, too many favours for this land of exile! Often my heart cannot contain them." In the manuscript she left unfinished, speaking of the hours she spent before the Tabernacle, she says, "I should have wished to remain there for ever. A magnet seemed to hold me to this enchanting spot. Could it be otherwise? Does the spouse leave with indifference her beloved? Can she look at or love anything save him? Jesus was for me, as for the spouse in the Canticles, 'the Beloved chosen out of thousands.' Oh, how heavenly are the conversations one then has with Jesus! How swiftly the hours flow! How delicious are His words! What sweetness is in them! How tender are His caresses! My very soul melted when He spoke with the fire of His words!" Her passionate love for her Lord seemed to make it morally impossible for her to tear herself away of her own free will from His Eucharistic Presence. She was divinely inebriated with love, for this holy intoxication is no mere metaphor of speech, but a marvellous reality: "Drink, O friends, and be *inebriated*, my dearly beloved," says the Spouse in the Canticles. He wills, not only that His beloved friends should drink of the wine of His charity, but that they whom He thus favours should through the rapture of their love lose, so to say, the very mastery of themselves. It is an excess in the world's eyes, but it is an excess where in fact there can be none.

It will be remembered that when she was as yet almost a child in years, and young in the path of perfection, Eustelle, after casting about to remove all that might displease Him, would with filial love and simplicity turn to her Lord and ask Him what more there was that she could do for Him. In this disposition and preparation of heart she had ever since remained; and Jesus had taken her at her word. Thus it is that He often deals with souls who in all sincerity make offers the extent of which they but imperfectly comprehend. "We can drink of Thy chalice," said the sons of Zebedee, ignorant as yet of the nature of that awful pledge; and Jesus replied, "Ye shall indeed drink of My chalice." When Eustelle offered all to Jesus, she knew not the import of that all; but He did not forget, nor did she ever repent the unreserved surrender she had made. The sacrifice, however, was not yet complete, and Jesus continued to ask so long as Eustelle had anything left to give.

CHAPTER X.

WORKS OF MERCY.

BEFORE speaking of the fresh vow which our Lord inspired Marie-Eustelle to make, we must give some account of the external life which she led after she had completed twenty-three years. At that time she ceased to go out for the day, and set up a little business at home. Soon after this change she left her parents' roof, and hired a room at some distance—either with a view to a more entire freedom in her devout exercises, or for the more convenient carrying on of her work. The last was probably the ostensible, as it was a sufficient, reason for a separation which must have been desirable in many ways. She continued, however, for three years to go home for her meals. She had now apprentices of her own, and showed herself a true mother to her adopted family. Not only did she bestow the tenderest care upon them, and treat them with the greatest kindness, but she was ever solicitous in providing for their highest interests, sparing neither charitable warnings nor affectionate vigilance to keep them in the right way. If one among their number continued obstinately deaf to her advice, then, like a prudent shepherd, who separates the sickly sheep from his flock, to prevent the contagion spreading amongst the healthy, she sent away the incorrigible offender, lest her evil example might be injurious to the rest. Remembering the snares and peril of her own early youth, Marie-Eustelle was fain to forego her devoted love of solitude, and assembled the little girls of the neighbourhood on

Sunday evenings, to prevent their going to the dancing, which was the common amusement* of the peasantry on holidays, and to which many were led, not so much from any particular taste for that diversion, as from lack of an occupation to fill their idle hours.

The girls to whom Eustelle was teaching her business, and who were the daily witnesses of her virtues, and especially of her admirable patience, felt the greatest veneration for her. One day, as some of them were talking of their holy mistress, a young person who was present became desirous of making Eustelle's acquaintance. It seemed a mere chance, but it was a particular providence, for her whole life, not to say her eternal future, was influenced by the intimacy of which this incident was the accidental origin. She soon experienced the charm which all who approached Eustelle found in her society ; and Eustelle, on her part, perceiving that her new-found friend had a heart well disposed for higher things, applied herself with her own exquisite tact, gentleness, and felicity to inspire this young girl with a distaste and hatred for the world, and to lead her to give herself wholly to God. The fruit of these lessons, and still more of the insensible influence she exercised, was soon visible in a marked change of life. Old acquaintances, old ways, and old places of resort were abandoned, and she began to set herself resolutely to follow Christ. As might be expected, this alteration was far from agreeable to friends, and Eustelle was blamed as the cause. The girl's parents were furious,

* Marie-Eustelle's biographer says that this deplorable custom is particulary prevalent in the central departments of France.

and forbade their child to go any more to see her. Eustelle, as usual, kept silence, but did not abandon her *protégée*. She would cheer her by a letter, or would contrive to meet her on the way to church on Sundays, in order to give her a word of encouragement or counsel. Among other pieces of salutary advice which she imparted, she especially urged her young friend to do nothing without her confessor's advice, and not to deprive herself of a single communion allowed her. In short, not all the abuse of which she was the object for her so-called interference could deter the charitable Eustelle from acting the part of an angel guardian to this young girl, until she saw her safe in the happy port for which by her vocation she was bound,—the religious life. This watchful care, indeed, followed her into the novitiate, for the novitiate is a period of probation, involving a heavy trial to some, who, after putting their hand to the plough, will then perhaps be assailed with the temptation to turn back. The terms in which Eustelle writes to the young novice of the privileges and blessings of the state to which she aspired, demonstrate how fully she appreciated its value, although she had not been called to it herself. "As for me," she says, "I should envy your lot, if such were the will of God."

Eustelle's affection had always God for its principle; consequently it partook of none of those weaknesses which so commonly attach to tenderness of the mere natural order. She knew how to be firm, as we have seen, when duty was in question, in spite of all the heart's pleadings, and how to teach others to be firm. The parents of the postulant refused at first to send her clothes to the convent, hoping, probably,

M

that she would come back to fetch them, and that
they would thus have another opportunity of working
on her feelings.   Eustelle saw the danger: "Do not
give way," she writes to her friend; "they will end by
yielding to your wishes."   Her charity was as full of
condescension as it was exempt from weakness.   There
is much condescension common in the world, proceeding from mere obligingness of temper, which
causes any personal trouble or inconvenience to be
preferred to the pain of refusing a request, or, at best,
from that unselfish readiness to prefer the wishes of
others which distinguishes some fine and generous
natures.   Amiable as such dispositions undoubtedly
are, they differ in character and principle from that
which was so remarkable in Eustelle.   Her condescension was altogether of a higher order, and its
motive purely supernatural.   A surviving friend
relates how at one time she would leave the church
after Vespers to take a walk into the country with
her and one or two companions.   It was for their satisfaction, as they well knew, not her own; yet she
never allowed them to feel this.   While her dis-
course, as usual, turned on heavenly things, she
knew how to mingle a certain cheerful sportiveness
with the most serious talk.   There was no solemnity
about her, no studied gravity of manner; her
superior sanctity never embarrassed or weighed on
those who were in her company; on the contrary,
so refreshing was her conversation that her society
was eagerly sought as a recreation and a solace.   The
little party was a merry one, and she was pleased that
they should indulge their lively humour, so long as
nothing was said to wound charity; but when one
of them began to make fun of a neighbour, Eustelle

gently checked her, reminding her not to say of
another what she would not like to be said of herself: a hint was sufficient, and not a single word of
the sort was again uttered. Eustelle's extreme
sensitiveness on this point was, indeed, matter of
notoriety; for even when she judged silence to be
imperative or discreet, a deep blush would reveal
the pain she suffered from hearing any uncharitable
word. But these pleasant walks, which were kind
condescensions on Eustelle's part, were not undertaken
with the mere view of amusing or obliging those she
loved; these young women could find entertainment
without her help, and her sole pleasure was to be
with Jesus. If then, she left Him, it was never
but for Himself. In this instance, her object in
thus sacrificing her predilections was for the sake of
a person who was harassed by scruples, and upon
whom this little diversion had a salutary effect.
The walks ceased with the occasion which gave rise
to them.

There was nothing Eustelle was not ready to do to
further the spiritual interests of those whom it was
in her power to help, and, above all, her zeal knew no
bounds when it was question of the salvation of a
soul and its reclaim from a life of sin. One of the
playfellows of her childhood had been for some time
giving much scandal, and was at last tempted by a
rich and profligate man to desert her home. Having
thus forfeited her reputation, she was, as the natural
consequence, cast off by such as cared to preserve
their own. But Eustelle, who had long been compelled to give up friendly intercourse with her, did
not forsake the unhappy wanderer. Laying aside all
repugnances and all fear of what evil tongues might

say, she sought out the poor sinner in her abode of
shame. More than once did she visit her, using every
endeavour to snatch her from perdition. Each time
the wretched woman, touched by Eustelle's charity,
and moved by the grace which, like a benediction,
seemed ever to attend her words, wept and promised;
but, alas! this was all. None the less, however, was
Marie-Eustelle's merit, although it was not granted
her in this instance to see her labours rewarded. But
this was by no means generally the case. Herself an
angel of purity, she had the special gift of attracting
her erring sisters back to the paths of virtue. Often,
touched with remorse, they would go to her of their
own accord, and such was the tenderness with which
she invariably received them that they could not refrain from laying bare their whole hearts to her. So
it is; the most removed from sin are ever the most
compassionate. The worldly Pharisee says, "This
woman is a sinner;" she may be a repentant sinner—
no matter, he will spurn her from him, and be scandalized that Jesus allows her to weep at His feet and
to kiss them. Immaculate Mary, upon whom not
the stain alone, but the shadow of sin never fell, is
the "Refuge of sinners," and it is to her that Eve's
penitent daughters first turn, nay run with confident
love to her maternal bosom, when a corrupt world bids
them stand aloof, or would fain crush them with its
virtuous scorn.

And how did Marie-Eustelle receive the voluntary
humiliations and confessions of these poor fallen creatures—she who blushed the deep blush of shame at
one slight word which could injure fraternal charity?
Did she tell them of the just anger of a Holy God?
Did she speak of the hideousness of sin, and of the

pit of hell and the everlasting fire? No, all these
things Eustelle might have descanted upon, but she
did not: it was not the time; the bruised reed she
would not break: she had drunk too deeply of the
spirit of the Son of Mary and of His compassionate
Mother to deal ungently with a returning sinner. It
was not her zeal but her charity that took fire as,
with a face beaming with heavenly love, she would
speak of the treasures of the infinite mercy of God,
and of the unimaginable tenderness of the Heart of
Jesus, as they only can speak who have the abundant
unction of that Spirit which "maketh eloquent the
tongues of the simple." Then light would dawn
before the eyes of these poor outcasts, who had come,
in the depth of their misery and remorse, to un-
burthen their grief, with hope almost extinguished in
their breast and love dead within them. How could
they love, when in God's pure sight they were so
unlovely and so vile? He could not love them; how,
then, could they dare to love Him? The same light
revealed to them the state of their own consciences
and made them tremble at the thought of the justice
of God, but with a new and salutary dread; not that
dread which drives to despair, but that filial fear which
is inseparably joined to hope and love. By her assistance many left their sinful courses; but if, weak in
resolution, some fell back into habits of sin, never
were they deterred from returning to their kind benefactress. She knew how to apply remedies to cases
well calculated to discourage the most sanguine, and
to prevail upon the sufferers, stifling all sense of
shame, to seek again the true physician of their souls.
Nor did Marie-Eustelle, in her charity, aid only such
as appealed to her for advice or help; she herself

sought out occasions of usefulness. She visited the
sick, wrote letters for the illiterate poor, aided the
dying to make a good end, and even buried the dead.
We have already seen what a peculiar gift of consolation was hers, a gift the efficacy of which was
attested by the numbers of persons who constantly
applied to her for relief in their interior trials. No
less was the esteem entertained for her advice ; and
it was a general impression that whoever followed it
fared well, but that trouble and anxiety were the sure
result of divergence from her counsels. " Jesus spoke
by her mouth," were the emphatic words of one who
bore testimony to the estimation in which this holy
girl was held during the last years of her life.

Amongst those in whom Eustelle took a peculiarly
lively interest was Armand Guérin, of Saint-Pallais,
the little Seminarist to whom we before alluded.
Eustelle loved him with the tenderest affection ; he
was, we may say, a kind of spiritual son to her, for
whom she felt a solicitude quite maternal—nay, a
purer and a higher, for with mothers the bodily health
and temporal interests of children must necessarily
engross a considerable share of their attention, and
natural love is so strong in their hearts that this
attention will have a tendency, so far, to diminish a
predominant and exclusive anxiety for the soul's
welfare. But Eustelle's thoughts were all concentrated on the " one thing needful." Young Armand
Guérin, indeed, was a tender plant of much promise.
" I knew him," says Cardinal Villecourt, " when he
was still quite a little boy ; he was at that time a
child of admirable candour and rare judgment. On
being placed at the college of Pons, he commenced
a little apostolate, which God vouchsafed to bless.

While at this seminary, Eustelle frequently wrote to him. As he advanced in the ecclesiastical course, his fervour was observed sensibly to increase. A few years after his ordination to the priesthood he went to rejoin Eustelle in heaven : I should not wonder if he had always preserved his baptismal innocence." This boy, who was not more than fifteen when she died, always cherished in his heart the counsels he had received from his dear benefactress. The deep veneration, indeed, which he felt for Eustelle led him, before his admission to the priesthood, to record his reminiscences of her, which he sent to Cardinal Ville- court when he understood that he purposed writing her life.

The whole of her correspondence with the young Seminarist turned upon one subject—need we say what that subject was ? It is all summed up in the first words of her first letter. " I love to believe," she says, "that your soul, O child of God, understands those sweet words, ' All through Jesus and for Jesus in the Eucharist.'" Then she adds, " The God of the Tabernacle is my word as He is my thought." To Armand Guérin she was, indeed, the Angel of the Tabernacle, ever inviting him to join her in her seraphic worship before the throne of the Hidden God. " Dear child," she says, " I love to speak thus to you, because I believe that Jesus, our Sovereign High Priest, wills to give you this attraction. I know that He has already caused you to taste its charms. Let your generosity and love respond to His favours, and, in order to this, go to the tabernacle, visit the God unknown, who desires to communicate Himself to your soul. There, as I have told you"—it was one of her frequent remarks—"we learn all by un-

learning all. There at the feet of this tender Master
we taste by anticipation heavenly joys. Ah! let
your young heart be enamoured of that which is enclosed in this asylum of love; above all, study the
incomprehensible humility which the God-Man there
teaches us, and always take these words for your
device, 'Humility and Love.'" It was not only that
Eustelle believed that she discerned in the fair soul of
this child an attraction to the devotion so dear to her
own heart, but Armand Guérin was to be a priest:
he was being trained for the sacerdotal office, for
which she had an unspeakable reverence. The hands
of that young boy were one day to offer the Divine
Victim, and so by anticipation she looked upon him
as a consecrated thing, the object of her tenderest
respect, and of the only envy which she was ever known
to cherish: for she had indeed a holy envy for this sublimest office—an office which never could be hers. She
betrays it in this same letter: "Do you," she says,
" whose hope is my envy, pray for me: ask of the
God who captivates hearts to captivate mine wholly
to Himself." The concluding sentence is a specimen of
her unaffected simplicity, and shows how the commonest
things were always associated in her mind with those
higher objects which alone were important in her
eyes: "Mind you do not make any more stains on
your surplice, and, above all, take care to make none
that may prove as hard to efface on your soul."

Often did she remember this child of her love before
the altar, and on one occasion we find her moved to
quit the spot from which we have seen how hard it
was to draw her, in order to converse with the young
Levite about Him whom she had just left. "I leave
the tabernacle," she writes, "for Jesus gives me the

thought to continue with you, the son of His charity, the sweet conversation I was having with Himself." How singular must have been the piety of the boy to whom she could write what follows: "Oh, how useful and consoling is this intercourse of souls, which enables them to unite together their most intimate sentiments. The sweet outpouring of the soul into its Creator is prolonged by this union, by this mutual communication, which makes us love God with one united love." She then goes on to describe what this their all-absorbing love ought to be; but soon she glides into her one ever-engrossing thought of God in the Adorable Sacrament, resulting, as usual, in ecstatic acts of adoration. The flame is ever ready to burst forth: "O prodigy of love! O Sacrament of my God! Divine Eucharist! It is not given me to express the thoughts, the lights, the sentiments which Jesus communicates to me in the participation of this ineffable mystery; and when I say that it is not given me to express, I mean that no human language is capable of conveying what Jesus alone can comprehend and express. How vast a gift of God to men! What return shall we make to Him? Oh, He is Himself the only gift which men can offer to God, the only gift which is perfectly worthy of His Supreme Majesty! Dear child, how happy you are! Try and realize all your blessedness in this Jesus, the Eternal Love. This God-with-us has made choice of you to raise you one day to the august and tremendous dignity of His ministry. This thought makes my soul rejoice for you; and then—it saddens me: Jesus knows the rest." Eustelle, in short, was jealous as well as envious. We shall meet more than once with these proofs of the passionate nature of the divine love that

burned in her bosom, a love so difficult for the great
majority to realize save in an appreciative manner.
Its vehemence recalls to us that of the Psalmist when
he exclaims, "For Thee my flesh and my heart hath
fainted away;"* and its intense personality is attested
by sentiments which bear a resemblance to those
very weaknesses which accompany the most ardent
and exclusive of human affections.

She was continually exhorting young Armand to
fidelity to his holy vocation. She reminds him that
it was in order that he might love Him with a purer
and more perfect love that Jesus had in His mercy
caused him to spend his early days in peaceful retreat,
far from the world and its vanities. "Beware," she
says, "of ever turning back . . . . I beg of our Lord,
with all the strength of my soul, to give you perseverance, until you attain to that day when, for the
first time, it will be granted you to hold in your hands
the Holy Victim immolated on the Altar . . . .
Doubtless you will have to encounter difficulties before
you reach that solemn moment, but be courageous:
He who calls you will know how to smooth them.
What an account you will have to render, should you,
through fault of your own, miss your vocation! But
it will not be so. Jesus calls you ; and you, faithful
disciple, you will obey Him. Nothing will seem hard
to you at the thought of what it is to which you
aspire." Then, to ensure his courageous perseverance,
she once more directs him to the tabernacle: "There,"
she says, "is the arsenal of the Apostolic soldier.
Jesus present there shall be Himself your invincible
armour. Oh, love Him well, this good and dear
Saviour ; strive to unite yourself more and more to

* Ps. lxxii. 26.

this pledge of His tenderness. Heaven is there; yes, all is there. Know and see nothing, breathe not, act not, save for Jesus. Let your example lead others to love Him; let your conversation be always of Jesus and Mary. Humility, peace, confidence, love, divine union, receive all from Jesus, and give all to your Jesus in return. Let Him be your Jesus by sacrificing you; your Jesus by consuming you; your Jesus by beatifying you. Think of my soul, in presence of our Love; beg Him to communicate to me His Eucharistic humility. When you wish to find me, seek me in the Adorable Heart of Him in whom I am entirely devoted to you." It was to this youthful servant of God that one of Eustelle's last letters was addressed, written in the midst of the burning heats of fever and the still more glowing flames of divine love, and when her hand was almost too weak to trace the words.

Among Eustelle's charitable labours we must class the truly marvellous number of letters which she wrote, marvellous indeed when we consider the hours which she necessarily gave to toil, and those which she daily spent in prayer, not to speak of her failing health during the concluding years of her life.* The time given to them is evidently often taken from the short period allotted to repose; and on more than one

* The greater part of Eustelle's letters which have been preserved were written during the last two years of her life; but we notice them in connection with the present subject as illustrative of her charitable labours. Her correspondence, which had been gradually forming, was but an extension of that work of charity to which we find her devoting herself at this period,—that of leading all over whom she had any influence to embrace and persevere in the life of perfection and to increase in love to the Adorable Sacrament.

occasion she speaks of the fatigue and headache caused by the prolonged effort.

We have already quoted a few passages from some of these letters, in which she exhorts her friends not to allow themselves to be deterred by vain scruples from a frequent reception of their Lord. It would be impossible, in a work like the present, to give any idea of the varied contents of these beautiful, these deeply spiritual, and yet truly simple and unaffected letters. Every virtue is in turns the subject of her pen, yet always intimately connected and associated with the central object of the Christian's love. In her estimation, indeed, no other motive, no other spring of conduct, no attraction, no desire, no purpose, can exist on earth worthy of influencing the human heart ever since a God-Man has come down to dwell in the tabernacle to draw us to Himself and to feed us with His Sacred Flesh. When therefore she is not directly speaking of this mystery, she is still always referring everything to it. The virtues most especially dear to the Heart of the Lamb of God are consequently those upon which she most frequently dwells—those virtues which, from their unpretending character, have been called the "little virtues," and of which S. Francis de Sales so often speaks, in his own sweet way, as the lowly flowers which bloom at the foot of the cross. If, indeed, there be a saint whose spirit, more than that of any other, Eustelle singularly reflects, it is that of the loving and most loveable Saint of Annecy.

She was consulted by numbers of persons, many belonging to a class superior to her own, in their spiritual difficulties and trials, and nothing is more remarkable than the frequency with which she re-

commends an abiding confidence in God and a childlike
freedom from anxiety and care. Simplicity, humility,
peace, and serenity of mind, detachment, inward
mortification—these are the constantly recurring
topics; but everything which falls from her pen is
so full of grace, freshness, and nature, that repetition
has always the charm of variety. "Courage, my very
good friend," she writes to a sufferer under trial;
"all for Jesus! Do not weary in the practice of
holy humility and sweet simplicity. Be not disheartened by the difficulties which the devil will not
cease to raise in this path, so arduous to nature, for
humility demands sacrifices; but then it gives to
the faithful soul peace and perfect liberty. Our
Divine and Good Master, the Eternal Truth, bids us
learn of Him, not to perform miracles, or raise the
dead, but to be meek and humble. Oh, how happy
is the soul which possesses herself! Jesus makes His
abode in her; she is His tabernacle, the throne where
He takes His rest, His garden of delights. Yes, it
is humility which makes Jesus be well pleased in
her; and with what torrents of joy do His heavenly
communications inundate her! He vouchsafes to
make known to her the sweetness of His presence,
He introduces her into the treasury of His Divine
Heart, into that sacred asylum whence the most profound adorations, love incomprehensible, and acts of
an infinite value ascend to the Eternal. Oh, unite
yourself more and more to this loving Jesus, this
dear Brother, this God-with-us. Shut up in His
Heart, think of, adore, and love the one only worthy
Object of love—Jesus all good. I rely on His promise:
He will grant you the fruit of the prayers I offer
for you; I am at this moment beseeching Him to

grant you more and more the science of the tabernacle: it is what I desire for myself and others."

Always is her active charity on the watch to discern symptoms of the baleful spirit of disquietude and discouragement, and, with the spiritual discernment which distinguishes her, she lays her finger on its root, self-love. We find her writing thus to a friend: —"To a truly interior soul united to Jesus, the Eternal Love, ought there to be any occupations capable of diverting it from a calm and loving attention to the Divine Presence? All our actions, be they what they may, can acquire a merit wholly divine by the perfection with which they should be performed. But so soon as agitation, disquiet, eagerness begin to animate them, destitute as are all these of a supernatural motive, self-love soon corrupts them. It is an incense offered to the devil, and which Jesus rejects. We must apply ourselves at the commencement of each action to purify our intention, and then act by Jesus, in Jesus, and for Jesus. He is the Prince of Peace; He loves nothing but peace in Heaven, and upon earth He bestows it on men of good will. Act, then, always with calmness, repose, gentleness, and tranquillity; let us remind ourselves that it is for Jesus our God, our Father, our Heavenly Friend, and the Companion of our exile." Again, in a short and very concise letter, written probably when time or strength was wanting for more, we find her, as usual, insisting on the cultivation of the lowly and quiet virtues, as the sure road to the extirpation of self-love. "All for Jesus—try to realize fully the meaning of these words. Be sure never to excuse yourself; never to manifest the least shade of coldness, but always a sweet equanimity and gentle compliance. You have not failed in charity in what you told me"—she here alludes to some scruple, which she hastens to dismiss by adding—"think no more of it. My health is as usual," she remarks by the way, and then quickly resumes the subject which occupies her. "Apply yourself, then, to extirpating from your heart this miserable old man. Distrust yourself. The love of the Sovereign Love, Jesus our ineffable delight, will reward your pains and sacrifices, even in this life, by filling your soul with the plenitude of His increated charity, hereafter to plunge it into its Divine flames throughout the everlasting reign of this dear, this good, this all-amiable Saviour. Adieu: I am all yours through His Blood, and I leave you with His love. Eustelle, the poor servant of Jesus." Distrust of self, trust in God—humility and confidence—these are the two poles of the spiritual life. Eustelle is ever passing from the one to the other in her letters. "I think," she writes to a person who had specially sought her friendship,* "you do not sufficiently abandon yourself to the spirit of confidence, and that you trouble yourself too much about what passes in your soul. No doubt, if you see anything there which can displease that jealous Friend, you must rid yourself of it, and tear up even the smallest weeds which unprofitably fill up any portion of the

---

* This was in consequence of some remarks made in one of his sermons by the Bishop of La Rochelle, who had taken occasion, when speaking of the friendship, all founded on virtue, which united St. Basil and St. Gregory, to recommend his hearers to beg of God the grace to find true friends and to follow their salutary counsels. Eustelle's humility, as usual, makes her deem herself unworthy, and she assures her correspondent that she has made a very poor choice; that she herself is a weak reed, and needs rather to be admonished of her own faults.

field of your soul. Such is the will of the Divine
Gardener, who desires to cultivate therein nothing
but His own plants, and to make them bear fruit.
But do not fancy that all which is displeasing in you
is owing to your fault; this is a snare of the devil.
Put such a thought away; have more confidence.
Allow yourself to be humbly led by Him who is the
Way, the Truth, and the Life. Lay your whole soul,
with all its miserable defects, in the Tabernacle. Jesus
will consume them in the fire of His Divine charity.
To tell you what I think, I believe that Jesus, our
Heavenly Friend, desires to lead you by the road of
love. What a favour it is to love this Saviour, who
is so worthy of all love. My wish would be that all
should think only of loving Him, never of fearing
Him. He is so good! His love is so sweet!"

It would be needless to multiply quotations. We
will, however, add one more, as illustrative of the
solicitude with which she never ceased inculcating a
spirit of filial confidence, and that entire immolation of
self which is the fruit of a multitude of small and
repeated sacrifices. After alluding to some little
incident which she feared might lead to her friend
being deprived of the liberty of visiting her, her
humility makes her add, "Not that it could be
esteemed a privation if you were forbidden to visit
my poor abode; what help can be found in leaning
on an arm of flesh, too weak to support itself? Pray,
pray, that Jesus, the Eternal Love, may deign, all
unworthy as I am, vile dust and ashes, to cast on me
His sweet and merciful eyes. May He kindle in my
heart, created for Him, the pure love of which His
own is the strength and the principle. I need this
fire to consume the innumerable sins which sully this

soul of mine, which Jesus daily makes His sanctuary and His temple. My weaknesses humble without discouraging me. I know what our dear Saviour is. I rely upon Him—no, He will not disappoint my hopes. Dear friend, have the tenderest confidence in His goodness: He refuses nothing to this good virtue coupled with humility—confidence in Jesus. O Crib! O Cross! O Sacrament! O love of Jesus!—these are the grounds of the Christian's confidence; these are the motives of my confidence and of yours. Take care not to wound the sweet and tender Heart of Jesus, by failing in a holy and a loving confidence. Oh, keep yourself in peace all the days of your exile; second more and more the designs of the Lord towards you; labour to die to yourself, to your own will, your own judgment, tastes, inclinations, and to clothe yourself with the new man, who is Jesus our God. These sacrifices, these victories over yourself, will put you in possession of divine charity. Then will the Spouse introduce you into His 'wine-cellar,' where He inebriates the souls that are dear to Him. There He will 'set charity in order within you;' that is, He will free you from those defects which too often alloy this gold, which ought to be entirely pure. Make haste, then, to burn with divine love, for I burn because this sacred fire does not inflame hearts as it ought to do. Jesus alone can appreciate what I suffer on that account. Pray that I may be the first to practise what I write to you on this subject. Is it for me to preach?" It was love made her speak, humility would have kept her silent.

An extract from a letter written, in 1838, to her former director will show how, in the midst of her charitable labours, she was ever watchful against the

temptation of spiritual pride.   After asking his
prayers for two persons desiring to return with their
whole hearts to God, but still held back by the spirit
of the world and by want of courage, and after
speaking of the pain which this causes her, she adds,
" I must here take occasion to tell you that I feel
pain of another kind also : it comes from this, that
many persons repose too much confidence in me.
You are aware that there are some who consult me
about their interior state ; others, again, ask my
advice ; and why should they thus seek payment in
bad coin ? I am afraid of these things making me
proud.   Yet it seems to me that herein I am animated by the pure motive of the love of our good
God ; but I suffer from the esteem in which I cannot
help perceiving that persons hold me.   Ah, it is because they do not know me.   God grant that I may
be in His eyes what I am in those of people here.
Beg, then, of God that I may never do anything but
what He asks of me, and that I may act, under these
circumstances, with much simplicity and humility.
Once more tell me sincerely your opinion about all
this."

We have given a few instances, taken almost at
random, of the practical character of Eustelle's teaching in the modest apostleship she exercised with her
pen.   She little knew how wide was to be its range ;
and the humility which dreaded even the appearance
of preaching to another village girl like herself, would
have shrunk abashed from such a thought.   What she
wrote was for one eye and for the benefit of one soul ;
it has this single object ; self has no share in her
purpose.   Had she wished to speak of self, she might
have told of raptures and ecstasies and visions ; all

these were hers, but not one word occurs in allusion
to them, not one hint of the glorious revelations of
the invisible world which her eyes were so often
privileged to behold. If she speaks of her own
feelings, it is only because the ardour of her love is
irrepressible, or because at times the least ostentatious
way of recommending virtue and piety is to make
audible acts of divine love, which, when they proceed
from the heart, have a sweet contagious influence on
those who hear them; but in all this she is guided by
her own refined and unconscious tact, which the Holy
Spirit had exalted within her into a supernatural gift,
and is not acting upon any deliberate or settled plan.
She does not sit down to write a letter of advice,
thinking over what would best answer the purpose;
no, pure charity makes her take up her pen, and
charity dictates its every word, a charity which needs
no instructor but itself. Hence, also, the remarkable
absence in her letters of all those terms of endearment
with which epistolary effusions are often so profusely
garnished, and with which the French language is so
richly provided—not to speak of that subtle and delicate flattery which scarcely ever is altogether absent
from the correspondence of even good and pious
persons—*not saints*. We do not say that Eustelle
was a saint, for the Church has not declared her so,
but we think we may say that her letters have a
singular resemblance to those which saints alone can
and do write. Eustelle's letters were, in fact, not
letters of mere kindness and affection; that is, her
correspondence was not directed to the object of
cultivating friendship or of testifying regard; nevertheless the absence of all tokens of a natural and
imperfect affection is far from imparting any air of

coldness to her writings; human affection is absent only because it is swallowed up in the divine. Marie-Eustelle cold and unloving would cease to be herself.

We have alluded to her early drawing off alike from friends and from friendships, but hereafter (as we then said) she was to knit new ties, of which Jesus was to be the exclusive bond. A short note of hers to one who seems to have been afflicted with various forms of scrupulosity will serve at once to show the spirit in which she cultivated an exalted Christian friendship and the holy liberty the soul of this true child of God enjoyed. "Dear sister," she writes, " notwithstanding my unworthiness, which ought to prompt me to keep silence rather than to teach others, I assure you that our good Lord entirely approves our meetings, in which our hearts mutually inflame each other more and more with the pure love of Jesus, our Spouse. No need for disquiet on this subject : humility and love. I quite understand all you say. Persevere, and receive in increasing abundance the chaste favours of the Beloved, who desires still more and more to captivate your soul. Abide in His Heart ; I am there with you to love Him and to bless Him. This evening He is to give us His Benediction : see how good He is! I will not fail to come and see you this evening. Adieu."

CHAPTER XI.

Vow of Poverty and Self-Detachment.

Jesus has yet something to ask. Until this demand has been made and conceded, the conquest is not complete, the trial is not ended. Eustelle has given herself, but she has still, so to say, a little life-interest in a few things. Trifling they are, it is true, but Jesus wants all. All—that word of deep import, which says nothing of much or of little, says nothing of the amount of what it contains or implies. The poor widow gave a mite, and Jesus pronounced that she gave more than did all the rich men who cast of their abundance into the Treasury; and this because she gave all she had to give. The Apostles, who had left a few poor nets on the seashore, and a life of hard and often ill-requited toil, said to Jesus, " Behold, we have left all and followed Thee, what shall we have therefore ?" Our Lord did not remind them of how little value were those things they had renounced for Him ; He accepted their assertion :—they had left all, for they had nothing more to leave, and He replied with the magnificent promise that in the great day, when the Son of Man shall sit on the throne of His glory, they also should be enthroned in splendour and made participants of His judicial power. Between *much* and *all*, then, there is an immeasurable distance, or, rather, there is no relative comparison. Not but that our Lord graciously accepts and repays a hundred-fold any and every sacrifice made for the love of Him; but, as such offerings are compatible with a certain withholding, they do not argue nor produce that perfect detachment of heart which He requires in chosen souls, and which He rewards, not liberally only, but with the full possession of Himself and of all the treasures laid up in Him.

Eustelle's offering of herself to Jesus had been a full and perfect offering in intention from the beginning. She had not been as one who step by step is drawn on to part with what conscience enlightened by grace denounces as incompatible with the life of holiness which our Lord requires, and without which He will not own us as His; from the very beginning her surrender of herself, and of all she had, was generous and unreserved, only it pleased our Lord to acquaint her gradually with the amount of the debt she had voluntarily and lovingly taken on herself. She was in the disposition of mind described as following her consecration of her virginity to God, when—probably some time in the year 1839—her Heavenly Spouse (she tells us) exacted from her a fresh sacrifice, but one which she esteemed no sacrifice at all: "I was poor," she writes, "by His own holy will and dispensation; my state in life had prevented me from having any share in this world's perishable goods; but He asked me one day, in a most loving manner, to bind myself to Him by vow to practise a still more perfect poverty. Above all, He required of me poverty of spirit, judgment, and will. Then was kindled in my heart an ardent desire to be faithful to this new inspiration. Besides, I had received from this dear Master a peculiar attraction for holy poverty; she was my sister, my inseparable companion; I loved nothing in the world so much as poverty. Pressed to bind myself by this new engagement, I hastened to ask permission. It was accorded to me ; I made a vow of poverty, and was happy to be able now to practise by obligation what before I had observed from inclination." For Eustelle, as we have seen, had felt herself continually drawn to self-despoilment, both internal and external ; and always from this same abiding motive of love.

It was little, as may be supposed, that one like her, poor by condition and still more poor by choice, possessed with which she could part. Yet some few trifles were still hers, which when we say they were superfluous, we must be understood to use the word in its rigid not its ordinary sense. She proceeds to give a little inventory of the things of which she retained the use after making her vow of poverty. She kept only a single change of the different articles of dress needful to her, and of shoes had never but one pair at a time. As for household linen, she had none of her own, her parents lending her such as was absolutely necessary. Her kitchen utensils hardly arrived at what was strictly indispensable, for the true lover of poverty courts inconvenience, and cannot esteem himself poor unless he is also uncomfortable. Of money, she never kept any provision by her ; she never saved from her small earnings, and often she lacked wherewithal to buy food. The furniture of her room was in keeping with the rest, and consisted of a poor little bed, a chest of drawers, a small table, and four chairs ; she even allowed herself a very limited number of devotional objects, and such as she permitted herself to keep had no intrinsic value. She would even have discarded some prints which hung upon the wall, but that she feared to grieve her father and mother Her beads were strung on a cord, and the crucifix appended was of copper. A rosary which she had

worth about a franc, she parted with when she made
her vow. She also kept very few books of piety, and,
as the reader will readily imagine, she had never
possessed any but such as were of a religious character. A very pretty copy of the "Imitation of Christ,"
and many little devotional prints which she had received as presents on different occasions, she gave
away only because they were pretty or were of some
small value, not choosing to retain anything for which
she could possibly feel the least attachment. Quite
irrespectively of the requirements of a vow, holy
souls have been often thus moved to deny themselves
whatever seemed to be a mere luxury to the spiritual
taste, albeit in the great majority of cases rather
a help and an aliment to the spirit of piety. In depriving herself of such devotional objects, Marie-Eustelle was acting under her Lord's special and immediate
guidance. He would not permit even the consuming
love which He had Himself kindled in her bosom for
the Adorable Eucharist to content itself at the expense
of the perfect detachment which He exacted. As it
was impossible for her always to be before the Tabernacle, she had entertained the idea of embroidering
a monstrance in gold and placing it in her room as a
continual memorial of the Beloved of her soul. Her
heart thrilled with pleasure at the thought, and if ever
a pure gratification was coveted, this would seem to
have been pure indeed; yet was it an indulgence which
Jesus would not permit her to enjoy. What might
have been almost a merit in another, He would have
esteemed an imperfection in His spouse, and He
prompted her to renounce for the love of Him what
she had desired for the love of Him. The parting
with those things which were associated with her

devotions, and which it appeared lawful for the most disengaged heart to love, since their whole value consisted in what they represented or suggested, seems alone of all the sacrifices she was called to make to have cost her something. For this reason, perhaps, it was that Jesus allowed of no exceptions in their favour : if she loved anything, in however small a degree, if she clung to it, so to say, by a mere thread, it was to be parted with; the thread must be snapped. A soft interior voice, which her all-attentive ear never failed to catch, required the sacrifice. One day a friend asked her for a print she saw in her room. For some reason it was dear to Eustelle's pious heart, and she was surprised into confessing as much. The friend said no more ; it was but a passing wish, probably forgotten long ere she reached her home, where, however, she was promptly reminded of it by the arrival of the desired object. Another time, a religious begged Marie-Eustelle to let her have her image of the Blessed Virgin. This seemed hard, but some people are bold beggars ; perhaps she knew Eustelle's spirit of detachment, and was trying it. If it were the dearly-loved and dearly-loving Sister Anastasia, the one chosen friend of whom we shall have to speak hereafter, this would furnish the probable explanation. At any rate, Marie-Eustelle momentarily failed under the trial. "A crucifix," she replied, "is sufficient for a religious,"—a rather rigid doctrine, it may be remarked, but to Eustelle it naturally occurred, no doubt, that if she was expected to be content with a crucifix only, and to be ready to dispense with the image of Mary, such poverty could not be reckoned so intolerable in a nun that she must needs supply the want at another's expense. If thoughts of this nature

flashed through her mind and found utterance in her
once quick tongue, they were instantly repressed, and
she at once acceded to the request.

But if to such things Eustelle held a little, a *very*
little, of all the rest she stripped herself with the same
or, rather, far greater delight than others feel in acquiring or in possessing. " Dear virtue," she said to
her confidante, Anastasia,—" dear virtue, oh, if I love
you so ardently, it is because Jesus loves you ! " She
delighted in wearing " very old clothes, very well
mended :" these are her own expressions, for she did
not like them to be in holes or tatters : that, she said,
is " slovenliness, untidiness, not virtue," a remark
which reminds us of S. Bernard's " *Paupertas semper,
sordes nunquam.*" It is true that God, who is admirable in His saints, has inspired some even to despise cleanliness for His sake, and in these our days
of luxurious indulgence and fastidious delicacy, it has
pleased Him that a beggar should, in the person of
Joseph Labre, be raised to the altars of the Church,
one who cherished his filthy rags for the love of Jesus
more than if they had been princely robes. But these
are obviously exceptional cases, the results of a special
inspiration ; for, speaking generally, want of cleanliness and a marked negligence in attire has no right
to shelter itself under the plea of disengagement of
heart or the love of holy poverty. We find Eustelle
herself objecting to the " singularity of dress" which
had been adopted by one of her correspondents,
apparently from a religious motive. Much as she
cherished poverty herself, she strove personally rather
to veil than to display it ; and, except in confidence
to a chosen few, a very few, she did not even speak
much of her love for it ; partly because such language

is unintelligible to the vast majority, or, at least, is apt to wear in their eyes an appearance of exaggeration, partly in order to avoid attracting notice to her indigence, lest kind friends should hasten to relieve it. Notwithstanding all her precautions, she already had something to endure on this account. She was now beginning to be as much the object of affectionate reverence as she had once been of reproach and contempt. Friends endeavoured to guess what she might most need, or they would observe some want to which she had taken care never to draw attention. During her absence they would place such articles in her room, and she had the disagreeable surprise on her return to find that she had been enriched in spite of herself. She would then lovingly complain to her Lord, "Why will not these good people allow me to taste so precious a gift in all its fulness?"

So entirely had Marie-Eustelle abandoned herself and all her earthly interests into our Lord's hands, that she made a complete mental sacrifice of the money she earned by the work of her hands. Poor as she was, she never applied for payment, but waited patiently, even when her purse was as empty of silver as her board was destitute of the commonest supply of food. "Jesus," she said to herself, "knows what is owed to me, and He knows also what I need. He takes care of my soul; He will also have a care for my body. I abandon myself to His fatherly providence." One day she was passing in front of the house of a person who owed her thirty sous. The sum was a very small one, so small that delay might sit lightly on the debtor's conscience, as is unfortunately too frequently the case with those who have not themselves known poverty, and who can scarcely realize the all-importance of prompt payment to their humble creditors. To Eustelle thirty sous was a large sum, for at that moment she did not possess even a cent. It naturally crossed her mind, " This person ought to pay me, and, if she did so, it would relieve me from my present embarrassment." But the thought was quickly followed by another: " Jesus, my Father and my Spouse, knows my indigence ; that is enough." Then, raising her heart to Him, she inwardly said, " O my Jesus, I wish for nothing, but leave all in Thy hands ; it is from those sacred hands that I will receive my money whenever it pleases Thee to send it me." She repaired to the church—it was Lent, and no sooner had she reached her place than her debtor entered, and, going immediately to where Eustelle was kneeling, presented her with the long-owed thirty sous.

Similar instances of our Lord's loving and special care were not unfamiliar to her. " Ah, as for me," she said one day to her friend Anastasia, " I can trouble myself about nothing any longer, absolutely nothing ; not even my faults and lack of virtue. Perhaps I have very good reason to do so ; but when I try to reflect on such things I find it impossible. The confidence our Lord gives me drives away every other sentiment. If anything could trouble my peace, it would be the having too much peace. But I have often consulted about it, and have been told to be quite easy on the subject: not to examine what passes within me, but to leave all to our Lord. This I have done, and I am happy." Eustelle was happy like a sleeping infant in its mother's arms, cradled in softness, with every want supplied, without toil or

solicitude of its own, nay even without the trouble
of asking for aught it needs.   Such is the privilege
of babes.   The Christian babe, whom the Saviour
takes in His arms, and bears with a love surpassing
that of mothers, has the still higher privilege, while
thus provided and cared for, of being conscious of its
felicity.   The holy Curé of Ars used to say, "Man,
when he has a pure heart, commands the Almighty as
if he were His master."   His own wonderful life was
a comment on this remark, and an exemplification of
its truth, of which those who are conversant with the
lives of God's saints will remember abundant con-
firmations.   All will call to mind that servant of God
who one day complained to Him that she often received thanks for the success of her prayers when
she had in fact forgotten the requests which had been
made to her.   "My daughter," Jesus replied, "when
thou placedst thy will in My hands, I placed My will
in thine."   So gracious was her Lord that He fulfilled
her unexpressed and even forgotten desires; and does
not the Holy Ghost also assure us that God hears the
"*preparation of the heart*"?   Eustelle has the same
testimony to give: "Our Lord," she said with a faith
full of humble confidence, "grants me everything I
ask."   One year she was very desirous to hear a
celebrated preacher whom she esteemed very highly
for his zeal and virtue.   He had been asked to preach
at Saint-Pallais on the occasion of the Quarant' Ore,
but refused, on account of a bad and obstinate cold.
"But why refuse?" said Eustelle; "I promise you,
on the part of our Lord, that if you will preach you
will be cured, and will then be able to undertake the
long journey you now dread, and devote yourself
freely to your apostolic labours."   This ecclesiastic

knew Eustelle well, he knew she was incapable
of uttering words at random, and that, if she
spoke with so much confidence, it was because she
was moved to do so. Accordingly, on the strength of
this promise, he mounted the pulpit, still suffering
from a violent irritation of the chest, but he descended
its steps so completely cured, that, although he continued to preach several times a week for two months
unintermittingly, he never felt the least return of his
indisposition. Unnumbered, indeed, were the proofs
which this holy girl was constantly receiving of our
Lord's love in His attention to her wishes in matters
of lesser moment; a regard to which we are accustomed to consider, in the case of human affection,
as peculiarly exhibiting at once its delicacy and its
depth. Saints seldom care for what by comparison
may be called little things, but when it so happens
that a passing wish of this kind enters their pure
minds, our dear Lord seems as if (to speak humanly)
He were actually rejoiced at the opportunity of gratifying them. Besides, what they ask for they are
always so sure that they will obtain; and our Lord
will not disappoint a confidence which is the offspring
of love. "Love our Lord very much," said Eustelle;
" love gives confidence."

The sort of reciprocity in liberality which exists between the Lord and faithful souls is the fruit only of a
perfect self-renunciation, internal as well as external;
and it was to interior poverty, so much more arduous
in practice than the outward, that Jesus had especially
called Eustelle. It is poverty of spirit which gives
true liberty, the liberty of the children of God, who
are admitted to a sweet familiarity with their Lord.
Nothing could exceed the strictness with which He

exacted of her the most entire abandonment of self.
In the soul that draws nearer to the blaze of the Sun
of Justice specks and imperfections become visible
which before were not perceptible; then, too, it is
that the holiness of God, like a purifying fire, begins
to act with greater force and intensity upon it, to
efface these stains and make that soul a more pure
and perfect mirror of His beauty. Jesus would not
pass over or excuse the most trifling failing in His
spouse, but He at the same time infused so bright and
penetrating a light into her intellect that she herself
perceived the loveliness and superhuman excellence
of that perfection which was required of her, and
passionately longed to make it her own.   Above
all, these demands of the Saviour were always
made in the form of the most tender solicitations
and accompanied with indescribable testimonies of
love.   When He asked something special of her,
He would show her His all-compassionate Heart,
and, casting on her a look of majesty and sweetness, would say, "Such is My good pleasure." At
times she beheld Him drawing aside His tunic,
to disclose to her His Sacred Heart, the furnace of
charity, and heard Him say, as He pointed to It, " It
is from hence that this desire of Mine proceeds ; it is
from hence that I invite you to this sacrifice." This
grace was vouchsafed to her frequently ; and can we
wonder, then, that gratitude for these touching favours gave wings to her will for the performance of
what was asked of her ?

A short time before her death, when she was pressed
with inquiries upon the subject by her confessor,
Eustelle was fain to acknowledge that she could not
remember having ever resisted any one of her Lord's

inspirations; but no sooner had the words passed her lips, which the spirit of obedience alone had extracted from her, than her humility took the alarm, and she exclaimed, "Ah, my All, my most amiable Jesus, I should be truly rash if I dared to assert that I am without reproach. Forgive me my failings, and deign to enlighten me for the future. Oh, let me die rather than ever grieve Thy Heart of infinite goodness.". The attraction which drew her, not only to conform herself to His will, but to lose her own will altogether in that of her Beloved baffles description. She called it her delight, her paradise, and with her eyes ever fixed on Him and her desires absorbed in His Holy Will alone, in God she saw all things, and accepted all things. To this Will she was united in the least things as in the greatest. Every event which can possibly occur in this changeful world—pains, sicknesses, vicissitudes of fortune, all than can result from the malice of men, calumnies, humiliations, disgrace, all those variations which attend the spiritual life, temptations, dryness, derelictions—all alike were viewed by this servant of God in the light of the Divine Will, and all were equally loved and rejoiced in. She confessed, indeed, that she felt it to be impossible to turn away her will for one instant from this loving and peaceful adhesion to the Will of God. In all distresses and afflictions she was ever uttering in her heart, if not with her lips, these words: "It is Thy Will, my beloved Saviour, and it is my will too: blessed be Thou."

In describing the different trials which Marie-Eustelle was called to undergo, we have made no allusion to any but such as were strictly personal; but it must not therefore be inferred that these constituted the

whole sum of them, and that she had not her share of
those sorrows of which we are all more or less par-
takers, the griefs which wound us through others.
Eustelle's family was not exempt from its portion of
domestic troubles, though her biographer makes but a
passing and covert allusion to them, probably because
any detailed account would have been distressing to
the feelings of survivors, and his narrative was sure
to be extensively read amongst Eustelle's relations
and friends. We have seen that she had a life-long
anxiety respecting the spiritual state of her father,
for it was not given her while on earth to witness any
satisfactory change in his religious conduct, and many
and bitter were the tears which she shed in private, not
only for his soul's sake, but for the sorrow which his
behaviour caused to another equally dear to her. Her
biographer, alluding to him without mentioning his
name, speaks of the ill return which virtue, patience,
and the most considerate affection received at his
hands. Eustelle exhorted the sufferers, probably her
whole family circle, to resign themselves with all
humility to the dispensations of God ; telling them that
these very sufferings might one day contribute to the
salvation of such as were the cause of them, although
it might be only at the hour of death. But this
sorrow also, lacking as it did much of the consolation
attending her own personal trials, which, in fact, she
did not regard in the light of sorrows at all, she cast
into that ocean of God's Holy Will where all her
hopes, fears, desires, pains, and griefs found their
blissful grave. Happy Eustelle! she had reached
the state in which she could give thanks in all things,
in adversity as in prosperity, in sadness as in joy ; for
to the loving adorer of the "most amiable Will of

o

God" there can no longer be either adversity or sorrow, since, come what may, that blessed Will is ever done. "O Jesus," she would exclaim, with the ecstatic love which this holy disposition inspired, "how good Thou art! Thou givest me in this world a foretaste of eternal felicity!" One cold winter's evening, as she sat before her fireless hearth in her room almost bare of furniture, suffering under one of those feverish paroxysms which mark the progress of the fatal malady which was upon her, a lady entered who truly valued and admired her, and began to express much concern at her illness and the comfortless condition in which she found her. Eustelle turned on her those eyes in whose mystic depths Heaven itself seemed mirrored, and with a radiant smile said, "You think me unhappy, then? Well, I would not change my state for the most prosperous and fortunate which the world has to show. Amid all my privations —ah, if you knew what happiness!" How much did these few words imply! It was not, "I am happy in spite of my sufferings and privations," but, "What a happy, what a blessed state is mine : *si scires donum Dei!*" The lady, however, owned that to her this answer was unintelligible.

Need we add that with her devotion to the Adorable Will of her Beloved, Eustelle's ardent love for the Blessed Eucharist continued to deepen? It seems hard to express this increase in words, without seeming to repeat what has already been so often said. At any given time since the moment that she became Its passionate adorer, Eustelle seems to have loved as much as it was possible for her to love ; but God can increase the soul's capacity for love, and Eustelle's faithful correspondence to grace merited, doubtless, this favour for her. Hence it is that we hear of the growing intenseness of the flame within her, which in its very beginnings seemed to be consuming the frail tenement in which it was lodged. To burn in mortal flesh with the ardour of a seraph seems to need a supernatural intervention of God's sustaining power; yet such was the life which Eustelle was to lead for the remainder of her days on earth. The trial is ended, the conflict is over; the all-conquering love of Jesus has won her wholly to Himself: henceforth He keeps His possession in peace.

PART II.
THE DAYS OF PEACE.

CHAPTER I.

EUSTELLE AND ANASTASIA.

IT remains to us to describe the three last years of Marie-Eustelle's life,—years so full of peace and holy joy. The winter was now past, the rain of tribulation had ceased; she had heard the voice of the Beloved saying, "Arise, my love, my beautiful one, and come." He had called His "dove" into "the clefts of the rock," He had caused her to repose under the shadow of Him whom she had desired.* True she still languished, but it was with the delicious languishing of love. The sinkings of bereavement, the groanings of absence are departed for ever, for He is evermore with her; His left hand is under her head, and His right hand embraces her. On earth, in heaven, there is no real joy but love; that joy was hers now : the love, the abiding love, the encompassing love of Him who is the Eternal Love, that name by which she so delighted to call Him. Even the world had now ceased to persecute; Eustelle had lived down prejudice; respect, nay veneration surrounded her. Of these days her own pen has left no record; it drops from her hand upon their threshold. Her increasing illness and extended correspondence, no doubt, ren-

* Cant. ii. 3, 13, 14.

dered her unable to complete her task; possibly, too, the humble servant of God shrank from drawing a detailed picture of the wonderful graces and favours which she received in those last years. Yet we were not to be deprived of the knowledge of them, and Providence so ordered events that we have little reason to regret the incomplete state of the auto-biography, in which, perhaps, she would have used more reserve than in her correspondence. To seculars, as we before observed, she never spoke of these super-natural favours; it is from her letters to two of her directors, already well acquainted with her spiritual state, that we obtain the information we possess on this interesting subject. We have already alluded to the priest who left Saint-Pallais in 1837 to exercise his ministry in another part of the diocese. With this ecclesiastic Eustelle kept up a tolerably active correspondence. Later she was moved to lay the state of her soul before one of the priests of Saintes,* but as he was often called to preach in other places, and was consequently absent for considerable periods of time, she was in the habit of communicating with him in writing, a circumstance which has secured to us some of her most valuable letters.

She had, moreover, a confidante—one only—to whom allusion has already been occasionally made, and with whom the reader must now make a nearer acquaintance. Sister Anastasia was a nun belonging to the convent of La Providence at Saintes, and employed to teach a girls' school which that religious house had established at Saint-Pallais. Nature had

---

* M. Briand; the same, no doubt, to whom Eustelle pro-mised the cure of his distressing cough, as related in the last ﹖ter.

not been bountiful of her external gifts to Anastasia.
She was low of stature, deformed, and lame; yet, in
spite of these personal disadvantages, she had been
warmly welcomed by the community, who were well
acquainted with her merits. Her piety was deep and
fervent, but she suffered from exaggerated fears of the
justice of God. A desire for consolation in these
interior trials first led her to seek Eustelle, who
extended to her the open arms of charity, and soon a
close friendship united these two hearts. Charity
formed its first bond, charity cemented, and charity
perfected it; no shadow of mere human and natural
love ever obscured this pure affection, which was all
for God and in God. Hence Eustelle reposed a confidence in Sister Anastasia which no other person
ever won from her. This good religious survived her
friend a very short time, but before following her she
diligently collected all the materials which might
hereafter serve to her glorification. In particular
she placed on record many of the conversations which
she had had with her, and in her own unadorned and
simple language has given a portrait of the holy girl
such as none but herself could have furnished, since
none else had the privilege of being admitted to a
knowledge of her hidden and interior life.

It was, as we have seen, in the course of 1839 that
Eustelle's inward trials, after 'becoming gradually less
frequent, finally ceased. It was early in that year
that she received the intimation from her Lord that
He willed she should henceforth devote herself to the
one only occupation of honouring Him in the Sacrament of His Love. Another time Jesus said to her
interiorly, " It is very pleasing to Me that you should
come and bear Me company ; I wish you to make it

your delight to be with Me, as I take Mine in being with you ; but I require from you a perfect detachment of heart."   With what generosity of spirit Eustelle responded to these demands of her Saviour has been related : she had given up all to Him, and henceforth He was all hers. Some months afterwards, He caused her, while engaged in prayer, to hear these words : "My daughter, it is no longer My will to keep any secrets from you ; be faithful to Me, and do not compel Me to leave you.   I desire to confirm you in My grace and My love."   Again, when Eustelle was one day disquieting herself with the notion that perhaps she was wanting in devotion to the saints— for she was so wholly absorbed in the contemplation and love of the Divine Eucharist that she seemed to forget all else—Jesus reassured her by saying, "It is My will that the Pledge of My Love should be your special occupation."   And Eustelle's forgetfulness, in fact, was owing neither to neglect nor to want of memory.   The devotion to which she was called super-eminently included all that it seemed to supersede.   As Jesus is honoured in His saints, so are His saints honoured in Him, the Saint of saints. Never is the soul nearer to those of whom Jesus is the joy and crown, and whose splendours are a portion of His own, than when He fills every thought and is the all-absorbing object of its contemplation.

In one of her moments of unreserved confidence with Anastasia, she said, "St. Paul exclaimed, ' I know nothing but Jesus, and Jesus Crucified ;' as for me, I know nothing but Jesus, and Jesus in the Eucharist.   He is my whole thought, my whole life ; day and night I think of Him."   " Do you never sleep ?" asked Anastasia.   " Very little," she replied.

"I am not able, I long too much for the day, that I may go and visit my Saviour. I hunger insatiably to unite myself to Him. So if ever you see me lie in bed of a morning you may say, 'Ah, Eustelle is certainly very ill this time; she is at the last extremity now.'" She quickly added, "But when that happens, it will be He who keeps me there. Blessed be He for that, blessed for evermore. Amidst all my privations I shall be happy in the thought that I am accomplishing His will. Oh, how I love that Holy Will! How happy we are when we will only what He wills, and when we see God in all!" Love seemed to give her at times supernatural strength to achieve what otherwise would have exceeded her power. As in persons who live a life of the flesh the spirit is weighed down by the corporeal frame, and comes to partake itself of the fleshy character; so in those who live an exalted spiritual life the feeble body at times seems almost to become a participant in the strength of its immortal and incorruptible companion. So it was with Eustelle. Always of a very delicate and fragile constitution, she had probably already contracted the seeds of a mortal complaint. Of food she was most sparing; rest it seemed impossible for her to take during the few hours she lay down at night; in the day she had to work hard for her subsistence; long hours she spent in prayer on her knees in the cold winter nights, and in the still more chilling winter mornings—on the bare floor of an unwarmed church. Add to which, she was always ready at the call of charity: she belonged, for God's sake, to all who had need of her, nay to all who thought they had need of her. And these were not occasional exertions; we are stating what was her ordinary practice; and when we have summed up all, we are struck with wonder that with her feeble health she should have been able to endure an amount of fatigue which, we cannot but feel, would have severely taxed the most hardy frame.

But if divine love was allowed to supplement her deficiency of natural strength, that same love sometimes deprived her of it altogether. She once asked Sister Anastasia whether she had ever noticed that after receiving communion she did not return to her place for some considerable time. Her friend replied in the affirmative. "And what did you suppose was the reason?" asked Eustelle. "I thought either that you felt ill or that something extraordinary was going on within you. When you leave the altar, one may read in your face what is passing in your soul." "Oh, how I suffer," rejoined Eustelle, "when this happens, from the fear of its being perceived! And then, too, there are persons very clever at that sort of thing who might take occasion to ridicule piety. They would certainly tax me more than ever with affectation; but what can I do? I am quite powerless in these matters." Anastasia took this opportunity to obtain a little satisfaction to her pious curiosity. "What do you feel at those times, my dear friend?" Perhaps no one but she could have ventured on such a question: certainly no one who had hazarded the inquiry would have been likely to obtain much information; but Anastasia was all simplicity, and Eustelle dealt with her in a similar spirit. "What I feel," she replied, "I feel without being able to express it; that is quite impossible. Before communion I am in a sort of fever of impatience; it passes into all my limbs, I can scarcely contain myself, and quite dread

lest those near me should perceive the state I am in.
But no sooner has Jesus touched my lips, and descended into my soul, than immediately all this ceases,
all is calm within me, and I am filled with an immense
joy ; I no longer feel myself, my limbs seem to be
made of wool, my strength forsakes me ; if I were to
rise I should fall at once ; I am afraid of fainting.
This state lasts some ten minutes or quarter of an
hour ; then I am able to return to my place. I beseech
our Lord not to allow this to happen in public, but
if He wills it, in order to humble me, may His will
be done. I have frequently seen our Lord between
the fingers of the priest, at the moment of communion,
under the form of a little child. How beautiful He
was ! Judge what my happiness must have been
when He thus manifested Himself to me ! Tears of
love, delicious tears, flowed from my eyes. How
free from constraint I should have felt if only I had
been alone ! But what distresses me at these times
is those little choir children who accompany the priest.
They have no respect for the most Adorable Sacrament : they fix their eyes upon you. They have often
seen me weeping, in spite of all the efforts I have
made to conceal my emotion. Ah, if I could do as I
like, they should stay in their places and not approach
the Holy Table." While Eustelle was speaking in
this strain, Anastasia would silently watch her, for
her face at such times beamed with radiance, and
when, in conversing, the Name of Jesus passed her
lips, or fell upon her ear, she seemed to take fire, as if
she beheld Him or was pressing Him to her heart.
"My Love ! My Love !" she would exclaim ; "for
Thee I desire to live, for Thee I desire to die !"

Her facility of being affected by divine things

sometimes well-nigh incapacitated her for taking her
part in singing the praises of God in church. She
had a beautiful voice, and her assistance was therefore
much valued in the village choir ; but if the canticle
happened, for instance, to celebrate the love of Jesus
for souls in His Sacrament of Love, the words so
deeply affected her that her voice would die away
amidst her tears. Her emotion could not always
pass unobserved by her companions, and they would
beg her to remain although she could not sing : " We
are enough without you," whispered her neighbour to
her one day ; " but I wish you to be always by me,
even when you cannot join your voice with ours ; "
and Marie-Eustelle, much as she disliked betraying
her irresistible emotions, kept her place in the choir,
in order not to disoblige her companions. They loved
to have her near them, for her vicinity seemed to
kindle their own fervour, and they loved herself too,
and for what she truly was, not, as her old worldly
friends had loved her, for · her mere amiable and
agreeable companionship. Her virtues had triumphed
in the end. The last little outcry we hear of was
when she took to dressing always in black, in token
of being dead to the world. Although there was
otherwise nothing singular in her attire, yet folly,
extravagance, and pride were once again imputed to
her. But the lustre of her virtues had become too
bright to allow the clouds which envy or prejudice
would raise to gather again about her ; soon they
were to melt away for ever and leave the aureole of
sanctity shining in undimmed splendour on her brow.

"The inhabitants of the parish of Saint-Pallais," says
the Abbé Guérin,* "had the utmost veneration for

* Armand Guérin, the young seminarist already mentioned.

her during the last two years of her life, and no
request she might make was ever refused. 'She is an
admirable girl; she is a saint'—such were the expressions even of an habitual scoffer after hearing her
speak for a few minutes." One day Eustelle was
leaving the house of an ecclesiastic when a gentleman
distinguished alike for his rank and personal merits
was entering. He had, of course, but a passing
glance, and, besides, was entirely ignorant who she
was, never having even heard of her ; but the first
words he uttered after greeting his friend were, " Oh,
Monsieur l'Abbé, I never saw a saint, but certainly
she who has just left your door is one. What an
angelic face !" We may add the testimony of a
gentlewoman of the neighbourhood, who averred that
the remembrance of Eustelle's "angelic countenance"
during her long thanksgivings after communion was
still a source of edification to those who had been
used to witness it. The very sight of her enkindled
fervour : accordingly this lady was in the habit of
getting as near as she could to her during Mass, and
those were happy days with her when she had enjoyed
this advantage, for she seemed (she said) to love our
Lord the better. She once asked Eustelle to accompany her to a neighbouring parish where there was
to be Benediction of the Blessed Sacrament; the
office being concluded, she turned to her companion
to ask her when she would be ready to go. Never
(she said) should she forget the countenance which
was raised to her, for never had she beheld anything
like its supernatural beauty. Eustelle seemed all immersed in the love of Jesus, tears were on her face :
" My request, I own," adds the lady, " must have
been anything but agreeable to her, yet, that I might

not suspect anything, she came away almost immediately."

But what Eustelle laboured to conceal, with the secretive instinct of those who have found "the pearl of great price," could no longer be hid : "All in this young girl breathes of Eternity," said one to whom she had simply given a letter which she had been commissioned to convey to her. If, however, much of Eustelle's saintliness penetrated the veil with which she sedulously endeavoured to shroud it, on Anastasia alone was the privilege conferred of contemplating it in hours of unreserve and confidence. "I thank, and shall ever thank, our Lord," she says, "for the great favour He granted me in permitting me to enjoy Eustelle's conversation. I was very timid, and had the greatest difficulty in opening my mind to any one when I needed advice ; this good Eustelle alone inspired me with so much confidence that by degrees I began to communicate to her all my anxieties, fears, and perplexities ; and in her I found all that I desired. My confidence was accompanied by a profound respect ; if I had been less reserved, and had ventured to question her, no doubt she would have told me much more concerning herself. Everything about her drew you towards our good God. Her heart was a furnace in which divine love was always burning ; and those who approached it felt its heat in proportion to their own desire to love the God of the Altar. I can venture to say that I never knew any soul so far advanced in the ways of perfection. Her conversation has been more useful to me than many sermons ; I ought to be ashamed of myself for having remained so far behind. Oh, what good this excellent friend did me !" Sister Anastasia then laments her inability to recall to mind all Eustelle's impassioned expressions of divine love. Her conversation, in fact, was all of love; and "the God of the Eucharist was all she sighed for. Him only she desired; Him only she sought; her heart carried her away, and then she said more than she intended to say. She was as one beside herself with love. One day in particular that she came to see me, three or four words escaped her lips which I cannot recall, but the effect remains: they were like flames which burned me, and I felt when I heard them an immense desire to love Jesus enkindled within me, accompanied by a clear inward light which manifested to me the saintliness of this favoured soul. I seem to see her yet with her face all on fire, ready to exclaim, like St. Francis Xavier, 'Enough, Lord, enough! I can bear no more!'" A witness to these transports of love, Anastasia inwardly humbled herself, candidly confessing, "and good reason I had to do so." All of a sudden Marie-Eustelle seemed like one awaking from a trance: "My dear friend," she said, "I fear I have been wanting in humility"—not knowing into what expressions she might have been betrayed during her enraptured state. "No," replied the sister, "be quite easy about that. It is God who permits it for my good: praise be to Him for it! I do not esteem you any the more: you count for nothing therein; I see only the goodness of Jesus and His love for your soul: it is He who works all within you; you have but to correspond to His graces." Sister Anastasia with true instinctive delicacy had made the only reply which could have reassured her friend. "Indeed!" replied Eustelle, quite charmed, and yielding again to her former movement, "you see things in this light,

P

do you? Ah, what pleasure you give me, how happy I am! I shall feel more at my ease with you now."

We have reason to be grateful for this good sister's prudent reply, since it was, no doubt, the key which unlocked many treasures which otherwise had remained jealously concealed ; for Marie-Eustelle, free now from the fear of scandalizing her friend, allowed herself occasionally the satisfaction of seeking a little relief by giving expression to the intense love pent up within her heart. Anastasia has left on record a few specimens of these rapturous outbursts, during which Eustelle ceased to address her listening companion, and at times seemed almost to forget her presence. "O my Love! O God of the Eucharist! why can I not remain day and night near Thy prison of love? Oh, may I at least be ever in spirit there where love keeps Thee enchained for us! I cannot think of Thee, my Beloved, without being carried out of myself, without being all transported into Thee, O my Joy, my Delight, my Life! I am not happy anywhere except with Thee. How I desire to love Thee always more and more, O my dearest Master! Would that I could make Thee known and loved by so many souls still sitting in darkness! How I envy the lot of those zealous missionaries who cross the seas, and expose themselves to tortures and death, that they may gain souls to Jesus Christ. O Lord, why hast Thou made me so worthless a thing, and hast given me high and ardent desires which I can never accomplish? I languish and suffer from the need I feel to sacrifice myself that I may win be it but one soul to Jesus. But why do I complain of these languors and sufferings? I love them. Augment,

Lord, both my sufferings and my longings; since I can do nothing, let them supply for my incapacity. May I procure Thy glory as far as it is in my power to do so. O Jesus, I would love Thee like a St. Teresa, like a St. Francis Xavier! May I love Thee, Lord, as much as Thou desirest I should love Thee! My heart is very small, but Thou canst enlarge it, and so fill it with Thy love that I may die of it. That is all my desire: grant it, sweet Jesus! People die of profane love: why, then, should not a very ardent love of God also cause death! O Jesus, Jesus! O Name so sweet to my heart! Jesus, do Thou kindle in me such a flame that I may expire at the foot of the altar, nigh to that tabernacle in which Love dwells! O beloved tabernacle, why cannot I take thy place? Thou knowest not thy happiness. Then should I continually possess my Jesus, as thou dost, night and day. But what am I saying? vain desires which never shall be satisfied! O Jesus, I seem to hear Thee say, 'What wouldst thou have more, my daughter? Each morning I come in communion to repose on the altar of thy heart.'" Here Anastasia interrupted her rapturous colloquy by saying, "That is true: what more would you have? You have all that can be given to you." "Yes," replied Eustelle, "but my desires increase in proportion. I would have our Lord ever sacramentally present in my heart, or, at least, be myself continually at the foot of the altar, from morning till night, and from night till morning. Ah, why," she continued, again borne aloft in spirit by her impetuous movements of love—"why am I not always shut up with this inestimable Friend in His dear prison—always, always! When I think of this, my heart leaves me to go to

Jesus; I am left without strength; 'stay me, for I languish with love.'" Such were Eustelle's ejaculatory prayers, which at every moment were going up, like incense, from her heart, but which it was given to this one favoured friend alone to hear audibly pronounced and to record for our admiration.

Anastasia asked her one day how often she thought of Jesus. "What a question you ask me!" replied Eustelle; "I should be very much puzzled to tell you how often." "That is because you are always thinking of Him?" rejoined her companion. "It is so sweet," said Eustelle, without making any direct reply to this query,—"it is so sweet to think of what one loves. You know our Lord told us that our heart is there where our treasure is. My good friend, let us love this God who is so little loved now because He is so little known. What pain this thought gives me! Thou art not known, my Saviour; and what makes me groan still more deeply is that Thou art not known by those who ought to know Thee best. Oh, wherefore is it not in my power to remedy this forgetfulness! O my Saviour, since I cannot effect what I wish, at least grant my prayers." We see here why Eustelle so constantly calls our Lord the God Unknown and the Love Unknown. She was ever mourning over the indifference of Christians, and making reparation to Him in her heart by acts of love. "One day,"—it is still Sister Anastasia who speaks,—"having something to communicate to Marie-Eustelle, I entered the sacristy. I found her all on fire with the love of Jesus, but much more so than usual. She could scarcely speak: her heart was full, oppressed; she would fain have relieved it a little by pouring it into mine, but the fear of wounding the

fair virtue of humility restrained her." Anastasia
knew her so well that she read her thoughts at a
glance, and was all attention to catch what might fall
from her lips. Eustelle's first remark gave the clue
to what was passing within her, and, indeed, some
explanation of her state seemed to be due to the in-
quiring look of her friend. "I fervently pray our
Lord to attract numbers of worshippers to Himself.
When I see a great many of the faithful come to the
church to testify to Him their love or their gratitude
I am filled with joy. I suffer much when I see Him
abandoned; and yet I prefer being alone at the foot
of the tabernacle. Can you understand that?" Sister
Anastasia replied in the affirmative. Instantly her
face became all radiant with heavenly light, and in a
transport of joy she exclaimed, "How! you understand? But it is not possible. Tell me, dear friend,
what you understand;" and her whole countenance
and attitude seemed to interrogate one who, as she
feared, had half surprised her secret. "Well," rejoined the sister, "when you are alone with Jesus
you follow the inspiration of your heart; your love
feels at its ease; and you do things from which you
would abstain if there were any one else in the
church." "What things?" asked Eustelle, whose
eager anxiety seemed far from allayed by this reply;
"what do you mean? Did you ever see me do anything? Explain yourself." "No, my good Eustelle;
but our Lord gives you so much love for Him, that
you cannot contain yourself, and you go as near to
the tabernacle as you can." Anastasia says no more,
and whether she explained herself further we know
not; but she had detected Eustelle's secret, and
Eustelle perceived as much. "You ought to have

seen her at that moment," observes the sister; "she was like one distracted, distracted with love!" "What an idea is this of yours!" she said, for still she would fain have concealed what her friend had discovered, or thought she had discovered, although her own impassioned emotions plainly confessed the truth of the surmise. "Would you not be scandalized at such conduct? Would *you* act in that way?" she inquired. "No, I should not act so, but I should not be scandalized." "Oh, is that possible?" Eustelle rejoined;—"a person like me!" The fear of scandal removed, she no longer attempts any disguise, but she is alarmed, and adds, "I will not continue, however, without consulting my director: I hope he will give his consent." "I do not think, my good Eustelle," replied Anastasia, "that your director can consent." "Yet I persuade myself of the contrary, dear friend; the burning ardour which I feel makes me so much need refreshment. But if he forbids, I will suffer and obey." And, in fact, she did submit; but many a time she said to Anastasia, "Death would be preferable to me: the fire which consumes me is too devouring." We shall return to this subject when we have occasion to speak of her letters to her director, where we shall find her giving more details than Anastasia has furnished or possibly knew.

We will now follow the two friends into a meadow near Saint-Pallais. It was one Sunday after High Mass, Marie-Eustelle having, contrary to custom, proposed to take a walk. "How have you been able to persuade yourself," asked the somewhat astonished sister, "to leave your 'dear sacristy' so soon, against your usual practice?" "Our Lord moved me to do so," was Eustelle's simple reply. "It is because your heart

is too full, is it not?" "Oh yes, indeed it is," Eustelle
candidly rejoined; and forthwith she began to speak
with so much unction and with such passionate
fervour of the love of God, that Anastasia felt the
infectious flame seizing on her own heart, and, like
the disciples at Emmaus, could have exclaimed,
"*Nonne cor nostrum ardens erat in nobis, dum
loqueretur in via?*—(Was not our heart burning
within us, whilst He spoke in the way?)" for Jesus
seemed to be speaking by the lips of His spouse. She
had, indeed, as Anastasia observed, been compelled to
leave the church, because she could no longer restrain
the inward fire, and must needs communicate of it to
another. Yet the sister was unable to recall anything
beyond mere fragments of the conversation: could
she have retailed it all, she would probably have
experienced no little dissatisfaction, and the reader
some disappointment, for words which come all
glowing from the heart are cold and lifeless by comparison when set down on paper. If this is the case
with mere natural eloquence, how much more when
it is the Spirit of Grace that animates the speaker!
And then there is the mute power of that speaker's
presence. Anastasia remembered how they sat together
on the grass in this pleasant mead, and how every
sweet sight and sound seemed to furnish fresh fuel to
the fire of divine love in Marie-Eustelle's heart. She
plucked a flower, and looked lovingly at it, for her
Beloved had made that flower; His wisdom had been
occupied on it, and His love had decked it with a
ray of His own beauty. "Admire," she said, "the
power and the greatness of Him who formed it! See
how good our Master is! His goodness shines even
in His creatures." "I cannot," said Anastasia, "call

to mind her expressions, but I remember that she talked to me about the pure love of God for His own sake, a love which loses sight of self and its interests. ' You think,' said I, ' neither of recompense nor punishment, is it not so?' ' I think only of loving God for His own sake, not mine,' was Eustelle's reply." The words she spoke were few and simple ; it was the look, the manner, with which they were spoken which so impressed the listener. Presently Marie-Eustelle interrupted herself, and said sweetly to her companion, " It seems always my turn to talk ; dear friend, do you speak too." But Anastasia was struck dumb by her admiration and delight, and was unable to do anything but listen : " Beg our Lord," she murmured, " that I may practise what I have heard." " How I loved," adds this holy woman, " to gaze at her when she was speaking of Jesus ! " A certain splendour seemed at those times to emanate from her and invest her whole exterior with a supernatural brightness. It was the love of Jesus, who had made her heart His tabernacle, which seemed thus to render itself sensible. Anastasia felt its warmth. She has already told us that Eustelle's words, when she spoke in the transports of her love, acted like fire on her own soul ; and now we find her confessing a secret desire she used to entertain, a desire in which human softness and tenderness had no part : " How often," she says, " when I was near her, did the thought come to me of laying my head on her bosom, as St. John on that of Jesus ; but I feared to pain her humility, and never ventured to express my wish."

CHAPTER II.

THE SACRISTY AND THE ALTAR.

OUR Lord, who had called Eustelle to the special life
of honouring Him in the Adorable Sacrament of the
Altar, placed her also in circumstances most favourable to the devotion with which He had inspired her.
It is common in the rural parishes of France to select
some good and pious young woman for the office of
attending to the altar, and taking care of the linen
belonging to it. The girl to whom this charge had
been entrusted, observing Eustelle's fervour, felt sure
that, in requesting her to assist her in her labours,
she should only be proposing what would prove a
most grateful employment. Eustelle joyfully assented,
and manifested such zeal and assiduity in her work
that the Curé afterwards gave her the entire super-
intendence of the sacristy. She thus became bound
by a tie of duty to the altar, to which love had long
attached her. Her whole life henceforth centred
round it. Who could attempt to describe the high
veneration which Eustelle entertained for the august
office with which she found herself invested ? How
few, indeed, even of those who discharge this function
with decorum and respect, can be said to rise to a full
conception of its dignity, and of the deep reverence
with which they ought to approach and touch the
altar, while not seldom, alas ! (as Eustelle's biographer
sadly remarks) mercenaries will acquit themselves of
their sacred charge in a cold, perfunctory spirit, which
too clearly betrays itself in their manner. The Curé
of Saint-Pallais, the same to whom so many of her

letters are addressed, obtained for Eustelle a special permission to touch the sacred vessels. We find her thanking him for it, and saying that, in the absence of the sacristan, she had several times availed herself of the privilege in preparing the altar for the Holy Sacrifice. When thus engaged, she loved to think of our Lady's* employment in the service of the Temple, and this reflection again added to her gratitude. " But to be worthy of this holy office," she says, " I ought to have the purity of the Blessed Virgin, which I am so far from possessing." And then she reproaches herself with being so entirely absorbed in the enjoyment she derived from ·her occupation, that she did not sufficiently reflect on the account she would have to render of these multiplied means of grace. As usual, love swallowed up, or, rather, converted every other feeling into itself; for it was love, after all, a love which supereminently contained every virtue, which rendered that enjoyment so keen as to make her seem unmindful of all else. Every object connected with the worship of God became an occasion to Marie-Eustelle to testify her love for Jesus in the tabernacle. All things in her mind converged to that point; every thought, every act tended thither. The Bishop of La Rochelle had sent some relics to the Curé of Saint-Pallais for his church, and Eustelle was

---

* The thought of uniting oneself in heart to the Blessed Virgin in adoring and loving Jesus, principally in the mystery of the Eucharist, gave rise to the community of *Marie-Réparatrice*, the plan of which was conceived on the ever memorable 8th of December, 1854. This congregation numbers now several houses, and is under the direction of the Jesuit Fathers, on whose rule its own is based. The *Archiconfrérie de la Communion Réparatrice* in union with Mary was instituted for the faithful at the same time, and in January, 1863, numbered no less than 25,000 associates.

employed to embroider the cloth on which they were to be placed. The work was very elaborate, minute, and arduous; but, as she remarks in a letter to a priest, "in working for the honour of the saints, we honour our Lord, that worthiest Friend of our souls. It is a means of adorning the house which He inhabits for us, for me—yes, for me. Oh, how this thought increases my love! Oh, how little worthy is this house of His greatness! What attractions ought not His tabernacle to possess in our eyes, since it contains Him who is all love, and all whose love is for us!" And then, forgetting entirely the relics and the embroidery, she proceeds to pour forth her whole heart in adoring praise of the Eucharistic God. "Glory, love to this Divine Master, to this dear Brother, to this Beloved of our souls! May He bless you when you kneel at His feet; may He inflame your heart when you possess Him. Like the spouse in the Canticles, let Him slumber upon your heart; His repose will refresh you; His closed eyes will open yours; the beatings of His Heart will cause your own to palpitate."

True love is never satisfied that it has done enough, or that enough has been done. It never acquiesces contentedly in its own incapacity to do more. It aspires even to impossibilities. Poor Eustelle, witnessing the bareness and destitution of the altars of God, inwardly groaned and sighed; she would have wished to see all the treasures of earth consecrated to the enriching and adorning of His sanctuary. Having herself no treasures to bestow, she offered her ardent desires in compensation, and laboured to the best of her ability to adorn, and induce others to help in adorning, the humble church which was the nearest object of her solicitude. She had a graceful way of her own in begging on such occasions : "I want two francs more," she said one day to an acquaintance ; "and you know the person very well who can give me them." On vigils she might be seen almost the entire day in the church ; and each time she passed the tabernacle, not satisfied with making her genuflection, she would remain on her knees for a minute in adoration. On these days she would often forget to eat, as her sister would discover afterwards by finding her food untouched. In the year 1841, she had a great desire to adorn the altar of Our Lady with a beautiful covering for the festival of the patron saint, but money was wanting. She knew not to whom to apply, or, might we not rather say, she well knew to whom to apply ? Prostrate before Mary's image she told her dear mother with a childlike simplicity and confidence how much she desired to make her this offering, but had not the means to gratify her wish. It was a Sunday : on the very next day the funds were supplied. Her friends observing—as who could fail of observing ?—that she gave herself no rest, and that her health was visibly declining, remonstrated with her upon the sacrifice she was making ; but she replied, "It is a need with me rather than a sacrifice."

The charge she had received did but add fresh fuel to the zeal for God's house with which she was devoured, and her affections were by no means exclusively concentrated on the little church of Saint-Pallais. A zealous interest will often be felt about the sacred edifice wherein we ourselves habitually worship, which fades almost into coolness when we step beyond our own loved neighbourhood. It has

necessarily the first claim ; but how often under this
specious plea does a real lack of love for our Lord
shelter itself, proving how much of self there is in our
apparently purest aspirations.   There was no selfish
narrowness in   Marie-Eustelle's zeal.   As Jesus
multiplies Himself and is enthroned in the Sacred
Host on thousands of altars, so would this holy girl
have wished to multiply her own homage, and adore
and minister to His glory everywhere.   It was a
favourite devotion of hers to transport herself in spirit
to those sanctuaries where the Blessed Sacrament was
the most neglected.   Many such she knew there were
in her own France, in little country places still poorer
than Saint-Pallais.   Deep was her grief at the thought
of their poverty, their meanness, their destitution, all
unworthy of their sacred destination ; but deeper far
at the remembrance of Jesus, the Lord of her heart,
abiding unvisited and unknown day after day within
those desolate walls.   And then she remembered with
profound sympathy and compassion the priests called
to minister therein, and the secret groanings of their
hearts seemed to find an echo in her own.   In March,
1840, she writes to the former Curé of Saint-Pallais,
telling him that she is forwarding to him six lavabos,
three purificatories, two corporals, an altar-cloth, and
two amices ; she excuses herself at the same time for
sending so little ; and not long after we find her
busying herself in the preparation of some sacerdotal
vestments.   A charitable association called *L'Œuvre
de la Miséricorde* had recently been formed at La
Rochelle, the object of which was to furnish poor
parishes with furniture and ornaments for the altar,
thus performing a work of charity towards the Man-
God under His Sacramental veils.   Marie-Eustelle

hastened to recommend this institution to every one
by word and example, exhorting all her friends to
join it.* The Abbé Guérin, that diligent collector and
recorder of the acts and words of the kind friend of
his childhood, speaks also of the zeal and vigilance
with which Eustelle tended the lamp which burned
before the Blessed Sacrament.   None but the Catholic
heart can appreciate the feelings with which the
devout children of the Church regard and cherish
that solitary light, that mysterious flame, which night
and day watches and burns, offering mute adoration
before the God who has made Himself mute for our
sakes in His Eucharistic prison.   Holy souls have
always felt a peculiar love for this perpetual adorer,
"the Lamp of the Sanctuary," who thus fills our
place and performs our office, the live-long night, and
alas ! too often is the solitary worshipper during the
live-long day.   "How I wish," said M. Olier, "that
I were of the nature of oil, that I might be ever consuming before the Most Holy Sacrament !   O ye
lamps of the sanctuary, how happy are ye to be all
consuming to the glory of the Lord !"   We shall find
Eustelle emulating this holy man ; day no longer
sufficed her, she ardently desired to adore by night
also before the tabernacle.   Often she begged the Curé
to let her have the key of the sanctuary : "But he
will not give it me," she said to Sister Anastasia, "so
of course our Lord does not will it either.   Indeed, I
feel that I should exceed all bounds, and should never
be able to tear myself away from the holy place.   Oh,
one is so happy near that furnace of love !   One

* This single association provided sixty poor churches with
furniture for the fitting celebration of the Divine Mysteries in
the space of less than four years.

thinks of nothing but loving and suffering for the Beloved Object."

The long-desired favour, however, was granted her before the festival of Corpus Christi and during its octave. At that time the procession of the Blessed Sacrament on the *Fête Dieu* was not permitted: the King of kings was not allowed to show Himself in public. Such (as Eustelle's biographer remarks) was the *liberty* men owed to the Revolution—that lying word which for half a century in France was employed to cloak every servitude and every apostasy. To compensate the faithful as far as possible for this loss, the good priest of Saint-Pallais purposed erecting several little temporary *reposoirs*, or altars, within the sacred edifice, upon which the Blessed Sacrament could be successively enthroned, and from which Benediction might be given. The preparation of the *reposoirs* was to be the work of his pious sacristan. It would require a considerable time, and so Eustelle must have the key. She asks for it, and her request is granted. She has it at last—that coveted key, the object of her sleepless longings. She has it now: and who can describe her joy? It seemed as if she had obtained the key of the Heart of Jesus. "She remained the whole time," says her friend, "in a continual state of contemplation, and the night passed away without her perceiving it." During those happy days, followed by still happier nights, if Sister Anastasia was able to seize an interval to speak with her, Eustelle would unaffectedly express her delight. "What happiness!" she would exclaim; "I am free to do as I please, there is no one to see me; I can indulge all my follies (*Je fais toutes mes folies*)." What these follies were we shall afterwards see. In a letter to her friend, the former Curé of Saint-Pallais, she thus alludes to her feelings during her night watchings : "How happy I was, thus alone in the presence of our good Saviour ! I should have wished never to leave Him. Oh, what joy one tastes, and what illumination one receives at the feet of the Eternal ; above all, in the silence of night ! There I was, with only the feeble light of the lamp, which, consuming itself before God, reminded me that I, too, ought to burn and consume away in His presence, to honour by the entire destruction of self His supreme greatness and sovereignty." As we think of this holy girl worshipping during those long nights in that obscure village church, we seem to behold one who in God's designs is helping to lay the foundation of that admirable devotion of our day, the nocturnal adoration of the Blessed Sacrament, which was established only a few years later at Paris.* She was at least preluding on earth the perpetual adoration of

---

* The biographer of Marie-Eustelle enumerates several works directed to the object of ministering to the honour and worship of God in the Blessed Sacrament, which took their rise but a few years after her death, and to the formation of which we may believe that her prayers and her example contributed their full share. Two, in particular, have spread with great rapidity. The *Œuvre des Tabernacles* was begun at Paris by thirty ladies belonging to the *Adoration nocturne à domicile* in the year 1847, for the purpose of supplying poor churches with all the requisites for worship. The value of the articles thus distributed, which as far as is possible are manufactured by the members of the association with their own hands, amounted a few years ago to between 50,000 and 60,000 francs. The *Œuvre des Lampes* was begun in 1855 with the object of providing lamps for the tabernacle in poor churches, under the condition of their being kept burning by night as well as by day. This association has been enriched by the Sovereign Pontiff with many indulgences. It had already had the happiness, a few years ago, of lighting 24,000 lamps in honour of the Blessed Sacrament.

Heaven. We have her own word for her having on one occasion spent four, and at another five, whole days consecutively before the tabernacle. Such prolonged elevation of the soul to God would be utterly impossible unless prayer had already become a kind of beatific rest.

Marie-Eustelle loved the sacristy. It was the vestibule of the sanctuary, the antechamber of the throne-room of the Eternal King, next to the church itself, the Holy of Holies, the most august and venerable spot in the world. She called it her "dear sacristy," to which expression we have seen Sister Anastasia allude, and not a few of her letters are dated from it. Many persons who desired her advice preferred seeking her there; and, indeed, it was there they were the most likely to find her : she would gladly never have left it except for the foot of the altar. Her office included that of washing the altar linen, and in this occupation she took an inexpressible delight. Angels watched and adored where the Sacred Body of Jesus had lain, and kept guard over the garments which had enveloped It; what numbers, then, may we conceive invisibly worship around every object which still, 'so to say, retains the perfume of His Eucharistic Presence ! Eustelle seemed to have borrowed of their seraphic ardour when her hands pressed the sacred altar linen, as precious in her eyes as the swaddling-bands of Bethlehem or the winding-sheet of Calvary. So occupied during the day was the servant of the Lord with this one thought, Jesus in the Eucharist, to which her new office had brought her as near as to her was possible, that in slumber her mind still dwelt on the same engrossing subject, and then her thoughts would take a body, and assume the sem-

Q

blance of realities.   Eustelle had too much native tact
and delicacy to entertain others, as the uneducated are
so prone to do, by retailing her dreams; yet once the
illusion was so vivid and complete, and withal so
sweet, that she could not resist confiding it to Anastasia.   She was at the altar, was saying Mass, had
already opened the tabernacle, was about to take the
ciborium in her hand—with what childlike enthusiasm
did she paint her rapturous delight, and then the
sudden awakening, with its sad, sad disenchantment:
it was but a dream after all.

A confraternity of the Blessed Sacrament had existed for some time at Saint-Pallais, established, no
doubt, by the zeal of one of its good priests, a zeal ill
responded to by that tepid little place.   The confraternity lingered on until the year 1839, when it was
suppressed because of the small number of the associates, and, still more, on account of their lack of
fervour.   The Exposition and Benediction customary
on the second Thursdays in every month ceased in
consequence.   Eustelle's grief may be imagined: "Is
it possible," she exclaimed, "that faith can be so
weak?"   She felt it to be a renewed call upon her to
exert herself to make amends to Jesus for the love
and homage denied Him by the coldness of others.
When communion was borne to the sick, Eustelle
always followed to do honour to her Lord: "You
cannot conceive," she said to Anastasia, "what I feel
at those times when I get a sight of the ciborium: it
is happiness indescribable.   I keep as near as I can
to the minister of Jesus, particularly when outside
the village, but just on one side, so as to fix my eyes
on the little prison in which is enclosed my Master,
my Love, my Life—all, in fact, that I love!"   Some

persons (she added)—a proof, it may be noted, that
the censorious spirit was not quite silenced—-taxed this
practice of hers with idleness, but she little heeded
their observations. "Ah! if they knew our Lord,"
she said, "they would do quite as much as I do; I
pray this good Master to enlighten them, and make
them understand that it is no loss of time to follow
Him. Yes, as long as I have any strength remaining
I will accompany my Saviour." She then went on to
describe the arrival at the house of the sick: "Ah!
there truly it is that I admire and contemplate the
love of my Jesus. He comes to console the afflicted
on their bed of suffering, to inspire them with the
hope that their pains will soon cease, and that a
boundless felicity awaits them in Heaven. The priest
prostrates himself, opens the ciborium, takes his
Master in his hand: O happy moment! a transport-
ing thrill runs through me as soon as I perceive the
sacred species. What delight! I envy the happiness
of these sick people." Here she interrupted herself
to offer a prayer that they might themselves appreciate
that happiness, and then proceeded: "But Easter—
that is the happy time! then we set out early, we
make a good prayer going and returning, we pass
from house to house." "But suppose," asked her
friend, "that the Curé should forbid your accompany-
ing him on account of your ill-health and the tattling
of the village." "Oh," rejoined Eustelle quickly,
"there is no fatigue in following our Lord; and our
Curé, who knows my motives, gives no heed to all
that gossip. If he were to say a word, I would leave
it off, cost me what it might; but he leaves me to
myself. Our Lord permits it to be so: may He be
blessed for this!"

Q 2

The Curé of Saint-Pallais had revived a good custom which had fallen into disuse since the Revolution, of appointing persons to visit the houses of those to whom the Viaticum was to be administered, and make such decent preparation as was possible for doing honour to the Divine Guest. The pious Eustelle was naturally selected by him as best fitted for the office, and she received the charge with fervent gratitude to her Lord, accompanied with a deep sense of her own unworthiness. "In the state which He has willed for me," she says, "what higher function could He allot me?" We detect here again a touch of the holy envy with which she regarded the priestly office. On these occasions she might be seen setting off, happy and recollected, bearing a crucifix and a box containing all that was requisite for making the needful preparation. In a letter of hers to M. Briand we have a description of one of these visits, and the sentiments with which it had filled her mind :—"This morning the Hidden God was borne to a sick person. I had been previously at the house to prepare a little altar; when I saw the sacred ciborium placed upon it, how I longed to press it to my poor heart! The remembrance still gives me a thrill of emotion; and Thou, O Jesus, knowest well the suffering which my soul experiences from this cruel privation. I content myself with pouring out my boundless desires before my God. But when my functions permit of my kissing the sacred corporal on which He has reposed —how my heart all melts within me. What a flood of happiness, joy, and love! The remembrance of the goodness of our Lord in coming to this sick man, and the thought of His greatness annihilated under these fragile species, was the occasion of my receiving a new favour from this Love of Angels in communion. My soul was represented to me as the cradle of Jesus; it was during my thanksgiving that He thus manifested Himself to me, as at the age of six years. What a divine slumber! What a ravishing countenance! What perfect calm in all His features! And although He slept, He appeared to be thinking of me! I seem still to see Him. After so many benefits, very dear father, silence, love, admiration become my ordinary thanksgiving; I offer to Jesus my powerlessness to respond to His benefits; I consecrate to Him my life, which, little by little, is wearing away." After reading these lines, we can better realize the nature of that joy of which she spoke so feelingly to Anastasia. She had said (as we have seen) that as long as her strength permitted she would follow her Lord when He was being borne to the sick. She kept her word; but the days came when she could no longer walk, and scarcely could drag herself along from excess of feebleness. Yet, although unable to accompany the priest with the Blessed Sacrament, she would still laboriously make her way to the sick person's dwelling, however distant it might be, to make all things ready for the visit of Jesus. One day, however, her strength altogether forsook her in the street, and she would have fallen if one of her sisters had not run promptly and caught her in her arms. As soon as she was a little restored she proceeded on her way to discharge her office. This was just before the Easter of 1842, when the hand of death was already upon her; but there is a love which is as strong as death: such was Eustelle's.

CHAPTER III.

The Three Directors.*

It has been incidentally observed that Marie-Eustelle remained for some time without any director in the high paths of spirituality to which her Lord had called her. Not but that she submitted every case of difficulty to her ordinary confessors, and never took a step of any importance without consulting them ; but she does not appear to have given them any account of the extraordinary graces which she received in prayer. Later, two ecclesiastics must be considered as having been her directors, properly so called. The first was the priest to whom frequent allusion has been made ; he followed M. Jouslain, and preceded M. Laage de Saint-Germain ; and it is to him that a number of Eustelle's letters are addressed. He was a man of sincere piety, yet he not only wanted for experience, but did not seem so much as to suspect that others were more experienced than himself. Eustelle was very far from deficient in penetration, and she soon observed the high esteem he entertained for her, and

---

* Much of the information given in this chapter is derived from three dialogues, true in substance though fictitious in form, appended to the collection of Eustelle's writings, which were published long before the Life. They were preceded by an advertisement to the effect that one who had been intimately acquainted with this holy girl had collected her pious sentiments and observations, and thrown them into the form of dialogues with an imaginary person. It transpired afterwards that Mgr. Villecourt was himself the author. This invests the matter they contain with a new authority, and explains also the manner in which much of the information respecting Eustelle's directors was obtained.

the admiration he had conceived for the extraordinary graces of which she was the recipient. Much danger might have arisen in many cases from such an unguarded course. Spiritual pride so easily insinuates itself, and is, indeed, the main peril to be apprehended for those who tread in these exalted ways. But Eustelle's deep humility, coupled with a peculiarly straightforward simplicity, was her safeguard. She saw that her pastor thought very highly of her, but she thought not one whit more highly of herself on that account. His partiality, indeed, for his penitent might almost seem to have been divinely permitted for her consolation, for one of its results was the care he took to comfort her in her interior sufferings, and the encouragement he gave her during that trying season. She much needed this sustaining aid, and he thereby did her, she affirmed, a real service, for which she ever preserved a warm sense of gratitude. No sooner, however, did Eustelle begin to emerge from this path strewn with crosses, than he manifested a marked eagerness to become acquainted with the divine favours which she was beginning to receive in such abundance. Here was another snare to humility, but Eustelle equally escaped it, although she willingly replied to his inquiries; and this not from vanity— for she never appropriated to herself these rich gifts of her Lord, for which she only felt herself the more deeply indebted to Him—but because the means were thus furnished her for relieving her soul of the superabundance of its heavenly consolations. And so she told her pastor, as she could tell none other, of the love of Jesus towards her and of her own love for Jesus. He listened and was edified; perhaps it was as much for his own benefit as for Eustelle's refreshment that he was permitted to manifest this well-intentioned but incautious curiosity.

Not only, however, did he show the high esteem in which he held this gifted soul, but he also gave plain tokens of considering himself as ignorant and cold by comparison with her, traces of which occur in her replies to his letters; and he was in the habit of recommending himself in a special manner to her prayers. Eustelle did not judge him at the time, nay, she never judged him subsequently, but she could not help perceiving, particularly when she was able to compare his unreserve with the extreme caution evinced by the Bishop of La Rochelle, that the admiration betrayed by a good and pious man for the spiritual graces and gifts with which she was endowed, might have been calculated to suggest the temptation of thinking that there was something in herself which attracted these purely gratuitous favours of her Lord. As it was, she had ever been deeply penetrated with the conviction, that in whatever emanated from the infinite goodness of God, she had as many motives for self-humiliation as for gratitude. Accordingly, the temptation never having arisen, she did not until afterwards perceive the peril she had incurred. She then saw the course which it would have been proper to pursue in her case, a course involving less display of partiality, a closer sifting of her interior, and greater caution in deciding points on which it would have been well to consult ecclesiastical superiors. Such an idea, however, never occurred to this good Curé. He seems to have been a mixture of timidity and confidence, for he was confident where timidity would have been simple prudence, and timid where a little decision would have been highly desirable.

It would, for instance, have quite alarmed and altogether upset him to have to pen a letter on the subject of spiritual direction to the bishop, or to one of his grand vicars, and yet he would himself pronounce opinions without the least hesitation upon the most difficult and delicate questions. When Eustelle first imparted to him her desire to take a vow of perpetual chastity, he formally asserted that the Pope had expressly forbidden such engagements being contracted by persons living in the world. This was incorrect, as no doubt he discovered, since we have seen that he allowed her to hope for the permission at some future time—a permission which was eventually granted ; but he certainly did not err in this affair through defect of caution, while on the other hand he saw not the slightest difficulty in the case of a vow of humility which she desired to make. In fact, he authorized Eustelle to bind herself by such a vow, renewable every year, and apparently would not have refused his sanction to an irrevocable engagement of that nature ; whereas we shall find the bishop pronouncing an opinion on this subject of a widely different character. This priest was young, and consequently wanted for experience, but Eustelle bore testimony to his being a true friend of God, and felt sure that age and reflection would bring their fruits in a more clear discernment of the order established by God in His Church for the direction of souls ; the faithful looking to their priests for guidance, and they in their turn looking up to their hierarchical superiors for instruction in all cases of doubt or difficulty.

The second ecclesiastic before whom Marie-Eustelle laid the whole state of her soul, and whom she acquainted with the favours she had received, was a man

of very superior qualifications and a far wider experience. She entertained a deservedly high opinion
of her own pastor, M. Laage de Saint-Germain, who
had been appointed Curé of Saint-Pallais in August,
1837, but she felt as if his incessant occupations and
extremely weak health imposed on her the obligation
of laying no additional burden upon him, and of
limiting herself in confession to the accusation of her
faults. Besides, she told Sister Anastasia in confidence that she was afraid M. le Curé had too high
an opinion of her. This was probably her decisive
reason for not seeking any special direction from him,
which would have involved the manifestation of much
that would, no doubt, have singularly increased his
esteem for her. Eustelle was, in fact, beginning to
feel more and more the need of some master hand
which would probe the depths of her soul, and which
would review and scan her whole spiritual state with
a rigid, unsparing scrutiny. Consolation she no
longer needed, for her soul overflowed with heavenly
joy, and directors suitable for one stage in the progress
towards perfection will be no ways fitted for another.
Perhaps she felt this instinctively. She had now
entered those high regions in which not to advance is
grievously to fall ; so that, if humility is all-important
at the beginning, nay, the indispensable foundation of
the Christian character—if it be the necessary condition of every advance in grace—its preservation and
increase attain an importance hardly to be estimated
upon those lofty heights, where by its protection alone
can the soul be preserved from turning giddy at its
elevation. As the tree rises, the roots must descend.
Eustelle had placed her treasure under the safe keeping of her humility ; but how was that humility itself

to be kept, which was the greatest treasure of all, because the security of all else depended on its possession? The fear of losing it was never absent from her; and just as the miser trembles when he sees even a friendly eye rest on the spot where he has concealed his hoard, so did Eustelle shrink from exposing her treasure to the view of any one whose admiration might endanger its safety. Besides, there are ways which none can understand but those who have themselves trodden them, or to whom the spiritual life has been the subject of close and enlightened study. A deep discernment is also required, in order to discriminate between the operations of God's grace and that spirit of illusion of which holy souls always stand in dread.

For all these reasons Eustelle suffered much from the need she felt of an experienced director, and confided her embarrassment to Sister Anastasia. "What I want," she said, "is a Jesuit father, very learned and very pious." The good sister named M. Briand: "He is worth any Jesuit father," she said; and she then proceeded to give the reasons for her confidence in thus recommending him. She had often heard him preach, and his sermons bore the impress of practical experience; they bespoke a soul replenished with the Spirit of Jesus Christ, whom he evidently loved most ardently, and of whom he was always speaking in the pulpit. This worthy ecclesiastic, who was not overrated by the sister, was one of the clergy of Saintes, and a canon of La Rochelle, Luçon, and Evreux. He was extensively employed in the work of missions, and had been often selected to give retreats to priests, both secular and religious, in different dioceses. He was also distinguished as a writer, and universally known and esteemed for his many works of charity and zeal. Marie-Eustelle herself had heard him preach in the church of Saint-Pallais on Ascension Day in 1838, and felt disposed to follow her friend's advice; but nothing was ever undertaken by her without prayer. Many pray when in perplexity or trouble, but forget to do so, or, perhaps, do not think it necessary when reason and human prudence appear to furnish sufficient light to guide them; but saints pray always and upon all occasions, and thus entitle themselves to a very special direction in all their actions, besides obtaining a peculiar blessing upon them. "We must ascertain," she replied, "whether the good God wills it; so let us pray a great deal, that our Lord may let me know His Holy Will." And so, although she appeared to possess all the information requisite for forming at once a reasonable and discreet judgment, and although she was extremely desirous of coming to a decision, she prayed and got others to pray for four months. At the end of that time M. Briand was preaching the Advent in the cathedral church of Saint-Pierre at Saintes, and Eustelle felt moved to lay her whole interior before him. She told him all that passed within her, gave him an account of her manner of prayer, and made him acquainted with the extraordinary favours of which she was so frequent a recipient. As Eustelle was inspired to have recourse to M. Briand, so also was he moved to correspond to the confidence she reposed in him. He received her with the greatest kindness, and made no difficulty, notwithstanding his multiplied occupations, in giving her all the requisite time and attention. After having, with the utmost care and caution, studied the

case submitted to his consideration, he could not fail
to recognize an extraordinary work of God in
Eustelle's soul. He was able, accordingly, to dispel
all her anxieties, and to assure her that the devil had
no share in what was being operated within her. It
was for this assurance Eustelle had so ardently
longed, and which she could not feel she possessed so
long as she communicated only with those who,
however much entitled to her respect and personal
gratitude and affection, had apparently little acquaintance with the ways she was called to tread.
She thus gives expression to her joy in one of her
letters to the former Curé of Saint-Pallais : "He
tells me that he has examined everything, analyzed
everything, and in all sees only testimonies to a love
of predilection on the part of our Lord towards me.
I am no longer the same person since my mind has
been thus settled, which for a long time it has not
been. The way by which God is leading me is not
unknown to this ecclesiastic. You can scarcely form
an idea of his faith and love of God. As for me, his
words quite set my heart on fire, and I see well what
great profit I may derive from him. I purpose going
about once a fortnight to acquaint him with what
passes within me. It is not," she adds, "that I want
for confidence in him who is my ordinary guide ; God
knows it. But it is the Lord's will that, in certain
states of the soul, we should receive light from Him
by this or that person to whom He communicates it.
Of this we are advertised by a special attraction or
interior voice, which cannot deceive us, because it has
nothing in it which in the least degree assimilates it to
the fancies or caprices of light and inconstant souls."
And then she begs her former director not to forget

her in his prayers and always to beg humility for her.
" It is," she says, " the ladder of heaven and the
foundation of sanctity ; I have need of it in proportion to the graces which I receive." To M. Briand
himself she writes, "What a consolation for my
soul, after so many privations and trials, to be able to
pour itself forth unreservedly into the bosom of a
good father, into the heart of a friend of Jesus !
What a joy to have found a support to my weakness,
a guide in the way by which God is leading me !"
May He be for ever blessed, and may He, while
you await the joys of our true country, bestow on
you the plenitude of the gifts of His Spirit of
Love." This gratitude Eustelle carried with her to
the tomb, nay beyond the tomb, for we shall find
her director receiving testimonies of her grateful remembrance after she had passed to her everlasting
reward.

If Eustelle thus highly appreciated the benefit of
M. Briand's guidance, he himself set no less a value
on the spiritual profit he derived from his knowledge
of this favoured soul. He writes to his bishop in
these terms : " I bless, and shall all my life bless, our
Divine Master, who has moved this holy girl, Eustelle,
to open her heart to me, by making me acquainted
with the treasures of grace and the admirable gifts
with which the Holy Spirit has vouchsafed to enrich
her. I am full of the memory of so many virtues."
Not content with this testimony to her merit, M. Briand
many years later, as though with a presentiment that
he was soon to follow Marie-Eustelle to the home of
bliss where they are now eternally united, desired to
leave a formal document, to be deposited in the
archives of the diocese, recording his firm conviction

of her exalted sanctity. It was in substance as follows :—

"After offering the Holy Sacrifice of the Mass to obtain of God the grace to state the truth, and nothing but the truth, I, the undersigned, honorary canon of La Rochelle, declare, as upon oath, to Mgr. Clément Villecourt, Bishop of La Rochelle and of Saintes, that, desiring, as far as lies in my power, to make known the perfection of the virtues of Marie-Eustelle Harpain, of Saint-Pallais, I can attest that this beautiful soul, moved in all things by the grace of the Holy Spirit, has never manifested in her words, her behaviour, or her relations with me for the direction of her devotion, the shadow even of a sentiment of the human and natural order. Her heart was filled only with the love of our Lord in the Eucharist ; she lived for the Saviour alone ; her mind, enlightened by the most lively faith, recognized in the person of her director only the representative and minister of the Man-God.

"Likewise I solemnly attest that, during the three years that it pleased the Lord to confide to me the charge of this innocent soul, I experienced the greatest benefit from the communications she made to me respecting her own interior. She inspired me with a high esteem and a profound respect for the gifts she had received from Heaven, and was for me an angel of peace, of charity, and of edification. The very sight of her made me cherish the virtues of the priesthood, and imparted to me a recollection of mind which inclined me to the love of God . . . . To have had the happiness of being the depository of the secrets of this chosen soul, to have known the treasure of extraordinary graces with which she had been enriched, will be to me a motive for gratitude to God until my last breath . . . . Marie-Eustelle has made me love our Lord.

"In testimony whereof, at Saintes, the Feast of St. Jane Frances de Chantal, 1852,

"L'Abbé Briand,
"Honorary Canon of La Rochelle,
"Luçon, and Evreux."

The Bishop of La Rochelle must be reckoned as Eustelle's third director, although his earliest interview with her appears to have taken place before she consulted M. Briand; for at the first meeting with Mgr. Villecourt Eustelle did not acquaint him with any of the wonderful operations of grace in her soul. This interview was brought about in consequence of a desire which she had expressed to her ordinary confessor, the Curé of Saint-Pallais, apparently with regard to some penitential practices. M. de Laage, feeling reluctant to pronounce upon the question, recommended that it should be referred to the bishop. Mgr. Villecourt was expected shortly to visit Saintes, but as some matter of business was taking Eustelle to La Rochelle about this time, he availed himself of the opportunity to furnish her with a letter to him. It ran as follows :—

"My Lord,—This letter will be presented to you by a young person belonging to my parish who is going to see two of her friends, postulants in the convent of La Providence. She would desire to obtain permission from your lordship to enter the convent enclosure. This young woman is the model of my parish, one of those privileged souls whose virtues are of a rare and exalted order. Last year she expressed to me her wish to wear a hair-shirt, but as in these matters I do not like to act upon my own authority, I deferred the execution of her desire to your earliest visit to Saintes, promising to consult you then, and procure her an interview with your lordship. As she was herself going to La Rochelle, she begged me to write to you; but if you would have the kindness to hear her once in confession, she would then feel more at her ease with you, and you would feel better acquainted with the state of her soul. I should also myself be better satisfied in regard to my decision on certain points which she will explain to you. I allow her to communicate daily. She lives by the work of her hands, and has very delicate health, two reasons which prevented me from acceding to her desire to wear a hair-shirt." This letter is dated the 18th of July, 1839.

We may imagine with what feelings of reverence Marie-Eustelle presented herself before her bishop. Mgr. Villecourt received her with a paternal kindness and simplicity which perfectly reassured her. Her heart seemed to expand, and she inwardly compared the difference between greatness of the spiritual order and mere worldly grandeur. To Eustelle, a poor needlewoman, Mgr. Villecourt, indeed, occupied an exalted station in both capacities, but she saw in him only her bishop and her father; she was, anyhow, too humble and simple to lose her self-possession, for much of that shyness and timidity with which persons are apt to be oppressed in the presence of their superiors, not unfrequently arises from an over-anxiety which has its source in self-love. After kneeling to receive

R

his blessing she handed him the Curé's letter, and
then remained silent while he persued it, inwardly
praying the Holy Spirit to dictate to her what she
ought to say. The bishop spoke first, and with the
gentlest consideration began to ask her questions so
pertinent to her needs that it seemed to her as if he
had been inspired with the knowledge of all that was
in her mind. She was filled with joy and gratitude,
yet the apprehension of appearing indiscreet made her
pass over in silence many points upon which she
would have rejoiced to be enlightened, especially with
regard to prayer. She could not have entered upon
this matter without manifesting some of the peculiar
favours she had received, and she had too much tact
not to perceive that the prelate himself abstained from
any remark which might imply the supposition that
she was the subject of any extraordinary operations
of grace. " If our Lord," she said to herself, " desires
for His glory and interests that I should discover my
whole soul to Monseigneur, he will himself furnish me
with an opening for doing so." She waited therefore
for the bishop to take the initiative, but, unlike her
former kind but incautious director, the prudent prelate in his first interviews practised much reserve, and
entirely concealed the high esteem he had conceived
for her. He well knew that humility is a plant of
very delicate growth, and that a breath of self-love
will be sufficient to tarnish the purity of the most
exalted virtue, nay sometimes to poison and wither it
in a moment. While his manner therefore was full
of the sweetest encouragement to her to open her
heart, he was at the same time quite ingenious in
contriving to suggest in all he said the humblest and
lowest views of herself. Eustelle, speaking of him in

confidence to the Sister of La Providence, said, "If you knew, my good friend, how Monseigueur humbled me! I can tell you that holy bishop well understands how to do it. It did me a great deal of good!"

Eustelle, in fact (to use a familiar phrase), saw perfectly well what the bishop was about; she honoured him for it, and was full of gratitude for the charity which prompted this treatment of her. More than this, her honest, simple, and truly lowly heart seconded his design, and realized its wholesome effect as fully as if she had not penetrated his purpose. Some persons are charmingly humble, so long as you exalt them. The monster, pride, is satisfied, and remains quietly beneath the surface, busy at his bad work, feeding on the roots of virtue. He does not show himself; he is not felt; but "touch the mountains and they will smoke." If such vain, imperfect persons are addressed in terms which imply ignorance of their worth, real or supposed, immediately they experience an uneasy sensation; and even should they, like Eustelle, discern the charitable motive which dictates the unpalatable advice, a craving self-love makes them suffer even at the very sound of depreciating words. For just as there are persons who will relish the grossest flattery, even when they have every reason to know that flattery it is; so there are others whose weak and sensitive natures cannot bear any language which does not satisfy their foolish longings for approbation and sympathy, however well-intentioned they may believe him to be who utters it. Such persons may, indeed, be said to be greatly deficient in this essential virtue, yet in nothing, perhaps, is the difference between the saint

and the ordinary Christian more strongly marked
than in this matter of humility.   The humility of a
saint is something which we recognize at once in its
peculiar fruits, although sometimes it surpasses our
comprehension.   Eustelle has herself recorded her
opinion that it is the rarest of virtues, speaking, of
course, of its more perfect exercise.   She was herself
unconsciously a model of this saintly lowliness of
soul, which, the more it is acquired, the less is it
believed by the possessor to have been attained.
Hence, in proportion to her love for it, was she
always coveting and courting whatever might nourish
and increase it ; and hence also she relished whatever
contented this craving, as a child relishes a sweetmeat.
Her satisfaction at the manner in which she was
received by her bishop is described in a few short
words, addressed to the servant, Marie, already mentioned, with whom Eustelle was on terms of familiar
intimacy : " I have just made the journey from
Saintes to La Rochelle, and have had the honour of
speaking three times to Monseigneur.   This bishop is
truly a saint, above all in humility and charity.   I
am really astonished at the very kind manner with
which he received me ; for, after all, you know what
sort of a person I am, and the high dignity of him in
whose presence I stood.   I to speak to a bishop !
And I am to have this honour soon again.   I seem to
hear you saying to yourself, ' What could she have to
say to him ? '   By 'r Lady ! that is my secret (*Dame !*[*]
c'est mon secret)."   She then passes to other subjects,
or, rather, to the one subject.

---

[*] This exclamation is the one solitary instance we have
observed in any of Eustelle's letters of the employment of an
expression peculiar to the inferior class from which she sprang.

We will now hear from the bishop's own lips an account of the impression which Marie-Eustelle made upon him in this first visit, but which he so well knew how to conceal from her eyes. "She presented herself before me," he said, "with every mark of the deepest respect joined to a confidence quite childlike. Her dress was without any pretension, exhibiting neither affectation nor negligence. Her language was correct, clear, precise; and was not wanting even in a certain dignity.' But, above all, every word which came from her lips revealed a soul taught in the school of Jesus Christ, habitually faithful to the impressions of grace and far advanced in the ways of the highest perfection. When she had left me, I remained, so to say, embalmed with an indefinable perfume of sanctity." If, then, the good bishop discoursed to Eustelle only of the ordinary lowly virtues with which every Christian soul ought to be adorned, it was not because he was unaware of the merits of her who stood before him. He needed not the Curé's letter to recognize them almost at a glance; nevertheless, he addressed her as a young beginner, or, at best, as one who had but just entered on the path of perfection. He exhorted her to be faithful to God in the least things, and to lead a truly self-denying and penitential life, less, however, as respected corporal austerities than interior mortifications. He spoke of that self-renunciation and bearing of the cross which our Lord declared to be essential in all who would come after Him, and, especially, he dwelt on the all-importance of a deep and genuine humility as the foundation and basis of the spiritual life. "Without humility," he said, "no virtues are possible, for it is humility which gives them birth; no virtues are

durable, for it is humility which preserves them."
And Eustelle listened with docile attention and submission ; she listened as if she had heard these things
for the first time, she who had so long and intimately
realized them and had herself so often spoken of them
to others in terms of glowing eloquence, allowing them
to penetrate and sink into her soul as they came all
fresh with the episcopal sanction and benediction.
She drank them in as the thirsty ground drinks in
the fertilizing shower, and, as her pastor spoke, his
words seemed to engrave themselves deep in her heart
in ineffaceable characters ; for Eustelle was one who
never let the blessing of the hour fall to the ground,
—a prize which fulness of self and lack of faith so
often miss.

Dear as humility had hitherto been to the lowly
maiden of Saint-Pallais, it now became, if possible,
doubly dear ; she felt to aspire after it with inexpressible ardour, and henceforward it was more than
ever the subject of her continued fervent prayer.
Her desire would have been to bind herself to its
practice by an irrevocable vow, but the bishop was
decidedly opposed to any such engagement, considering that a vow of this nature was more likely to
burden and harass the conscience than the three
vows taken in religion, on account of the multitude
of occasions so continually arising, which are calculated to furnish an aliment to self-love. He permitted
her only to renew it daily, so long as it did not become
a source of disquiet to her soul. She persevered to the
day of her death, and as it not unfrequently would
happen that every memory but that of the Blessed
Sacrament was banished from her mind, she offered a
general intention to our Lord of reiterating this vow

each morning; a pious contract, of which Sister Anastasia was the depository.

The bishop heard Eustelle's confession a few days later, when he came to Saintes, a privilege which she greatly valued. A short letter of thanks which she addressed to the bishop at this time has been preserved :—

" My Lord,—May I beg you to forgive my indiscretion, and permit me to write a few lines to your lordship? The profit which my soul experiences from the holy counsels you had the charity to give me, moves me to testify to you my lively gratitude for them. Would that I might have the honour to be guided by your lordship in the paths of humility, that virtue of which God makes me feel all the worth, and for which He vouchsafes to give me a special attraction. I recommend my soul to your remembrance before God, that He may speedily grant me the desire of my heart, by bestowing on me that holy virtue which I love, and which I practise so little and so imperfectly. I long to fulfil my sacred engagement for its exercise, which I renew each day. I humbly request your lordship to be pleased to offer your prayers for this end in behalf of her who, with sentiments of the deepest respect and veneration, has the honour to be,

" Your lordship's humble and obedient
" servant and daughter,
" EUSTELLE."

We subjoin the bishop's reply :—

" Courage, dear daughter ; labour incessantly to

acquire true and perfect humility, but do not believe to have attained it only because you experience a desire for it. There is an incalculable distance between the desire of a thing and the possession of it. It seems to those who are at the foot of a mountain, as if they would be able to touch the sky with their hands when they have reached the summit ; but the higher they mount the further do the heavens recede from them. If the Lord should grant you the grace to make some progress in holy humility, the more you advance the better will you understand at what a distance you are from that marvellous good. But do not therefore be discouraged : act like those who are digging in the earth for a treasure which they know to be hidden at that spot ; the deeper they delve the more does their courage rise. Do not forget, moreover, the saying of a great master of the spiritual life : that it is difficult, while yet young, to be far advanced in perfection. The young may be rich in desires and in good will, but for want of experience and trial they are generally poor in the possession of real treasure. Do not act imprudently respecting your health ; it is much weaker than you imagine, and it is the Lord's will that you take care of it. I have been much consoled this morning by the return of a stray sheep : pray God to bring us more. I give you, my dear daughter, my paternal blessing.

"CLEMENT, Bishop of La Rochelle."

We see from this letter that the bishop nourished this lamb of his flock on very plain food. He knew that it was safe and wholesome diet for all, the highest as the lowest.

The consent to wearing a hair-shirt was refused.

"Monsieur le Curé," she remarked to her friend with a gentle playfulness, "had been beforehand with me, and had spoken to Monseigneur ; he did me a mischief, for Monseigneur believed him." The appearance of Eustelle, indeed, was not likely to invalidate the Curé's statement, and she even received a prohibition to fast, when she saw the bishop again the following Lent. "Monseigneur," she writes, "has scolded me very much for being ill (as he says) through my own fault. He insists on my eating meat this Lent. I shall obey since such is his will, and, indeed, I have already begun. I said to myself as I was returning, he is ignorant of the source of my malady. If he did but know how the love of Jesus treats me!" But if Eustelle was debarred from fasting, she knew how to season with the bitter herbs of penitence the food which her infirmities compelled her to take. "I am not allowed to fast," she says ; "see what I am good for—not even to observe the Church's precepts ! Poor, useless member ! But since I cannot fast, I will try this Lent to be entirely converted to God."

She saw the bishop again in the July following, when she visited La Rochelle. She had not yet renounced all hopes of obtaining a permission to practise some austerities, but he was not disposed to make any concession of the kind. Upon this occasion she appears to have spoken more fully to him of her state, without, however, mentioning any of the extraordinary graces with which she had been favoured. The fear which she perceived him to entertain lest she should be tempted to set any value on her own proficiency, contributed to deter her from a manifestation to which the bashfulness of holy souls ordinarily disinclines them. She spoke to him now only of the interior pains she had suffered, of her manner of prayer, and of the vows she had taken, and he gave her many salutary instructions, particularly upon the subject of mortification. These were naturally suggested by the repetition of her desire for the hair-shirt and the discipline. While expressing his conviction that the saints have invariably been the enemies of their flesh, and consequently lovers of mortification, he added that nevertheless there were dangers of excess especially to those who in their ardent beginnings give themselves up unrestrainedly to the impulses of their zeal. He pointed out all the evils incidental to such rashness, not to speak of the merit of obedience lost by this self-will. He instanced the error committed by that great servant of God, Henry Suso, to whom the Lord revealed that He did not make any account of the cruel rigour with which he had treated himself, because in all this he had only done his own will. He enlarged upon the necessity of strictly adhering to the rules laid down by the confessor, as respects not only the character of the penance, but its frequency, its duration, and the rest. Persons, he said, who are given to talking of their corporal austerities to others besides the directors of their conscience, or who would be likely to value themselves in consequence, must not be allowed to practise them. They need instead to be severely humbled. All the instruments of penance must be carefully concealed, and if there be danger of discovery, that is sufficient reason for their retrenchment, except in religious communities where the discipline forms part of the rule. Their use must not in general be permitted to individuals of feeble constitution or suffering from any delicacy of the chest. They are profitable for the

most part to persons of robust health, and to such as
are naturally prone to sloth and heaviness. As regards sleep, the bishop pointed out the necessity of a
due medium; for, not to speak of the injury likely to
result to health from any imprudent abridgment, a
kind of incapacity for fulfilling our daily temporal
and spiritual duties is apt to ensue. Even as regards
the fasting and abstinence enjoined by the Church,
all scruple was to be dismissed when competent authority has spoken. No regard is to be paid to any
doubts which may arise in the mind, because in cases of
doubt we may always take the side favourable to health.
Besides giving these instructions upon the practice of
penance (the substance of which we have extracted
from one of Eustelle's letters to her former director), he
dwelt again very forcibly on the subject of humility,
advising her to make its acquisition the subject of her
intention in fifteen of her communions each month,
which was, in fact, to offer the half of them to that end.
He carried (she adds) his own humility so far as to beg
her from time to time to offer her communion for him,
and exhorted her to be constant in very fervent prayers
for such of her relations as seemed to stand specially
in need of them. With the recommendation of humility this good bishop's addresses to Eustelle always
began, and they closed in like manner with the same
earnest advice. Eustelle treasured up his words in
her heart, but they had the effect in a great measure
of sealing her lips. The day was to come, however,
when they were to be unlocked, and that too, as we
shall see, at the bishop's own desire.

Before quitting this subject we will subjoin a few
additional instances illustrative of this prelate's great
caution, his extreme fear of exaggeration, and his

jealous love of the strictest orthodoxy both of expression and of sentiment. Eustelle assuredly not only was a most submissive and docile child of Holy Church, but had no tendency to indulge in over-strained ideas or singularity of conduct, and no disposition, on the ground of the exalted favours of which she was the recipient, to cherish or adopt imaginations of her own. Yet the bishop used as many precautions to guard her against the illusions of false mysticism as if he had perceived indications in her disposition calculated to excite his alarm. One day, when Eustelle was giving expression to her sentiments respecting conformity to the will of God, she said that she felt her own will so united to that Adorable Will, that she would resign herself to be cast into hell if she knew that such was God's will; and that, although the whole attraction of her heart was to the love of God, she was ready to consent not to love Him, if it pleased Him to reject her love. In making so startling a declaration Eustelle could hardly be considered as putting forth a deliberate statement. Saints themselves have given utterance to sentiments not very dissimilar; sentiments which nevertheless cannot stand a scrutiny, and must be regarded simply as struggles after the expression of a love which is unutterable. As human language contains no terms adequate to represent the intensity of what these great lovers feel, they have recourse to hypothetical impossibilities with corresponding paradoxical protestations of self-devotion. The bishop, however, took the alarm at once: "What is that you are saying, my daughter?" he exclaimed, with a look of much displeasure. "Know that such suppositions concerning God are supremely injurious to Him; and I forbid you ever to give them admittance into your mind. The Church cannot endure such sentiments." Eustelle was going to observe that she had met with similar observations in some book of piety, and that she had been charmed with the generosity of soul they seemed to manifest ; when the bishop, interrupting her, said, " Repeat to me. the second petition in the Our Father." Eustelle replied accordingly, " Thy kingdom come." " Recite now the first commandment of God." " Thou shalt love the Lord thy God," &c. " Every day, then," continued the prelate, when she had finished, " you pray that the kingdom of God may come—it is Jesus Christ Himself who puts this prayer into your mouth—and yet you can admit into your mind the absurd supposition that God requires of you a willingness to be cast into hell. It is as if you were to suppose that God should will you to live in mortal sin. His desire, St. Paul says, is that we all should be saints ; and, since He desires us all to be saints, He also desires the salvation of all, for His sanctity does not permit Him to condemn those who are not worthy of punishment. Besides, there is something presumptuous in so resigning oneself to hell, which cannot be pleasing to Him who loves and receives only such as are humble. Jesus Christ reproved St. Peter, who boasted that he was ready to give his life for Him ; and yet simply to give one's life is nothing in comparison with devoting oneself to hell. I say the same of the strange, not to say monstrous, supposition of being willing not to love God if such were His will ; as if it were possible, without the most palpable absurdity, to admit such an hypothesis. God cannot contradict Himself. As He loves Himself with a necessary love, we cannot,

without insulting Him, suppose that He could wish
a soul not to love Him ; and so the Church has justly
condemned an analogous sentiment in the doctrine of
Molinos, although one less formal and less explicit."*
Eustelle, as may be supposed, was greatly confused at
having entertained a thought which she would not
for an instant have harboured if she had suspected
that it was not in harmony with the teaching of the
Church.

So fearful was the bishop of anything which might
possibly suggest ideas bordering on the errors of
Quietism, that he forbade her reading several books
which might appear in occasional passages to favour
exaggerated notions regarding pure and disinterested
love, although some of them having been written
before the condemnation of those errors, we may
justly put a good construction upon them, and conclude that the writers would have used more guarded
language had they lived later.   For this reason Mgr.
Villecourt would not allow her, for instance, to read
the works of P. Guilloré.   She thought that Boudon's
writings at least would be permitted her ; but even
here the bishop hesitated, and clearly evinced his
preference that she should abstain, on account (as he
said) of some propositions to be met with therein,
which, taken literally, wanted for strict exactness.
With such jealous care did this venerable prelate
guard the treasure of sanctity he recognized in this
holy girl, for whom his high veneration was afterwards so strikingly manifested.   Further proofs of
this same unrelaxing caution will appear in the course
of the narrative.

* Propositions 12 and 13, condemned by Innocent XI. in
the Bull, *Cœlestis Pastor*.

CHAPTER IV.

The Two Attractions.

Marie-Eustelle's heart was swayed by two attractions leading her in apparently opposite, but not contrary directions. The one tended to fix her within herself, the other to draw her forth. These opposite inclinations are often exemplified in the lives of saints : the explanation is obvious. It is Jesus they seek, whether they abide with Him in contemplation, or minister to Him in His suffering members. We have already noticed Eustelle's attraction to retirement, and how she never allowed it to interfere with her attention to the claims of fraternal charity. Her love for silence and solitude were now increased ten-fold. In proportion as our Lord had vouchsafed more intimate and unreserved communications to her soul, the more had her own interior become to her a paradise of bliss, which she never desired to leave. But such words are feeble to express the hunger and thirst, the longing desire she had to be alone with her Lord ; and when creatures came to tear her from this enjoyment, it required all the proportionate increase of her burning charity for those whom in God she so purely and devotedly loved, to enable her to obey the call. For it was not that in so doing she put compulsion on herself from a mere sense of duty ; it was rather that an equally powerful force drew her in that direction without superseding the opposite attraction, which, continuing still to operate, produced the intense pain of separation which she experienced upon these occasions. " I should wish to be always alone," she said to Sister Anastasia; "I should wish never to appear in the world. I prefer my solitude. O dear solitude, how I love thee! Be ever in my memory and in my heart, O my beloved Master; let me never lose sight of Thee!" Her love of solitude was, as these words revealed, no self-indulgent preference of her own mental repose or gratification of her spiritual tastes; it was the pure love of Jesus, with whom in solitude and silence she could more freely converse. "The conversation of creatures," she often said, "is insipid when one has been conversing with the Creator." The Abbé Guérin says that Eustelle would have even wished, like the "Solitaire des Rochers," to fly to some desert place in order to be at perfect liberty to hold uninterrupted communion with God, but that she was checked by the remembrance of the Eucharist. To go far away from the world, she must go far also from the Presence of Jesus in His Adorable Sacrament, and she could no longer daily receive Him.

Notwithstanding the powerful attraction which thus drew her within herself, she ever received those who came to consult her, or simply to edify themselves by her conversation, with a smile of welcome. Not one momentary chilling glance or transient fall of the countenance, which not all the graciousness of manner which may instantaneously succeed will obliterate from the recollection of the visitor—for that glance has told him that he is an intruder—ever betrayed the pain which these constant interruptions must have caused her; and they were continually on the increase. But as they increased, so did her spirit of self-sacrifice increase; for the love of Jesus, whom she beheld in these souls, she daily, and, not unfrequently, many times a day, left Him that she might devote herself entirely to their relief, although amongst them were often inconsiderate persons who would trespass on her time without adequate cause or beyond all reasonable measure. She would put off every-thing—meals, employments, needful rest, all, in short, which could be postponed at the expense of only per-sonal inconvenience to herself—in order to listen to what they wished to say, never making the least effort, however allowable, to curtail their stay. More than this, she took the utmost pains to conceal the physical sufferings which these prolonged conversations caused her, as well from the fatigue and exhaustion they produced, as from the extreme delicacy of her chest. How difficult it is on such occasions to suppress all outward indication, however trifling, of the distress experienced will be readily appreciated by those who have made the attempt—an attempt, however, from which many would consider themselves to be legiti-mately dispensed.

The secret of her patience is to be sought in her union with God. She never left Jesus, and so Jesus never left her to herself and to all those distracting per-turbations of which the soul becomes the prey when, engaged in external occupations, it goes out of itself, and abandons its hold on the Divine arm. Eustelle, while stretching forth the hand of charity to her neighbour, with her other always held the Spouse of her soul closely embraced. Hence not only could she employ herself in external acts without detriment to the fervour of that love which is nourished in con-templation, but she performed them in one and the same spirit of love. "Many a time," says Sister Anastasia, "did she impose on herself great privations

8

merely to satisfy some person or other, so much did she delight in giving pleasure."

It is from Anastasia also that we learn what was the condescension which of all others cost this servant of God the most. Eustelle said to her one day, " You cannot imagine what I feel every evening when I have to quit the holy place. What violence I have to put upon myself ! My heart is rent in twain. My soul seems ready to abandon me. My strength forsakes me ; and if our Lord did not support me, I should be unable even to get back to my room. What adds greatly to my suffering is to find some one waiting to speak to me as I leave the church. Oh, what an effort I have to make not to allow any sign of what I feel to appear ! Jesus, who sends these persons to me, gives me special graces for their spiritual good ; were it not so, it would be impossible for me to say a word to them. But if I followed my own inclination—ah ! how much I should prefer to live unknown. I do not believe I have done anything to attract these persons to me, and I wonder at people coming to ask advice of me, which I am not capable of giving. It is a humiliation : Jesus wills it, and I will it too, and I try as much as I can to be useful. But my own personal wish would be, after my evening adoration, to regain my solitude in perfect silence." While thus unburdening her heart, Marie-Eustelle quite forgot at the moment that the person addressed had herself not unfrequently intercepted her at the church door ; but poor Anastasia well remembered it, and began to make excuses. Eustelle, perceiving her inadvertence, endeavoured in the kindest manner to reassure her friend, begging her not take to herself any observation she had made, but to continue to wait for her as usual, whenever she wished to speak to her. These assurances and entreaties were most sincere, for Eustelle (as we have seen) was far from desiring to avoid those who she believed were sent to her by her Lord. The following letter was in all probability written on this occasion :—

"July 24th, 1840.

"Blessed be Jesus for all and in all! May this merciful Lord forgive me the pain my words have caused you. He knows, however, that the meaning you put upon them is far from my heart; and His will alone would enable me to support the sad and painful privation it would be to me to be unable, through my unworthiness, to be any longer of use to the souls for which I would give my blood. I call Jesus to witness that such is my heart's desire and aspiration. Oh, may He be known! May He be loved! May He look favourably upon what He knows, and grant my desire. Ask this same Jesus to make known to you the prayers I offer for you. Be it far from me to seek the esteem of creatures: Jesus, nothing but Jesus! But for Jesus in my neighbour, charity! Promise me never to recur in thought to the moment when such distressing reflections found access to your mind. As for me, who, notwithstanding my faults, have never had the thought that a visit of yours could prove wearisome to me, I am afraid lest these slight suspicions may have the effect of rendering them less frequent. For the love of the good Jesus, whom I desire you should love more than I love Him myself, if such be His will, be pleased not to deprive me of what I love for Him, in Him, and

s 2

through Him. All God's—yes, let us be all God's, by
the bond of the most perfect charity : God's in time,
God's in eternity. Yes, we shall be God's and in
God, to bless and love Jesus, our God ; to immerse
and lose ourselves in Life Eternal, which is God
Himself. Always, and more than always, all yours.
Christians love each other for eternity. May Jesus
tell you the rest of my thoughts.

> "EUSTELLE, the poor servant of Jesus."

With what affectionate earnestness do we here see
her endeavouring to efface a painful impression which
she had unwittingly conveyed ; all her tender and
loving heart is manifested in these lines ; and yet she
never allows human weakness to make her unsay anything, or for one instant to descend from the high
supernatural ground whence she drew her motives
and into which all her affections had been trans-
planted. She feared that her incautious observation
might have not only grieved but closed a heart which
desired to open itself to her ; yet, while she spares no
pains to restore its familiar confidence, she never
lowers herself to those protestations of personal
affection which to the many would have appeared
the most obvious and most appropriate remedy to
apply where the feelings had been inadvertently
wounded. Indeed, in all her correspondence we can
never detect one word which reveals a merely natural
and human affection.

Eustelle's attraction to silence sometimes even
affected her physical powers, and she felt not only
unwilling but almost unable to speak. This powerlessness seems to have been an approach to a suspension of the senses, such as takes place altogether in

the ecstatic state. Notwithstanding the life rapturous love which this holy girl was called to live, notwithstanding the marvellous communications which she received, and (as we shall presently see) the visions with which she was frequently favoured, we have no recorded instance of her falling into a perfect state of rapture. She seemed rather to enjoy the effects of rapture without passing through its state; but this is far from a proof that her visions were not of an exalted order,* or that love in her was not much more than sufficient to have produced a suspension of the faculties in other souls. There was

---

* "Raptures are marks of imperfection, and of a certain remaining earthliness, when they happen to a soul simply because it is as yet unaccustomed to the objects which throw it into rapture; but when they proceed from the greatness and the extraordinary excellence of the light communicated by God, they are not marks of imperfection. . . . When the soul, being perfectly strengthened and habitnated to the most wonderful communications of grace, is no longer liable to be ravished out of itself, it experiences the effects of rapture without being actually in a state of rapture. The impressions of grace are then purely spiritual, and act no longer on the body, as was the case when it was not perfectly subject to the spirit, and as pure as it is now become. For it is a maxim of philosophers, that 'everything received into a subject is received therein according to the disposition of the subject.'"— "The Spiritual Doctrine of Father Louis Lallemant," p. 310.

The same writer says that when God imparts some new and very extraordinary light, the soul will still fall into rapture, although it has become accustomed to those objects which heretofore produced rapture, but had ceased to do so. The state of suspension of the faculties, then, commonly called rapture, would seem to be dependent upon the mutual relation between the soul and the object presented to it by God, and, viewed apart from such relation, cannot be taken as the measure either of the exalted character of the vision or of the soul's advance in spirituality. A perfect proportion between the two would seem to prevent the occurrence of these bodily phenomena. We do not hear of our Lady falling into any raptures or ecstasies, and the blessed, who see God face to face, are exempt from such affections.

something in Eustelle's silence, as she came forth from the sanctuary in the evening, so supernatural in its character, that some, instinctively feeling its influence, although they might not understand, were drawn to respect it. "The veneration with which my holy friend inspired me," writes a lady of the neighbourhood, "was such that many a time I did not venture to break · in upon her silence. One day it was nearly a quarter of an hour before she could attend to what I was saying to her;" so completely had the Presence of our Lord, whom she had just left, absorbed all her faculties. The same thing would not unseldom occur when she went to speak to M. Briand about the state of her soul. This ecclesiastic, knowing that she had come for that very purpose, was naturally surprised the first time this silence occurred, and inquired the reason. "Excuse me, father," she replied, "I can say nothing; our Lord takes possession of my soul, and I am unable at this moment to acquaint you with its state." Tears rolled down her face in streams as she spoke these words : it was like the countenance of a beatified spirit. Those few words, those tears, that countenance must have said enough. In a letter of explanation which she thought proper to address to M. Briand upon some like occasion, we see her double attraction to silence and to works of zeal and charity manifesting itself.

"September 7th, 1841.

"All for the love of the all-amiable Jesus! Did you not find me a little silent last Monday? It was because the suffering love of the most loving Jesus filled my heart, and that heart suffered much—oh, much! But what sweetness there is in that kind of suffering! O my father, this disposition deprived me of the power of speaking; I was thinking of Him who is my life, my thought, my memory. To-day I have spoken more; but I have talked only of my holy love, of Jesus, and for Jesus, my Beloved, whom alone I love. I cannot shed my blood for Him, but if I cannot shed it, I will drain it, dry it up, consume it. I desire, as much as I can, to consecrate my voice, and exhaust it even to the end, to make Him known who is not known; Him whom you know, my father; whom you love; who is your occupation; Him whom, by His grace, I know a little; for whom I live, and for whom I desire to die."

Many instances of her entirely putting aside her love of solitude and silence have been recorded by survivors. One while we find her endeavouring to calm the distracted mind of a poor woman who, a prey to the most absurd and extravagant imaginations, was led to the verge of despair, and even tempted to commit suicide. Eustelle, mingling wise counsels with affectionate treatment, offered to go and spend the day with her, and succeeded in persuading her to place herself in the hands of an enlightened and charitable priest. At another time we find her devoting herself to watching, with the care and love of a guardian angel, a young woman who, having wandered from the paths of virtue, had recently been reclaimed, mainly (it would seem) through the lessons and example of Eustelle herself; warning her of the obstacles she would meet with; and by her kindness and friendly offices encouraging her to bear up against the sarcasms of her former evil associates, who were endeavouring by the potent weapon of ridicule to win her back to those worldly courses which had proved to her the occasion of sin. All such good deeds, of which these are but a slight sample, implied a sacrifice of her personal attraction, which fully to appreciate, it would be necessary to share it. "Eustelle's charity," writes a lady, "was extreme; and to gain souls to God nothing seemed difficult to her. She often expressed to me her regret not to be able to labour for the conversion of the heathen in foreign missions. One day I said I should wish to resemble her, but to succeed in that would give me much to do, and I lacked the courage." Eustelle's *naïve* reply is worth recording, so thoroughly was it unlike what a false humility or the awkward desire to appear humble would generally dictate. "Ah," she rejoined, jumping at the idea, "if I only could take your soul! But of course I would not keep it as it is : how very soon it would be changed! Then, when the labour was over, I would give it back to you, and you would only have to take care of it." And she seemed quite to rejoice at the thought, and only grieved that it was not possible to realize it.

Unable to have a share herself in the Apostolic labours of conversion, she was consumed with a zealous longing to promote them and to engage others to render a like aid by their prayers and alms. The Association of the Propagation of the Faith was peculiarly dear to her. "Oh, why," she would exclaim, "are Catholics so wanting in generosity, when the Protestants of England give so much money to disseminate their errors!" Hence her prayers were continually offered with special fervour for priests, that they might correspond to the holiness of their vocation, and thus win many souls to God. Her heart wept tears of blood when she contemplated the deplorable condition of her own native district, Saintonge : the majority of its people given up to vanity, pleasure, or money-getting ; holy days profaned ; religion often publicly insulted ; the laws of God and of the Church outraged ; the rest of the Sunday so neglected that in many places scarce one or two families abstained from business ; indifference wide-spread ; infidelity common ; the holy offices of religion neglected ; sacraments unfrequented ; men and women living as if they had no souls, ignorant of the essential truths of Christianity, often caring little to have their children baptized, and themselves dying like the beasts. Such is the picture drawn by one well qualified to judge : it was sufficiently discouraging, but Eustelle was never disheartened ; there was prayer, and there was the Heart of Jesus. She remembered how St. Eutropius, the first Apostle of her country, finding his missionary labours fruitless, returned to the Sovereign Pontiff and begged to have another field of work assigned to him ; and how the Vicar of Christ refused to accede to his request, and sent him back to persevere in cultivating the ungrateful soil of Saintonge, which he was to water with his blood : the harvest came at last, and by his labours, his martyrdom, and, finally, his powerful intercession, the land was entirely converted to the faith. Nothing, Eustelle believed, could be refused to the prayers of the ministers of the sanctuary ; and fain would she have raised her voice and exhorted them to fulfil their sacred mission with zeal and courage, and continually to lift up their consecrated hands in supplication. The holy familiarity with which she was able to address the former Curé of

Saint-Pallais allows her to manifest these her ardent desires without in any way overstepping the modesty and humility which became her.

" In expressing to you," she writes, " the sentiments of my heart, I feel that it is not yet satisfied ; I feel the thirst I have to love God, and make others love Him, as yet unrelieved. Oh, that I could communicate to my brethren the devouring fire which consumes me ! God knows that such are my most ardent desires : would that they might be fulfilled ! I am happy when no day passes without doing some service to my neighbour. To God alone be the glory ! As for me, I am nothing and can do nothing. Let us pray, then, without ceasing, that the spark of faith kindled upon earth may not be extinguished. Oh, how feeble it is, how pale it is ! O Jesus, author and perfecter of faith, revive this sacred torch ; dispel by its light the darkness of error, bring back into the fold Thy wandering sheep, and those which are separated from it : I conjure Thee, O my Saviour, by the bowels of Thy infinite charity and by Thy precious and divine Bloodshedding." And again, " Let us love so good a God. In desiring His love for myself I desire it also for you. Love Him, then, this good, this all-amiable Master ; love Him, and labour with all your strength to make others love Him . . . . Forgive me if I take the liberty to speak thus to you. It does not befit me ; but God knows the motive. I would wish to love Him, but I am unworthy of the degree of love to which I aspire. I desire it, then, for others . . . . I desire it, not for them only who, like us, have the happiness of belonging to the Holy Church of Jesus Christ, but also for such of our brethren as are outside this ark of salvation and live in darkness, strangers to truth. Happy they whom God has placed in the Church to labour in bringing back to the heavenly fold these erring sheep, who by their sincere return shall gladden the Heart of the Good Shepherd."

On another occasion she writes, " My prayers for you to the Good God are ever the same : that is, they have for their end His greater glory, looking only to His dearest interests in desiring to see all hearts possessed by that sacred fire which He came to cast on the earth, and with which He desires to inflame the whole universe. It is yours especially which I wish to be consumed with this divine fire, and, believe me truly, solely for the glory of our common Master. I am aware that you already possess this heavenly love, more perhaps than you think ; but you know that we can increase it more and more, until it has attained the last degree of perfection which it can reach in this life. It is this degree of perfection which I should desire to possess, but of which I am unworthy ; and it is this which I wish for you with my whole heart, in order that you may love Him for me and for those who refuse to know Him. Oh, how I rejoice in God and for God that by your state you are specially bound to love and to cause Him to be loved ! and, believe me, I never cease begging our Lord to pour down His heavenly benedictions upon the souls committed to your charge, that even in this life they may become, as St. Paul said of the Christians of Corinth, your joy and your crown, awaiting the time when in Heaven they may, as so many jewels, help to form the diadem which God prepares to reward your fidelity."

In another letter, written about two years before

her death, we find her thus expressing the longings of her soul :—"Consumed with the desire to sacrifice myself for the glory of God, and seeing my powerlessness,—unable to share the toils of Evangelical labourers, and longing to see them all priests according to the Heart of Jesus—I have made to this God, full of love, the sacrifice of my health and of my life, beseeching Him to accept this most unworthy oblation ; relying nevertheless with an entire confidence on Himself alone to obtain for these highest members of the Church the accomplishment of His will in each one of them. And now I often conjure Him from whom this thought came to me, not to delay the completion of my sacrifice. M. Briand,* to whom I mentioned this, said, 'My child, the Lord will grant your prayer ;' and so I venture to believe. But Jesus has caused me to know that the time is not yet come, and that I have yet sufferings to endure for His sake." The nearer she drew to her end, the more ardent did this devotion to souls become, and in her letters we find it ever intimately blended and, as it were, confounded with her love of the Lord of souls. When we compare this burning charity for her neighbour, drawing her continually to external acts in their behalf or prompting aspirations after such as were to her impossible, with her deep longings to be alone with her Beloved in the silence of contemplation, we feel that we have the clue to the import of those few simple words, found among the papers to which she had committed her inmost thoughts :— "Vehement desire for solitude and procuring the

---

* A blank is here left in the original edition of the Letters, probably because M. Briand was still living when they were first published.

glory of God." In Heaven alone shall such desires no longer contend together, but find at once their full and simultaneous satisfaction. There shall each beatified spirit enjoy that eternal and inaccessible solitude with God of which He has implanted the desire in the souls created to His image, the image of the Ever-Blessed Triune God, who after, as before, the creation, dwells alone in the blissful enjoyment of Himself. To the enjoyment of that beatitude He calls each predestinated soul, which is its own special possession; and this it is which enables each Christian soul, while saying "Our Father and our Lord," to say also, "My God and my Saviour," as truly as if Jesus had lived and died for him alone. This singular happiness each of the redeemed shall taste in everlasting conjunction with that communion of love which makes him a partaker of the joy of all the rest; and in this blessed society the glory of God, which has been the life-long passion of holy souls like Eustelle's, shall also be the never-ending source of their delight and the perpetual theme of their triumphal songs.

CHAPTER V.

SECRETS OF THE INNER LIFE.

SIMPLE as Eustelle was in her outward demeanour and careful to shun all appearance of singularity, her extraordinary sanctity could not be altogether hidden. Her very countenance spoke of heavenly communings. Hence a desire was excited among the devout to know what passed in the depths of that

pure soul, and persons would visit her actuated by
this species of inquisitiveness, who had not even the
good taste to conceal it. One day a young lady of
rank, who had sought an interview with Eustelle, was
fain to rise and take her leave without having
satisfied her curiosity. Eustelle was on the point
of seeing her to the door when the lady, determined
to give herself a final chance, and thinking perhaps
that her position in life, as compared with that of
the young workwoman, entitled her to use a freedom
which in another would have been judged impertinent, began to ply her with direct questions, even
asking her in so many words whether God had ever
shown Himself to her in visions—("si elle voyait
le Bon Dieu"). Eustelle inwardly shrank from this
rude intrusion on the sacred privacy of her heart :
"My good lady," she said to herself, " you are very
indiscreet ; you shall know nothing ;" she, however,
quietly replied, "But whom do you take me for,
Mademoiselle ? A poor creature like me to see the
Good God ! What are you thinking of?" "In
short, I got out of it as well as I could," she added,
when relating the incident to her confidante. "As
for me," said the sister, "I should not have stood
upon much ceremony with one who treated me with
so little, and should have given her a bit of my
mind." "I did not wish to pain her," Eustelle
gently replied. "As for you, dear Anastasia, if I
open my heart to you, it is because I know your
prudence. It is not well, as you are aware, to confide in all the world, but it is very allowable to have
one friend ; and indeed, with the exception of my
directors, you are the only person to whom I make

known the goodness of Jesus to His unworthy servant."

"*Secretum meum mihi*—my secret to myself," said the prophet ; and Eustelle was cautious to keep hers. We have just seen her give an indirect recommendation on this point to her trusty Anastasia, and we frequently meet with passages in her letters to the former Curé of Saint-Pallais, in which she entreats his perfect silence with regard to anything extraordinary which she had confided to him. "Pray do not show my letters to any one," she writes ; "you know the world ; join prudence always with simplicity, and be mindful whom you trust. This is the advice of the author of the 'Imitation,' and I do not remind you of it without cause." This priest's great admiration, and even veneration, for his former penitent made it perhaps a little difficult for him to keep such things strictly to himself. "Always consider," she writes on another occasion, "that my letters are only for yourself ; " and again, "The good parishioners of Saint-Pallais do not know me"—this observation is elicited by their accusing her of being ill through her own fault—"and it is not fitting they should know me. Divine operations are not to be thus unveiled. I shall be more secret than ever ; not," she adds, "that I have ever talked much." And in another letter, written only three months before her death, she says, "When you have some sufficient reason for communicating to any one what I write, pray never read anything which may seem extraordinary. Many might take occasion to ridicule what I do not think at all a subject of laughter ; others, perhaps, might be seized with the idea of imitating me in certain things, and this latter result would be much more serious than the former."

So completely had she succeeded in shrouding from the view of those about her the marvels of grace of which her soul was the theatre, that many remained quite ignorant of them until after her death. "We were far from thinking," said her parents to Eustelle's biographer, "that our daughter would ever be so much talked about." They saw, they felt, her goodness; her wonderful piety and devotion could be a secret to no one; but the communion she was holding with the invisible world, whose glories she was so often inwardly contemplating while she moved so quietly and simply through all the little ordinary affairs and charities of her humble daily life, was entirely concealed from their sight. It is to Marie-Eustelle's correspondence with her two directors that we are indebted for becoming acquainted with the secrets of her inner life. With her first director, the former Curé of Saint-Pallais, a certain familiarity mingles with the respect which she never for a moment forgets. As a priest of God, he was the object of her deepest reverence, while, as one who had been her personal director, she felt she owed him a special debt of gratitude. He had comforted and supported her in her interior trials, and his removal from Saint-Pallais had not abated the lively interest he felt for this chosen one of his former flock. The tone, however, in which she addresses him often approaches to a certain equality, which finds its explanation in the altogether exceptional character of their relations. We do not possess his letters, but it is plain from many of Eustelle's replies, that he used to lay bare the state of his soul to her, deplore his deficiency in fervour as being

immeasurably inferior to her own, detail his trials
and temptations, and seek almost a kind of *direction*
at her hands. It is natural that this should influence
her manner of addressing him, though perhaps nothing
can manifest a more delicate tact, or a more perfect
sense of the bounds imposed upon her by their respective positions, than the way in which she avails herself
of the opportunity he thus affords her of encouraging
and consoling him. In her later letters it is observ-
able that she habitually calls him her " brother,"
whereas she never gives M. Briand any appellation
except that of " father." In a letter dated June, 1840,
we find her beginning by seeking consolation at his
hands, before venturing to administer it :—

" United to Jesus by the Eucharistic bond, I feel a
desire to converse with you awhile. The sentiments
which fill my soul, and which Jesus Himself inspires,
move me to seek some consolation from you. Not
that I want for consolation, on the contrary I have
too much, and the desires which hence arise in my
heart, being incapable of satisfaction on account of
my unworthiness, cause me to experience a species of
martyrdom which is known only to God. I feel that
Jesus alone, who is the cause of my sufferings, can
put a term thereto. Not that I wish not tó suffer,
but I mean that if I could promote His glory and
sacrifice myself for Him, the fulfilment of my desires
would diminish this hunger and thirst which He more
and more excites in me. O my brother, with what
a holy cruelty the love. of the Beloved Jesus afflicts
my soul ! But do not think that I complain of this ;
it is the excess of my happiness which makes me suffer.
What can I do to correspond with so much love ?
Ah ! unite with me to bless our common Benefactor,

T

and believe that your soul is always in my thoughts
when I am kneeling at His feet.   I will not have you
entertain the sad thought, sad both for your heart
and the Heart of Jesus, that our lot in Eternity will
not be the same.   What! I shall behold my God, I
shall bless Him, and you shall be a stranger to that
happiness.   Why do you thus wound the goodness
and infinite mercy of this dear Saviour?   Why will
you suppose that He will allow one to be lost whom
He has chosen and placed in His Church to labour
for the salvation of His beloved sheep?   Do you
doubt Him?   I know all you think at this moment,
and all you might allege if you were with me; but, in
spite of this, it is not your will to lose your soul: and
it is that alone which could cause your reprobation.
I know that sinners will not be saved simply because
they assert that they do not wish to be lost, for to
transgress, as they do, the laws of God and of His
Church is to will their own perdition.   No, no, death
shall not separate us from Jesus : of this I am sure.
We shall meet again, to love Him eternally who has
been so often the theme of our conversations here
below.   Receive, then, from the Heart of Jesus these
temporal and spiritual trials which I beg you to
accept as coming from His love.   I feel sure that
Jesus will grant me what I ask for you.   Tell me all
your sufferings as far as you are able.   It is true that
I cannot myself heal them, but I will go and lay them
on the altar of Jesus ; and the confidence with which
this good Saviour inspires me makes me firmly believe
that you will receive the fruit of my prayers.   Oh,
how powerful is prayer with the Heart of God!
What can He refuse to a humble and truthful prayer!
Beg of Him to give me this precious humility ; I need

it more than ever: you shall know why another time."

A few days later we have another letter of affectionate interest, in which Eustelle consoles her former director under his trials, and tells him that he must not suppose them to be the result altogether of his own faults; nevertheless, if he really believes that they are so, she exhorts him to use all his endeavours to clear the garden of his soul of those little weeds which might prevent the Heavenly Spouse from taking His repose therein with complacency. "Oh, I entreat you," she writes, "do all in your power to acquire peace of soul. How I should bless my dear Saviour, if you could give me this joyful news! But you will not think that I wish you to be without the Cross. I seem to know the way by which God leads you. You will always have some persecutions, some humiliations; and besides, your own natural disposition will ever be the source of some suffering to you. It is the interest I feel for you that makes me speak thus. O my God, how desirous I am that you should become a saint! Make haste to become one," she playfully adds, "and then—who knows?—you may perhaps make me one afterwards: but, joking apart, let me know the state of your soul." In another letter we find her assuring him that he loves Jesus. "Do not say that it is not His design that you should love Him as much as certain chosen souls for whom He has a perfect love, and from whom He exacts a reciprocal affection. I do not say so, and do not think so." This good priest had alluded to herself; but Eustelle is inflamed with the desire to raise him to a degree of holiness, we do not say commensurate with her own—for her humility would not have allowed

T 2

her to entertain such a thought—but to that which is the object of her own aspirations. From this letter it appears that she had special reference to him and to another person in the sacrifice she had made of her health and life, a sacrifice which we know she also made for her father's conversion.

The following letter strikingly exhibits the freedom and confidence with which her late director had encouraged her to speak to him of his own spiritual state :—" Do, then, tell me," it begins, " whether your soul fares better, and in general how you are as respects all your troubles. Why should you fear to speak to me of them? I never saw anybody like you. All you have told me, and all you could tell me, will make no difference to me, I assure you ; in my thoughts you will be neither a greater saint nor a greater sinner. I know very well that you do not owe me any such disclosure, but you are well aware that, if I interest myself in your soul's welfare, it is only for the glory of God. I desire to know that you are happy and full of love for Him. It would be to me a special consolation if I knew that you are as you would wish to be, as Jesus would have you to be. I often beseech this God whom I love to enlighten you, to make you His captive, His possession,—to animate you more and more with an ardent zeal for His glory. May your soul find its food and its very life in the sacred flames of His love. Would that I could share with you that which Jesus imparts to me ; but, indeed, you already love Him more than I do : it is for you to communicate to me of your superabundance. Fain would I persuade you to spend before the sacred tabernacle all your disposable moments. Indeed, I know that this is what you already do ; only I would pray you to go as often as you possibly can. What charms ought it not to possess for one individual soul, seeing that it encloses the Beatitude of the Saints in Heaven, the one, the only good, Jesus, our Friend, our Brother, our Spouse, our All! O how happy we are to be able to love Him! Let us, then, love Him as much as it is possible to love Him here below."

These examples may be sufficient to explain the intimate affection which bound these two souls to each other. Theirs, indeed, was an intimacy to which that of mere earthly friends, however closely associated they may be, is but an outside acquaintance. For how often do those whom even the dearest bonds of relationship unite go through a whole life mutually ignorant of what passes in the depths of each other's souls and of all that most nearly concerns them. It is the Holy Ghost Himself who forms such pure and holy friendships as that which subsisted between Eustelle and her former pastor, friendships which the world cannot and is not worthy to comprehend. To this beloved brother in Christ, then, Eustelle unreservedly confided the transports of her love for Jesus in the Eucharist, and the gracious manifestations of His love towards her. The Saviour often showed Himself to her in the Blessed Sacrament. " Death only, Monsieur l'Abbé," she writes in the beginning of 1840, " can put a term to what I suffer from the desire to love and to cause others to love:—Jesus alone is the depository of it. You could scarcely believe how many special graces my soul receives from Him in prayer. I saw this amiable Saviour a few days ago in the monstrance under the form of a child. With one hand He showed me His Sacred Heart, the other He extended towards me with the most touching

expression. This lasted about a quarter of an hour.
I will give you more details later." She tells him
that she had mentioned all to M. Briand, who had no
hesitation in assuring her that this vision was of
heavenly origin. She then goes on to speak of the
fruits which grow in the garden of our soul, and which
the spouse in the Canticles invites her Beloved to
come and eat.* They are the fruits of His own trees,
trees which He Himself has planted out of His own
gratuitous liberality. "Thus," she says, "you
cannot be ignorant that nothing in me can have
merited those fruits which Jesus has made to ger-
minate in my heart; they are, in all the force of those
terms, fruits of the trees of my Saviour. I only
marvel that He should have chosen my soul as the
field for such operations. Believe me, it is the
desire of His glory alone that animates me; and, if I
tell you these things, it is only that you may know
His goodness and His love, and that with me you may
bless Him. Love, then, this tender Saviour, and do
not say again that He does not wish you to love Him
as much as I do. Go often to the tabernacle; you will
learn from the Sovereign Priest the duties which your
sacred ministry imposes; there you will receive light."

We find these visions always producing in her the
same effect of humility, which was, doubtless, what
stamped them in M. Briand's eyes with the seal of
genuineness. Another of their results was increase
of charity. It was as if one threw fuel on an already
blazing fire; for this fire, as she frequently tells us, was
unceasing, and it was to assuage it in some degree
that she felt compelled to be always writing or speaking of Jesus. "When it is granted me to behold this

* Cant. v. 1.

Divine Saviour in the monstrance," she says, " a kind
of universal transport seems to seize me; I do not
know what there is I could not do. And yet, notwithstanding this state of rapture, it would be impossible for me to be only occupied with myself; I
offer my prayers for all who charitably interest
themselves for me: you may conclude therefore what
place you hold in my remembrance. And our poor
town of Saintes, how I recommend it to the tender
Heart of Jesus! And all sinners, what an interest I
feel for them! With what urgency do I beg for
their sincere conversion! At these moments I feel
inebriated with aspirations and with love; my tongue
is powerless to utter a single word; I leave all to
faith and to my heart. I can no longer make petitions while engaged in prayer (*Je ne peux plus prier
dans l'oraison*); to contemplate and love is my sole
occupation. Then, when I quit this exercise, the fire
that has been kindled within me is so vehement that
I cannot restrain myself from speaking of it, that I
may move all whom I know to the acquisition of this
heavenly love. Ah! why does Jesus make me thus
to languish? Wherefore does He so long delay the
accomplishment of my desires? Why, since by my
state I am precluded from promoting His glory, does
He leave me to live a dying life and to die a living
death?" And then she remembers His adorable Will,
and submits herself to be "a useless member in His
Church, since such is His good pleasure." To get
nearer to that fire which is consuming her is her
abiding desire; hence she covets the priesthood,
though it cannot be hers. The priesthood here, or
that happy country where we shall be kings and
priests for ever with our great King and High Priest

—Heaven above, or the priesthood on earth—this alone could slake the unquenchable thirst of her love.

An interior communication which she received in prayer added inexpressibly to its intensity. Jesus one day caused her to hear those deeply affecting words which He uttered during His dolorous Passion while hanging on the Cross, and which He still utters in the loving depths of His Sacred Heart, and will continue to utter till He has gathered all His elect into His bosom: "I thirst." "O compassionate Saviour," she exclaims, "Thou thirstest! I understand this thirst of Thine; Thou didst thirst in the bosom of Thy Father before Thy Incarnation; Thou didst thirst during Thy mortal life; Thou didst thirst in the garden of Gethsemane; Thou didst thirst on Calvary; and now I hear Thee again complaining in the Eucharist that Thou thirstest. Ah! I understand it: this thirst will never be satisfied until the consummation of ages. O my brother in Jesus, let us strive, then, to share the thirst of this dear Benefactor; He thirsts for our hearts; He thirsts for our love: can we refuse Him? Ah! I seem to see Him in the recesses of His tabernacle; He regards me with kindness, and my heart turns towards Him. O Heavenly Friend, how my soul loves Thee! But, my God, do I love Thee enough? Beg that I may love Him more. Why cannot I die of love? Ah! I hope I may; pray that I may obtain this boon." These words of her Lord appear to have made a peculiarly deep impression on Eustelle's mind, for although, in her correspondence with secular friends, she never relates any supernatural manifestations of which she was the subject, yet in her letters we find frequent allusions to the "thirst" of our Lord, in

which we trace a reminiscence of the interior voice of
Jesus, when He deigned to repeat again in her soul
one of His seven last words.

Her visions were, as we might naturally expect,
generally connected with the presence of Jesus in the
Eucharist. "How often," she writes, "does He grant
me the favour of beholding Him under the Eucharistic veils! Frequently, after my thanksgiving,
grieved to have to leave Him alone in the Sacrament
of the Altar, I have left with Him my heart and my
affections, uniting myself to those blessed spirits who
ever surround this throne of love. Then would this
Heavenly Friend often vouchsafe me the favour to
present me His Sacred Feet to kiss before I departed.
This favour is always present to my mind, and I
seem still to behold his Adorable Feet." She thus
describes this same manifestation in a letter to M.
Briand :—" There is a grace which this tender Friend
of souls often grants me when, being alone with Him,
I love to kiss the foot of the altar before leaving
Him. He deigns to manifest himself to my soul,
and to show me His Sacred Feet, inviting me to
imprint upon them the kiss which I was about to
give to the altar step." This regret at leaving Him,
which frequently made her turn back to say a few
last words and take another last look, as persons do
when bidding farewell to those whom they love so
dearly that they are loth to lose sight of them, was so
pleasing to our Lord, who (as she said) loves these
little testimonies of affection, that He one day rewarded it with another vision of Himself. As she
stood at the church door gazing at the tabernacle, she
beheld His Sacred Heart in the Blessed Eucharist
surrounded with flames. "How good He is!

What return can I make for so much love!" is
all she can say; and then with childlike simplicity
she promises a meeting on the morrow : " à demain,"
and so takes her leave. The next day (it is to M.
Briand she relates both these visions), when contemplating Jesus on the altar, after the elevation, as
an immolated victim, she heard Him say, "I offer
Myself for My sinners." "Mark these words,
father," she says : " My sinners." She understood
in them the tender love of Jesus for those for whom
He died, and they filled her with fresh confidence in
His pardoning mercy, and renewed tenderness and
compassion for souls so dear to Him. Every one of
these visions seems, indeed, to have worked a special
effect upon her at the time, the echo of which we
meet with in her subsequent letters.

Sometimes she seemed to see her own soul in the
chalice all empurpled with the Blood of the Redeemer ; and upon more than one occasion she was
the recipient of a grace which must be regarded as of
a very high order. " On Sunday last," she writes,
"after having reposed in Holy Communion, like the
beloved Apostle, upon the bosom of Jesus for nearly
two hours, I prepared to adorn the altar of the
Blessed Virgin, when, on approaching the tabernacle"
—it will be remembered that the Blessed Sacrament
was reserved also at our Lady's Altar—"I was
minded to kneel down again because Jesus was
near me. At that moment I felt myself all transformed into our Lord, in suchwise that I no longer
saw myself or had any conscious sensation of myself.
I had never been before in a similar state; the
Adorable Humanity of Jesus seemed to absorb my
whole being, and I marvelled at what I experienced,

seeing and feeling in my limbs only those of Jesus.＊
Then I recalled to mind what the Apostle says :
' I live, but it is Jesus only who lives in me.' "
Words, indeed, seemed to fail her to express the
operations which were so frequently passing in her
soul. Writing about a week later, she says, " O my
father, read in my heart : there is something more ;
but I cannot say it. Jesus knows it, and you understand it." The very number of the graces she daily
received in this Divine Sacrament made it impossible
for her to report them all. She can only entreat for
more love, more gratitude, and more humility :
humility especially is the object of all her ambition—
humility, which (she says) " is to the soul what sugar
is to fruit."

A few days afterwards she takes up her pen to
record a fresh gracious manifestation of her Lord.
He had again shown her His Sacred Heart. It was
during Mass that she beheld It, placed as it were in
the midst of a wide space which It seemed to fill with
the flames of love which issued from It, and darted in
far-reaching rays into the measureless distance. Our
Lord caused her to understand thereby His desire to
inflame the whole universe with His love. She
beheld at the same time many angels in human form
adoring the Sacred Heart. " You can imagine, my
father," she says, "what must have been the state of
my soul as long as I beheld It. My spirit was as if
lost in this ocean of all good, and I understood that
I could not understand it." In the same letter she
tells her director that another day, while assisting at

＊ Similar states are recorded in the lives of Saints ; e.g.,
V. Margaret of the B. Sacrament, who was specially called to
propagate the devotion to the Infant Jesus.

Mass and meditating on the grandeur of the sacrifice which was being offered, after the Gospel she no longer saw the priest at the altar, but our Lord Himself, who with exceeding majesty was offering to His Heavenly Father the Holy Victim, which is none other than Himself. "A God offering Himself to a God—what a sacrifice! My mind cannot grasp its value! It was, above all, at the moment of consecration that my soul was filled with awe and love. The sight of this God-man consecrating His own Body and Blood penetrated me with joy and happiness. With what avidity did I long for the moment when the Beloved of my soul would come and bring me the Bread of Angels, Himself giving Himself to me. I was forgetting to tell you," she continues, "that I saw two heavenly spirits serving Him during the Holy Sacrifice, and I think that I perceived them near Him when He was giving me Holy Communion. All this took place mentally, and I seem still to see and feel what I experienced in my soul during those precious moments. It appeared to me as if it was on the altar of my heart that this Sacred Victim offered Himself; and I united myself thereto to be immolated with Jesus and by Jesus. Blessed be He for ever!" Then she assures M. Briand that she has not forgotten his recommendation to prefer one act of the will, one good desire, to all the extraordinary lights she might receive. "Believe me," she says, "I feel no attachment to these things, and a desire for the glory of our Divine Master alone occupies me at such times." Neither, she adds, do they fill her mind at other times; she recalls them only to make them known to him, and if Jesus should require her to be absolutely silent on the subject, she would joyfully submit.

She had beheld Jesus offering Mass in the person of the officiating priest on earth ; she was now to see this same representative of her Lord celebrating the Adorable Mysteries on the great heavenly altar. " On Saturday, my very dear father," she writes, " I hope to assist at the Holy Sacrifice in heaven, for the last time I heard your Mass I was no longer upon earth. I saw you in those regions where Jesus manifests Himself unveiled by clouds ; a multitude of blessed spirits surrounded the August Victim, Jesus my Beloved, Jesus my Love. As for me, of whom I would rather never speak, I was at your feet, my soul abyssed in the contemplation of the wonders being enacted upon that sublime altar by the ministry with which Jesus has entrusted you."

Another time we find her relating a very remarkable vision of the same character. " It was on Sunday, during Mass," she says ; " and Jesus filled my mind with the same sentiments as those which you mentioned yesterday as having yourself experienced during this great action. It was near the moment of consecration, about five minutes previous to it, when I felt my mind raised up to heaven ; then I beheld a ray, or rather, a path of light reaching from this abode of glory to the altar. It was about four feet wide, and was bordered by a hedge of clouds of silvery whiteness. Upon these clouds rested numbers of heavenly spirits, who seemed to be awaiting the solemn moment when the Saint of Saints was, if I may so say, to traverse by this road the immense space which separates heaven from earth, in order to abase and annihilate Himself in behalf of His senseless and ungrateful creatures. I cannot tell you in what way my mind was enlightened, but so vivid and penetrating was this light that it must have been supernatural. It seemed to me that in the sight that presented itself to my soul, I beheld far more than my bodily eyes would have been capable of beholding. What I felt was in accordance with what I witnessed. I seemed to be freed from the bonds of the flesh, so clear was my intelligence. This is the manner in which I am always enlightened at such times. No self-love then : I do not give self a thought, yet I may be allowed in your presence, a presence in which I beheld Jesus Christ alone, to acknowledge the continual gifts which I receive from the Divine Creator. Oh, I understand how great they are, but it is only to humble myself the more. Yes, the more prodigal Jesus is of His favours, the more humble I will be ; and the light which He shall deign to communicate to me, will serve also, I hope, to make me know and feel my unworthiness, my weakness, my poverty. Scarcely had the Holy Victim been laid on the altar of sacrifice, when I perceived Jesus fastened to the cross by two barbarous executioners; then, like another brazen serpent, He was raised between heaven and earth. He seemed to be occupied with the souls of those kneeling at His feet, but the greater part of whom were there in the body only. With my eyes fixed upon this divine cross, I prayed this dear Saviour to permit me to immolate myself with Him, and not to let me have the pain of seeing Him expire without me. 'What ! my Adorable Master,' I said, 'it is but an instant since by a love the most marvellous of all loves Thou hast descended for us upon this altar, and already Thou longest to pour forth all Thy Blood for us. Thy Heart burns to testify the insatiable love for us ᵕh consumes It.' Then all words and all reflections gave place in me to a silence of admiration and love. Jesus was immolated!"

Eustelle's life seemed now almost one continual ecstasy. "The beloved disciple," we find her writing, "does not rest alone on the bosom of the good Saviour; it is granted to His poor servant also lovingly to repose thereon, and to feel the throbbings of this Heart which beats for her. United to this Adorable Heart, she feeds on love. Hence she draws the unction which instructs and enlightens. Ah! it is from this Heart one learns all that it is important to know. I desire no other book. There all the hearts that belong to Jesus live by the life by which He Himself lives in the bosom of His Heavenly Father. O perverse world, vanish from my sight. I have found on the bosom of Jesus that holy ignorance which is preferable to all the lights of the learned, and that sacred folly of the Cross, which is of more value than all the pretended wisdom of philosophers. As for me, I will know but one science, that of my Jesus, who teaches me to attach myself to Him alone, to love nothing but Him or for Him." And again, "Yes, my father, He is my existence; He is what I cannot express: God grant you may understand it. My soul is beside itself, but is in peace, because the good, the amiable, the all-desirable Jesus, occupies it, fills it with rapture, and consumes it. And how does all this take place? I do not know. In the Eucharistic union Jesus manifests Himself, and causes Himself to be felt, in a manner surpassing comprehension. I seem to rush forward to lay hold upon Him. Oh, how this good Saviour burns in me with the zeal of the glory of His Heavenly Father! How He excites in my heart the thirst of Calvary!

And all the while I am but a poor feeble girl, powerless, incapable of anything. Blessed be He for it.
I desire to be such, if it be His will. I suffer from
the wound of His love. Oh, how sweet is this suffering! It makes me die, and raises me to life at one
and the same time." This wound of divine love,
of which saints have discoursed, can be described in
their own language only, and even this has been
totally insufficient to express its united joys and pains.

She had seen and felt herself resting on the Heart
of Jesus; and again, after receiving her Beloved in
the Eucharist, who at the moment of consecration had
manifested Himself to her as a mystical lamb, we find
her contemplating Him in His Sacred Humanity, as
He reposes in the sanctuary of her soul, beams of
splendour radiating from His glorious Body, and
filling this new heaven wherein He had placed the
throne of His Majesty. "Acknowledge," she says
to M. Briand, in the same letter in which she recounts this vision, "that I am very unworthy of
the favours of my Jesus, and that in Himself alone
can He find the motives of the love He bears me.
But you must also understand to what a degree I
desire to love, and cause others to love, this God
who is alone worthy of love. I am so transported
at this very moment, as I write, that if I did not
restrain myself, I should fill the paper with a thousand extravagances. Oh, then, love Him who is
Love Itself." With a timid respect she then ventures
to invite him not to leave their Divine Master alone,
but to visit Him as often as possible, begging him on
the morrow to lay at the feet of the August Victim
her desires and her helplessness. "O my father,"
she says, "I conclude, but my soul is not satisfied:

I think of the Eucharist, and I feel my heart in-flamed anew."

In a letter written near the close of her life, she recounts a vision in some respects similar, only much superior to that with which she had been favoured two years before, and of which she gave an account to the former Curé of Saint-Pallais. It will be remembered how, as she lingered at the church door from reluctance to leave her Beloved, He had shown her His Sacred Heart; and on the present occasion the grace she received seems to have been attracted, as it was preceded by like sentiments on her part. "I must tell you, my father," she writes, "that when, after having received our Love, I have to retire from His Eucharistic Presence, I experience such acute pain, that as I am leaving the church, when I am alone there, I keep turning my eyes again and again towards the holy tabernacle, testifying with the liveliest expressions of sorrow the bitter grief it is to me to leave Him alone in His prison of love. Some days ago, when kneeling at His feet, I besought Him, since it was His will that I should leave Him, to deign to shut me up in the ciborium which I so love to contemplate. I prayed Him to unite my heart to His Divine Heart, to transform it into It by a kind of transubstantiation. Then this Divine Master showed me His Heart filled with incomprehensible wonders, which I felt, but cannot utter. My own was also shown to me united to His by an indissoluble tie. Soon I saw it melt, flow, and lose itself in this furnace of love; so that now I no longer beheld anything except the infinitely holy and adorable Heart of my Saviour. Jesus Himself assured me that night and day I was always present to Him

U

in His tabernacle. This grace consoled me much, but
it has only served to augment my love. Ah! my dear
father, you tell me that every evening you shut up
your soul in the gilded prison where Jesus dwells; I
do the same; consequently I always meet you in that
holy retreat." Eustelle was soon to need the consolation which this beautiful vision gave her, when,
languishing on her sick bed, she was no longer to be
able to visit the tabernacle; and precious, indeed,
to her in those hours of privation must have been
the sweet assurance which Jesus had given her that
she was ever with Him in that sacred home of her
affections.

The fruit of Eustelle's visions, then, was ever a
deepening of her humility and an increase of her
love; and we cannot better conclude this chapter
than by quoting some of her own words, taken from
the same letter in which she records the vision of the
Sacred Heart. After other rapturous addresses to
the Beloved of her soul, she exclaims, "O my tender
Brother,"—that being the relationship under which
she specially delighted to consider her dear Lord—
"the words I employ do not express all that I see,
all that I feel, all that I comprehend of the mystery
of Thy love. And yet, O Jesus, I am but an insignificant creature, a worm of the earth, a heap of corruption, and, through my iniquities, the instrument
of Thy death. Do I, then, deserve thus to participate
in Thy favours? Jesus, my God, pardon my boldness. But it is Thou Thyself, it is Thy love, which
makes me so bold. O Jesus! O Jesus! O Jesus!
my soul is consumed in Thee, by Thee, and for Thee.
It is not only the innumerable graces which Jesus
bestows on my soul which excite in me such lively

gratitude and love, but much more the love which prompts Him to abase Himself in order to communicate Himself to me, a creature so poor and vile.   O infinite charity!   In Thyself alone canst Thou find the motive of the love which Thou bearest me ; for in me there is nothing but what is fitted to repel Thee. . . . . . Notwithstanding my poverty, I pray much for you, my father, as well as for the souls you evangelize. That is all I can do ; to offer some prayers, which Jesus, I hope, will not reject.   He is so good, so good, so good.   My confidence in Him is boundless. Beg Him to make my heart according to His Heart. . . . . . My health is very bad, I suffer much, which rejoices me much.   I am very thankful to Him for it. I leave you that I may seek His feet.   I ardently desire to die for His love.

"Your daughter in His Heart,

"EUSTELLE, His very little servant."

CHAPTER VI.

EXCESSES AND MARTYRDOM OF LOVE.

WHEN the liquid boils in the full vase, it runs over, it *exceeds ;* and so it is with ardent love.   When love is too strong for ordinary words and ordinary actions to express its vehemence, it takes refuge in demonstrations which are excesses, if not follies, in the eyes of others.   Such demonstrations naturally seek the shade.   We have seen that Eustelle's love was of this character ; and we have seen, too, how much it cost her to keep it within such tranquil bounds as might escape the charge of singularity, and how it became to her almost a necessary relief to pour out of the super-abundance of her fervour to those few chosen souls who could understand her, or, where they could not follow her to her lofty heights, would not misunder-stand her. But if it was difficult for her in the inter-course of daily life to repress all manifestation of the ardour which glowed in her bosom, it may well be imagined that when alone in the solitude of the sacred edifice, prostrate before the tabernacle, where that furnace was for ever burning, and whence her inward fires were being perpetually fed, the passionate expression of her seraphic love burst forth with un-controllable energy. These transports, common to the saints, have found their relief in divers ways. Some have had the gift of tears, their eyes have become fountains whence streams, not metaphorical but literal, have issued. The floor where St. Aloysius knelt used to be wet with the tears he shed. Others have been separated, as it were, for hours from their corporeal senses, the body, rapt in a mystic slumber, being thus spared for the time that participation in the consuming fervours and sublime flights of its immortal companion, which it languishes to follow, and which it attempts to follow only to languish and die.

We have seen that with Eustelle the use of her senses and bodily faculties was seldom, if ever, en-tirely suspended. In her solitary ecstasies, ecstasies in which others have been surprised raised from the ground, or praying in unconscious immovability, Eustelle's passionate and restless love led her to commit what she calls her "follies." But if follies

they were, it was overflowing love which alone
impelled her to commit them; with less love they
had been irreverent acts, and even love equal to
her own would have been insufficient to excuse
them unless they had been the result of a like invincible attraction. For we cannot but believe that
it was our Lord Himself who drew her to give Him
these testimonies of tenderness, if only for this reason,
that, although she calls them "follies and extravagances," although she dreads their becoming known to
any one to whom they might give scandal, although
she has certain misgivings as to obtaining any authoritative permission for her conduct, yet—albeit her conscience was so acutely tender—never for one moment
does she allude to these practices as possibly wrong
or implying any fault on her part. She will allow
others to blame them, but she never condemns them
herself. She could not help them, she feared she
should die if she were hindered, and yet she mentions
them; considering, doubtless, that the silence of her
directors would be a virtual consent. No priest,
indeed, could formally authorize such acts, and our
Lord, who prompted them, did not will that they
should have any such positive sanction. We have
Sister Anastasia's testimony that her friend did at last
receive a prohibition, or what she construed as such;
for we must understand her as alluding to what
passed between Eustelle and the Bishop of La Rochelle
a few months before her death, when we shall find
her interpreting some of his observations in that
sense. But he could not have given a positive prohibition, since he was not acquainted with the facts, and
certainly she never received any from either of her
other two directors. As for the former Curé of

Saint-Pallais, so great was his veneration for Eustelle, and so unattainable by himself did he consider the love which she bore her Saviour, that he probably never thought of discouraging any mode in which she was drawn to express it.

It is in her correspondence with this priest that we first find mention of the subject. In the month of March, 1840, after telling him of the bodily weakness and exhaustion which at one time she experiences in prayer and communion, and of the supernatural force which at another time they would impart, followed, however, by renewed prostration of strength, she adds, "I do not complain of this, I am unworthy of it, and I beg of Jesus to increase my love of Him, although I know that this will only augment my sufferings. Do not pity me, I can manage to get on. The fact is, that the way by which I am led is, as M. le Curé told me the other day, extraordinary and uncommon. And yet he does not know all—not as much as you do. I must now acknowledge a very bold action of mine. I will even allow you to condemn it as reprehensible, unless you should reckon it as one of those transports which precede reflection and become excusable because they are not deliberate. The other day, being alone in the church, all of a sudden I left my place, and in a moment I was before the holy tabernacle ; I even dared to ascend the altar, and to kiss the door of the sacred prison where His love confines Him. My confession is made. Let us love Jesus : love Him, my dear brother, but love Him calmly, tranquilly, without anxiety or weariness." No regret, no apprehensions, are expressed : she only says, " Let us love Jesus "— the conclusion at which she ever arrives—and accompanies the exhortation with an affectionate counsel to the troubled soul she is addressing.

Less than a week later, we have another letter to her former director, written on her birthday, in which the following passage occurs:—"O minister of Jesus, what will you think of the temerity of my love, and of the extravagant desires with which it inspires me? Would you believe that I am always envying the happiness of priests, to whom it is permitted so often to open the holy tabernacle, and to hold in their hands the vessel of love in which Jesus deigns to repose? The very thought makes my whole frame thrill with emotion. I feel it at this moment; my limbs tremble, and my pen can scarcely trace the sentiments of my heart. I feel a mixture of happiness, awe, and veneration; but, above all, of love: what do I say, love? it is an inexpressible transport. Do you remember how I once asked you to open for me an empty ciborium? I did not then tell you all that was passing in my mind; I was imagining to myself this ciborium filled with Hosts consecrated on the altar by virtue of the sacramental words, and I said to myself, 'Ah, if only I were allowed to press it to my heart!' This morning the same thought tormented my soul, which is ever thirsting, languishing, consuming away, because I burn with a desire which the Church cannot permit me to satisfy. Sometimes I am almost obliged to turn away my eyes from the holy tabernacle, that I may not be tempted to go and press my burning lips against it. The sacred ciborium awakens in me a like strange emotion; with the eye of faith I contemplate within it our imprisoned Love; but fain would I contemplate also the sacred species with which He tenderly enshrouds Himself. The presence of persons in the church, placing as it does a constraint upon the need I feel to shed abundant tears, to sob at my ease, and utter exclamations of love, is sometimes a cause of suffering to me. When there is no one in the holy place, I am at liberty, it is true, to give full vent to the feelings with which my heart is surcharged; but then I become a prey to temptations which may be regarded as a species of insanity. My soul is, as it were, inundated and consumed at one and the same time; my heart beats violently; I long to cross the space which separates me from Jesus; I covet the bliss of holding in my hands the happy vessel which encloses Him, and which would be a thousand times more blessed than myself, were it capable of comprehending its blessedness. I wish to embrace it, to hold it pressed to my lips, to open my heart and place it therein. If such a thing were possible, the most agonizing wound would be to me the sweetest and most ravishing delight. Sometimes my consciousness nearly forsakes me, my limbs stiffen and become cold; I feel my strength gradually ebbing away, and I can no longer form words wherewith to address Jesus; its last burning sighs seem to escape from my heart; and my whole body languishes and faints. Yet from time to time I seem to arouse myself to exclaim, 'O Jesus, how I love Thee; make the sinners I commend to Thee to love Thee! O my Beloved, my soul cries out for Thee; I cannot live without Thee. My dear Jesus, why am I not allowed to carry Thee away with me? I feel all the weight of my unworthiness; nevertheless I am drawn to Thee by an invisible and invincible force. This force is the love I have for Thee, the love which makes me die.' Sometimes I address myself to the blessed spirits who surround the invisible majesty of my God hidden under the Sacramental veils, and I say to them, 'It is not for you that He is here ; it is for me.   Leave, then, to me the place which you occupy so near to Him.   Why do you rob me of Him ?   Does not Heaven suffice you, where you contemplate His glory ?   Give place, I conjure you, to His exiled lover, who asks, as the only consolation in her banishment, to approach nearer to the throne of His love.' "

This letter was not finished the day it was begun. The ardent desires which it expressed had proved irresistible, and she has to add another " confession " before closing it.   " In the afternoon of the same day," she writes, " I returned to the foot of the holy altar.   I was suffering a hunger and a thirst which I might in vain attempt to describe ; those alone who have experienced the same could understand it.   I was alone, and, without considering that I might be surprised in the act, I crossed the sanctuary, and went to press my lips against the sacred altar.   Oh, how often did I kiss it !   With what a flood of tears did I bedew it !   . . .   In fine, my brother, I cannot tell you all : there are things which cannot be expressed in words. I found it almost impossible to take any nourishment, absorbed as I was in the thought of Jesus and of His love.   Oh, how I love Him !   Do you also love Him. No, our Lord will not be displeased with me for the excessive familiarities I have permitted myself ; it even seems to me that in exceptional cases He would permit more, were it not needful that the holy rules which He has prescribed to His Church should be of general application.   I receive these holy rules with the deepest veneration.   They would, doubtless, be less severe, and would leave us nearer access to Jesus in the Eucharist, if all the faithful were devoured with the pure flames of holy love. I pray you write to me your thoughts upon all that I have been telling you. I will work at your stole and banner. Adieu, the clock calls me. Preserve the most inviolable secrecy with respect to the contents of this letter. Love the God of Love. Your sister EUSTELLE."

What her correspondent's expressed opinions on this subject may have been we are ignorant, but there are no traces in her subsequent letters of having received any censure or check. She evidently had an intimate conviction that she was committing no real act of irreverence. Love was her safeguard, as it was in the early days of the Church, when to be a Christian was all one with being ready in very deed to die for Christ, and the faithful were allowed to carry the Blessed Eucharist to their homes, and take it in their hands when they received communion. For such a privilege Eustelle would have been willing to undergo a daily marytrdom. Her letters continue to manifest, in varied ways, this same intense longing for a more intimate union with Jesus, which finds its expression in the most passionate cravings for a greater local nearness. "I leave you," she says, in concluding a letter; "it is time to go and take my repose with Him near His paternal bosom. Oh, why, then, can I not be nearer to His altar ?" Another time she says, "When Jesus is placed upon the altar, when I perceive the monstrance in which He is exposed, or the ciborium in which He rests, I experience a feeling of reverence and love which penetrates and fills my whole being. To feel Him so near me replenishes me with heavenly joy ; I would gladly die where I kneel.

I attach myself specially to the contemplation of the
Host in the monstrance; Jesus is there as if unveiled before me; then on your behalf, and on that of
the whole Church, I give utterance to the one great
aspiration of my heart. But in saying I give utterance, I do not rightly express my meaning, for faith
and love are my sole language." Then follows a fresh
avowal of the unrestrainable transports of her love.
"Finding myself alone in the church one day," she
says, " I could not refrain from going to kiss the door
of the holy tabernacle; but this is not all. This week
I had received permission to ascend the altar to clean
the image of our Lady. You know that our Lord is
also in the tabernacle of this chapel—well, pray do
not scold me : having got up to acquit myself of the
office with which I had been entrusted, I knelt down
close to our good Jesus, then, throwing my arms round
the tabernacle, I gave it a thousand kisses. I next
embraced the image of our good Mother, our sweetest
friend, our sister, for so I love to call her ; I arranged
her, adorned her, and from time to time permitted
myself to kiss her face and hands. After thus spend-
ing three hours, I was fain to leave a place so dear to
my heart, and return to love Jesus in my own simple
dwelling." But it was not to the former Curé of
Saint-Pallais alone that Eustelle made these confessions; M. Briand, her then director, was not left in
ignorance. "The other day," she writes, "nobody
being in the church at the time, I could not resist
going to kiss the door of the holy tabernacle. If I
did wrong, I hope you will forgive me. I will not do
it again if you should forbid me ; but until you do, I
will not answer for not giving way again to the same
temptation." That he did not forbid her may be

inferred from finding her in a subsequent letter telling
him how one day she had ascended the altar, embraced
the tabernacle, and was about to give a like testimony
of affection to our Lady, when she heard the outer
door of the church opening, and had only time to
descend before the entrance of a person who, she says,
would have been much scandalized at detecting her in
such an act.

It was the same resistless attraction drawing her to
the altar which made priests the objects of her constant envy as well as her affection. Unable to share
their privileges, she longed at least to honour and
love Jesus through them, and to procure their greater
sanctification. "Ah, my brother," she writes to the
Curé, "how is it possible not to die of love? How is
it possible not to have thought and memory filled
with Jesus in the Eucharist? I implore you, love
only this only Love of the Heavenly Father ; see Him
alone in all things ; breathe only, act only, for Him.
Him alone ! Him everywhere, Him always ! Ah,
priest of Jesus, how happy you are ! You may love
Him much more than I can, if you will." And again,
" O what happiness to be able in this land of banishment to love Jesus, and, above all, in the Eucharist!
Sacred Manna, I die of hunger for It, and yet I feed
upon It daily. Ah, my brother, I suffer wonderfully
from the love that Jesus gives me for this ineffable
mystery. My life is but one continued languor, and
He knows it, this good Master. I cannot express
what I feel ; no human language is adequate. Love
Jesus, then, much, my brother—you whose word
He daily obeys. O, how happy are you, priest of
Jesus ! Wherefore must useless desires consume me,
who envy a blessedness which on earth cannot be

mine ?" Then we find her thus reasoning and remon-
strating with herself: "When Jesus had reascended
into Heaven, His holy Mother was content to receive
Him daily in communion, and did not allow herself
to indulge in those innocent caresses towards the
Eucharist which she had lavished on the Child Jesus.
She forbade herself those kisses which she had formerly imprinted on His heavenly face ; she did not
press this Sacred Manna to her heart before placing
It in her virginal mouth ; she did not ask to bear
about with her on her own person this memorial of
the infinite love of Jesus Christ for men, although
there never existed upon earth a tabernacle so pure .
or so lovely in the eyes of the Lord as this spotless
lily."*

* Eustelle, as is evident, was unacquainted with the pious
belief, which has authorities of weight to support it, that Mary
was the perpetual tabernacle on earth of her Divine Son from
the moment she received Him on the night before His Passion,
the sacred species remaining within her uncorrupted, and so
retaining the Presence of the Incarnate God. Sister Maria de
Agreda, in her vision of the " Mistica Ciudad di Dios," says that
our Lady was communicated by angelic hands, when our Lord
offered the first Mass in the Cœnaculum ; and that her bosom
was thus the sole tabernacle in which the God-Man, who had
come to be ever with us, dwelt while His Blessed Soul was in
Limbo. This miracle was renewed each time she received her
Divine Son in the Eucharist. This belief singularly recommends itself to us, both as a mark of the peculiar love of Him
whose delights are to be with the children of men, and as an
honour most congruous to the dignity of His Mother, who
thus, from the moment that the Archangel saluted her with
the address, " Dominus tecum," and that she gave her consent
to the ineffable mystery of the Incarnation, was never to lose
His presence. Thus, too, would our Lord, who had promised
to be ever with us, have provided a tabernacle for Himself
wherein to be reserved during the earliest days of the Church.
Marie-Eustelle's biographer, after alluding to the pious belief
that the Adorable Sacrament remained unconsumed in Mary's
bosom from one communion to another, adds, " and if, as some
have thought, and as we love to conjecture, the last Host con-

Eustelle's longings for the sacerdotal office had a double source, as her aspirations show. She considered that priests enjoyed the advantage of being able to love Jesus more than others, through the great increment their devotion must receive from the ineffable relation in which they stand to the Lamb of God offering Himself by their hands, and that they had, besides, fuller means of satisfying their love. " I am transported with His love," she exclaims ; "so transported, that I do not know what to say. How can He lavish so many favours on me ? Why can I not respond to them with the love of the Seraphim and of all the united choirs of angels ? Would that I possessed a thousand million hearts, and a thousand million voices, that I might consecrate them to the love of Him who is Love, and make others love Him ! Happy, shall I for ever repeat— happy are the ministers of the sanctuary ! The thought of a priest fills me with rapture. O my brother, and you are one ! It is this character I love in you. Wherefore must I be possessed by a kind of

secrated upon earth shall be borne at the consummation of time into Heaven, to be there eternally venerated by the elect, is it not to be presumed that the August Trinity will place It in the most pure and most holy Heart of Mary, the true golden Monstrance of the endless Exposition ?" What a peculiar depth of meaning does this idea seem to give to the "*Dominus tecum !*" She is the true Ark of the Covenant, which held the Manna ; and it will be remembered that St. John, in the Apocalyptic vision, when the nations have been judged and the kingdoms of the world have become the kingdoms of the Lord, saw the Temple of God opened in Heaven and the Ark of His Testament within it (Apoc. xi. 19). If this interpretation be admissible, and that Ark was Mary bearing in her bosom the Sacred Manna, we may recognise in the concluding words of the "Salve Regina" a special meaning very glorious to our Blessed Mother : "*Et Jesum, benedictum fructum ventris tui, nobis post hoc exilium ostende.*"

folly, which impels me to envy a vocation which my sex renders impossible to me? Wherefore does Jesus permit me to pine with such strange regrets for things which I know to be out of my power? Ah, dear good Master! He knows whither all the desires of my heart tend. And you, too, know : it is to the tabernacle, that abode of love, that obscure and mysterious prison, wherein, however, by the illuminating light of faith we are enabled to discern the King of Heaven in all His splendour. And it is the priest who reproduces Him there!"

The hunger and thirst which were never satisfied except by the Eucharistic Banquet, increased in intensity the nearer she drew to the term of her mortal life. It is the perpetually recurring topic of her letters. In the autumn of 1841, she writes thus to her late director :—'· My soul is more and more attracted to its centre, which is Jesus. It dies a thousand times from the longing to have what nevertheless it so intimately possesses. Always does the same hunger devour it; always does the same fire consume it. Ah, wherefore cannot I find in the place where I dwell a heart which loves our good Redeemer as I should wish Him to be loved in the Sacrament of His Love? Wherefore is the light eclipsed even in those in whom it ought to be so bright? . . . I feel His blessed presence in so intimate a manner, that I know not what to do or what to say to appease the thirst with which I am consumed. The zeal of His glory dries me up; His love fills me with rapture; and yet I can scarcely do anything for Him. . . . To calm a little the excessive ardour of my soul, it would be needful to have the God of the Eucharist perpetually in my heart. You may think, perhaps, I exaggerate, and yet what I say is as nothing. Last Sunday Jesus redoubled this suffering by augmenting the love which already consumes me. I felt so ill that I left the tabernacle, and retired into the sacristy, that I might give free course to the burning sighs which oppressed me. I knew not what to do. Oh, would that the adorable, the delicious Eucharist could be received several times a day! What adds to my martyrdom is the sight of the indifference which the greater part of creatures manifest for the God I love. . . . If it is not possible for you, cruel brother, to satisfy my sometimes extravagant desires, at least take pity on me, and relieve my pain by talking to me of Jesus." And so, on another occasion, she takes him to task for not talking to her enough about her Lord, and says that in this respect his letters are not worth the five sous he pays to frank them ; adding, however, that he knows she says this only in jest.

The spirit of reparation, so closely united to the love of Jesus in the Blessed Sacrament, was very strong in Eustelle, and she suffered a daily martyr-dom from her inability to make amends to the God of Love for the little love His creatures show Him. Hence she is always going, as it were, a-begging for love for Him. For as light and love daily increased in her own soul with the increasing favours of her Lord, she perceived with the greater clearness and sorrowed with the deeper sorrow for the indifference of men and the outrage which such indifference offers to Him in the Sacrament of His Love. "This sight," she says, "afflicts me beyond measure; I should wish to en-counter it with all my strength, and I find only inability and powerlessness. O dear brother, if Jesus in the Eucharistic union did not alleviate this pain, it would be impossible for me to live, so closely do His interests touch my heart. Pray, then—let us all pray—that His love may dispel so much coldness and indifference. Redouble your efforts to love Him more and to make Him loved." In another of her letters she again tells him that without a particular disposition of her Lord she could not live long; and she is obliged, she says, to speak and write continually of Him in order in some degree to quench her thirst. The happy, the blessed moments of communion are short; and, though the remembrance of her morning's communion is sweet, yet it is sad also, because it recalls a past happiness.

Long before, our Lord had made known to Eustelle, while in prayer, that she was to be His victim. She understood the meaning of His words, and had abandoned herself to be immolated according to His good pleasure. She knew, as she often said, that death alone would terminate her sufferings, for they had their source in a love which in this mortal flesh never can be satisfied. Hence what she utters are not so much complaints as plaints; she would not exchange her pains—we do not say for all the joys on earth, but even for the bliss of Heaven, till such is her Beloved's will. "How far I am," she says, "from desiring the close of this languishing life!" "I suffer much, my father," she writes to M. Briand, "but how blessed are these sufferings! I languish ever, and often borrow the words of the spouse in the Canticles, begging Jesus to stay me with His fruits and His flowers. You know what those fruits and flowers are; but, besides what you take them to mean, I understand also crosses, humiliations, perse-

X

cutions, contempt; above all, and better than all, I
love the most holy and most sweet flower of the Divine
Will.   No; in spite of all I wish to be and to do for
Jesus, I desire only the accomplishment of His good
pleasure.   When will He permit me to speak with
you and communicate to you my pious longings?
Some there are which cannot be realized in this life, and
yet it is my Jesus who seems to excite them.   What,
then, does He desire of me?   That I should leave
this earth?   Ah! here I am, ready to take wing for
my own country, to prostrate myself at His feet, and
cast myself into His arms, that I may be inebriated
with His love.   What does He wish?   That I should
remain still in my banishment?   I consent : but let
Him either satisfy my desires or temper their
ardour;" and then she immediately contradicts
herself and says that she does not desire any abatement of what makes her so happy while it makes her
suffer.   Again, in a letter to the Curé, she thus expresses herself : " What I can simply say is this—that
the love of Jesus makes a martyr of me by that which
He operates in my soul.   Jesus alone is the witness
of this inward torment, which nevertheless I assure
you is most sweet.   M. Briand, who knows all this,
has told me I shall die of it.   Blessed be God !   I
await the day ; but it is with resignation."   Never,
indeed, in her letters do we meet with any absolute
desire for death expressed upon her own account, or
for the sake of personal relief from suffering, although
many and many a time do we find her desiring to die
for the love of Jesus ; to die of love and for love, and
that even daily ; to die at His feet, before the Adorable
Eucharist, that she may be united to Him for ever.
It is the death of love she longs for : she dies that

she cannot die.   And then again she says that to live
or to die is indifferent to her ; it is His Will alone
she loves.   At other times she will say it is true that
to die is gain, but it is always to die of love, and to
be united with her Beloved for whom she is longing ;
as when she exclaims, " Why cannot I hold Him in
my arms, like St. Gertrude or St. Anthony of Padua,
and protest a thousand and a thousand times that I
am altogether possessed by His love ?   O death,
dearest of friends, come, then, and restore me to the
Object of all my desires ! "   Her love sometimes
makes her seem even to forget Heaven itself, so completely is Heaven to her in the Blessed Eucharist.
" Our good Saviour," she says, " augments more and
more my love for the Holy Eucharist. . . . What a
martyrdom !   I do not beg for it to end : it is too
sweet to me to suffer for Him, for whom I would
willingly give my life a thousand and a thousand
times.   O Holy and Divine Eucharist—Heaven is
nothing to me ?   O Host, so little and so frail, Thou
enclosest all I love and all I wish to love."

She suffers from the excess of her own love, and she
suffers from the deficiency of love in others.   She
suffers because the love of Jesus in His Divine Sacrament is so intimately known to her, and she suffers
because it is not known to others, and therefore is not
felt.   Men are blind to it and outrage it by their con-
temptuous neglect.   " How is it," she cries, " that so
few are won by its secret loving solicitations ?   Yes,
Jesus is a God outraged and unknown." She deplores
the absence of faith and of Christian practice in this
perverse age : " God alone," she says, " knows what I
suffer on this account, and it is His will alone which
enables me to endure the hunger and thirst for His

justice which He makes me feel. The more He is offended, the more does this hunger increase, and the more does my life languish. But be He ever blessed for this; and may I thus obliterate the many years passed in the forgetfulness of His divine law! He knows that I have now no other desire, so long as I continue to languish on earth, but to die of love for Him, and to see before I depart the knowledge of Jesus implanted in all hearts. Ah, why am I so far from doing for this dear Master all with which gratitude inspires me? But my powerlessness is in the order of His will. Pray, you who are His ministers, pray that His kingdom may come into the souls where it is not established, and ask this King, this Father, this God-with-us to accept the poor and unworthy sacrifice I have made Him of my life, for the needs of the Church, our mother, and the conversion of those amongst her children who every day afflict her tender heart by the most shameful desertion and the deliberate contempt of her commandments, which are themselves all love."

It was with this special view that Eustelle had made the sacrifice of her life for the sanctification of priests, as being the great means of kindling love in others, and of converting sinners to God. "I love sacerdotal souls," she says, writing to M. Briand in the spring of 1841; "and Jesus knows why. Pray that He may accept the sacrifice which I have made for them." "My father, O my father," she again exclaims, "beg this loving Saviour that, if He leaves me in His Church, I may at least not be a useless member. The desire of saving my own soul occupies me less than that of saving the souls of others. . . . . Oh, if Jesus, the Heavenly Friend of my heart, was

but loved, if His ungrateful creatures were less insensible to His benefits, the zeal with which He
animates me would be satisfied, and the insatiable
thirst which devours me would be appeased. I
rejoice to suffer, but I must have the Adorable Love
made known."

"Console yourself, good Eustelle," says her biographer; " soon, soon, the ardent desires of your soul
shall be fulfilled. Scarcely shall a few years have
elapsed after your death when, at the voice of holy
Pontiffs of the Church, the Host of Life shall be
lifted up on high in the capital of France and in many
places throughout the land. Pious Christians like
yourself, filled with love for Jesus, shall gather from
all sides and range themselves in adoring circles round
the throne of the Lamb of God. Like you they shall
offer themselves as victims in union with the Saviour,
and, raising towards the Eucharist their suppliant
hands and tearful eyes, shall utter unceasingly that
imploring cry for pardon on a sinful people: '*Parce,
Domine, parce populo Tuo*—(Spare, Lord, spare Thy
people)'. Then shall be inaugurated before Jesus,
exposed in His Divine Sacrament, a public and
solemn reparation, which shall be perpetuated from
sanctuary to sanctuary, which night itself shall not
interrupt, and which shall last, we hope, until the
end of time. May the grace of the Lord, zeal for
God's glory, charity for the erring, love of sacrifice,
mingled with the divine attractions of the Most Holy
Sacrament, draw together a multitude of fervent
Christians, holy women, devoted souls, and assemble
them under the banner of that 'Perpetual Adoration
and Reparation' which is destined to save the
world."

CHAPTER VII.

EUSTELLE AND HER BISHOP.

IN the year 1840, Eustelle's health began sensibly to
fail. She was constrained to give up a portion of her
beloved occupations in the sacristy, and soon became so
weak that she could scarcely even write. This state
of debility was accompanied by much suffering and
acute pain in her chest. Two doctors were consulted,
and one of them pronounced it to be a very serious
case. She herself, bearing in mind the offering she
had recently made, thought at first that her Lord was
taking her at her word, and willed that she should at
once complete it. Ignorant as yet, however, what
might be His design, she would not allow herself any
of those eager hopes or anticipations which are so
many manifestations of the vitality of self; or, rather,
self was so dead within her that she was incapable of
making any other acts but those of conformity to
the Divine will. "To live or die, according to His
good pleasure," she said. "It is true, nevertheless,"
she would add, smiling, "that I feel a taste for the
heavenly country; but, if our Lord thinks I can still
be of use on earth, I am willing to prolong my stay."
In the mean time she gave no thought to those many
wants which press so heavily on the poor in time of
sickness. She forgot herself for Jesus, and Jesus, according to His promise, thought of her and provided
for her. When she saw everything she needed arrive
just as it was wanted in her humble dwelling, where
she was now confined to her bed, she observed, " The
Lord has fulfilled in me the words of the holy Evangelist, 'Seek ye first the kingdom of God and His

justice, and all these things shall be added unto you.'" She saw her Beloved's hand in the kind assistance and consideration of her friends. She was grateful to them, but all was ultimately referred to Him.

She continued for a considerable time in the same precarious state, unable to sustain the slightest fatigue or make the least active exertion, and rallying occasionally only to suffer fresh relapses, when news reached Saint-Pallais that the Bishop of La Rochelle purposed visiting the place on the feast of the patron saint. Marie-Eustelle desired, notwithstanding her weakness, to resume her functions on this occasion; and she found strength in her courage, or, we might say with more truth, was fortified by Him who took pleasure in gratifying the wishes of His servant; wishes which were always prompted by her love for Him and by her zeal for His interests and honour. Her object at present was to contribute her endeavours to add ornament and splendour to the approaching ceremony, and for two days she displayed so much activity, that those who were aware of her previous feeble condition could scarcely believe their eyes; nay, she herself was surprised at her own strength. She tells the Curé, in a letter written on this occasion, that our Lord had really performed a miracle in the amount of work He had enabled her to accomplish. "How good He is," she adds, "and how sweet it is to trust Him!" The festal day was observed with great solemnity, the sacred edifice could not contain the crowd which sought access to it, and numbers, unable to enter, were fain to cluster round the door. Never, in the memory of all, save the survivors of the last genera-

tion, had the parish church of Saint-Pallais looked so
glorious. "M. le Curé was enchanted," writes
Eustelle; "our church was truly magnificent." It
was to her own exertions that it was in a great measure indebted for the beauty and taste with which it
was adorned, and no one would have had a better
right than herself to drink in a little innocent pleasure
through her eyes by beholding the pomp and glory of
the ceremonial. Mgr. Villecourt, although he had
been previously at Saintes, had never before paid a
pastoral visit to Saint-Pallais, and he preached upon
this occasion surrounded by a large number of his
clergy. Eustelle considered herself to be singularly
indebted to him, and at that moment her heart was
warm with feelings of the tenderest gratitude from
having learned that, when he heard that her illness
would probably deprive her of the satisfaction of
seeing him, as she had hoped to do, he had kindly
observed that he would himself go and visit her.
Yet during the whole of the ceremony Eustelle
deprived herself of the gratification of raising her
eyes even for once to look at him. Such mortifications in her case were not so much the result of a set
purpose, urging her to deny herself everything which
might be a source of sensible enjoyment, as the spontaneous promptings of an ever-energizing love. As
there are persons so liberal and open-handed that they
cannot, as we say, keep money in their pockets, so
Eustelle could not retain any pleasure for herself, but
was continually impelled to give all to Jesus and
renounce everything to please Him. After Mass she
was amply rewarded for this little sacrifice, for
Monseigneur having entered the sacristy, where she
was engaged in some arrangements with the choir-

children, the Curé called her forward to receive the bishop's blessing.

M. Briand clearly foresaw that Eustelle's days on earth would be short. No one, indeed, could anticipate a long life for one of so fragile a constitution, and who so unsparingly taxed its feeble powers; but he had additional reasons, grounded on his knowledge of her spiritual state. It was not her want of physical strength alone which menaced her earthly existence, there was a flame within which was gradually consuming its victim. He availed himself therefore of his authority and influence as her director to induce her to record in writing the operations of grace of which her soul had been the theatre. He made the first overture, it would seem, in the May of 1840, and, in order to avoid everything which might by possibility have rendered such a request perilous to her humility, he suggested the idea at first in a half-jesting way. But Eustelle knew that he was serious, and her first feelings, as he plainly saw, were those of extreme repugnance. We have her own account of the matter in a letter to her former director, in which she reminds him that he had himself once made a like proposal to her. From this letter it appears that her repugnance was not grounded on sentiments of humility alone, but resulted also from the fear of any possible risk such a task might involve of impairing or tarnishing that virtue, so hard to gain, so easy to lose—the only fear, indeed, which she ever expressed, and which made her so vigilant a guardian of that inestimable treasure. Deference to her director's wishes and the spirit of obedience alone probably withheld her from giving a refusal, but she suggested the necessity of consulting our Lord in prayer, and to this M. Briand agreed. Meantime she begs the former Curé to pray that if there were any danger to her soul, or any snare to self-love in this undertaking, the Lord would apprise her of it. A change, however, had evidently come over her since the proposal was first made, for she says that she does not herself believe that it would be the occasion of any such peril to her. " O Monsieur l'Abbé," she says, " believe me, if I yield to this request and accede to my director's wishes in performing the work, I shall be actuated by nothing but a desire to promote the glory of Jesus. I need not tell you of my unworthiness, you know it; you know that I am nothing, and even less than nothing, for I offend Him who has created me, and who has never ceased pouring His graces on my soul in such profuse abundance. I am therefore unworthy to occupy, either now or hereafter, the thoughts of creatures—utterly unworthy. I know it, and it needs no humility in me to say so. Nevertheless, if God, who is sometimes pleased to use the feeblest instruments to promote His glory, wills that I should obey His voice in obeying that of His minister, I acknowledge in all simplicity that for His pure glory, and from the desire I have to make Him loved, I should willingly resolve to undertake this writing, in which I hope He will vouchsafe to guide my pen; for I leave the care of all that to Him." Viewed in this light, the idea seemed to grow upon her and to wear a different aspect. It would be sweet to record her Lord's mercies to her soul, and to give free expression to her own love for Him. Yet time wore on, and the manuscript was not begun. In July we find her writing to her friend the Curé, " M. Briand, whom I saw last week, told me he knew I was going to another world. I cannot say whether he will prove a true prophet; my health is sometimes better, sometimes worse. . . . He again asked me to put down in writing a full account of myself. My life, indeed! this would be very interesting, would it not?'" she adds with a little playful irony. "I confess I have thought of undertaking it; but then I have scarcely time. Pray that Jesus may inspire me. His holy will be done!" She must have begun to write soon afterwards, as she mentions in the following October having made some progress in her task: M. le Curé (she said) was aware of it, for M. Briand had consulted him on the subject. Fortified by the opinion of these two priests who had the immediate care of her soul, and urged by their strongly expressed wishes, Eustelle no longer hesitated, and even found great pleasure in recording, under obedience, the benefits which her Saviour had showered upon her. It was from a quarter whence we should have least expected it to proceed, that she was to receive a final and still more authoritative command, sufficient to have removed any lingering doubt, had such existed.

In the beginning of the year 1841 she had another very serious illness, which confined her to her room for several weeks; her doctor, indeed, scarcely expected her to rally. As she had a large open wound in her side which gave her acute pain, one of her friends, aware of Eustelle's spirit of mortification and ardent love of Jesus, took it into her head that she had been endeavouring, after the example of some saints, to cut or burn the Adorable Name of the Saviour over her heart. She ventured on the question; Eustelle smiled: "No," she said, "it is not on the good side that our Lord has sent me this suffering ;" and she ingenuously acknowledged to Sister Anastasia that she would have been very glad had it been on the left instead of the right side. Expecting little from their remedies and medicaments, Eustelle, nevertheless, like other holy persons who have fallen into the hands of the physicians, submitted patiently to their treatment and followed all their prescriptions in the spirit of penance. During the whole of her painful illness she received those who sought her advice with the same readiness as if she had been enjoying perfect health, her countenance retaining all its accustomed sweetness and tranquillity. To those who knew what she must be experiencing, this was a source of no little edification. But she had a privation to endure far more distressing to her than the sharpest bodily pain. Confined to her sick bed she could no longer receive daily the Bread of her soul ; she could no longer visit the tabernacle. In this, to her the only suffering, she found her chief relief in speaking of the love of Jesus. "How good He is !" she said to Sister Anastasia ; "seeing my inability to go to Him, He Himself comes to me, on Sundays and on Thursdays, to appease a little the insatiable thirst I feel for His Adorable Blood, and to feed me with Himself." So also we find her telling friends who visited her of His goodness in having come to her that morning, or saying in her letters, " He will return to-morrow." The Blessed Sacrament was, in fact, her life : the memory of the last communion and the anticipation of the next alone seemed to enable her to drag on her feeble existence during the interval ; and when, after long weeks of comparative privation, she was again able to go to Mass, these expressive words fell from her lips : " O how hungry I was ! "

Profiting by her amendment, to the doctor's extreme surprise, she promptly set to work, with an activity ill suited to a feeble convalescent, and began forthwith to clean the great silver lamp which hung before the altar, and attend to all her other customary occupations about the church. She was much exhausted, as might have been expected ; but to suffer in the presence of Jesus was, she said, not really to suffer at all. She had risen from her bed of sickness with a still higher degree of that luminous faith which in her almost resembled sight ; a reward, no doubt, of the love and resignation with which she had borne her illness. The infinite value of Him who has given Himself as our redemption-price, was so clearly present to her mind that she would gladly have sacrificed her life to make Jesus known, were it but to one single soul. She felt herself continually impelled to say, " Love Jesus." Then, meeting with scarcely any who could understand the language of her heart, the arrow of love which had pierced it only sank the deeper.

Towards the latter end of the September of this year, Eustelle determined to seek counsel from the Bishop of La Rochelle. M. Briand, it appears, was opposed to this resolution. Perhaps he judged such reference unnecessary, and objected, on the score of her health, to what seemed to be a superfluous exertion. Eustelle, who regarded God alone in all the actions of her life, and made every step she took the subject of assiduous prayer, had come to a different conclusion ; and nothing can better prove that her usual docility and submission were the fruit of grace,

and not the result of native timidity, than her perseverance on this occasion in spite of the unwillingness of
her director, whom, we know, she regarded with the
highest veneration. In thus acting contrary to his
advice, Eustelle was well aware, however, that she did
not in the least degree infringe the duty of obedience
to him as her spiritual guide. The chief pastor of
the diocese possessed an authority superior to his,
and to all other, with the exception of that of the
Supreme Pontiff himself. She thus writes to her
director : "I will not go, you know where, without
a reason which renders this course indispensable to
me. The tabernacle suffices me; everything else is
devoid of all attraction to me. Oh, if Jesus would
withdraw me from all created objects, how I should
bless Him for it ! But I adore His just and holy
will. Do you fear that my health might suffer from
this journey? You are too kind. Ah, Jesus has
many other ways of reducing my bodily strength ! If
I were but able to tell you all His dealings with my
soul last week ! O my father, may you learn this
from Himself ! I feel that I must die in order to love
as I desire to love. Or do you fear that Monseigneur
might lead me to talk too much ? The Lord will give
me the strength to say all that may be for His glory
and the good of my soul. I do not fear being guilty
of indiscretion. There is a time to be silent; but
there is also a time to speak. What can I fear in
discovering me whole soul to him who on earth repre-
sents my Jesus to me ? God will inspire him to ask
what it is expedient he should know, and will dictate
to me what it is fitting that I should reply. I ought
rather to be on my guard against a certain timidity
which would incline me to be silent in presence of the

chief pastor of the flock, who ought to know and direct all his sheep. Even if he should upon some points be of a contrary opinion to yourself, you would, I am sure, have sufficient humility to prefer his decision to that which you have pronounced. It is the Holy Spirit, I believe, who requires me to take this step. I should take it even if I had no other motive for my journey. To explain all this would take me too long. To-morrow, at five o'clock in the morning, the companion of my journey will join me : it is Jesus Christ Himself ; I have arranged so as to receive Him before setting off. I should be very much grieved to act against your will ; but I am sure that it would not be acting against it to do that of our Adorable Jesus. I beg you, therefore, to rest assured that it would make me miserable to disobey you."

This letter appears to throw light on the cause of M. Briand's reluctance that Eustelle should seek an interview with the bishop. She was evidently moved to be more explicit with Mgr. Villecourt than, from motives of humility and timid reserve, she had as yet ventured to be. There was a time to be silent, as she said : that time had gone by, and now she was urged and pressed by her inward Monitor to make him fully acquainted with her whole state. It entered, doubtless, into the designs of God for the glorification of His servant that her bishop, who was to be the great means of publishing her merits, and who was to lend the high and venerable sanction of his testimony to her rare sanctity, should have full personal knowledge of the ways by which she had been led. We need scarcely say that any such ideas were quite foreign to the mind of the lowly Eustelle, who, it is more than probable, was prompted to enter into fuller expla-

nations with her bishop, solely that she might enjoy
the most authoritative assurance attainable with reference to the supernatural communications she was
so constantly receiving. Remembering, however,
her former perturbations of mind through fear of
illusion, which he had been himself the means of
entirely removing, it would not have been surprising
if M. Briand should have dreaded on her account any
re-opening of a question which he justly considered to
be most satisfactorily settled ; particularly when he
recalled to mind the extreme apprehension entertained
by Mgr. Villecourt of furnishing any temptation to
vainglory, and the care he had always manifested to
maintain in Eustelle a humble estimation of her own
spiritual progress. Were she to be as open with the
bishop as she had been with himself, might she not
possibly misinterpret the caution with which he was
sure to reply, and the doubts he might think it prudent to suggest, and disquiet be thus raised anew in
her mind ? That he had some such misgivings is,
perhaps, not a very hazardous conjecture, and Eustelle's letter to him, after the desired interview, seems
to favour this conclusion.

But this interview was not to take place immediately. There is no record in her extant letters, or
in any of her notes, of her having seen the bishop
while at La Rochelle. Either he happened to be
absent at the time, or she may have found him much
engaged ; and hearing that he purposed visiting Saintes
shortly, she may have deferred executing her purpose
until he came into her own neighbourhood. On reaching La Rochelle she went to the Convent of La Providence, where she was received within the enclosure,
and conducted to the choir to witness the profession

of one of the sisters. To be present at this ceremony was evidently the other motive of her journey to which she had alluded. Two of the religious who beheld Eustelle for the first time, were so struck with her air of modesty that they conceived at once the highest veneration for her, and felt the greatest wish to converse with her. Eustelle had several friends among these good sisters, and they did not find it difficult to persuade her to spend the day with them. " Here at least," she said, giving a reason characteristic of her, " I shall have full freedom to talk of our good God." The nuns naturally wished to know what she had thought of the morning's ceremony. She replied with all simplicity that she had not seen it, such having been our Lord's good pleasure. It is quite impossible to describe how completely she was a thing in His hands, with no desire or thought but as He prompted, nor even the use of her bodily senses but as He permitted; not so much conforming her will to His, as having her own will transformed into that of Jesus. Sister St. Vincent, to whom we owe these reminiscences, observes that, when speaking of the goodness of God to her, and of the love which consumed her, Eustelle added that she longed to publish these things to the whole world that she might make her Saviour loved." We have had occasion to remark Eustelle's timid reserve in the early days of her spiritual life, a reserve to which her own modest nature had not alone inclined her, but which had been prompted by the Spirit of grace ; how great, then, must have been that love which now made her even desirous of proclaiming what formerly she had striven to withdraw from view. But it was the same Spirit who dictated conduct and desires seemingly opposed; as she

Y

had herself said, there was a time to be silent and
a time to speak. Here, indeed, there was no restraining motive for silence; she was with those
who had retired from the world to give themselves
by profession to the exclusive love of the Heavenly
Bridegroom. "How happy I am," she said, "to
converse with you who are His spouses!" She
spoke, indeed, of nothing but Jesus all the time
she remained with them. During the repast she
continued conversing on the same theme, and was
so transported with Divine love as to be unable to
eat. But she looked at the sister who served her,
and said, "It is for Jesus you do this, is it not?"
so ardently desirous was she to bespeak every intention for her Beloved: that was her meat and
drink. One of the nuns was suffering from a secret
temptation to repugnance for her employment, and
found an opportunity to make a passing remark on
the subject to Eustelle. "Dear sister," replied the
holy girl, "beg, then, for courage; look at Heaven
which awaits you" — few and simple words, which
any one might have uttered; but, as Sister Anastasia
before observed, it was the way in which they were
uttered which gave them their effect: they brought
peace and consolation to the troubled mind of the
religious. Eustelle was accompanied by her youngest
sister, a good and piously disposed girl, but who, with
the curiosity natura to her age, was desirous to see a
little of the town, and kept importuning Eustelle to
walk out with her. It was getting late, but Eustelle,
always kind and accommodating, could not refuse, and
took her down to the sea. We should have been glad
to know the thoughts of the maiden of Saint-
Pallais as her eyes rested on the measureless expanse

of waters, fit type of that infinite ocean of the Supreme Love in which her soul was ever engulfed; but perhaps, like the convent ceremony, she saw it not.

Nothing struck the nuns of La Providence so much, in this her last visit, as Eustelle's complete forgetfulness of self when speaking of herself; so difficult, perhaps so impossible a thing to do with entire simplicity, and, so to say, unconsciousness, in the early stages of the spiritual life. "She would have wished," says Sister St. Vincent, "to lay bare her whole soul to us, in order that by so doing she might make us love our Lord the more." Surprised at the change which had taken place in her, her friend could not help noticing it. "How different you are," she said, "from what you were when I left Saintes!" Eustelle did not deny it. "I was then," she said, "like those little birds who dare not fly for fear of falling; I was too fearful of offending the good God in my actions; but now His love devours me;" adding, apparently from the connection always present to her mind between joy and sacrifice, "and I seem to have suffered nothing." Her whole behaviour, as described on this occasion, marked the progress she had made in the interior life. She had arrived at that perfect liberty of the children of God, who can do and say unreservedly what they will, because the life of Jesus alone lives in them. Perfect love in them has cast out fear, for fear has no longer anything whereon to exercise itself. God is love, and, being love, He is also joy; and He dwelleth alone in them. Souls arrived at this state scarcely know whether they are speaking of themselves or not.

On the 10th of February, 1842, Mgr. Villecourt arrived in Saintes to preach the Lent. His voice had already been heard in the capital of Saintonge two years previously. Evidence had then been given that the old Huguenot bigotry was not extinct in its ancient stronghold; for the bishop received several anonymous letters, written in a menacing tone, to induce him to avoid all controversial topics. We need scarcely say that these intimations had no effect. He declared that he desired only the salvation of his whole flock, and that, as on the one hand it was not his wish to give pain to any one, so on the other he was not disposed to keep back anything which concerned the welfare of souls. And so he fearlessly pursued his work, and delivered a series of sermons in which he presented a picture of the sufferings and victories of the Church from its cradle to the present days. This we learn from one of Eustelle's letters. And now the venerable prelate had returned to Saintes, to occupy once more, during the Lenten season, the pulpit of its ancient cathedral. She records with satisfaction the concourse of people that attended on this occasion, and, in particular, the encouraging circumstance that a large proportion of them were men. Next to her hunger for the Bread of Life was Eustelle's eager desire for the Bread of the Word. Her love for sermons, indeed, reminds us of that of St. Teresa; and it is not a little remarkable that those favoured souls who have enjoyed the familiar communications and immediate teaching of their Lord, have always had the highest reverence for the ministry of the word from the lips of its ordained dispensers; in this how widely differing from those exterior persons who, barren of all unction and grace, and never receiving one sweet confidence from God's loving Spirit, will nevertheless habitually listen in the attitude of judges, not learners, to their appointed teachers, deeming themselves deep and penetrating because they possess the very inferior faculty of criticism. If Eustelle honoured God's word so much in the mouth of His ordinary ministers, we may imagine how high a value she set upon it as coming from her bishop. She never missed one of his conferences, although to hear them she had to walk a considerable distance, and return after the cold February night had closed in ; and that, too, at a time when, as we learn incidentally from her correspondence, she was suffering acutely from pain in her chest. Her usual companion was a lady living in the neighbourhood who entertained a great affection for her. Every evening Eustelle called at her house and they proceeded together ; but if the lady was prevented from going, then Eustelle pursued her way alone. Her friends used to try and persuade her that she ran no little risk in returning along the long, narrow, unprotected bridge over the Charente in perfect darkness, but she laughed at what she called their vain fears. "What have I to dread ?" she would reply ; "does not Jesus walk by my side ?" The Abbé Guérin, who related these particulars, added that Eustelle used to say, "I will go to hear the word of God as long as I can drag myself along :" expressions equivalent to those which she employed with respect to Mass and the reception of the Eucharist. It was Jesus in another form irresistibly attracting her.

Eustelle was now able to execute her purpose, and we have an account from her own pen of two interviews which the bishop granted her. She had previously addressed the following letter to him :—

" My Lord,

 " The beloved Jesus having permitted that you should understand the way by which He leads me, I beg to be allowed to give you in detail, so far as I am able, a connected account of those things of which you were so good as to let me speak to you. Your lordship is aware of the motive which has induced me to keep silence on the subject of the graces with which Jesus so good vouchsafes to favour me. I now desire to lay open my soul to you with simplicity, and submit it entirely to your judgment. It is in a state of perfect tranquillity, nevertheless I still dread illusion, so dangerous, so subtle, so easy in these matters. I would beg you, however, to observe that this fear never diminishes in the slightest degree the unutterable peace which I enjoy ; I seem to find myself in a state of absolute incapacity to disquiet myself about anything whatsoever. Forgive me, my lord, if I allow myself to speak so freely to you ; but as I see only our Saviour in your person, I find it impossible not to speak to you as to Himself. O how long I have desired to lay open to you my whole soul ! But the Divine Spouse, no doubt, has not permitted it sooner ; and, as I love nothing more than His holy will, I have always submitted to this privation. However, it is not for the sake of any personal satisfaction that I desire to acquaint you with the heavenly favours which the Lord is pleased to grant to His unworthy servant ; Jesus being the sole author of His gifts, it is for Him alone that I desire to speak to you of them in all simplicity. My poor heart cannot contain the fire which our Lord is pleased to kindle in it ; and often I feel as if it were about to burst, so violent are the effects which this love produces in me. Indeed,

I must even say that if our good Saviour had not sustained me, my feeble health would have been unable to support such vehement transports ; and, if He had not restrained me, I know not to what extravagant actions I might have been impelled. Some things, indeed, I have done which were known only to my dear Jesus. I would not have you even divine, my lord, what they were, for I will not say more till you know all my poverty and littleness. Believe me, I have a sincere and an entire conviction of my unworthiness, and that it would therefore be quite impossible for me to attribute to myself the least of the graces which I receive from our most lovable and beloved Saviour. If I did not fear to trouble you, I would venture to beg your permission to speak to you some day next week. Be pleased, my lord, if you see fit to admit me, to have the kindness to give your reply to Mademoiselle de Saint-Légier. O good Jesus, O my God, Thou alone knowest how I love Thee! and it is only through Thee, O my Beloved, my mercy, my pardon, my All ! Bless, bless our chief pastor.

" Accept, my lord, the profound respect and veneration of your unworthy servant and daughter,

" EUSTELLE,

" The poor servant of Jesus."

The bishop received her with even more than his usual kindness—just like his child, she says ; his gentleness and simplicity making her feel quite at ease with him. He at once referred to the subject of her letter, and inquired why she had not acquainted him more fully before with the ways by which she was led ; that he quite approved of her not laying open her soul to every kind of person ; but that, as

for himself, he ought to know all, because he had
received from Heaven the mission and the necessary
power to judge and decide upon the state of souls.
This was precisely what Eustelle herself had felt.
Being therefore thus directly questioned, she replied
that, from a fear of self-love, she did not like to be too
ready to talk of what passed in her interior. Mgr.
Villecourt then required an account of her manner of
prayer, of the effects it produced on her both
spiritually and physically, and of the special graces
with which our Lord had favoured her. With respect
to her visions, she was as concise as was compatible
with sincerity. "I mentioned to him only three,"
she writes in her report to M. Briand : "our Lord's
appearance to me during my interior pains ; His
manifestation of Himself as He was when Pilate
showed Him to the Jewish people and said, 'Behold
the Man ;' and the last favour which, as I related to
you, took place at the moment of consecration. And
what," she continues, "do you think his lordship has
decided as to all those things upon which you yourself
have given your decision? His opinion coincided
with yours ; he even added that, as in what I had
told him there was nothing affecting the senses, he
recognized with more certainty a supernatural origin ;
that in such intellectual visions illusion was much less
to be apprehended, provided we have not in any way
prepared and disposed our imagination for their occurrence. This was certainly not the case with me ;
indeed, I have never, so to say, gone forward to meet
our Lord's operations within me : all has invariably
been unexpected, and has come as a surprise to my
soul. When these things have occurred, I was only
thinking of humbling myself before my God, anni-

hilating myself and loving Him. The picture I beheld was presented all of a sudden to my soul; nothing had prepared the way for it; it was God who did all; neither my imagination nor my desires had any part in its production. See, my father, how our Lord has permitted that the decision of our chief pastor should be a repetition of your own."

The bishop, she then goes on to narrate, proceeded to give her precisely the same injunction as she had long before received from her director, namely, to write a detailed account of her spiritual life; in which she should describe the change of her earthly affections into pious affections, and the subsequent transition to a supernatural state. This was no new thought in the mind of the venerable prelate, as we learn from himself. "From the moment," he said, "that God caused us to be acquainted with the treasures of grace with which He had enriched His servant, the thought occurred to us to engage her to detail, according to the measure of her ability, all that regarded her interior: her first steps in the spiritual life, the various combats which she must have sustained, the victories which by God's help she had achieved, and the graces she had received." For three years, however, he had hesitated to manifest his desire, partly from the fear of endangering her humility, by giving so strong a proof of the esteem in which he held her, before he was fully assured that his own movement was the dictation of God's Spirit, and partly from that very caution which his own high position rendered the more imperative; for he feared lest pious directors, wanting for experience, might take occasion from his example to act with imprudent confidence in cases which they might erroneously deem to be parallel.

But all these reflections had been kept secret in his own bosom, and Eustelle was not a little surprised at receiving such an order from one who had hitherto shown so much reserve. It was, however, a complete reassurance to her mind as respected the task upon which she had already entered. Yet she did not think good to tell Monseigneur that M. Briand had given her a similar injunction.

Never before had the bishop spoken to her in such unreserved terms of intimate union with Jesus, and the familiarity with which this good Saviour deigns to treat the faithful soul thus united to Him. It is true that Eustelle herself had never before led the way to such topics, but even so his previous demeanour had hardly prepared her to hope for so much openness and freedom on his part. Thus encouraged, she was preparing to be much more communicative in her next audience, but she found her pastor somewhat differently minded on this occasion. Doubtless he had been making his reflections, and perhaps feared he had been somewhat deficient in that caution which, as we have seen, marked his whole behaviour to Eustelle. Anyhow he seemed disposed to administer an antidote. She observed that (to use her own expressions) he was extremely preoccupied with the fear lest she should esteem herself to be something on account of the favours which the Lord had granted her; he pointed out to her the precipice which lies always very nigh to the most signal gifts of Divine mercy; he bade her remark how, when the Apostles came to relate to their Lord the miracles they had worked in His Name, He immediately reminded them of Satan's fall from his high pinnacle of glory. Self-love, he said, would in an instant substitute the devil for Jesus Christ in a soul; and, to add force to his words, he narrated several appalling cases. One was that of a woman who, in the first instance sincerely pious and given to contemplation, conceived so high an idea of herself on account of the admiration which she believed she inspired, that she became the victim of the most absurd delusions. Another, and a worse, was that of a priest who was led on to feign visions and ecstasies. The third instance was that of a girl who pretended to read the souls of others and to enjoy the gift of prophecy. An excellent priest—a man, indeed, who might be called a confessor of the faith—was induced to place such unbounded confidence in her pretensions, as to write at her dictation what proved to be a mere farrago of rhapsody and nonsense. Ecclesiastical superiors, informed of the reputation for sanctity which this wretched impostor had acquired, took measures to put her humility and obedience to the test; the result of which was to expose her utter deficiency in those virtues. Her death was accompanied by frightful circumstances; yet all was insufficient to cure the infatuation of some among her blinded followers, who continued to regard her as a saint.

Eustelle also noticed that, when referring to the supernatural ways by which she had been led, a detailed account of which he had previously enjoined her to commit to writing, the bishop was much more guarded than at their first interview. In her letter to the former Curé—for we have a double account from her pen—she says, " He took particular pains to make me feel that there is often nothing more dangerous to the soul than uncommon and extraordinary ways. He seemed to be mightily afraid lest, by being

too much occupied with myself, I should be exposed
to the most perilous of temptations, that of self-love.
This was his ruling thought, which he presented again
and again in every possible shape. Dreading for me
the subtle snares of pride, I saw what trouble he took
to make the least of all that was extraordinary in the
Divine communications I had received; he intimated
that they were more common than was supposed,
although they generally remained concealed through
the modesty and reserve of those privileged souls who
were favoured with them; adding that no soul had
been privileged like Mary's, yet she neither wrote nor
caused others to write any account of the Divine
favours of which she was the object : no one so silent,
so reserved as this most gifted of creatures ; so that,
with the exception of a few scattered words, she has
left us no memorial of her sentiments save the
Magnificat." The bishop concluded his admonitions
with an exhortation to his hearer to advance, as far
as depended on herself, in the ordinary path, assuring
her that this would not hinder the action of the Holy
Spirit if He willed to lead her by another way.

Eustelle listened to all Mgr. Villecourt said, not
only with the deepest respect and submission, but
with a perfect acquiescence of her will and judgment.
Perceiving his object as clearly as if he had openly
avowed it, this circumstance, as on previous occasions,
in no way tended to neutralize the effect of his
counsels. She accepted and cherished the lessons she
received from her pastor as much as if she needed
them, and as if she did not discover the secret thought
which prompted them. Yet we can scarcely be surprised that his tone and manner had the effect of
silencing her. " I had many things to say to Mon-

seigneur," she writes, "but I withheld them when I heard him speak in this way. I felt that such was the language which became a bishop, and I inwardly blessed the Lord for allowing a chief pastor to descend into these details with the least of his flock; but I dared not say more, lest he should think I was actuated by an eager and ill-regulated desire to pass for a soul peculiarly favoured. However, thanks be to God, I did not recognize in my heart any leaning towards that vanity against which my bishop wished to set me on my guard. I made my profound obeisance to him and took my leave, while he recommended himself to my prayers."

Eustelle had intended to acquaint the bishop with the acts upon which she had ventured when under the influence of her transports of love; but the tenour of his language made her afraid of saying more than was sufficient to extract an opinion which in her estimation virtually settled the point, though it was opposed to her own inclinations. When she spoke to him of certain unreasonable desires with which she was seized at the sight of the altar and of the sacred tabernacle, he smiled, but said, "It is quite enough for you to be a daily communicant. We must love Jesus Christ much; but our love for Him must ever be accompanied with the deepest reverence. The Church does not permit the priest himself to forget, through an indiscreet familiarity, the veneration due to the Most Holy and Most Adorable Sacrament of the Altar; he is not allowed to open the sacred tabernacle without having on at least a surplice and a stole, and his head must be uncovered." "When I heard these last words," remarks Eustelle to her director, "I felt their whole import; and I took care not to

tell Monseigneur all the extravagances to which my
transports of love for Jesus in His Holy Sacrament
had sometimes impelled me."

It may be asked why, since Mgr. Villecourt entertained so strong a persuasion of Eustelle's sanctity,
he used such extreme precautions? Why was he
always so bent, as he clearly was, upon humbling her,
and, if possible, even blinding her to the fact that she
was favoured in a very remarkable degree with the
choicest graces? It is quite impossible to suppose
that he had seen anything in Eustelle herself calculated to awaken his fears; such a notion would be
altogether irreconcilable with the estimation in which
we know, from his own testimony, that he had held
her from the first moment that he saw her. On the
contrary it was the high opinion he had formed of her
virtue which made him so jealously vigilant to preserve
its purity unsullied. In Marie-Eustelle her bishop
beheld a humble lily of the valley, and he wished to
keep this flower of grace in the green protecting
shade, lest the sun should look upon it, to mar perchance its snowy whiteness and impair its delicate
fragrance. Besides, he must have felt that, thus
referred to as an authority, his words had all the
weight of his high office. It is wonderful, however,
considering this prelate's cautious reserve and her own
bashful timidity, that Eustelle should have been led
to lay her soul open to him, which in all essential
respects she certainly did; and that for this purpose
she should have so earnestly sought these last interviews, although not impelled thereto, as she herself
avowed, by any disquietude of mind. In all this
we cannot but see the hand of God, who willed
that the graces and merits of His servant should be

proclaimed to the world for His own glory and for
our benefit.

When Eustelle and her bishop had their final conversation, her weeks on earth were numbered. If
she saw him again, as from one of her letters it appears she purposed doing, it must have been only
to take her leave of him, as we have no record of any
other conversation between them.

CHAPTER VIII.

EUSTELLE'S SPIRIT AND CHARACTER.

BEFORE we conclude our narrative and describe the
last closing days of this saintly girl, it will be well to
pause a moment and take a glance at her distinctive
character, as it comes before us in all the charms of
its high graces engrafted on a happy nature. Grace
always reconstructs, but in many it has much to cast
down and root up, so opposed to its workings does it
find the nature which is its basis. Until the work is
arrived at its more perfect stages a certain constraint
and ruggedness will be apt to betray itself in such
persons through the conflict involved in their transformation, the result of which is to impair their outward attractiveness. In others the nature is so rich
in good qualities, that although grace has even here
to do an entirely new, not a supplementary work, yet
is there less that requires forcible removal, less to offer
resistance, and the transformation accordingly seems
to be not so much a substitution of what is foreign to
the native disposition as a substitution of motives,
and an exaltation, a refinement, and a sublimation of

what already existed. The work of renovation in these souls, if not more meritorious, is at least more harmonious, more gentle, more even, and its outward exhibition is always peculiarly pleasing. In a large measure such was the case with the subject of this biography.

Of the eminent degree in which Marie-Eustelle possessed the great Christian virtues, little remains for us to add to what has already appeared in the narrative of her life. The three theological virtues shone in her with singular lustre. Her faith was so vivid that it resembled sight. "All things appear so clear to me," she said, "that I seem no longer to have the merit of faith;" and it may be here observed that during the period of her inward temptations the enemy of souls was never permitted to assail this servant of God with any doubt of the truths of our holy religion. Almost every one of the letters which Eustelle has left furnishes proof of the sublime degree in which she possessed the virtue of hope. The reader will recall to mind how she was supported and fortified thereby when passing through the season of darkness and trial, and how she was ever ready to exclaim with holy Job, "Though He slay me, yet will I trust in Him." The spirit of confidence which so eminently distinguished her was the fruit of this abiding virtue of hope, and was for ever offering to God a homage most acceptable, because it so specially honours His great attribute of mercy. And what need be said of her charity? Her whole life is but a record of the burning love which was as the very element in which she lived. We might in like manner, were it not superfluous to do so, enumerate the gifts of the Holy Ghost each in its turn, and notice the eminent degree in which she possessed them, as well as His fruits, the infused virtues; all this, however, would be more or less a recapitulation of what the reader is already acquainted with. Besides, our present purpose is to exhibit rather her character and spirit than the eminence of her sanctity.

Immense is the variety in unity of God's works. No two leaves which rustle in the breeze, no two flowers which unfold their petals to the sun, are exactly alike. No two faces are altogether similar; so no two souls have the same identical lineaments. No two human characters affect us in quite the same manner, for, besides their dissimilarity in detail, we notice something in the general which may be called their distinctive spirit, and which produces upon us a corresponding impression. The same beautiful variety prevails in the kingdom of grace, and God uses it for His own purposes in the accomplishment of His designs, throughout the various ages of the Church and according to its peculiar needs. It has pleased Him to exhibit to the world in this century, and in that country which is more exposed perhaps than any other to the observation of men— in that France which possesses such a special pre-eminence amongst those nations which were formed by our great mother, the Catholic Church, and whose doings and sayings, thoughts and feelings, circulate with electric rapidity through other lands—two saintly souls living at the same time, burning with the same seraphic love, and manifesting His glory each in an obscure rural parish; both designed in their several ways to give a most powerful impulse to the devotion of their compatriots, but presenting most striking contrasts in many of their personal

z

characteristics. Need we name those two marvels of grace, Jean-Baptiste Vianney, the Curé of Ars, and Marie-Eustelle Harpain, the sempstress of Saint-Pallais! In the one we see a man who, had he not been a *saint*, would have possessed, we do not say nothing to attract attention or captivate the admiration of the world at large, but nothing even to win for him any particular influence in his own humble circle. Not only was he ignorant in respect to human learning, but he had a limited capacity for acquiring knowledge, so that it was a matter of difficulty for him to pass through his preparatory studies for the priesthood. In person he was unprepossessing, his gait was awkward and heavy, his air timid and embarrassed; and although his saintliness afterwards imparted a strange fascination to his ascetical aspect, there is nothing to lead us to suppose that without this marvellous indwelling grace his countenance would have been anything but most ordinary. His language not only possessed no graces of style, but was provincial to vulgarity; his pronunciation was akin to that of the peasant class from which he sprang; and, notwithstanding the amount of education which he necessarily received while passing through his ecclesiastical training, he continued frequently to offend against grammar and syntax, not to speak of literary taste, of which he did not so much as possess the rudiments. Yet we all know, not only how amazing was the work which God performed by the instrumentality of this seemingly weak instrument, but how potent was the indescribable influence of his mere presence. The beauty of holiness penetrated and transfigured the rugged envelope in which it dwelt. Grace in him appeared, so to say, visible;

his soul rather than his voice seemed to speak ; and we need not here recount how the fame of the poor Curé of Ars spread throughout France, and converted the cottages of that little, rude, unknown village into so many hostelries, and its impracticable roads into beaten highways, along which countless vehicles were ever bringing multitudes of pilgrims to consult him in their difficulties, confess to him their sins, or simply to gaze at the man.

The work which the humble sempstress of Saint-Pallais was called to accomplish was to be of a more silent and secret character ; not that we are attempting to draw any comparison between the fruit of their labours, still less to estimate the respective merits of these two servants of God, we are but simply pointing out a contrast, which exemplifies the multifarious means which God employs for accomplishing His divine purposes. If grace triumphed over personal ungracefulness in the Curé of Ars, in Marie-Eustelle it came to enchance and elevate natural recommendations of a remarkable order ; physically, mentally, and morally she was cast in a beautiful mould. Like Jean-Baptiste Vianney, she sprang from the peasant class, but unlike him, whom the advantages of education failed to fashion, she, who only learned to read and write in her village school, spoke and used her pen with a grace, an accuracy, and an elegance not unworthy of any rank in society ; nay more, she at times employed language so remarkable for the sublimity of the ideas it conveyed and the eloquence with which they were enunciated, that the most competent judges, literary men of incontestable talent and prelates of the highest dignity, have united in expressing their admiration of her

writings.* "Even to the very last lines she traced
with a trembling hand a short time before her death,"
writes Mgr. Villecourt, " we still find her expressing
beautiful thoughts in a language always lucid and full
of that sacred fire with which her soul was inflamed.
No observation foreign to her purpose or out of place
ever disfigures her writings ; she says all that she
ought to say in the most appropriate, the most natural,
and the most agreeable manner. And this because
there is no better school than that of the Holy Spirit."
M. Léon Aubineau, himself a writer of no ordinary
merit, says, " The most innocent and pleasing images
flow in profusion from Marie-Eustelle's pen. All the
mystics have loved language of this kind. The
mouth speaks from the abundance of the heart, and
the innocency of their minds made them attach themselves by preference to all those pleasing, graceful, and
pure objects which are to be found in creation. The
birds, the flowers, the waters are constantly recurring to their imagination, and are reproduced
by their pen. Every one knows what a charming
use St. Francis de Sales has known how to make of
these things, and how much beauty his constant
allusions to all that is sweet and lovely in nature
imparts to his writings. Nor is any one surprised at
meeting with graces of language and exquisite taste
in the Bishop of Geneva. But where did this young
and illiterate girl acquire the talent of forming these
delicious *bouquets ?* Who taught her the secrets and

* The unaffected beauties of style and language which abound
in these letters are necessarily lost to a great extent in the
process of translation. Besides, as it was important to render
the meaning of the original with the strictest and minutest
fidelity, every other consideration has been made subordinate
to this primary object.

the graces of that beautiful, energetic, and finished diction which past centuries have bequeathed to us ? How has she become mistress of its most delicate turns ? From whom did she learn how to use it with a freedom, a precision, and a purity to which, we must confess, we have become strangers since the seventeenth century ?"

To this high panegyric we will add that of an author better known in this country, M. Auguste Nicolas, to whom we are indebted for several justly esteemed works in defence and elucidation of the faith. "The action of Christianity," observes this thoughtful and able writer, "is incessant and incalculable, although it is sometimes hidden; and, after the lapse of two thousand years, it still puts forth flowers as sweet and fruits as rich as ever. In the month of June, 1842, there died at Saint-Pallais, near Saintes, a young girl of lowly station, who had earned her subsistence by the work of her hands, but whose sanctity was distinguished by extraordinary characteristics. Of one of these the whole world can judge, as it is conspicuous in the writings she has left. These writings, the effusions of the pen of a young needlewoman, indited amidst the alternations of fatigue and suffering, unveil to us a soul truly superhuman in its knowledge and love of the things of God. We do not hesitate to say that in their simplicity, precision, correctness, elevation, and even sublimity of thought, sentiment, and style, they remind us of Fénélon, and sometimes seem to attain to the level of Bossuet. This young girl was Marie-Eustelle." * Of the practical effect of her writings we shall speak elsewhere.

* "Etudes Philosophiques sur le Christianisme," tom. iv. cap. vii. § 1.

Eustelle (as already remarked) was gifted with a
poetic turn.   Not only does it evince itself in the
graceful imagery with which her letters abound, but
she frequently expressed her religious affections in
verse.   Some of these effusions have been preserved,
and if they do not manifest poetic talent of a high
order, they at least display facility, tenderness, and
sweetness.   The versification is smooth, and bespeaks
an ear naturally attuned to harmony, for she was
possessed of no science to direct her, and could have
had few opportunities of cultivating any of her mental
endowments.   She was fond of sending these little
poetic *impromptus*, addresses to the Saviour or His
Holy Mother, to her most intimate friends, and
especially to the former Curé of Saint-Pallais, whom
we find her sometimes playfully reproaching for not
making her the return in kind which she expects.
" By the bye," she writes, " you will not, then, send
me the couplets you have added to the cantique :
' Lo ! the sacred door unfolds.'   Is it because they are
your own composition ?   What humility !   I follow
your example very badly.   Pray let me have them."
The delight she took in giving vent to her ecstatic
love in poetry accompanied her almost to her last
days.   She seems to have composed verses with the
greatest ease, her ideas running almost spontaneously
into metre and rhyme.   This exercise appeared to
afford her at once relief and refreshment.   An analogous case is mentioned by St. Teresa of a person
who, in the intoxication of holy love, would, although
not ordinarily possessed of any poetic talent, compose
on the spot verses full of feeling : " This," observes
the saint, " was not a labour of the mind, but the

product of love; love spontaneously breathed itself forth in a poetic melody."

Eustelle lived, it may be said, in that region where true poetry dwells, for all earthly harmony, to whatever sense, external or internal, it may be addressed, is but an image and an efflux of those eternal harmonies which surround the throne of God, and of which the primal source is in Him who is all beauty, as He is all goodness and love. Like the spouse in the Canticles she abode with her Beloved in a spiritual garden, the air of which was redolent of sweetness, and on whose balmy breezes strains of angelic song were ever floating. There she dwelt, playing as it were amidst its roses and its thorns with the joyous innocency of a child. Her letters, indeed, are full of metaphors and images drawn from the Canticle of Canticles, the mystic meanings of which her tender and impassioned love for the Spouse of souls rendered her peculiarly capable of penetrating and relishing. All the mysteries, all the joys, all the pains of the most holy of loves, that which exists between the faithful soul and Christ, which are there portrayed, were by her recognized with an ever-growing delight, and their language adopted and interwoven with her own, as that which best rendered what passed in the secrecy of her breast. The same love which was the source of poetry in Eustelle seemed also to have educated and refined her taste. She was always much distressed at the manner in which our Lord is often represented in common prints and pictures: "Only a saint could paint Him fitly," she would say. Upon one occasion she was fortunate enough to meet with a picture of the Saviour, apparently in some lady's house in the vicinity, which corresponded with her ideas. She remained for a whole hour in contemplation before it, and shed such abundant tears, that she was ashamed to rejoin the company. "It was Himself," she afterwards said to Sister Anastasia; "it was Himself. Oh, if you had seen that countenance, the sweetness of those eyes; that mouth which seemed to wish to speak to me! I really think that the painter who could thus represent Him must have beheld Him."

Eustelle possessed a faculty which is perhaps much more generally allied to the poetic temperament than is ordinarily supposed; we mean that of appreciating the humorous. The power of comparison seems to enter largely into this appreciative faculty, which lies at the root of wit, as it does into the gift of imagination. The connection between the two is therefore not surprising; and whatever may be said or believed of the melancholy temper of poets might, we think, with quite as much truth be alleged of their joyousness. Eustelle's disposition was certainly joyous, not melancholy; and we have seen that she had an early turn for pleasantry, which in her days of thoughtless levity betrayed her into faults of the tongue; faults which furnished her afterwards with matter of severe self-accusation. But this turn of mind, in itself not harmless merely, but a graceful quality, continued to reveal itself in many a little pleasing touch in her letters to her equals, but particularly in those addressed to the former Curé of Saint-Pallais, whom on the one hand she treated with the familiar equality of a sister, while on the other she reverenced him as the priest of God. This slight vein of humour which mingles so artlessly with the highest themes, reminds us of the gentle gaiety and lively freshness which give such a charm to the writings of the Saint of Annecy, whose spirit, indeed (as we before observed), Eustelle reflected in a remarkable degree.

Her perception of the ludicrous is evinced in the following extract from a letter to the Curé of Saint-Pallais : "I have heard," she says, "a little incident which I will relate to you. It happened the first Sunday that M. l'Abbé said Mass at the prison. When it was over, the prisoners came up to the sacristy to speak to him, and ask for books, as they had been in the habit of doing with you. M. l'Abbé, who was not aware of this custom, was so frightened that he barricaded his door ; and so these poor people had to go away again. I fancy they were not very well satisfied, particularly as self-interest had not a little to say to bringing many of them there." "Mademoiselle N—," she writes in another letter, "has her head in a pretty confusion. She amuses us much ; but she does not like me, because she says I am dead to the world, and as for her, she wishes to live a little longer in it. It is quite a comedy." A little gentle irony is also sometimes apparent in her letters to her spiritual brother, the Curé, who, we suspect, was given to certain procrastinating and unmethodical habits. Eustelle wished him to write often, as she longed to console and encourage him under his trials. "I would forgive your silence," she says on one occasion, "if it was the effect of your mortification, but I do not think so at all ;" and again : "The remorses of your conscience for your neglect in writing to me have been, I perceive, very soon stifled. Truly, if I remain upon earth after you, I shall have to invoke St. Negligent, and I hope he will obtain for me the grace not to be neglectful." But it is not only for his

carelessness as a correspondent that she ventures to
take the Curé to task : "I should much like to know,"
she writes, "whether you are grown more reasonable
now, and if you say your office earlier ; the bad habit
you have contracted of putting it off made you go to
bed very late ; and this, I know very well, did not
suit M. le Curé at all. If I were near you I should
scold you often, all for your own good. You injure
your health by depriving yourself, from want of order,
of the rest you need." At other times she gaily
quizzes herself; sometimes for her verses, of which
scrawls of hers, she says, her friend the Curé will soon
have quite an interesting collection ; or again, for the
pleasure she took in the beauty of the altars she had
adorned : "We have made a very pretty chapel for
Holy Thursday," she tells him. "I ought not to say
so, for it was I who did it; but, as you know my
vanity very well, it will not surprise you." The
solitary instance on record of her having asked or
hinted for the supply of any need—her usual complaint being rather that her friends would not allow
her to bear the cross—was in the form of a little joke
intended to give pleasure to a kind and good person.
A lady, observing the worn-out state of Eustelle's
gown, asked her why she did not get another. "Because I leave that care to you," she replied.

Nothing was more remarkable in Eustelle than her
perfect freedom from all affectation or constraint. As
grace seemed to dictate each act, without the need of
special reflection on the separate virtues, so a certain
exquisite tact appeared to teach her the appropriate
manner of addressing every one, high as well as low
(for she had correspondents in both classes), and the
fitting thing to say upon all occasions, without study

or effort. There is never the smallest aim at effect in anything which flows from her. Immediately after passages full of all the eloquence which impassioned love, combined with a poetic and ardent imagination, could dictate, and in the very midst of the sublimest flights of thought, she will turn with the utmost simplicity to some common topic which occurs to her, resuming her former strain at once with the greatest ease. As when we find her, after some rapturous expressions of love for the Divine Eucharist, interrupting herself to say, "Our pigeon is well, and I am very fond of it," and then returning quite naturally to speak of Jesus, all unconscious of any contrast or abrupt transition. It is like what we witness in children, whose deep thoughts (for some children have very deep thoughts), come out side by side with common observations. But Eustelle was as truly a child of nature in one sense as she was a child of grace in another. If the Curé of Ars, had he not been a saint, would have possessed no attraction to arrest the eyes or win the heart, Eustelle, even had she not been a saint, would still have been very charming as a mere wild-flower in the waste. So it is : God in some builds, so to say, in a comparative void, and in others re-casts, and beautifies, and transforms what already exists in a lower order.

In noticing Eustelle's characteristics we must not omit her thoughtful kindness, which so often exhibits itself on comparatively slight occasions. We say kindness, not charity, for many have much charity who yet are deficient in what may properly be termed kindness ; anyhow it has to be learned by them as one of the more delicate fruits of charity. The common sufferings of humanity are intelligible to all, and

unless the heart is hard and selfish, they excite pity and compassion in most persons when
brought under their notice; but there is another
class of sufferings occasioned by the sensitiveness of
the human heart, which are often overlooked or
disregarded by those who do not possess a large
amount of sensibility. Eustelle's letters abound with
proofs that her all-absorbing desire for the sanctification of the souls of others had not led to the smallest
forgetfulness of the pleasure or pain which is constantly resulting to those around us from a host of
minor and what may be called insignificant acts. Not
only does she herself always manifest, even in trifles, a
tender regard for the feelings of others, but she frequently suggests little kindly actions to her friends.
For instance, we find her reminding them to thank
others for presents or slight attentions, to write to
some relative on his fête-day, as she knows it will
give pleasure, and in many other ways showing all
that delicate consideration which distinguishes affectionate and sensitive dispositions, and which endears
them to those around more, perhaps, than greater
deeds of charity.

The affectionateness of her disposition is another
leading trait in her character. Although the love of
God had absorbed and transformed all the feelings of
her heart, it had effaced nothing, it had dulled and
dimmed nothing. She loved otherwise, not less. Grace
has impelled some, it is true, to trample on and set
aside their human affections, to forget their own
people and their father's house, but God draws His
children to Himself by different paths, and this was
not the way by which He was pleased to lead Eustelle.
After she had engaged a separate apartment for her-

self she always went to take her meals with her own family, where her appearance was like a gleam of welcome sunshine. Two years before her death, however, she gave up this practice, but they continued to supply her with what she needed. Her sister Angèle related afterwards the trouble which their dear Eustelle used unwittingly to cause them on this account, because she so completely forgot herself on all occasions that they could never feel certain that she would eat anything unless reminded to do so. If they left the food provided for her in her room, it was a chance if they did not find it untouched. Then they took to following her. "We even used to go into the church," said Angèle, "cup in hand, to get her to swallow a little soup at least." Assuredly this was the only vexation which the loving Eustelle ever caused her family. So oblivious of all that only concerned herself, she never forgot the sorrows, cares, and interests, especially the spiritual interests, of those who had the nearest claim upon her. She would profit by even a few minutes' leisure to run home and cheer the drooping spirits of her good mother, by talking to her of the heavenly country, and of God, our eternal reward after this our exile. René's temper was passionate, but the very sight of his angelic daughter always calmed him. Eustelle took the tenderest interest in her sister Angèle's welfare, and we find frequent proofs in the course of her correspondence of the maternal solicitude with which she watched over her.*

Perhaps nothing is a greater touch stone of sterling

---

* Marie Angèle survived her sister sixteen years, living a holy and edifying life, and making a happy death in the year 1858.

virtue than the behaviour of persons in the bosom of their own families. Many motives of self-restraint which keep us in check elsewhere do not operate there. Hence it is rare, we conceive, to meet with persons so free from small defects as to stand the daily scrutiny of years of domestic life. Great, then, was the edification of Eustelle's biographer at witnessing the embarrassment of Eustelle's mother and sister, and the difficulty they evidently experienced in framing a reply when, adjuring them to tell him frankly the entire truth, he asked what faults they had ever remarked in Eustelle; for (he added) certainly some faults she must have had. They remained silent awhile, looking at him, then muttered something inaudible. He pressed anew for an answer. Again they examined their memories, and both agreed in observing that they never heard her utter a word of detraction. But this was a merit, not a defect: he must know whether they had ever noticed anything which might be considered a fault. At last, after much consideration, Angèle recollected that her sister sometimes said to her, "I choose you to do that—(Je veux que tu fasse cela)." "And how long were you with her?" "Ten years." An occasional slight peremptoriness of manner, perhaps not uncalled for, to a younger sister whom she was instructing in her business—this was all that could be recalled after a diligent retrospect of ten years' constant association.

We do not find Eustelle's friends ever complaining of any lack of personal affection to themselves, although it would appear that her director taxed her, not intending, it may be imagined, any very serious reproach, with loving only Jesus and forgetting all, Mary not excepted, for Him. After recording, in one of her letters to him, the favour, already mentioned, which she had received from our Lady, when, kneeling before her altar, she had begged her to send her the means to adorn it, she adds, " So never say again that the love I have for her Adorable Son makes me forget His holy Mother. I love her as a true daughter must love the best of mothers." No one, indeed, can take the most cursory glance at her letters without being convinced of Eustelle's deep and filial devotion for the Blessed Mother of God. Mary is her mother, the best and tenderest of mothers ; she is her refuge, her defence in trouble ; she owes all to Mary ; she is, after God, her hope ; she is her sister too ; she loves to call her her sister ; and we know how tender a regard she had for the fraternal bond, for there was no relationship under which she better loved to view her Lord than as our Brother. Tender devotion to Mary is a sign of predestination ; all graces come through her, and Jesus can refuse her nothing : such, and many more like them, are the expressions scattered over the pages of her correspondence. How, indeed, could she who so loved the Son forget the Mother ? How could she who so valued intercessory prayer, fail to place the utmost reliance on the most powerful and, so to say, omnipotent intercession of the Queen of Saints, the Immaculate Mary ?

We may here mention an instance of the perfect confidence she reposed in the Blessed Virgin. In the year 1840, her brother became liable to be drawn for the conscription. The other young men similarly situated wanted him to go and spend the evening with them at the tavern, with the view of drowning care during the anxious hours that preceded the drawing of the lots. His father seconded

their solicitations. He had taken one of those strange fancies into his head which often obtain possession of ignorant persons whose minds own no religious influence. It would be unlucky to refuse. "If you do not do like the others," he told his son, "the lot will fall only on you." "No," said Marie-Eustelle, "that is not the way to get the Blessed Virgin's protection;" and she confidently assured her brother that he would draw a favourable number if he placed his whole trust in this all-powerful Bene-factress. Charles Harpain followed her advice, went to Mass on the morrow, and when he put his hand into the dread urn, repeated the prayer which his sister had suggested to him: "O Mary, conceived without sin, pray for us who have recourse to thee." All his companions who had wished him to share their drinking-bout the night before were drawn; he alone escaped. Some one ran off to carry the good news to Eustelle. It was no surprise to her; she calmly answered that she knew it. She knew still more; for she foresaw her brother's future vocation. "How often," says Sister Anastasia, "did she speak to me of her dear brother, hinting to me that he had another vocation than that of a thatcher"—his father's business—"and that *later I should see.*"*
"If," adds the good sister, "he is now at the seminary, undoubtedly it is to Eustelle that he owes it." Eustelle had asked this grace for him, and had asked it, as she did his exemption from the con-scription, believing she should receive.

Eustelle's affectionate devotion to the saints cannot be questioned any more than her tender love for

---

* Charles Harpain still survives, and is at present the Curé of a parish in the neighbourhood of La Rochelle.

Mary, although we once found her expressing a fear that she neglected them, so absorbed was her whole soul in the adoration of the Blessed Sacrament. Our Lord on that occasion reassured her by causing her to understand that it was He Himself who drew her to this one engrossing object. Such forgetfulness is not forgetfulness. The human mind in its present condition is incapable of dwelling intensely in an *explicit* manner upon several objects simultaneously ; much more, then, will that which eminently contains, withdraw the mind from detailed reflection upon that which is contained. As well might a saint raised to the sublime contemplation of the Adorable Trinity be taxed with forgetting or neglecting the Sacred Humanity of Jesus, which at such times will cease to be a distinct object of consideration, as one so specially absorbed in the adoration of her Eucharistic Lord be held responsible for being incapable of finding place in her mind for any other and secondary thought, however good or holy. We might quote frequent passages in her letters* which show her familiar acquaintance with those great servants of God, and her desire at once to imitate their virtues and enjoy their patronage ; but this would be a

---

* It may interest the reader to know that Eustelle had a very special devotion to the Venerable Grignon de Montfort. Thus, in a letter addressed to a lady whose family were in affliction, we find her strongly approving their intention of making a novena to that holy servant of God, in whom, she says, she places a boundless confidence, and mentioning an instance in which much benefit had been experienced from his invocation. A candle had been kept burning during the novena before his image, but, as her correspondent has the facility of so doing, she recommends, in preference, lighting it at his tomb. She had probably imbibed this devotion when, as a child, she used to visit the Congregation of the Filles de Sagesse, who owed their foundation to that holy man.

needless task. That Eustelle loved those who were
most like and are now most near to her only Love, is
self-evident. It is, however, perfectly true that she
was unable to speak long of anything that was dear
to her, be it friend on earth or saint in heaven,
without reverting to the one great centre of her
thoughts and affections. For instance, after speaking of the joy which she experienced in hearing
her bishop relate the triumphs of St. Eutropius, the
glorious apostle of his diocese, and of her own
patroness St. Eustelle, who had won the double
palm of virginity and martyrdom at Saintes, of
which her father was the governor, she blesses God
for having allotted her the name of this pure and
intrepid virgin, and aspires, after her example, to the
happiness of giving her own life for the faith and for
the love of Jesus; but no sooner have the words
"love of Jesus" flowed from her pen than she takes
fire and, forgetting her two holy patrons, she exclaims, "It is too little to give one's life once for
Him. O good Saviour, the sacrifice Thou offeredst
on the cross did not satisfy Thy love; Thou must
needs renew it millions of times each day, and that
unto the consummation of ages. O the prodigy of the
charity of a God to His creatures! He alone was
capable of this excess of love. Oh, how is it possible
not to desire to die for Jesus!" And in this strain
she continues rising, as the lark rises higher and
higher, singing as it ascends towards the orb of day,
until she poises herself on the wings of contemplation
in that region which the sun of the Eucharist alone
illuminates.

The spirit of Eustelle, then, may be characterized
as singularly winning and attractive, combining the

loving and the lovable, the gracious and the graceful, the ardent and the tender, the simple and the poetic. Not a harsh feature, not an austere lineament, can we trace in her who was chosen for the one special office of proclaiming to the world the delights of that Manna "which contains in itself all sweetness." This was to be her one theme, her one strain, like some beautiful melody which the accomplished musician presents ever new, yet ever the same, under an endless succession of enchanting variations. Such in spirit did it become her to be who was to appear in this our generation as the great lover and songstress of the sweetest mystery of our faith; who was to strike the note which countless voices were to take up and swell that choir of perpetual praise and adoration of our Eucharistic Lord which seems to be the abiding occupation of His Bride in these latter days.

Devotion to the Blessed Sacrament and to the Sacred Heart may be said to be, indeed, the great devotion of these last times. This is the evening of the world, and the cry of evening goes up from the heart of Christendom: "Abide with us, for the day is far spent." The noon is past, the shadows are lengthening, the weariness of the hour is on us, and the soul muses on rest in the bosom of its God. In the austere morning air man goes forth to labour; he thinks little, he speaks less of his feelings, be they joyous or be they sad; but when the faint vesper sweetness is on the breeze the heart turns towards its home to seek repose on the heart which it loves. Jesus, we have forgotten Thee often during the glare of busy day; our eyes could not behold Thee, though Thou wast with us, in the heat and dust of the road; but now we cannot, we will

not be without Thee, for all is gloom and darkness
save with Thee. Abide with us, Lord, call us near
Thee, for the day is far spent. Let the lamp of Thy
tabernacle be the light of our dwellings; let us
with Eustelle gather round it; and, as every other
light is one by one extinguished, let us trim the
sacred flame and watch before Thee till the everlasting day shall dawn.

CHAPTER IX.

MARIE-EUSTELLE's LAST DAYS.

A MELANCHOLY chapter in common human life is
that which gives the closing scene. In the case of
the good Christian the sadness of death is, indeed,
tempered by consolation and hope, but in that of the
saints, of those who have already died to all, that hour
is a joyful and a blessed one; for the first notes of
the eternal Alleluia are already sounding in their
ears, and their eyes have opened to a vision of " the
far off land" and of "the King in His beauty."*
Eustelle had first to pass through a short season of
suffering; of suffering from the only privation she
was capable of feeling. It was a little before the
Easter of this year 1842, that she had swooned in
the street, and the exertions which her office involved during Holy Week gave the finishing blow to
her now rapidly failing strength. She dragged herself rather than walked to the church on Easter
Tuesday; it was the last time she entered its walls,

* Isaias xxxiii. 17.

the last time she knelt before the tabernacle. "To-day," she writes on the 12th of April to the young seminarist in whom she took so lively an interest, "begins for me the painful privation I experience from my inability to go and prostrate myself before the tabernacle, where, from love, our God conceals Himself. O Will of Jesus, Thou art my paradise, notwithstanding the sacrifices Thou requirest of me. Dear child of God, these sacrifices are great : none but Jesus, who wills them, can form an idea of what they are. I suffer in my body, but my soul suffers incomparably more, on account of what our Lord makes it feel through its zeal for His glory. O, my God, what a martyrdom ! but it is sweet, oh, too sweet ! Jesus gives me too much joy, too much peace and happiness in my sufferings. How attractive is His Cross, how lovable, how precious ! The Eucharist is the abridgement and the august memorial of the Cross." We see here, as ever, how the Eucharist is to her the compendium of all ; she sees all the mysteries of the faith in It, and she sees It in all the mysteries of the faith. It will be remembered how she said to Anastasia that St. Paul declared that he knew nothing but Jesus and Him crucified, and that as for herself she knew nothing but Jesus in the Eucharist. In this, apparently her last letter to young Guérin, she renews her exhortations to frequent communion, and this again recalls the thought of her own coming privation. "In a few days, perhaps, I shall be deprived of the joy of uniting myself to Jesus. I submit my will for ever to that of God ; yet, in spite of my submission, my eyes are already wet with tears." But she loves too much not to trust that Jesus will have pity on her. "Ah, my dear Jesus, Thou wilt come to my humble abode, when

I am no longer able to seek Thee in Thine; Thou wilt come and annihilate all that Thou art in the poor receptacle of my heart. O Jesus, Thy love reduces me to silence, but my heart is not hidden from Thee; it lives for Thee alone, suffer it to expire for Thee only, at Thy feet, in Thy tabernacle. . . . I can write no more, being in a high fever. Oh, how good is its fire joined to that of Jesus—is it not?"

The enemy of souls saw that the end was nigh. Long before, the servant of God had vanquished him; in the strength of the Lord she had trodden on the basilisk, who remained bound beneath her feet. But Satan knows that whatever else the soul may merit, and whatever treasure of past merits it may have laid up, one grace, the crowning grace, the grace of final perseverance, it can never absolutely merit; and so he would make another and a last assault, and God permitted it, that Eustelle might add a fresh jewel to her crown. The tempter rose, then, from the abyss, and once more presented himself and his infernal suggestions to the mind of this pure spouse of Christ. With what peculiar temptation he assailed her we know not, and it matters little. All we know is that she no sooner perceived his presence than she broke forth in piercing cries; and our dear Mother hastened at her call. Mary appeared to her dying child; the light of her sweet and heavenly countenance brought instant peace and consolation; and the baffled fiend slunk away into darkness.

Eustelle knew that all the skill of the physician would be powerless against the malady which had so long been undermining her health and consuming her vital powers. It assumed, indeed, many of the outward symptoms of that fatal complaint which we call consumption, and which selects so many of its victims from amongst the young, the fair, and the gentle ; but she knew that its source lay deeper, and that it was no mere natural fever which burned in her veins. She did not, however, refuse the medical aid which friends were solicitous to procure her. The doctors were called, and soon pronounced her case hopeless and her end imminent ; one of them, M. Bougé, using these remarkable expressions : "She has a burning fire in her bosom which is consuming her." Eustelle's disconsolate friends, hopeless of human aid, now raised their supplicating hands to heaven, entreating that they might not be deprived of so precious a treasure, so bright and perfect an example. One of them, witnessing her sufferings, could not restrain her tears. Eustelle began to laugh, and asked her why she wept. "You fear to see me die," she said ; "but, O my God, I desire nothing else." This desire in no way interfered with her holy indifference. To a lady of Saintes, who addressed her in terms of commiseration, she replied, "Whatever our Lord wills : I ask neither for life nor death." From the day that she was obliged to take to her room, never more to leave it, she was like one no longer inhabiting this earth. Her state of prayer was unceasing, and she rarely spoke. It seemed, indeed, to require no little effort on her part to reply to questions addressed to her ; nevertheless she always answered with her habitual sweetness, only very briefly. Her sisters would occasionally read to her passages from the books she had specially loved ; such as the Annals of the Propagation of the Faith and the Life of Mme. L'Amouroux ; but her mind was habitually drawn inwards. Her calmness and serenity were admirable to behold, and were in no way disturbed by the few painful regrets which her pure and disengaged soul was capable of feeling. These she at times expressed, but always in terms of the most entire resignation. "My God," she would say, "Thou knowest that I do not regret to die; but the church of Saint-Pallais—who will take care of the church of Saint-Pallais?" She acknowledged also to Sister Anastasia that her mother's grief at losing her was a source of pain to her; and some time previously she had told another person that when she thought of her poor mother, she felt some sorrow at leaving her. But it is plain that whatever pangs of this kind she experienced, all proceeded from the most disinterested love and compassion; for herself she regretted nothing: to go to Jesus was not to leave anything. "No," she said, "I regret no one; I only feel a little anxiety about my youngest sister,* who has not finished her apprenticeship."

A devout lady who came to see her, and found her in a 'very suffering state, said, "My good Eustelle, you have so often obtained the recovery of others by your novenas, why not make one for yourself now?" "No, madam," she gently replied; "I will not ask for health; I am quite satisfied to be ill, since the good God wills it." But the lady insisted: "Still you prefer health to sickness; it is certainly more agreeable." "No, madam." Marie Eustelle saw that that *no* of hers pained the lady; "but I could not say *yes*," she afterwards observed when relating to Anastasia what had passed, "because it would not

---

* Madeleine Anastasie, who still survives, and lives with her brother the Curé.

have been true." What the lady could not understand was that Eustelle showed no personal preference on the subject. Resignation was intelligible, but
health in itself could not be matter of indifference.
Eustelle then changed the conversation. "That dear
lady," she afterwards said, "cannot understand the
pleasure I take at seeing the holy will of my Saviour
accomplished in me. 'Ah,' I often say to Him,
'Thy will, not mine, be done.' No doubt it is a
great privation to me to be confined to my room, and
not to be able to go and visit Him whom I love ; but
it is He wills it; my body is imprisoned, but my
heart and my soul are not. Here I can love, and here
I can think of what I love. This is my solace ; this
it is which assuages my suffering." Sister Anastasia
could not refrain from testifying her grief at the
prospect of their separation, and of soon having her
no longer with her. " My good friend," said Eustelle,
" how imperfect that is ! Do not attach yourself to
anything. Have you not our Lord ? He alone
ought to suffice you, and stand to you in the place of
all. Besides, you must not distress yourself, for, if I
leave you in exile, I will not forget you in our own
country. Come, dear friend, courage. God only !
God only !" She kept her word, for Anastasia has
assured us that she is convinced that she often
received aid from Eustelle after her departure to
Heaven. What she urged upon others was strikingly
exemplified in herself. Everything was referred to
Jesus and accepted from Jesus. Her friends were
affectionately assiduous in offering her anything which
they thought might tempt her appetite and help to
sustain her strength ; she thanked them for all their
kindness, but she thanked our Lord still more. "See

how good Jesus is," she said one day to Sister Anastasia. "A good lady has brought me the earliest fruits of her garden this morning; that is, she has offered its fruits to Jesus, and Jesus has sent them to me: it is to Him in truth that I am bound to return thanks. These things often come at a moment when I least expect them. How Jesus loads me with favours, both spiritual and temporal! I have ever abandoned myself with an entire confidence to His tender charity, and He never abandons such as confide in Him."

She suffered acutely during the two months and a half of her last illness, but not one of the numerous friends who almost contended for the privilege of nursing her ever heard her utter the slightest complaint. Indeed they might have remained in complete ignorance of the increased intensity of her pains, but for the replies which she was obliged to make to the inquiries of her medical attendants. When they expressed their compassion for her, and their regret at being unable to do anything for her relief, she would beg them not to distress themselves, and tell them that what she suffered was nothing, absolutely nothing, when she reflected on what our Lord endured. "It deserves not the name of suffering," she said. "It is well with me, since I am as Jesus wishes me to be. My great suffering is to be debarred from visiting Him in His temple; but this dear Master is so good that He comes Himself to visit me in my poor dwelling. What gratitude do I not owe Him!" But to her trusty Anastasia she would express her regrets at not being able to receive Him more frequently. "My dear friend," she would say, "beg this good Saviour to inspire those who can grant me this favour to give

it me, if it be His holy will and if it would be for my
benefit." A lady of Saintes who was affectionately
attached to Eustelle declared that she felt convinced
that the pain which she underwent from being unable
any longer to receive the Holy Eucharist daily, caused
them to be deprived of her much sooner than they
would otherwise have been. "I had frequently the
happiness," she said, "of being with this angel when
our Lord was brought to her. It was a real happiness to me to behold her. Before communion she
was sometimes so weak that one could scarcely hope
that she could live even a few minutes longer; but
no sooner had she been nourished with the Bread of
the Strong, than her sufferings seemed all removed,
and she was able to sit up in her bed for half an hour.
The tears which would then pour down her face made
her look singularly beautiful." Some one having
asked her whether Mgr. Villecourt would not come
and see her, she smiled, and said, "Who am I that
Monseigneur should condescend to visit me?"
"Jesus visits you," was the reply; "so why should
not His bishop?" At the mention of Jesus,
Eustelle's whole thoughts were instantly turned
towards her Beloved. Without further noticing the
observation that had been made, she said, "To-
morrow that good Master is to come. I invite you
to accompany Him." "How can I describe," continues the narrator, "the touching spectacle I then
witnessed? Paler than the white sheet extended
over the bed, and propped up on her cushion,
Eustelle appeared to have neither life nor consciousness save for the God she was about to receive. And
when the priest had taken our Lord in his hands,
and she heard those consoling words, '*Ecce Agnus*

Dei—(Behold the Lamb of God),' her eyes suddenly
lighted up with all their pristine brightness, and her
countenance seemed on fire.   After communion she
remained all lost in Him whom she possessed."

As her end approached, her friends were still more
assiduous in their visits ; they seemed reluctant to
lose sight of her.   But it was not friends and neighbours only who gathered round Eustelle's dying bed ;
there might be seen persons of the highest rank, mingled with those of humble degree, begging her to
remember them before God, and recommending to her
the special needs of their own souls or those of others.
As during the whole of this her mortal illness Eustelle
appeared almost unceasingly absorbed in God, it would
not unfrequently happen that persons in affliction,
who had come to solicit her prayers, would be unwilling to disturb her rapturous silence by relating
their troubles to her.   Eustelle at such times would
seem to receive some secret intimation of their wish,
and, returning to herself, would forestall their desire
by addressing to them in the sweetest tone a few con-
solatory words which restored peace to their souls ;
then in an instant she would resume her beatific repose,
interrupted only occasionally to bestow a momentary
smile of recognition or of kindness upon any fresh
visitor who drew near to her bedside.*

* The description of Marie-Eustelle's appearance during
these last days of her life strongly reminds us of that which
the Estatica of the Tyrol, Maria Mörl, now gone to God, habitually presented.   All who had the happiness to see this holy
woman will remember the sweet and childlike smile which,
when recalled to earth from her state of rapturous contemplation, she would bestow on those who stood around her bed,
her silently expressed acquiescence in their requests, and her
graceful distribution of holy prints, often strikingly suitable to
the spiritual state or circumstances of their respective reci-

She seemed to know but two days in the week, the Thursday and the Sunday, and to live and remain on earth only for those two days : all the rest was as a blank, a kind of non-existence. One day Sister Anastasia, on returning from Mass, called to see her friend, rather, however, to edify and console herself than to comfort the sufferer. She sat in silence, gazing at her on her bed of pain. By-and-by Eustelle became aware of her presence, and looked at Anastasia in return. But what a glance ! how much it did convey ! A minute after she said, " You come from Mass, do you not ? and you have received Communion ? " Anastasia assented. Another silence, as expressive as the look had been. The sister who, fearing to fatigue her, still sat watching her without speaking, now beheld the big tears coursing each other down her cheeks, and the sight distressed her greatly. Eustelle appeared to be aware of this, and said, " You understand why ? do not be disedified ; I am resigned, but I feel the deprivation. Ah, how long it is from Sunday to Thursday ! How I suffer ! If they only knew what I feel, they would not let me fast three days. All the pains of the body are not to be compared to this suffering ; and I would willingly consent to remain for all eternity on this sick bed, if that were possible, provided I might have Holy Communion every day." " In Heaven," replied Anastasia, " you will be united to Him whom you love." " Would you believe it ? " she rejoined, " I scarcely think of Heaven at all. Jesus alone is my whole thought." " But is not Jesus Heaven ? " said the sister. " That is true," was Eustelle's reply ;

pients. That smile especially can never be forgotten, blending as it did what we witness only on the face of early childhood with what we figure to ourselves in the angelic countenance.

"still it is in the Sacrament of His Love that I always see Him." She expressed similar sentiments to a lady who visited her either on this occasion or during a former illness. "I think, Eustelle," said her friend, "you will be very glad to die, the sooner to possess Him whom you love with so much ardour." "No," she said, "I do not desire to die; I desire only the will of God. If He sends me death, I accept it with submission; if He wills me to remain on earth, I abide here contented. It is happiness to be in Heaven, no doubt, because it is to be with Jesus; but have we not almost the same happiness here? Do we not possess Him in the Most Holy Sacrament! Ah, did we but know how to profit by His Divine Presence, we should in some sort have no reason to envy the inhabitants of the celestial city. And besides, here we can suffer for Jesus, and win hearts to Him." To suffer and to love—such is the sole joy of the saints on earth, almost converting this land of exile and vale of tears into a Paradise of anticipated bliss.

Faithful until death to the friends whom she loved, and to whom she considered herself indebted, Eustelle, on the 12th of May, asked her sister for pen and ink. It was to trace a few lines of farewell to the former Curé of Saint-Pallais. The writing is almost illegible :—

" May the Will of Jesus be our will. . . . You are wondering and uneasy at my long silence; but I must tell you that I have been ill ever since Easter, and shut up this month past. I keep my bed, and as yet feel no improvement. Do not let this news alarm you : we must submit. You know how I love to converse with you about our Lord, but weakness

compels me to cease. My poor brother, we have our
crosses. . . . Pray for me; I pray for you.
"EUSTELLE, servant of Jesus."

A short time before her departure Eustelle was to
enjoy a great consolation, for which she was indebted
to the kindness of her bishop. Hearing of her state,
and knowing well how insatiable was the thirst which
consumed her, he empowered a priest to give her communion occasionally in private, without the usual
attending ceremonies. By this means she might have
the alleviation of receiving oftener than it would have
been judged fitting to carry the Blessed Sacrament
publicly to a sick person. One morning, then, at
seven o'clock, this ecclesiastic entered Eustelle's room.
Eustelle was not expecting him; she knew nothing,
as yet, of the favour designed her; and nothing in the
priest's outward garb betokened that he bore his God
concealed upon his bosom. But no sooner had Eustelle's
eyes rested upon him than a ray of ineffable joy lighted
up her pallid countenance. "Minister of Jesus," she
said, "you bring me my Saviour, do you not? You
have Him with you! You have Him with you! I
feel His Divine Presence!" Nothing, of course, was
in readiness; and while preparation was being hastily
made, the priest, witnessing Eustelle's ecstatic joy,
was moved to render her felicity complete by holding
up the while before her eyes the precious Treasure
which was soon to be hers. She opened her hands
with an expression of reverence such as we picture
to ourselves in the blest spirits that surround the
Throne, and remained thus immovable in silent adoration. Peace unutterable reigned in all her features;
her eyes were gently closed, and the tears rolled

softly from beneath their lids. Eustelle's soul was rapt in God. He who beheld this scene thanked his Lord for having permitted him to behold it. A quarter of an hour passed thus, and then he gave her communion. "May the Saviour reward you," she said to him a few days afterwards, "for your fatherly charity. What happiness it was to my soul! I must be in Heaven to be able to thank you worthily for this favour." Three weeks before Marie-Eustelle's death the doctors ordered a seton—they must of course always be doing something, even when the case is hopeless; she meekly submitted, and only observed, "They prescribe remedies; but they do not understand my malady."

The tenderness of her heart made her most anxious to avoid giving pain to her parents, and it was noticed that she never spoke to them of her approaching death; she would even use a little pious artifice to cheat their sorrow, by taking when they were present some apparent interest in little future arrangements, as though she still expected to prolong her stay with them on earth. Her weakness so much increased in the beginning of June, that it was resolved to administer the last sacraments to her. She received them with full consciousness in the afternoon of the 12th of June. One feeling of sorrow she expressed. As might be anticipated, it had no reference to herself, but had its source in that pure disinterested love of Jesus which, as we have seen, had caused her, so long as her feeble strength permitted, nay until she fainted for very exhaustion on the road, to follow her Lord, when borne to the houses of the sick and dying, that she might do Him honour on His passage. "What grieves me," she said, "is that from the church door to my poor dwelling many souls have refused Him the tribute of reverence and adoration which is due to Him. Poor Jesus! O God ignored!" Eustelle was better after she had been administered. How often this is the case is well known to those who are conversant with death-beds; when the anointing and the prayer of faith do not restore the sick, as many a time they have done, their power is continually shown in this temporary revival. Eustelle's friends were led to hope for a moment that they might still retain her, but her race was run; she had finished her course, and already the crown was suspended over her head.

On the 20th of June M. Briand came to see her, and told her she would soon be united to her Beloved. Notwithstanding her weakness, she wrote a few lines to him the following day :—

"Jesus is all. Very dear father, how happy you made me yesterday by the hopes which you held out to my soul! I have thought of nothing else. To be eternally united to Jesus—what joy! To that Jesus for whom my soul so hungers! Dear Spouse and Friend of my heart, Thou art all my life. Dear Object of my soul's affections, towards whom it ever tends with an incomparable eagerness! My dear Jesus, how I love Thee! O dear half of my soul, I wish to die for Thee. All for Jesus!

"EUSTELLE."

On the Monday which preceded her death she lay silently expectant ; at last, as the hour advanced, she said to her sister, "They are not, then, going to bring the Good God to me to-day." She had measured time by her own feelings, and it seemed very long to her. Her sister reminded her that she had received the day before, and that communion would not be given to

her again until Thursday. Eustelle made no reply.
Two days passed by, when, towards five o'clock on
the Wednesday morning, the 29th of June, the festival
of St. Peter and St. Paul, she heard the church bell.
" I hear the bell ringing," she immediately said ; " our
Lord is coming." " But it is not to-day," replied her
sister, " that you are to communicate ; this is only
Wednesday." " Ah, I believed it to be Thursday !"
exclaimed Eustelle, and then relapsed into deep silence.
Sister Anastasia was convinced that she then received
her death-blow. Her heart was unable to endure the
delay, and her frame was too feeble to bear so great a
shock. Truly Eustelle may be said to have died of love,
the death she had so ardently coveted. A few minutes
only had elapsed when the dying girl's watchful sister
perceived unusual signs of agitation in her ; she
seemed seized with dread. " Pray, pray our Lord
for me," she said. The last awful combat of the soul
was taking place, some terrible sense of dereliction,
the shadow of that which drew the " *Deus Meus,
Deus Meus*" of Calvary from the Redeemer's Heart,
was passing over His spouse. It was momentary—
the dark shade was gone. Eustelle pronounced the
Holy Name several times, and then they heard her
say, " My God, I commend my spirit into Thy hands."
Mary's name also mingled on her lips with that of
Jesus ; her eyes were fixed on heaven with an expression most angelic ; her lips still moved, but now
the tones of her voice could no longer be caught on
earth ; at last the lips, too, ceased to move. Eustelle
has fallen asleep in the embrace of her God.

CHAPTER X.

SCARCELY had Eustelle breathed her last, when the news spread through the town of Saintes, as of an event in which all must take the deepest interest. There was no talk but of her virtues, and although prayers were offered for her in accordance with the spirit of the Church, a much greater inclination was felt to implore her patronage before the Throne of God. Her friends were meanwhile hastily dividing the scanty but precious spoil she had left—those few otherwise valueless things which had belonged to the votary of poverty. A little contention occurred about her rosary; and then there was displayed that pious eagerness which is usual in the case of persons who have departed with the reputation of high sanctity, to bring medals, pictures, beads to touch the venerated body. Eustelle had injured her knees from her continual posture of adoration; a kind friend had consequently nailed down a little cushion at the spot where she was used to pray. This was speedily removed, to be preserved, no doubt, by some pious family as a dear relic of the departed. Scraps of paper with her handwriting on them were eagerly snatched up; and even the leaves which she had pasted in her books of devotion, and upon which she had written a few words, were torn out and greedily appropriated. When Eustelle's biographer visited Saint-Pallais in 1855, everything which could be regarded as a memorial of this saintly girl had disappeared, and her good mother, who was then living, deprived herself for his sake of the last lock of her child's hair which she still possessed. He was not able to keep it long, but in his turn felt constrained to resign it in favour of a Carmelite father, to whom he had displayed his treasure.

Eustelle's mortal remains were accompanied to the tomb with deep religious recollection; and at her funeral Mass a great number of young persons received communion, as if it had been a festival day. This was in accordance with a wish expressed by Eustelle herself, a final and touching proof of her desire to multiply communions. Pious hands placed a cross at her grave, with these words carved upon it : " Je repose en Jesus—(I repose in Jesus)." Ten months after Eustelle had been committed to the earth in the churchyard of her native village, the collection of her writings was published with the authorization of the Bishop of La Rochelle, and preceded by an address of that prelate to the faithful of his diocese. In it he acquainted them with the deep impression which his very first interview with the maiden of Saint-Pallais had made upon him a few years previous—an impression only confirmed by his subsequent knowledge of her. He was now as eloquent in exalting the sublime virtues which had distinguished Marie-Eustelle, and especially her ardent love for the Divine Eucharist, as he had formerly been cautious in his observations and sparing in his praises ; in short, his whole desire now was that the example and writings of the sempstress of Saint-Pallais should become extensively known, and thus contribute, as he hoped, to renew devotion to the august Sacrament of the Altar. Such strong expressions on the part of so reserved and prudent a prelate could not but excite attention and stimulate a pious curiosity. Yet would not this high recommendation alone be sufficient to account for the extraordinary and almost electric rapidity with which Eustelle's writings were known and read in all parts of France; still less would it explain the wonderful effect produced by their perusal in so many hearts.

During the years which immediately followed Eustelle's death there was a continued resort of persons to visit her tomb and the room in which she had lived. "They came to Saint-Pallais," says M. Briand in a paper he gave Cardinal Villecourt, " as to a place of pilgrimage, from the very extremities of France; many for the purpose of thanking Eustelle for graces they had received or cures they had obtained through her intercession." On the occasion of the translation of the relics of St. Eutropius (of which we are about to speak) so many visitors presented themselves, that the member of the family who was commissioned to show her room became so exhausted from sheer fatigue that a priest was obliged to supply her place. Letters were often sent to Eustelle's relatives with a request that they might be buried in her grave; and one young man, they remembered, who, having been converted by her writings, visited her tomb on two several occasions to satisfy his devotion, and went afterwards, as they believed, to Rome to embrace the religious life. The Curé of Saint-Pallais at last judged it prudent to take the key of the cemetery into his own keeping, that he might be able, if needful, to put a check upon any public demonstration of *cultus*, as such demonstration is forbidden previously to any decision on the part of the Holy See, and would even place an obstacle in the way of future canonization. "Ah, I did not know," he afterwards remarked, "what trouble I was entailing upon myself, such was the number of comers and goers, whose inquiries must needs be satisfied, and who all wanted to see the grave."

In conclusion, we will lay before the reader a few striking facts as testimonies, all tending to indicate the saintliness of the subject of this biography, and to demonstrate the virtue ascribed by many to her intercession. In so doing we simply relate, giving what we have received upon most trustworthy authority in the same spirit in which it has been stated, without attempting to enforce any opinion of our own, or to forestall any future authoritative judgment.

Eustelle's director, M. Briand, when he saw her eight or nine days before her death, made two requests of her : one was that she would acquaint him with her eternal blessedness when in Heaven ; the other was that she would obtain for him from our Lord the grace to discover St. Eutropius's tomb. She replied, "Yes, my father, be assured I will. I promise you." Accordingly, upon the day on which she expired, M. Briand besought God to vouchsafe him a sign of the bliss of the departed, *solely for His own greater glory*. He himself selected the sign which he humbly begged might be granted him. It was that a general in the army, who was eighty-one years of age, and who had never even made his first communion, should express a wish to go to confession, a proceeding for which he was aware the old man was anything but inclined. He renewed his petition the following day. He had asked a hard thing, and, doubtless, designedly so, that, in case he succeeded in obtaining what he sought, he might be the better assured that it was a token from God. But would he succeed? He had kept the matter a profound secret, when, at nine o'clock on the evening of the third day, the general's daughter asked to see him. She had come to inform him that, to her great joy and contrary to all her expectations, her father had just bidden her go and request him to come and hear his confession on the following day. "No one," said the general, when he received M. Briand, "has ever moved me to take this step; but yesterday this good thought was suggested to my heart." The old officer survived two years, which were spent in a truly Christian manner. This remarkable incident rests on M. Briand's own testimony, who recorded it on the margin of the Abbé Guérin's memoir.

He was equally successful as respects his second request. Saintonge had been the special scene of the sacrilegious outrages of Calvinism in the year 1547, when its sectaries spread devastation throughout France, desecrating and pillaging churches; the relics of the saints being the special objects of their hatred and fury. The religious who had the charge of the tomb of St. Eutropius, the first bishop and martyr of Saintes, hearing of the excesses committed by the Protestants in the neighbouring isle of Oleron, hastened to conceal underground the precious body of which they were the guardians. This was, of course, effected with the utmost secrecy, and as little as possible was said about it. Living in the continual apprehension of the storm bursting on their own heads, they would have wished that, so far as might be, the existence of these relics should be forgotten by the world. The Protestants took possession of

Saintes in 1562, returned in 1568, and again in 1578,
and committed so many sacrilegious horrors in their
several visits that it might have been believed that
nothing had escaped them; and, indeed, they boasted
that they had utterly destroyed everything in the
church of St. Eutropius. Meanwhile the religious had
been obliged to retire to Bordeaux. All these circumstances, combined with the menacing attitude which
Calvinism continued for the space of thirty years
to maintain in these parts, up to the capture of
La Rochelle in 1628, led to a loss of the traditions.
If amongst the faithful some aged men still spoke to
their children of the mysterious interment of the
relics, these communications, transmitted from one
generation to another, came at last to be regarded as
mere popular rumours, which had no claim to credi-
bility. At the time of Marie-Eustelle's death, then,
it was the general belief in France that the body of
St. Eutropius had shared the fate of so many other
holy relics, and had been profaned and destroyed by
the heretics in the days of their triumph. M. Briand,
however, who was no less remarkable for his learning
than for his piety, and who had written a history of
the church of Saintes, did not entirely share the
public opinion on this matter. He had his doubts,
and he had his hopes: this is why he recommended
the affair to Eustelle when she was on the brink of
the tomb; and we have seen with what confidence she
gave her promise. It was not to remain unfulfilled.
The answer seems to have come in an extraordinary
impression conveyed to his mind as to the spot where
the relics would be found. In a writing which he placed
in the bishop's hands, he described himself as being
irresistibly led to the conviction that the tomb of

St. Eutropius was under the site of the ancient altar in the crypt. This site he indicated precisely; and there, in fact, the tomb of the saint was discovered, a year after Marie-Eustelle's death, on the day preceding that of her namesake, the virgin martyr Eustelle.

That day will be ever memorable in the annals of the Church of Saintes. The truly Catholic heart of the people displayed itself on that occasion as it has ever been wont to do in the Church's history. As the news spread rapidly through the town, the cry seemed to arise in all quarters almost simultaneously: "The tomb of St. Eutropius is found." The enthusiasm was indescribable. Men, women, and children left work, business, amusement, to run to the spot and assure themselves with their own eyes of the truth of the report. The crypt was soon full to overflowing. The Bishop of La Rochelle proceeded without delay to institute the strictest investigation, according to the rules prescribed by the Council of Trent, and after two years of most patient and rigorous scrutiny such a mass of evidence was collected as left the authenticity of the relics beyond dispute. The bishop solemnly pronounced his decision in the old cathedral of Saintes on the 8th of September, 1845; and on the 14th of October in the same year the body of the martyr was borne in procession by eighteen ecclesiastics round the walls of the city. Four hundred priests followed in their train, the solemn spectacle being witnessed by an immense concourse of the faithful, not of the diocese alone, but from all parts of France, who had hastened to Saintes to take a part in the glories of that triumphant day. The innumerable visits paid upon that occasion to Eustelle's lowly dwelling sufficiently attested the connection which existed in the general mind between this happy discovery and the saintly needlewoman of Saint-Pallais. Saintes will ever believe herself indebted for her recovered treasure to Marie-Eustelle Harpain, and will ever join in the declaration made by the preacher who opened the novena preparatory to the translation of the relics : "An angelic soul," he exclaimed, "has flown with a message to Heaven ; and behold the hour of awakening has sounded. The mists of a night of three hundred years have been dispelled, and the tomb of Eutropius has appeared like a radiant sun, once more to revive in our hearts the glorious light of faith."

We will now proceed to give a few instances of the graces and favours which have been attributed to the intercession of the holy maiden of Saint-Pallais, together with the testimony rendered by several pious persons to the influence exerted by her writings.

Some little time after Eustelle's departure, one of her friends, when engaged in prayer before the Blessed Sacrament, lamented to our Lord the separation which death had made between herself and her friend ; immediately she had an intellectual vision of two hearts above the tabernacle, which seemed to sink and lose themselves together in the Heart of Jesus, while an interior voice was heard to say, "Behold our union." This fact is solemnly attested by the narrator. Another went one day to pray at Eustelle's tomb ; scarcely had he knelt down when he fell into a state of profound recollection, and began to address petitions to Eustelle. All of a sudden, and quite unexpectedly, an interior voice said, "You must be more regular in prayer. *Prayer and the Eucharist save souls.* You must rise at four o'clock ; I will awake you, . . . and you will pray with joy." This person had been in the habit of rising at five o'clock, but after this visit to Eustelle's tomb, he always awoke at four o'clock, and used to pray with much spiritual joy until five. He was convinced that this was a heavenly favour granted to him through Eustelle's intercession. He added to the written record which he left in M. Briand's hands, that he could not explain its nature, but that he fully believed in the reality of the interior voice which he had heard. Eustelle's biographer, who examined this paper, thinks that there are good reasons for attributing it to an ecclesiastic. Our thoughts revert at once to the former Curé of Saint-Pallais, in whom Eustelle took so tender an interest, and to whom she ventured to offer advice while yet on earth. This, indeed, is a pure conjecture, but it is strengthened by the recollection that in many of her letters Eustelle most pressingly exhorts her afflicted " brother " to have recourse to M. Briand for direction.

We have seen how great a gift of consolation Eustelle had possessed ; we have now before us a testimony to her continued exercise of that same gift in Heaven. It is given in a letter which was placed in Cardinal Villecourt's hands. The writer therein expresses the pleasure he felt in offering to his sister now in glory the homage of his love and his regrets. These regrets were inspired by the recollection of the incredulity which he had previously entertained respecting her. It was when he visited Saintes in the August of 1842 that he first heard of Eustelle ; he found many of his acquaintance in the place regarding her as a saint, while others attempted to revive against her the old accusations of insanity and pride. Without entirely sharing the opinion of irreligious friends, he was inclined rather to side with the detractors, and at any rate disbelieved altogether the alleged heroism of her virtue. However, out of pure curiosity he visited her grave, and when he read those simple touching words: "I repose in Jesus," he felt deeply moved, and experienced a sensation of indefinable joy during the few moments he lingered on the spot. The five succeeding months brought him much trouble and anxiety of mind ; his worldly affairs went ill, and not loving our Lord sufficiently to derive any support from the consolations of religion, temptations to despair and even to self-destruction would at times assail him. In one of these dark hours of desolation the remembrance of Marie-Eustelle recurred to him. If she was as holy as people pretended (so he thought to himself), she would pray for him, and her prayer would certainly be heard. Half in a spirit of bitter irony and doubt, but with a latent hope in his breast, he went to kneel at her tomb. At first he could only weep. "If you are in Heaven," he said at last, "take pity on a heart over-whelmed with sadness ; find me an employment, but, above all, teach me to love Jesus ; I need this love so much." He also made a novena to her, and on the third or fourth day had two unexpected offers which were the means of setting his mind at rest, so far as concerned his temporal anxieties. Full of gratitude, he now begged Eustelle's pardon with sentiments of the liveliest sorrow, and ever after entertained the deepest veneration for her, accom panied by the sweetest confidence. She became to him as it were a dear sister, companion, and monitress. He seemed to have her continually present with him, and many a time did she prove a guardian angel to him in danger and temptation. How would Eustelle

have acted on such and such occasions?—the answer
to this self-asked question had an all-powerful effect
in restraining him from evil or impelling him to good.
Moreover, the reading of her writings made him
love the God of the Eucharist and ardently desire to
receive Him often in communion. Eustelle had
obtained for him his two petitions, notwithstanding
the somewhat ungracious spirit in which they
had been preferred; and she had given him besides what he had not asked, the abiding influence of her presence, to shield him from harm, to
direct him to good, and to kindle fervour in his
breast.

This is by no means a solitary instance; a like
favour was granted to others. In particular, a great
servant of God, whose name is not recorded, transmitted
to Mgr. Villecourt a full account of the graces which
he had received by means of the writings of Marie-
Eustelle, and the personal devotion to her which they
had excited in him. "Blessed for ever," he says, "be
that dear Spouse of souls for having opened to me a
path so easy of attainment, and given me so sweet
a guide to direct me in it." His love for Eustelle,
and his sympathy with her, as he describes them, have
something quite marvellous about them. "The mere
sight of her picture (he writes) is sufficient to rekindle divine love in my soul. Never did I feel such
attraction for any of the saints, or was so forcibly
drawn to their imitation. I never tire of musing
on and contemplating this fair model. The virgin of
Saint-Pallais seems to impart to me her own ardent
love for Jesus." And he then goes on to describe how
the attraction which he feels for Eustelle scarcely
attaches to herself at all, so rapidly does it direct him

to Jesus; his love for his Lord always increasing in proportion to the attraction he feels for His servant. She seemed ever present in all his pious exercises; and this was particularly the case in the early stages of his devotion to her. When he travelled she was his inseparable companion, animating him to the endurance of his fatigues by reminding him of the many weary steps she had herself taken from obedience and love; she seemed, as it were, to bear and support him on his road. But, indeed, on almost every occasion the remembrance of her would be suggested to him, and the pattern of her virtues presented before his eyes. For a considerable time it was his practice, when visiting the Blessed Sacrament, to transport himself in spirit to the church of Saint-Pallais; where he seemed to behold Eustelle adoring with seraphic ardour the God of the Tabernacle, and to catch some portion of the heavenly flame. But still more was his soul all on fire with devotion to the Most Holy when he was able to visit in person that sacred spot, that temple which to him was "all redolent of the perfume of love which had exhaled from the burning heart" of this great lover of the Divine Eucharist. He avers that he had not contributed to excite the sensible impression which he habitually enjoyed of the saintliness of Eustelle by any consideration or reflection of his own: it existed in him without his co-operation, nor would it have been easy for him to divest himself of it; he believed it, in short, to be supernatural. Much more does this servant of God say to the same effect; adding, in conclusion, "From all that I have told you, my lord, I have drawn a certain presage that God has chosen Marie-Eustelle to excite souls to the love of Jesus in the Holy Sacrament."

The testimony of Auguste Marceau,* the heroic and saintly captain of "L'Arche d'Alliance," will be considered of no little value. The writings of Marie-Eustelle singularly affected him; her words fell on a congenial heart. "The transports of this passionate lover of Jesus in the Eucharist," says the author of his life, "were for the soul of Marceau like so many burning coals. One would have said," he exclaimed, "that these pages had been written at the dictation of a cherub." From beyond the seas, from far-off transatlantic wildernesses—from heads of religious houses, from visitors-general of missions—came letters telling the same tale of the spiritual delight and renewal of fervour caused by the reading of her letters; nay, of the awakening of feelings never hitherto experienced towards the Blessed Eucharist even in souls long given to piety. There was all the difference, we might say, between appreciative love and love as a passion; yes, a passion for the Eucharist—this it is which Eustelle has come to kindle in our bosoms. "I read fifteen years ago," says the superior of a religious congregation, "the Life and Letters of Marie-Eustelle; and I shall ever retain a blessed remembrance of the impressions which I then received. I may even say that to me it was the dawn of a signal grace. . . . Ever since, I have daily recommended myself to the prayers of this holy lover of the Divine Eucharist. I feel convinced that the maiden of Saint-Pallais has been the precursor of that triumph which the worship of the Adorable Eucharist is having in our day."

We have selected instances of the spiritual effects

* The life of this admirable man will form the subject of a future biography.

produced by the words and example of this holy girl
in preference to those which relate to bodily cures ;
not because these are wanting, but because the former
have a nearer connection with the scope of this work.
We will conclude with an instance which combines
something of the two.   A priest who had suffered
for twenty-five years from a serious affection of the
throat has, in gratitude to Eustelle, recorded the benefits which he had received, as he confidently believed,
through her means.   His complaint appears to have
been of a chronic nature, and frequently incapacitated
him from saying Mass.   In the year 1855 he visited
her tomb, and made a retreat of several days in the
church of Saint-Pallais, before the very altars where
she had worshipped, his chief object being to renew
the fervour of his own devotion to the Divine Eucharist by the help of her intercession.   Entirely
unknown at Saintes, he felt himself to be in a desert
peopled only with those holy thoughts and images which
he had come to seek.   It was a happy and a blessed
time with him, which remained ever fresh in his
memory.   On the 5th of June, which was the Tuesday
preceding the Festival of Corpus Christi that year, he
said Mass in the church of Saint-Pallais, uniting himself in spirit to the saintly Eustelle, and desiring to
honour her thereby as far as the rules of Holy Church
would permit.   From that morning he was able to
celebrate Mass every day for a whole year, a thing
which for a long time had never occurred.   To Marie-
Eustelle he was assured that he was also indebted for
many graces received during his retreat.   With
respect to his health he had made no special request,
but as time went on the conviction arose in his mind
that he owed the inestimable favour of being able to

say Mass daily to her spontaneous charity. Gratitude for this as well as for other benefits ought (he said) to have moved him to have made a pilgrimage of thanksgiving to Saint-Pallais. Besides, he felt that he had given his benefactress a sort of half-promise that he would return. Yet, although he continued to have a vague intention of fulfilling it, he did *not* return, and exactly a year (ecclesiastical) after his cure, on the day before the Feast of Corpus Christi, his old malady attacked him again, and he became so ill that he could not offer the Adorable Sacrifice on the Thursday consecrated to the special honour of the Blessed Sacrament, nor yet on the Friday, nor even on the Sunday, to which day, it may be observed, the solemn celebration of the feast is in France transferred. It was then that he recalled to mind the impression which all through that year he had felt, that he owed his relief to Eustelle, and he deeply reproached himself for having suffered this thought to slumber, allowing it to come and go like any other indifferent idea, without giving it sufficient reflection or acknowledging the benefit in any definite way. Five years more elapsed, when, wearied in spirit at his constant occurring inability to say Mass, he resolved to have recourse to his former benefactress. "Good Eustelle," he said, "let us make a little compact by which both of us will profit. Whenever I feel, as I so often do, utterly incapable of celebrating on account of the pain in my throat, I will, cost what it may, in memory of your love for the Divine Eucharist, say Mass anyhow, even though I seem to be at the last extremity. It will be a Mass which, but for you, would never have been said; a Mass which the August Trinity will consequently in some sort owe to you. I shall have thus procured you, so far as in me lies, the felicity of which you were so covetous on earth ; and you, on your part, good Eustelle, will undertake that I shall not suffer more after saying Mass than I did before, notwithstanding the apparently extraordinary and imprudent exertion I shall have imposed upon myself. I do not ask for relief, I simply ask for the *statu quo*." The compact was to apply only to days when otherwise he would have felt himself compelled to abstain from the attempt. The agreement was to all appearance accepted ; and except where his inability was the consequence of fatigue incurred by unnecessary conversation or other little indulgence of some unmortified inclination, he had always hitherto been able to offer Mass, however ill he might be, without detriment to his health. Often and often, as he commenced the *Introibo*, he would be seized with dismay at the prospect of the half-hour of inexpressible suffering before him; it seemed as if he never would be able to complete what he had begun, and that he was guilty of presumption in making the attempt. But Eustelle always supported him, and he generally experienced a certain degree of relief after the oblation.

Some persons may be disposed to say, here is no miracle, but only the effect of a strong imagination : be it so, but (as Eustelle's biographer remarks), call it what you please—impression, sentiment, imagination —thanks to that power, real or imaginary, Masses have been said with which Eternity would never have been enriched. "*Tantum valet,*" says St. John Chrysostom, "*celebratio missæ quantum valet mors Christi in cruce.*" If these Masses have not been due to the intercession of Eustelle, they have at least been an effect of the influence she has exerted.

Blessed, then, be she, the very memory of whom draws hearts to the Adorable Victim of the Altar. Fruitful, indeed, in good effects, not on individual pious souls alone, but on whole classes, has been her memory and her example. For instance, a person who had heard Marie-Eustelle spoken of in a retreat given at Mans in 1845, procured her Letters, and on her return home used to assemble the neighbouring work-women at her house and read this book to them. The change wrought in numbers of her listeners, the majority of whom were thoughtless young girls, was very wonderful. Balls and other frivolous amusements, to which they had hitherto been devoted, were given up, and they began to frequent the sacraments with the most edifying fervour.

Other striking facts might be adduced, but our object is, however inadequately, fulfilled. We have set before our readers' eyes a simple uneventful life, but a life that is sublime in its very simplicity : a life with one dominant purpose, one all-absorbing passion —the love and the worship of our Incarnate God in His Most Holy and Most Divine Sacrament. Marie-Eustelle loved much and she prayed much : this is sufficient to make a saint. When such a one is laid in the ground, be it in the obscurest nook of earth, then it is that the life which is now ended, and which, it would seem, has but to undergo the lot of other humble lives—to be forgotten—begins to act upon the world. Many saints have worked wonderful effects during their mortal lives, yet all, perhaps, have accomplished more after their departure to glory. So, in their measure, may it be with all God's favoured children : in more than one sense, "their works follow them." Of Eustelle may this be said with peculiar truth. While on earth she was ever mingling lamentations of her own powerlessness to do aught for the glory of her Lord with the rapturous expressions of her love; but the imperishable words in which she breathed it forth were afterwards to fly like winged seeds over the globe and produce an abundant harvest, of which, it may be, only the first fruits have yet been garnered. "When God would move the world," says Eustelle's biographer, in whose steps we have humbly followed, and with whose words we cannot do better than conclude, "He rests His lever here below upon the saints. Under whatever form this character may appear—whether it be clothed in rags, like a Benedict Labre, or girt with the sword, like an Auguste Marceau; whether it exercise the sacred ministry, like a Muard or a Vianney, or ply the needle, like a Marie-Eustelle Harpain—a saint is the continuation of Jesus Christ, and Jesus Christ is ever a Saviour, whether in the Tabernacle where He hides Himself or in Heaven where He reigns."

WYMAN AND SONS, PRINTERS, GREAT QUEEN STREET, LONDON, W.C.

LIBRARY OF
RELIGIOUS BIOGRAPHY.

EDITED BY

EDWARD HEALY THOMPSON, M.A.

———◦○◦———

THE object of this series is to present Examples of Eminent Personal Holiness, under widely different circumstances and in various conditions of life.

The Biographies selected will be those of Saints and Saintly Persons who have adorned the Church of God in modern times, and especially (though not exclusively) of such as have practised heroic virtue or have attained a high degree of perfection, wholly or partly, in the secular state.

Care will be taken to make the contents of the several volumes as diversified as possible, consistently with the scope and character of the series ; and those Lives will be preferred which are capable of being treated in fullest detail within the limits assigned.

Each Biography will be an original composition, based on the best and latest authorities, and will be submitted to the revision of a competent theologian.

The volumes will be printed in foolscap 8vo, on fine paper, and in a handsome, readable type, and will be bound uniformly in cloth, lettered.

———————

Volumes already Published :—

I. THE LIFE OF ST. ALOYSIUS GONZAGA, S.J. 5s.

II. THE LIFE OF MARIE-EUSTELLE HARPAIN, the Sempstress of Saint-Pallais, called "The Angel of the Eucharist." 5s.

In immediate Preparation :—

III. The Life of ST. STANISLAS KOSTKA, S.J.

IV. The Life of M. ORAIN, Parish Priest of Fegréac.

This volume will be illustrated with details of the sufferings of the Breton Church during the " Reign of Terror."

V. The Life of V. MARIA CRISTINA of SAVOY, Queen of Naples.

To be followed by Lives of

M. Marceau, Captain of the Missionary Ship *L'Arche d'Alliance.*

The Baron de Renty.

The Count Louis de Sales.

Armelle Nicolas, the Servant Girl of Campénéac.

Three Nieces of St. Aloysius Gonzaga.

V. Maria Clotilda of France, Queen of Sardinia.

M. Gabriel de Vidaud, Model of Christians in the World.

M. Leclerc d'Aubigny, Advocate.

English Missionary Priests during the Elizabethan Persecution.

Father Baptiste Muard, Founder of the Benedictine Preachers of the Sacred Hearts of Jesus and Mary, &c.

V. Anna Maria Taigi, the Roman Matron.

Virginia Bruni, the Roman Widow.

V. John Baptist Jossa, Model of pious Laymen.

Father Louis Lallemant and his Disciples.

Cardinal Cheverus, Archbishop of Bordeaux.

Esprite de Jesus, Tertiary of St. Dominic.

Father Charles de Condren, Superior of the French Oratory.

M. Emery, Superior of St. Sulpice during the Great Revolution.

&c. &c.

₊ The progress of the series has been accidentally delayed, but it is intended for the future to issue the volumes at regular intervals.

THE THREE MISSION BOOKS,

Comprising all that is required for general use; the cheapest books ever issued.

1. *Complete Book of Devotions and Hymns: Path to Heaven*, 1000 pages, 2*s*. This Volume forms the Cheapest and most Complete Book of Devotions for Public or Private use ever issued. (25th Thousand.) Cloth, Two Shillings. Also in various bindings.
2. *Complete Choir Manual (Latin) for the Year*, 230 pieces. 10*s*. 6*d*.
3. *Complete Popular Hymn and Tune Book (English)*, 250 pieces. 10*s*. 6*d*. Melodies alone, 1*s*. Words, 8*d*.; cloth, 5*d*.

Prayers of St. Gertrude and Mechtilde. Neat cloth, lettered, 1*s*. 6*d*.; Fr. morocco, red edges, 2*s*.; best calf, red edges, 4*s*.; best morocco, plain, 4*s*. 6*d*.; gilt, 5*s*. 6*d*. Also in various extra bindings. On thin *vellum paper* at the same prices.

Devotions for the "Quarant' Ore," or New Visits to the Blessed Sacrament. Edited by Cardinal Wiseman. 1*s*., or in cloth, gilt edges, 2*s*.; morocco, 5*s*.

Imitation of the Sacred Heart. By the Rev. Father ARNOLD, S.J. 12mo, 4*s*. 6*d*.; or in handsome cloth, red edges, 5*s*.; also in calf, 8*s*; morocco, 9*s*.

Manual of the Sacred Heart. New edition, 2*s*.; red edges, 2*s*. 6*d*.; calf, 5*s*.; morocco, 5*s*. 6*d*.

The Spirit of St. Theresa. 2*s*.; red edges, with picture, 2*s*. 6*d*.

The Spirit of the Curé d'Ars. 2*s*. Ditto, ditto. 2*s*. 6*d*.

The Spirit of St. Gertrude. 2*s*. 6*d*.

Manna of the New Covenant; Devotions for Communion. Cloth, 2*s*.; bound, with red edges, 2*s*. 6*d*.

A'Kempis. The Following of Christ, in four books; a new translation, beautifully printed in royal 16mo, with borders round each page, and illustrative engravings after designs by German artists. Cloth, 3*s*. 6*d*.; calf, 6*s*. 6*d*.; morocco, 8*s*.; gilt, 10*s*. 6*d*. The same, pocket edition. Cloth, 1*s*.; bound, roan, 1*s*. 6*d*.; calf, 4*s*.; morocco, 4*s*. 6*d*.

Spiritual Combat; a new translation. 18mo, cloth, 3*s*.; calf, 6*s*.; morocco, 7*s*. The same, pocket size. Cloth, 1*s*.; calf, neat, 4*s*.; morocco, 4*s*. 6*d*.

BURNS, OATES, & CO., 63 PATERNOSTER ROW, E.C.

Missal. New and Complete Pocket Missal, in Latin and English, with all the new Offices and the Proper of Ireland, Scotland, and the Jesuits. Roan, embossed gilt edges, 4s. 6d.; calf flexible, red edges, 7s. 6d.; morocco, gilt edges, 8s. 6d.; ditto, gilt, 10s.

Epistles and Gospels for the whole Year. 1s. 6d.

Vesper Book for the Laity. This Volume contains the Office of Vespers (including Compline and Benediction), complete for *every day in the year.* Roan, 3s. 6d.; calf, 5s. 6d.; morocco, 6s. 6d.

The Psalter in Latin, 1s. 6d. *Do. in English.* New edition (*in the press*).

Easter in Heaven. By Father WENINGER, S.J. 4s. 6d.

The Spirit of Christianity. From the French of NEPVEU. 4s.

Considerations on the World. By PIOT. 1s. 6d.

The Touchstone of Character. By the Abbé CHASSAY. 3s.

Crasset. Meditations for every Day in the Year. From the French of Père CRASSET, S.J. 8vo, 8s.

Sancta Sophia. By Father BAKER, O.S.B. 5s.

Lombez on Christian Joy. 1s. 9d.

Spirit of St. Francis of Sales. 8s. 6d.

Our Faith the Victory. By Dr. McGILL. 10s.

Spiritual Maxims of St. Vincent de Paul. 1s. 4d.

The Beauties of the Sanctuary. From the French of LEBON. 2s. 6d.

The Art of Suffering. From the French of St. GERMAIN. 1s. 6d.

Method of Meditation. By Father ROOTHAN. 2s.

The Genius of Christianity. By CHATEAUBRIAND. Complete edition. 8s.

The Martyrs. By the same. 6s.

Hecker (Rev. J. T.). Aspirations of Nature. 5s.—Questions of the Soul. 4s. 6d.

Mission and Duties of Young Women. 2s. 6d.

Guide for Catholic Young Women. By Father DESHON. 4s.

Maynard on the Teaching of the Jesuits. 3s.

Mary, Star of the Sea. 3s. 6d.

Paradise of the Christian Soul. Complete. 6s.

The Words of Jesus. Edited by the Rev. F. CASWALL. 1s.

Lyra Liturgica : Verses for the Ecclesiastical Seasons. By Canon OAKELEY. 3s. 6d.

---o---

BURNS, OATES, & CO., 17 & 18 PORTMAN STREET, W.

Select Sacred Poetry. 1s.

Instructions in Christian Doctrine. 3s.

Letters on First Communion. 1s.

Flowers of St. Francis of Assisi. 3s.

Manual of Practical Piety. By St. FRANCIS DE SALES. 3s. 6d.

Manresa; or the Spiritual Exercises of St. Ignatius. 3s.

The Christian Virtues. By St. ALPHONSUS. 4s.

Eternal Truths. By the same. 3s. 6d.

On the Passion. By the same. 3s.

Jesus hath loved us. By the same. 9d.

Reflections on Spiritual Subjects. By the same. 2s. 6d.

Glories of Mary. By the same. New edition.

The Raccolta of Indulgenced Prayers. 3s.

Rodriguez on Christian Perfection. Two vols. 6s.

Stolberg's Little Book of the Love of God. 2s.

The Treasure of Superiors. 3s. 6d.

Archbishop Hughes' Complete Works. Two vols. 8vo, 24s.

Sermons. By Father BAKER. With Memoir. 8vo, 10s.

Devout Instructions on the Sundays and Holidays. By GOFFINE. 8vo, 9s. 6d.

Sermons by the Paulists of New York. First Series, 4s.; 2d ditto, 6s.; 3d ditto, 5s. 6d.; 4th ditto, 6s.; 5th ditto (1865-6), 7s.

A Hundred Short Sermons. 8vo, 8s.

Preston's Sermons. 7s.

Spalding's (Bishop) *Evidences.* 7s.

Spalding's (Bishop) *Miscellanies.* 12s. 6d.

The Gentle Sceptic. By Father WALLWORTH. A Treatise on the Authority and Truth of the Scriptures, and on the Questions of the Day as to Science, &c. 6s.

Family Devotions for every Day in the Week, with occasional Prayers. Selected from Catholic Manuals, ancient and modern. Foolscap, limp cloth, red edges, very neat, 2s.

Aids to Choirmasters in the Performance of Solemn Mass, Vespers, Compline, and the various Popular Services in General Use.

P.S. Messrs. B. & Co. will be happy to send any of the above Books on inspection.

A large allowance to the Clergy.

BURNS, OATES, & CO., 63 PATERNOSTER ROW, E.C.

RELIGIOUS BIOGRAPHY AND HISTORY.

St. Aloysius Gonzaga. 3s.

St. Charles Borromeo. 3s. 6d.

St. Vincent de Paul. 3s.

St. Francis de Sales. 3s.

The Curé d'Ars. 4s.

St. Thomas of Canterbury.

Wyndham, Waynflete & More. 4s.

The Blessed Henry Suso. 4s.

M. Olier of Saint Sulpice. 4s.

The Early Martyrs. 3s. 6d.

St. Dominic and the Dominican Order. 3s. 6d.

Madame Swetchine. 7s. 6d.

The Sainted Queens. 3s.

Blessed John Berchmans. 2s.

St. Francis Xavier. 2s.

St. Philip Neri. 3s.

St. Ignatius. 2s.

St. Frances of Rome. 2s.

Heroines of Charity. 2s. 6d.

Saints of the Working Classes. 1s. 4d.

Sister Rosalie and Marie Lataste. 1s.

St. Francis and St. Clare. 1s.

Lives of Pious Youth. 3s. 6d.

Modern Missions in the East and West. 3s.

Missions in Japan and Paraguay. 3s.

Religious Orders, Sketches of. 4s. 6d.

The Knights of St. John. 3s. 6d.

Anecdotes and Incidents. 2s.

Remarkable Conversions. 3s. 6d.

Pictures of Christian Heroism. 3s.

Popular Church History. 3s.

Missions in India. 3s.

Lives of the Roman Pontiffs. By De Montor. Fine engravings. 2 very large vols. 50s. (cash 36s.)

Darras' History of the Church. 4 vols. Edited by Fr. Spalding. Imperial 8vo. £2 2s. (cash £2).

Butler's Lives of the Saints. 4 vols. cloth. 20s.

The Life of Bishop Baric. 2s.

The Life of Mary Ann of Jesus, the Lily of Quito. 3s. 6d.

Life of St. Ignatius. By Bartoli. 2 vols. 14s.

St. Ignatius and his Companions. 4s.

The Life of Abulcher Biciarah. 2 vols. 3s. 6d.

Life of Mme. de Soyecourt. 3s.

Life of St. Angela Merici. 3s. 6d.

Life of St. Margaret of Cortona. 3s. 6d.

Life of Princess Borghese. 2s.

Life of P. Maria Ephraim. 5s.

Life of Mrs. Seton. 8s. 6d.

Life of Mme. de la Peltrie. 2s.

Life of Father Felix de Andreis. 4s. 6d.

Life of St. Stanislaus. 1s. 6d.

Life of St. Philomena. 2s. 6d.

Life of St. Cecilia. By Gueranger. 6s.

Lives of Fathers of the Desert. 4s. 6d.

Life of Bishop Bruté. 3s. 6d.

Life of Pius VI. 3s.

Life of St. Bridget. 2s. 6d.

Life of St. Mary Magdalen. 2s. 6d.

Life of St. Zita. 3s.

Life of St. Francis of Assisi. 2s.

Life of St. Catherine of Sienna. 3s.

Life of Bishop Flaget. 4s. 6d.

Life of Dr. Magian. 4s. 6d.

Life of Cath. McAuley, Foundress of the Sisters of Mercy. 10s. 6d.

Shea (J. G.). Perils of the Ocean and Wilderness. 3s. 6d

Shea (J. G.). Missions in the United States. 9s.

Shea (J. G.). History of the Church in America. 7s. 6d.

Indian Sketches. By De Smet. 2s. 6d.

History of the Society of Jesus. By Daurignac. 2 vols. 12s. 6d.

BURNS, OATES, & CO, 17 & 18 PORTMAN STREET, W.